PAST MADE PRESENT

A JAKE HOUSER MYSTERY (BOOK #4)

BO THUNBOE

WESTON PRESS, LLC

Published in 2020 by Weston Press, LLC

Cover Design by Jeroen ten Berge (jeroentenberge.com)
Interior Design by Kevin G. Summers (kevingsummers.com)

ISBN: 978-1-949632-06-4 (trade paperback)
ISBN: 978-1-949632-07-1 (ebook)

Weston Press, LLC
Naperville, IL
www.thunboe.com

As always, for Diane

ALSO BY BO THUNBOE

CHAPTER ONE

Detective Jake Houser leaned harder, his foot on Alan Mitchell's back, pressing him into the oil-stained gravel. The junkyard's Dobermans sensed their master's distress and started barking and howling. Jake shot a glance that way when the one with the red fur launched itself against the chain-link fence of their enclosure. The gate was latched and the fence was tall. He was safe.

"You're lucky your punched missed. But that's still assault on a police officer," Jake said. "I'll let that go if you tell me where she is."

"I don't know!" Mitchell scrabbled at the ground. "I keep telling you."

The problem was, Jake believed him. It might be the only thing the man had said that turned out to be true. Everything else he'd told Jake about Kate Ballard—where they met, where they spent time together, and who else they spent time with—had turned out to be lies. They met here at the junkyard when Kate Ballard was buying a cheap taillight assembly before her mom noticed the damage to her car, not at a party at a mansion in Weston. They spent time together in the trailer at the back of the junkyard, not going out to dinners and movies. They saw no one else, not all her friends from college.

Kate Ballard wasn't even in college. She was a high school senior who went missing the Friday night her spring break began, ten days ago. Kate's mother called in her disappearance the following Saturday morning, and Jake had worked it ever since without developing a single, solid lead. One friend was sure Kate had hitchhiked to Colorado to go into the backcountry with her dad, but spring break was over and Kate was not back and her dad was still in the mountains. Unreachable.

So, Jake kept coming back to Mitchell, the secret boyfriend no one knew about.

Jake pulled his foot off Mitchell and the man scrambled to his feet, wiping off gravel that was stuck to his face. Blood began to well from small wounds on his chin.

"You're crazy, man." Mitchell backed away, Jake following him, step for step. The air smelled of old oil and dog crap.

"Run through it all again." A cold spring wind whipped across the junkyard, whistling and howling through the twisted wreckage of hundreds of cars. Mitchell backed into a stack of rusted fenders. He startled, glancing behind him as if there might be a monster there. When he turned back around, his eyes—wide with fear—locked on Jake's.

"All what?"

"Everything," Jake said. "How you met. Where you went. Who you saw. Everything. For every time you saw her."

Mitchell started babbling. He'd already run through it at least three times so was getting better at keeping things straight. But Jake interrupted him anyway, forcing Mitchell to jump forward and backward in the chronology to test everything the man said. Nothing new came out of it.

"And I swear I thought she was in college, man."

"She wasn't."

"I know. I mean *now* I know because you told me. But she told me she was in college. North Western College. And the way she talked made me think that was true, man. She was super smart."

There! "*Was* smart?"

Mitchell shook his head, backing up again, rising on his toes against the stack of rusted metal. "I just meant back when I talked to her she sounded smart. She still is smart and alive and everything as far as I know." A trickle of blood ran from one of the little wounds and Mitchell flicked at it, smearing it across his face. He looked at his finger. "I'm bleeding, man. You gotta leave me alone. I called *you*. Remember? Why would I do that if I did something to her?"

Mitchell *had* called in. One of the few calls to the tip line that had gone anywhere. But that didn't mean he was innocent. Some criminals liked to insert themselves into the investigation of their crimes. It happened all the time.

"You called in, but told a lot of lies."

"But now I've told you everything!" Mitchell's voice rose even higher. The dogs howled. "The whole truth and nothing but the truth."

Jake believed him. Which meant he had nothing. He fished his sunglasses out of his shirt pocket and put them on. "I'll be back if I find out otherwise."

Mitchell's gaze slipped around, trying to see Jake's eyes through the dark lenses. "You won't, man. I'm telling you. She and I were over months ago."

Jake said nothing, letting the silence stretch until Mitchell swallowed, his Adam's apple bobbing. Jake spun and walked through the yard and out the gate to the parking lot. Back in the Mustang, he checked his phone. One text from Erin. Her official title was Civilian Investigative Support but she was a lot more than that including his eyes and ears at the station. He avoided the place and the constant political boil as much as possible.

Braff wants to see you right NOW!

Jake texted back that he was on his way and headed for Weston and the station.

* * *

Jake survived the greetings gauntlet that now occurred every time he came into the station. It had become a thing a few months before when a new desk sergeant started announcing Jake's presence over the intercom whenever he came in. Jake didn't like it.

Deputy Chief Braff's door was open and Jake found his boss behind his desk with Detective Callie Diggs sitting across from him. Callie and Jake had a romantic history together, but all that remained was a casual friendship and the habit of calling each other by their first names. Jake stopped in the doorway. "Callie." He nodded to her. "Want me to come back later, Deputy Chief?"

"Get in here, Houser. And close the door."

Jake did as he was told. Callie greeted him with a small, sorrowful smile.

Not good.

"What is it, Chief?"

"I'm cutting you off on this Kate Ballard thing. You—"

"It's not a thing. She's missing. She—"

"Do *not* interrupt me."

Jake closed his mouth.

"I've read your case file. You have no fresh leads and working your old leads has turned into a harassment complaint." Braff picked up a pink message slip and shook it. "Alan Mitchell's boss claims you smashed the boy's face into the ground and stood on him."

Jake returned Braff's hard stare. "Mitchell took a swing at me."

"Then why didn't you haul him in?"

"Because I deserved it," Jake said. He'd pushed the man hard.

Braff frowned. "Do I need to worry about you and this guy?"

"No."

Braff crushed the paper into a ball and tossed it in his trashcan. Then he propped his elbows on his desk. "I need you back on the opioid thing."

"But I—"

"I gave you the weekend. Today is Monday. I kept my side of the deal. Now you backburner this."

"We can't just quit on her, boss. She's out there—"

"Yes. She's out there. But we have zero evidence she's out there against her will. She's eighteen so *can* be out there, doing whatever she wants to do."

"She's still in high school. And her mom is sure she *is* missing."

"Her mom is a miserable drunk who doesn't even know what day it is."

"We can't hold that against her daughter."

"I am *not* holding it against her daughter. I'm holding it against her credibility. And her best friend is sure she hitch-hiked to Colorado to visit her dad."

Jake fumed, but Braff was right. Jake had no new leads and he wouldn't be able to disprove the friend's story until Kate Ballard's father returned from the mountain survival course Kate supposedly went out there for. That trip would explain why her phone was off and her social media accounts had no new posts.

"When the dad gets home, we'll all sigh with relief. Or ramp back up." Braff leaned back. "Diggs will brief you on what's going on in the task force. There's a meeting tomorrow morning. Be there." Braff's gaze dropped to the paperwork on his desk. "You're dismissed."

In the hall, Callie grabbed Jake's arm. "I can take the task force meeting, Jake. You can keep on with—"

"No." Jake shook his head. "Braff's right. Until something new pops, her dad comes home or her body... uh, she's found... I need to step away from it."

CHAPTER TWO

Eddie Shaw checked his word count for the day: nineteen thousand six hundred and forty-two words. At this rate he'd be done writing the book by noon Thursday and could spend that afternoon and all day Friday cleaning up the manuscript. Five days to write a first draft. It would beat his personal record by six days. But writing these books was the easy part. Finding the right crime to write about and convincing the people involved—victims and witnesses and suspects and cops and coroners—to talk to him was what took time. When the research was done he spent a couple weeks letting it all percolate until he found the narrative thread that tied all the threads together. Then he banged it out. Presto. A true crime book of the Eddie Shaw brand chock full of illicit sex and sudden violence.

His phone rang. Caller ID said it was his agent. He considered letting it go to voicemail, but he'd played that game too many times recently. He took a deep breath and answered.

"Hey, Gavin." Eddie got up from his desk and took the phone over to the window. He squinted against the sun, and gazed down at the afternoon bustle along Court Street.

"You're avoiding my calls." Gavin Ellison spoke with that rapid-fire New York urgency Eddie hated.

"But I got your text, Gavin." It had reminded Eddie of his blown deadline and finished with "and we need to talk." Gavin used that phrase when he had bad news. Eddie didn't like bad news.

"And?"

"They didn't need to see the first three chapters. I'll have the whole thing to them by the end of the day Friday just like the contract says. I *am* a pro, Gavin." Eddie had learned that saying his agent's name sometimes softened him.

"Professionals don't miss deadlines."

Eddie ground his teeth, but said nothing.

"I've re-assigned you to one of our newer agents." Gavin paused, but Eddie had nothing to say. "The missed deadlines, Eddie. Those are my deadlines, too. My promises. My reputation. I can't—"

"I understand," Eddie said. The only surprise was how long Gavin had stuck with him through this long slow decline in sales.

"I *am* sorry, Eddie. But you'll like your new agent. She's young and full of energy. Her name is Haley Jones. She'll call you."

The line went dead. Gavin had hung up on him. Eddie put his phone in his pocket, his gaze finding the movie poster centered on his wall. *Trackside Hunter*. His first book. His big one. Gavin had landed Eddie that book deal and negotiated the advertising budget that propelled the book to number eight on the New York Times bestseller list. Then Gavin sold the story to Hollywood and the real fun began—fancy dinners, morning talk shows, long lines at book signings. Gavin had helped deliver that, but Eddie had done the work. Chasing the interviews that freed a man and put the real murderer behind bars—a train-hoping serial killer whose crimes, until Eddie's book, had never been recognized as linked.

Eddie shuddered at where that work had taken him. He'd nearly been killed twice while working hobo camps that most people thought had disappeared after the depression.

Since then he'd focused on lesser stories. Stories that didn't put him at risk. Stories with emotional hooks he amped up with titillating photos and evocative captions.

Since then, he'd played it safe, relying on his writing to thrill the reader when the material didn't do it. And that suited him.

He frowned, flexed his hands, and got back to work.

CHAPTER THREE

Jake didn't go straight home. He drove, radio off, windows down. The spring air whipped through the Mustang and cooled him down. Maybe Kate Ballard *had* gone to her see her dad in Colorado and was now deep in the Rocky Mountain wilderness with him roasting marshmallows over a campfire.

Jake hoped so.

But his gut told him Kate had never left Weston.

A girl going backpacking in the Rockies wouldn't leave her hiking boots behind. Jake had hiked in the Rockies many times. Good boots were essential to avoiding a sprained ankle or broken foot.

He parked at the curb in front of Ballard's apartment building, but decided against going up. With the sun dropping Kate's mom would already be halfway into her bottle of vodka and a sloppy mess. He had nothing good to tell her, and bad news can always wait.

He drove home, his thoughts turning to Anna. They'd spent most of the weekend together but it had felt off. Out of synch. Lots of long silences. She would look at him, then look away. Open her mouth to say something, then close it. Saturday night she left his place almost immediately after dinner, explaining she was worn out from her long week in court. It was the first Saturday night they'd spent apart in at least a month. On Sunday they went to lunch and a movie but then she pushed him out of her townhouse to take a call from her mom.

That had never happened before. She'd often used Jake's presence as an excuse *not* to take a call from her mom.

Just a few months earlier he'd been happy, or at least content. The ache of losing his wife—Mary had been murdered more than ten years before—faded to a blunt ache. Then he met Anna, and now a couple awkward silences had him twisted up. *Face it, Houser. You're in love.* It was third time he'd accused himself of it today. Maybe he needed to say it to Anna. Maybe that's what was bothering her.

And he did love her. He hadn't said it out loud because he still loved Mary. Her death had not changed that. Using that same word with Anna seemed… disloyal.

Jake slowed as he drove through the gate onto his property. It was a five-acre parcel on the end of Spring Street with a concrete block commercial building surrounded by the fading evidence of the landscaping business his dad had run from here for decades. Jake had converted the second-floor offices into an apartment and used the old shop area as a garage and basketball court.

He parked the Mustang inside and climbed the stairs to the apartment. It was warm here, the setting sun beaming through the wide windows that faced west across the old equipment yard to the Burlington Woods.

He changed into jeans and a Chicago Bears T-shirt, then sat down at the kitchen island. Braff was right about his investigation having gone cold, but that didn't mean Jake would drop it. His gut told him Kate Ballard was in trouble and he trusted his gut. He flipped open his laptop to review everything he'd entered about the case. Maybe he'd missed something and reading through his file one more time would reveal it.

Kate had spent the afternoon on a computer at the library watching videos. This was confirmed by security camera footage and her library account record. She spoke briefly to two girls who Jake identified and interviewed.

She left the library at 6:43 p.m. to walk home. A trio of girls from her high school had seen Kate in the Starbucks on Main at 6:49pm where she bought an iced coffee to go. Four security cameras caught her image as she cut west on Jefferson, then north on Mill toward the apartment she shared with her mom. The last image was captured three blocks south of the apartment. Kate was not seen again.

Close examination of every camera feed available showed no one following Kate.

Mrs. Ballard was sure her daughter never came home that evening.

If true, Kate had disappeared in that three-block stretch.

Jake interviewed all her neighbors and friends and acquaintances. He had found her passwords and reviewed all her social media accounts. Patrolmen canvassed the entire neighborhood and the entire stretch of her walk home, twice.

They found nothing.

Then Alan Mitchell called in. The only hinky thing in Kate's life. But Jake was sure he was clean.

Jake closed the laptop. He hadn't missed anything.

"Kate is in Colorado." Saying it out loud didn't convince him of it.

His stomach growled, reminding him he hadn't eaten.

Jake had planned to get dinner with Anna but now that he was on his own, he had to scrounge something up. He pulled the pan of lasagna left over from Saturday out of the fridge. As he cut a slice he wondered why only half of it was left; he'd only had one slice on Saturday night. He plated the slice and put it in the microwave, then poured himself a glass from the open bottle of red wine. He sipped the wine while the microwave hummed.

The microwave dinged. When he opened the door the sharp scents of tomatoes and sausage made his mouth water. He took the plate to the island counter and ate. This wasn't the first time Anna had been moody, but it was the first time she'd kept the reason to herself.

Done eating, he put the plate in the dishwasher then took the wine to his recliner and turned on the TV news. A few minutes later his doorbell buzzed.

He hopped out of the chair and bounded down the stairs a smile growing on his face.

But it wasn't Anna. It was Doug Rieser, Chairman of the Weston Board of Police Commissioners. The Board was responsible for hiring, firing, and setting policy. Anything the Board had to say should be filtered through several layers of police department hierarchy before it got to Jake.

This visit couldn't be good.

CHAPTER FOUR

Jake stood in the open door and watched Rieser scan the property. The man wore jeans and soft brown leather shoes and a blue windbreaker with the hood puddled on his shoulders. When his gaze came to the door Rieser startled. "I didn't hear the door open."

"Come on in, Doug."

He led Doug between his Mustang and his C10 pickup—Anna did *not* like riding in the truck—to the back half of the shop. He had floored it with rubber and installed a basketball hoop and some exercise equipment. In the corner he'd set up a lounge area with a pair of couches, a giant TV, and an old oak bar against the wall. He had also gutted and rebuilt the bathroom his dad's workmen had used, adding a small bank of lockers and a shower.

Jake gestured to one of the couches and Doug sat perched on the edge, looking over the space. Interested, or reluctant to get to what had brought him here. Jake sat on the other end of the couch and watched him. He knew Rieser, they'd gone to high school together. But he didn't know him well.

"Is this really where you live?"

"It's convenient."

"It's the world's best bachelor pad."

"Thanks." Jake knew Rieser meant it as a compliment, but the comment still bit. Jake was a widower, not a bachelor.

"What was this place before?"

"My dad ran his landscaping company out of here for over forty years."

The gas-fired heaters ignited with a *whoosh*. Doug flinched and looked around until he spotted them high up against the ceiling.

"What brings you here, Doug?" Jake spoke loudly over the heater noise. Their roar would continue until the temperature rose to sixty-five degrees.

"Police business."

"You mean police *commission* business."

"Not exactly," Doug said.

Jake was about to ask Rieser what the hell that meant when he remembered a connection they shared. "You dated Bev, didn't you?" Bev Warren was Jake's cousin on his mother's side. She was also the current sheriff of Paget County.

"Dated?"

"Back in high school."

"Oh right." Rieser went silent.

Jake waited. He was good at waiting. A long silence could crack open even the toughest witness. Rieser's gaze wandered the big space, hands squeezing his knees. When his gaze came back to Jake, he said, "I'm actually here because of a letter Sheriff Warren received and forwarded to me." He pulled a folded piece of paper out of an inside pocket of his windbreaker and held it out to Jake.

Jake didn't reach for it. Whatever was in the letter should be routed through the proper channels. Back door communication always burned the low man involved. Jake leaned back.

Rieser lifted the paper. "It's about Ballard."

Jake frowned. "If it's about my case, a Weston case, why was it sent to Bev?"

"The woman who wrote it doesn't trust the Weston PD. And because Sheriff Warren transferred the Professional Standards Department to the Weston PD, she has no official way to look into the letter's allegations. So, she gave it to me."

"The letter should go there. To Weston's Professional Standards department."

"It should, but it can't. Read the letter and you'll see why."

Jake didn't like that answer but he was hooked. He took the letter from Rieser and unfolded it. It was printed on bright white paper with a slick sheen.

Dear Sheriff Warren,

My dad James T. Larson killed himself while in prison for a murder he didn't commit. I finally know who did it. For a long time I thought Mose Belker was the real killer because the murder my dad was convicted of was exactly like the two Mr. Belker confessed to. When I turned eighteen I started visiting Mr. Belker in prison. I tried to get him to admit it and clear my dad's name. He wouldn't. He talks a lot, but mostly to himself, and about bible stuff. But today I told him about the disappearance of Kate Ballard because it reminds me of those girls back then. When I showed him the picture of her from the paper he said "Mike's at it again." He didn't even know he'd said it out loud until I asked him "Who is Mike?"

He was shocked to hear me say that name I can tell you. But he hardly said another word that wasn't from the bible while I was there. But when the guard was taking him away he said "The Weston cops knew the truth about your dad." That means they knew my dad was innocent and they let him go to prison where he was treated so horribly he had to kill himself!

I have a clue as to who Mike is. One time when Mr. Belker was telling me stories about growing up—this is before he got stuck on talking all about the bible—he said his friend Mike got him a job laying concrete.

Because of what Mr. Belker said about the Weston police I can't talk to them.

Please help me!

Thank you.

The sender's name was printed "Donna Larson" and signed in unreadable purple loops.

"Mose Belker?" Jake remembered the name but not much more. He'd been living in Chicago back when it hit the news. "Refresh my memory, Doug."

Two young women, Amy Smith and Linda Brown, were killed in 1982. Both murders went unsolved. In 1999, a Weston detective remembered the semen found on Smith's body and tracked down the man the original investigating detective had liked for the murder—Mose Belker—to get a DNA sample for comparison. While interviewing Belker, the man suddenly confessed to both murders.

"What about the murder James Larson went down for?"

"Beth Lachey, 1986. In Glenbard. She was strangled, not stabbed."

"Could Belker have done that one too?"

Rieser shrugged. "Larson was convicted."

"Anything ever come out about Belker having an accomplice?" Jake held up the letter. "A guy named Mike?"

"No."

The whole story was probably just a ploy by Belker to string more visits out of this woman. She was probably a looker. Even if she wasn't, a guy who'd been in prison for twenty years was thankful for any kind of visitor. This story guaranteed she'd be back.

Jake scanned the letter again. "I don't see why the letter can't go to Weston's new Professional Standards department."

"Because Deputy Chief of Patrol Stewart runs it. His father was chief when these two girls were killed and when Larson was convicted of killing Lachey. He was also acting chief when Belker confessed."

Abe Stewart. Jake had met the man and heard the stories. If someone in the Weston PD had known Larson's dad was innocent, Abe Stewart had also known it. Sam Stewart could not investigate his own father.

"Why didn't you take this to Braff or Chief Arvind?"

"Bev was only sure about you."

Jake shook his head. She was putting him in a tough position.

"What if Belker *does* know who took Ballard?"

Jake gritted his teeth, but Rieser had him. "I'll work the Kate Ballard angle but not the rest of it," Jake said. "And no back-channel reporting to you. No follow up from you. No interference from you."

"Agreed."

After Rieser left, Jake went back upstairs and signed into the department system to read up on the Smith and Brown cases, but their murder books were too old to be online. He switched to Google and found dozens of newspaper articles on both murders, on Mose Belker, and on the Beth Lachey murder. He downloaded them all into a file on his hard drive he labeled as "Mike." He decided against adding it to his Ballard case file. So far it was nothing more than a daughter's wishful thinking and a confessed killer's rambling. He needed to confirm the story before he put it in his case file. When he did—*if* he did—it would raise a lot of questions and he needed to have answers.

His phone rang: Bill Coogan.

"I'm just sitting here wondering if my best friend since second grade had any news for me."

"What kind of news, Coog?"

"How was Anna this weekend?"

"Well, things between us felt off." He told Coogan about Saturday night and how she'd rushed him out of her house on Sunday when she got a call from her mom. "How did you know to ask?"

"Judy saw Anna at the pharmacy buying pre-natal vitamins."

Jake's face flushed as the weight of Coogan's words rushed through him. That explained Anna's increased appetite and staying away from the wine. "She's… pregnant?" Jake popped up from his chair and started pacing the room. "Are you sure?"

"Judy was sure about what Anna was buying, but pregnancy is just a logical guess."

Jake stopped in the middle of the wide window that looked west to the forest preserve. The sun had now set, the forest canopy backlit by the twilight bleeding over the horizon. The image blurred. He rubbed tears from his eyes. "I'm going to be a dad."

"Congratulations, my friend."

"I can't… " He took a breath. "Mary and I always… we just kept putting it off."

"I know."

Jake resumed pacing, his heart hammering. "I'm too old."

"Nonsense."

"Why do you think she hasn't told me?"

"Well… Maybe she, uh."

Jake stopped pacing. "What?"

"Her body, her choice."

Jake squeezed his eyes shut against the possibility that phrase pushed into his mind. "But if she bought the vitamins—and she didn't drink any wine Saturday night—that means she's made her choice, right?"

"Maybe. Or maybe she's keeping her options open until she decides."

Jake stopped pacing again, Coogan's words echoing painfully through his head: *Until she decides.* If Anna was pregnant and it was his—of course it was—then he should have a say. He was getting old; this might be his last shot at being a dad. "I should go over there right now."

"Or maybe you should sleep on it before you talk to her," Coog said.

Jake sat down. His pulse fluttered, and his legs trembled. Was that excitement, or fear? Or guilt. Anna was on her way to a distinguished career at the States Attorney's office. Having a baby would screw that up. Hell, she'd never once mentioned wanting children and he'd certainly never brought it up. They were just getting—

"You still there, buddy?"

"I'm here," Jake said. "You're right. I'm going to sleep on it." But Jake didn't anticipate getting much sleep.

CHAPTER FIVE

Paget County Sheriff Bev Warren loved that her job kept her busy twenty-four hour a day, seven day a week. As a single woman with no hobbies, no husband or children, and an ever-dwindling collection of friends, the job kept her too busy to mope about missing out on those things. But as she entered her forties, she'd begun to resent her job for the same reason: without the job, maybe she *would* have hobbies, a family, and time to keep up with friends. But now things were changing, on the job and off. On the job she'd gotten fit, working her body back to the lithe athletic form she's last had in high school, and she'd climbed out from behind her desk to manage her people from the streets. Off the job, she had a man in her life who often made her feel like a teenager again. Probably because they'd dated in high school.

Tonight, she was back behind a desk reading a file, but she wasn't at work, and this file had nothing to do with her position as Paget County's top cop. This file was one of nearly two dozen she had found in a safe hidden in her dad's home office after he died. Every file held a piece of leverage over a local politician, businessman, or government bureaucrat. She liked to think her dad had only used the files to encourage the men named in them to help with one of his many social justice programs. But just before his death she learned he wasn't exactly what she'd always thought him to be.

When Bev inherited the house, the files became hers. She'd left them in the safe, knowing that saving them meant she was, to some degree, like her dad.

But she had never used one.

Until now.

If her plan worked—and it would—she knew the players and how they thought. She would get to lay this file down like it filled an inside straight, forcing a lesson on the man who had once forced the same lesson on her.

Her phone dinged with an incoming text. It was from Forensic Investigator in Charge Duke Fanning: *Urgent—read my email and the attached report NOW!*

Duke Fanning rarely used exclamation marks so she immediately pulled her laptop out of her bag and read what he'd sent. Fanning was the county's best forensic investigator, but hope made her question his conclusion when he answered her call. "You're absolutely sure about this?"

"Positive. I ran the test three times. Both victims overdosed on heroin spiked with carfentanil. Synthetic. One hundred times stronger than fentanyl, which is one hundred times stronger than morphine. The stuff's deadly. Back in 2016—"

"In Ohio. I remember." One hundred and seventy-six overdoses resulting in over seventy dead.

"We need to act fast."

"I'll put out a press release."

"You'd mean it as a warning but the addicts would take it as a quality alert. They'd want some, sure they could dose themselves right and ride that high. It's happened to other towns."

"Then we need to find the source and shut it down," Bev said, knowing the "we" was really her. She headed the countywide opioid task force and with every new overdose her bosses—and the press—reminded her where the buck stopped. "Right now. Tonight."

"If we can."

"Okay, Duke. Thanks for the alert. This is on me now." After the call Bev got back on her laptop and sent a message to every detective on the opioid task force to gather in the war room immediately. She also called the judge on warrant duty and let her know she would get some faxes at home tonight.

Bev grabbed her keys and her bag. The front door opened.

"Hey!" Doug broke into the wide smile that always pulled a smile to her own face.

"Hey, yourself." She rose onto her toes and kissed him. A soft lingering kiss that left her legs shaky. Like a schoolgirl.

"You heading out?"

"I have a minute. What did Jake say?"

"He read the letter and said he'll—Hey, I didn't know you had a safe in here."

Shit! "My dad kept his important papers in there, mortgage, birth certificates. Stuff like that." She scooped the file off her desk then knelt on the hardwood and stuffed it back in the safe. She swung the door shut and closed the fake drawer front over it.

"That really disappears."

Bev stood back up. "So… Jake?"

"He didn't like me coming to him outside the chain of command because someone in the department is dirty. But he understood and said he'll work the Ballard part of it. All exactly like you thought."

"Thanks, Doug." Bev grabbed her coat from the rack and headed for the door. Jake would start with the Ballard allegation, but she knew he wouldn't stop there. He would get to the bottom of the entire sordid mess. She counted on it.

"Where are you headed?"

"I'll tell you about it later."

"You want me to stay? Wait up?"

"Stay, but don't wait up." She kissed him again and got moving.

CHAPTER SIX

Eddie Shaw got up early because he was finally ready. The paperback novel sat on the table by the front door where it had been sitting for a month as he worked up the guts to make this play.

He washed up, put on his jean jacket and grabbed the novel. He went downstairs, around to the alley, and got in his Mercedes. He headed west toward the Drake Diner for breakfast.

And to deliver the book.

He parked the Mercedes in the middle of three empty spaces and took a moment to look at the car before going inside. He'd paid cash for it when he got the option money for the movie. Twenty years old now, the paint was fading and it no longer turned heads as it had. But neither did Eddie.

Eddie paused inside the diner to scan for Penny. The place was packed with businessmen eating giant breakfasts and wait-staff and busboys rushing back and forth to keep up with the crush of diners.

"Eddie!"

Hearing Penny say his name always made him smile.

She waved to him from near the long curve of windows that looked out over the patio. She ushered him to a small table for two still wet from the bus boy's rag. She slapped down a paper napkin wrapped around cutlery, set a coffee mug in front of him, and filled it, raising the coffee pot as she poured until it was above his head.

"Show off," he said. The coffee smelled strong enough to wake the dead. Perfect.

"What'll you have?"

He ordered a Denver omelet and watched her work while he sipped coffee and waited for his meal. Penny dashed around the tables in a high-energy ballet, hips twitching under tight polyester. She was bigger now. Who wasn't? But she still had that hourglass shape that slayed him in high school. Back then she'd been the apex of the IN crowd and he'd been less than nothing. She left Des Moines the day after graduation and spent ten years knocking on Hollywood's door before coming back home.

He'd run into her at their high school reunion. She remembered him from a poem he'd read out loud in English class, reciting a line as they stood in line for drinks. They ended up in the sack together.

Ever since then he'd been trying to turn that into something more, without luck. She was unimpressed with the books he wrote, telling him they were "not to her taste" which ran to the cozy mystery novels she read when things were slow. She'd gotten mad when he laughed and told her anyone could write one of them. "So why don't you?" she said.

So he wrote three, self-published them, then bought her copies on Amazon and had them delivered to her apartment. And waited. Finally, last week, he spotted her reading one of his Lake Lodge Mysteries and asked her how she liked it. She loved it as he knew she would because he'd read all her favorites and wrote his three-book series exactly to her taste: the aging amateur super-sleuth with the devoted gay nephew, the wide circle of quirky friends, and the secret source inside the police department.

"Here you go." She slid the huge plate onto the table and refilled his mug with another high-flying pour.

"You should take that show on the road."

"Don't tell me you're reading a Lake Lodge Mystery now?"

"That's for you," he said, and slid the book to the edge of the table. "Signed by the author."

"Eddie! How cool." She put down the coffee pot and snatched up the book. She opened it, flicked through to the title page and read the inscription. "Penny. I told you I could write one of these." Her brow furrowed and she looked down at Eddie. "You signed this."

"I wrote it."

"Inez Swanson wrote it."

"A pen name. Check the copyright page."

She flicked to that page and her finger ran back and forth until she found his name. Her cheeks turned red. "You're an asshole."

He hadn't expected the anger. "I… You said you didn't like my books and I just wanted to show you I'm a good writer."

"No! You wanted to show me that the books I love are crap."

"Not at all." This was going sideways. "They're good books. The cozies I wrote are good books. And my true crime books are *good books*."

She crossed her arms. "You told me you write those in a couple weeks."

"So?"

"How long did it take to write *Trackside Hunter*?"

"What?"

"I just finished it last night. That book is a lot different than the *stuff* you write now."

"It was my first book."

Penny leaned forward, her still impressive cleavage spilling out of the top of her uniform. He kept his eyes off it. "Did you really solve those murders while you were researching that book?"

"I did," Eddie said. He couldn't keep the pride out of his voice.

"Why don't you do that anymore? Those other books—*Killer Coed* and *Mad Mother-in-Law* and *Deranged Divorce*—they're nothing like that first one. That book *helped* people. If you can investigate something like that and *solve it*... bring *closure* to all those families. Deliver *justice*. Then why are you wasting your talents on the stuff you're writing now?"

Eddie set his fork down. "People like my books."

She straightened up. "But you can do more. Solving a murder seems so much more... *important*."

"What you do isn't important." As soon as the words left his mouth he regretted them. Her job, which she loved, was a sensitive subject. She wondered if something was wrong with her for settling for this job after all her big plans. Every time she brought it up he'd told her that was nonsense. Now he'd made a lie of his support.

Penny's lips compressed as she pushed back from the table. "I feed people and brighten their mornings. It's worth doing, but if I could do more, I would." She got up and hustled off.

His face reddened with shame.

He finished his omelet and left.

She never came back to refill his coffee.

* * *

Eddie brooded about what he'd said to Penny the entire drive home. He'd lashed out because she was right. Writing *Trackside Hunter was* the most important thing he'd ever done.

Back home at the condo he'd bought with his earnings from the Trackside movie he sat down at his desk. He set his phone on the desk next to him, waiting for—hoping for—her forgiveness. Knowing that he didn't deserve it.

He flipped open the laptop and put his fingers on the keyboard. He needed another twenty thousand words today. Twenty thousand words of sensationalism and exploitation. He slammed the laptop closed and shoved it aside, knocking a stack of mail off the desk. He rubbed his face then picked up the mail and turned on his desk lamp. He'd handle this mess then get back to work.

Procrastination was every writer's enemy.

He sorted through it, saving the bills and tossing the rest of it into the garbage can until he got to a white envelope addressed in purple ink. The return address said it was from Donna Larson in Weston, Illinois. He didn't know a Donna Larson and had never heard of Weston, Illinois. But he knew what would be inside. He used to get so many letters like this one he couldn't even read them all. But this was the first one in a long time.

Dear Mr. Shaw.

My dad James T. Larson killed himself while in prison for a murder he didn't commit. I finally know who did it. For a long time I thought Mose Belker was the real killer because the murder my dad was convicted of was exactly like the two Mr. Belker confessed to. When I turned 18 I started visiting Mr. Belker in prison. I tried to get him to admit it and clear my dad's name. He wouldn't. He talks a lot, but mostly to himself, and more and more about bible stuff. But today I told him about Kate Ballard disappearing while walking home and he nodded like he knew all about it and said "Mike's at it again." He didn't even know he'd said it out loud until I asked him "Who is Mike?"

He was shocked to hear me say that name I can tell you. But he hardly said another word that wasn't from the bible until the guard was taking him away. Then he said "The Weston cops knew he did that girl, not your dad."

Don't you see? This guy Mike killed Beth Lachey, not my dad. Can you please help me? I have a clue on who Mike is. One time when Mr. Belker was telling me stories about growing up he said his friend Mike got him a job laying concrete. Just so you know, I sent a letter to the Sheriff here, too.

PLEASE HELP ME!!

Eddie read the letter again, his excitement building. If what Larson alleged was true, this story might even be better than *Trackside Hunter*. A wrongfully convicted man. Crooked cops. A killer still on the run. And a missing girl.

But it might be even more dangerous to investigate.

Eddie stretched out on his couch to think it through. The dual angles could really amp up his narrative: the wrongfully convicted man who killed himself in prison and the real killer still out there in the world, abducting, raping, and murdering young women.

Naming the real killer had propelled *Trackside Hunter* to the New York Times bestseller list and landed Eddie the movie deal. Could he ride this story that far? It certainly had potential—if he could identify Mike and tie him to the current case.

But chasing a killer on the loose had nearly gotten Eddie killed twenty years ago. Twice. Those close calls were why he now wrote about settled cases with lurid story lines. Safe stories where the killer was in prison and all Eddie had to do was weave an entertaining narrative.

But Larson's story had so much potential he had to chase it. There might even be two wrongfully convicted men. If the murder Larson's dad went to prison for *was* identical to the murders Belker confessed to, maybe this *Mike* committed all three and Belker was also innocent. Maybe Eddie could limit his investigation to the cold parts of the story and leave the search for the missing girl to the cops. That way he would stay off the radar of both the killer and any crooked Weston cops. Could he find all the answers he needed in the past?

Eddie went back to his desk and started researching what was available online about the old murders. Every big newspaper in the country was digitizing its old editions and he had subscriptions to all the biggies.

Amy Smith and Laura Brown were murdered in 1982. The murders did look nearly identical: the teenage girl snatched off the side of the road, stabbed to death with an identical knife, raped post mortem, dumped on vacant land outside Weston. Belker had known Smith and was questioned in both cases but never charged and he soon moved to Iowa. In 1999 a Weston detective took up the Smith case because her killer had left semen behind. The detective drove to Iowa and got a court order to obtain a sample of Belker's DNA. Within hours Belker confessed to killing both Smith and Brown.

Beth Lachey was murdered in 1986. Like Smith and Brown, she was snatched off the side of the road, murdered, raped, and dumped on an abandoned railroad siding in a town north of Weston. But Lachey had been strangled: a much more controlled and personal way to kill someone than the mad stabbing Belker used to kill Smith and Brown.

So Larson's original premise that the Lachey murder was exactly like Smith and Brown was wrong. But some serial killers did change their methodology as they perfected the fantasy they were living out.

But James Larson, Donna Larson's father, had known Lachey. He had been her high school English teacher and creative writing advisor. According to long and erotic passages in Lachey's diary they had been involved in a torrid affair. James Larson claimed the diary entries were pure fantasy. He testified that Lachey read a lot of romance novels—which had been confirmed—and was planning to be a romance novelist herself. Larson had been awaiting appeal when he was gang-raped in prison and committed suicide the next day. A horrible end if the man had been innocent; deserved if he'd been guilty.

Eddie read what the internet offered about the girl currently missing. All he found were a couple articles in local papers—the Daily Herald and the Patch—asking people to contact a tip line with information.

Eddie went back to the letter. The idea that Mike was "at it again" as Belker had told Larson, seemed off. Serial killers didn't take time off. Either 'Mike' had been killing all this time or something had interrupted his work. Prison, most likely.

Or Mike was imaginary—a sick game Belker dreamed up to amuse himself and keep Donna Larson coming back to talk to him.

Belker *had* confessed to the first two murders. Juries—and readers—believed confessions. Coerced confessions did happen, but mostly in big cities where the police department was overwhelmed: Chicago, New York, LA. Was Weston near Chicago?

Eddie googled the town. It was a suburb about 35 miles west of the city. But it wasn't a sleepy little town. It was the fifth largest town in Illinois. It had a high median income, an award-winning library, and was continually ranked A Great Place to Live and A Great Place to Raise a Family. A suburban Shangri-La according to one over-the-top article.

But it also had a very low crime rate.

Eddie could spin that. The suburban Shangri-La had so little crime that when confronted with a murder the in-over-their-head cops railroaded a local loser.

He found the Weston P.D. website and submitted his standard Freedom of Information Act requests to see the files on the two murders from 1982. The law gave the city up to ten business days to respond which was too long to do him any good, but maybe he'd get lucky. Maybe an eager FOIA officer would jump right on it.

Or maybe Eddie had just signaled the dirty cops in Weston that eyes were on them.

He pushed the laptop away.

That mistake could get him killed.

CHAPTER SEVEN

Deputy Chief of Patrol Samuel A. Stewart III was third generation Weston Police Department royalty. Both his father, Samuel A. Stewart, Jr.—"Abe"—and his grandfather, Samuel A. Stewart, Sr.—"Sammy"—had been chiefs of the department. The city hall rumor mill said current Chief Arvind was getting ready to announce his retirement. Whoever Arvind recommended as his replacement would get the job and there were only two real candidates—Sam, and Deputy Chief of Detectives Braff.

"I'm twice the cop Braff is." Sam started talking to himself after his wife left him. Without her the house was just so damn quiet. He tried leaving on the TV or the radio, but couldn't get used to either. He'd decided it was a harmless habit, but now he was doing it at work, too. "So what?" he asked himself.

"What was that, Deputy Chief?"

Sam looked up from the manpower reports on his desk to find Sergeant Massey standing in his door. He was a big man who stood straight and tall, projecting an air of confidence and capability that no doubt explained why the men responded so well to him.

"What is it, Sergeant?" Sam checked his watch. "I can't authorize overtime when you're working in records."

"I need to talk to you."

"About?"

"Something… private."

Sam frowned. Managing people was a never-ending string of reasons why they couldn't work: illness, injury, doctor's appointments, cable-TV hook-ups, appliance repairmen, parent-teacher conferences, and on-and-on. He eyed Massey, but the big man was in uniform and looked shipshape, alert, and healthy. He probably wanted to whine about his reassignment. One of Sam's first actions as the new head of Professional Standards had been to put Massey in the records room to punish him for fixing a misdemeanor drug possession charge for a city councilman's son.

"Come in, then."

Massey came in and shut the door.

"*I* decide when my door is to be closed, Sergeant."

Massey sat down in the guest chair across the desk, pulling a bulky black nylon briefcase onto his lap. "You'll want it closed, boss."

Sam leaned back in his chair. Massey was awfully sure of himself. "Out with it."

"We got two Freedom of Information Act requests this morning on old murder cases. The '82 murders of Amy Smith and Linda Brown."

Sam remembered his dad talking about the cases. Not back then, but fifteen or twenty years later when they arrested someone. "Closed cases, right. By confession if I remember correctly."

"That's right. Mose Belker. In '99."

"And?"

Massey paused and swallowed. His gaze flitted around the room, never landing back on Sam. He'd lost his cool.

"Spit it out, Sergeant."

"My dad was on the force with your dad, Chief Abe Stewart. And they were pretty tight. Dad had your job back then. Anyway—"

"I'm losing my patience, Sergeant."

"Your dad will want to know about this. Immediately."

"Because?"

"My dad wouldn't say."

Of course not. No one talked about Abe Stewart's business without his okay. Sam frowned. "Tell me what *you* remember about this."

Massey rubbed the briefcase, his rough hands making a soft whistle against the ballistic nylon fabric. "The chief at the time—this is '99—went out with a detective and got Belker's confessions. A few weeks later that chief resigned and your dad left his job with the city and came back as acting chief. The cases were closed and Belker went to jail. A few months later they hired a new chief."

"None of that seems… sensitive."

"I don't know, *personally*, what went on."

What went on. An apt phrase to describe lots of things Sam's dad got into. "But you've heard enough to be sure of this move you're making here. Accusing my dad, a decorated chief of this department, of doing something unseemly that a FOIA request might uncover?"

"I'm thinking of your promotion, sir. And the department." Massey rubbed the briefcase again. It was stuffed thick, something with hard corners.

Damn right. Getting the chief spot *would* be good for the department.

"Who made the FOIA requests?"

"Eddie Shaw. I googled him. He writes true crime books. Wrote one that became a hit movie. *Trackside Hunter.* Remember that?"

"I don't watch movies." Sam didn't understand people's obsession with movies and TV shows. You knew they were fake when you watched them so they meant nothing. It was no better than listening to someone describe their dreams.

"Anyway, I thought you should know about it."

Why now? Sam wondered. It had been twenty years since Belker confessed. Massey rubbed the briefcase again.

"What's in the briefcase?"

"I brought you the Smith and Brown murder books. I thought maybe you would want to look through them before I make copies for the writer."

"Let's have them."

Massey pulled two thick three-ring binders out of his bag. Their covers were dog-eared and loose pages stuck out in various places. He held the binders out.

Sam didn't reach for them. A hand-off would feel like an exchange—the file for something in return. A quid pro quo. Sam didn't do quid pro quos. But he did need to see the files. "Leave them on the desk and you can go."

Massey set them down and rose to leave.

"And mark both FOIA requests for a ten day response and send the copies out by regular mail."

"Will do, Deputy Chief."

"Hold it," Sam said. If there was some dirt on his dad to be uncovered by the writer then Massey was right that its disclosure could ruin Sam's shot at the top job.

Massey turned back.

"Let me know what else you hear about this writer. If he requests any other files or whatever."

Massey smiled, and why not. He'd gotten what he wanted. He was doing the boss favors, and now was owed favors in return. Sam didn't like to owe favors to people under him, but this time it couldn't be helped.

He would not let his dad's dirty hands ruin his shot at the top job.

CHAPTER EIGHT

Jake woke with his brain buzzing about Anna's pregnancy. He'd changed his mind after talking to Coogan and driven over to her townhouse, but she didn't answer her door. Or his phone calls. Or his texts.

Maybe that had been for the best. By the time he got to her house he'd been angry: At Anna for keeping her pregnancy secret and at himself for his role in putting this impossible decision on her.

Hoping for the clarity and focus that exercise often brought him, he went for a run. The spring air was cold and thick with humidity. He cut through the forest preserve on the wood-chip path spongy from the wettest May on record, then took the long curve of Douglas to Jefferson.

He did not doubt Anna was pregnant. It explained her behavior: eating more, not drinking wine, talking to her mom, not answering his calls. And it explained how she looked at him Saturday night. She'd been gauging his acceptability as a father and partner.

And maybe as a husband.

What had she seen? A work-obsessed widower who kept to himself when away from the job. A middle-aged man living in a commercial building customized for his hobbies. He didn't sound like partner or father material even to him.

He ran on the Riverwalk south through downtown then came home on surface streets.

He showered and dressed, then sat down at the kitchen island with a bowl of oatmeal. He shouldn't pressure Anna—he would wait for her to come to him.

After he finished eating he opened his laptop and clicked through to his "Mike" file. He'd given the material a quick read when he downloaded it, but now examined it much closer. He found nothing hinting at Belker having an accomplice, at Belker having anything to do with Lachey, or at anyone named Mike.

But he found one interesting thing. Although the express purpose of the trip to see Belker in Iowa in 1999 was to get his DNA sample to compare to the evidence found on Smith, no newspaper articles reported a match. Apparently, his confession had finished the story in the reporter's minds except for one final article when Belker was sentenced.

But the DNA must have matched. Confessions were not accepted at face value. They were tested, probed, and confirmed.

The Smith murder book should answer that question.

And prepare Jake to interview Mose Belker.

Jake closed his laptop and slipped Larson's letter into the inside pocket of his blazer. He equipped himself from the drawer in the kitchen: Glock in its belt holster, badge, pocketknife, two sets of latex gloves, three sets of plastic zip cuffs, notebook and pen. He checked his phone on his way down to the garage, but found nothing from Anna. He jumped in his Mustang and headed for the station.

As he made his way down to the to the basement records room to get the murder books on Smith and Brown, the intercom announced a 'Houser Sighting.' Jake ignored it and kept moving.

The civilian clerk at the records counter took Jake's order and disappeared into the stacks. A few minutes later a uniformed officer—a patrol sergeant according to his insignia—appeared from the stacks. He was a tall, thick-chested man who wore his complete equipment belt even though he wasn't on patrol. A serious cop. His nametag said SGT. MASSEY. Jake knew the name but had never worked directly with the man.

"You asked for the books on two closed cases, Detective?"

"Yes."

"I thought you were on the Ballard thing… the missing girl?"

"I am. What's the problem?"

"We started reorganizing the back of the stacks and things are in a jumble."

"Did you lose the books?"

"We'll find them, Detective. It's just a manpower issue. Priorities. I can have a volunteer look for them tonight and—"

"I need them right now, Sergeant."

"On the Ballard thing?"

"What's the problem, Sergeant?"

"No problem. We'll get right on it and I'll call you when we find them."

"I'll wait right here," Jake said.

Massey nodded and disappeared into the stacks.

Jake shook his head in frustration as he sat down on the padded bench. He pulled out Larson's letter and read it again. Was he wasting time here? Probably, but he had nothing else going right now. He put the letter away and leaned back against the wall and waited.

CHAPTER NINE

Deputy Chief of Patrol Sam Stewart went through both murder books. He flipped past the crime scene and autopsy photos, but pored over the written reports. Despite spending only one short stint in the detective division—investigating a string of vandalism incidents on city artwork—he could tell the assigned detective had done a thorough and competent job. He interviewed Belker for both murders because Belker had known the first victim. Even with his twenty-twenty hindsight, Sam didn't see anything in either Belker interview transcript that gave the man away.

The only thing that grabbed Sam's attention came at the end of the Smith book. A semen sample had been collected off Smith's body in 1982. In 1999 a new detective went to Iowa to get Belker's DNA swab to compare to the evidentiary sample. Belker immediately confessed. Sam saw notations for both the evidence collection and the DNA swab in the case chronology, but there were no matching forensic reports. A handwritten entry at the end of the chronology said, "BELKER'S DNA MATCHED."

Sam picked up the book and brought it closer to his eyes. It was his dad's handwriting. The DNA test had to be what his dad was—

"Boss?" Massey. Leaning in the open doorway, one hand on the jamb.

"What, Sergeant?"

"I need to talk with you about what we discussed earlier. Houser—"

"Get in here. And close the door."

Massey closed the door and sat down without being invited.

The man needed an adjustment. Being owed a favor by his boss apparently made him feel like he could take liberties. "Stop calling me boss. It's Deputy Chief."

"Of course, Deputy Chief."

Sam leaned back. "What is it?"

"Houser just came down and asked for both these books." Massey gestured at the binders.

First the writer, now Houser? That couldn't be a coincidence. "What's he working on?"

"That missing person's case. The girl who—"

"Kate Ballard," Sam said. He had her picture in every squad car, like procedure dictated, even though she most likely had just run off to Colorado to spend time with her dad or was hiding out with another secret boyfriend.

"I asked him if it was for that and he didn't answer me," Massey said.

Some detectives considered themselves above patrol, but Sam had never gotten that vibe from Houser. Which meant he had a reason for avoiding the question.

"What did you tell him?"

"That it would take some time to find the books and he sat down to wait."

Sam frowned. Whoever had tipped off the writer must have also tipped off Braff and he put his favorite detective on it. If Braff could smear Abe Stewart the taint would stretch to Sam and he'd lose his chance at the top job. Braff was playing hardball.

Sam closed the Brown book, stacked it on top of the Smith book and pushed both across the desk. "Take them."

"You don't want to… edit them?"

"Take them!"

Massey scooped them off the desk and stood up.

"Wait," Sam said. "Houser does some kind of book like this on missing person's cases, right?"

"A case file. It's online."

"Do you have access to it?"

"As the database administrator I'll be able to read everything in the file but I can't enter anything myself."

That's exactly what Sam needed to keep an eye on Houser. "Give me your access codes."

"Boss—I mean Deputy Chief—that's asking—"

"I'll reassign you to patrol as soon as I can."

"You can do it now."

"Right now I need you where you are. Listen, this is Braff's play for the top job. If he gets it, he'll reallocate budgetary resources to the Detective Division. We can't have that. Policing starts on the streets, Massey. We have to protect that."

"Okay." Massey recited his codes while Sam wrote them down. He was getting in very deep to Sergeant Massey.

It couldn't be helped if Sam wanted the top job, which he very much did.

How far was he willing to go to get it? he asked himself.

Pretty damn far.

CHAPTER TEN

Eddie stared at his laptop for a long time, wishing he hadn't submitted the FOIA requests. Maybe he'd get lucky and the FOIA officer would be a civilian employee paper shuffler and no one with any authority or hook into the past would hear about them.

Or maybe he should drop the story. He was making a living. But Penny was right. His books were lurid—that's why people read them. Penny made him want to do better. To *be* better. She was always challenging what he thought and even what he felt.

He needed her. He wanted her.

This story had everything *Trackside Hunter* had, and more: innocent man, killer on the loose, a missing girl. And dirty cops.

He rubbed his face, then went back through what he'd found.

He didn't buy Belker as a serial killer. The man had moved to Iowa immediately after being questioned in the Brown murder in 1982. He'd gotten married, found a job he held on to for sixteen years, and became a leader at his church. All without an incident of any kind.

Eddie had researched a lot of serial killers and two things were so universally true they'd become rules: once the killer got started, he kept at it, and once a killer found a methodology—a ritual, an MO—he stuck to it. The first two murders—the pair of girls from Weston—were committed close together and were nearly identical in all aspects. Clearly the work of one man. But the Lachey murder in 1986 didn't follow the rules; it came after a four-year gap and the modus was different. And Belker had moved to Iowa so wasn't even around for Lachey.

If the same man killed the Weston pair in 1982 and Lachey in 1986, then he'd spent those four intervening years killing other women and developing his ritual into the modus he'd used on Lachey. When Eddie identified those murders, he'd be able to see the killer's transition from the mad stabber to the controlled strangler. And, maybe, get a handle on who the real killer was.

Eddie bent over the laptop and researched murders between 1982 and 1986 around Belker's new home in Iowa, looking for a string that would lay out Belker's transformation. But he found only one unsolved murder and one missing person and both victims were men.

If Belker was a serial killer, where were the killings?

So maybe Mike was a real person. A serial killer who had gotten away with it in the eighties and then moved away. But now he'd come home and taken the girl who was missing from Weston.

Which put the killer in Weston.

If Eddie went there and started investigating, he'd be in the killer's orbit. Eddie broke into a sweat and his hands shook. He clamped then together and squeezed them between his thighs. If he was going to do this he had to put his fears and doubts behind him.

If he did this?

It was a stark choice. Continue on as he was, alone. Or take the risk in the hope that it might result in a future with

Penny. His mind spun into that future, waking up with her, eating meals with her, laughing at stupid TV shows with her. Growing old with her.

Eddie gathered all the clean clothes he had and figured it was just enough to get him through Friday. He packed his suitcase, then put his camera, laptop, and notes in his messenger bag. On the way out he grabbed the 1964 Roosevelt dime on the table by the front door. Penny had given it to him one morning at the diner. "The last dime made of real silver," she'd said. "For luck."

He put it in his pocket and headed east.

He left all the materials for his current true crime book behind. He was done with that crap.

* * *

It was only ninety minutes from Des Moines to the river, where Eddie took Highway 67 north. After cutting through LeClaire the highway picked up the touristy name The Great River Road. It was a picturesque drive: nothing between Eddie and the mighty Mississippi but a single line of railroad tracks and a strip of greenery that sometimes widened enough to hold a string of houses. He rolled the windows down and the cool spring air slapped at him, Big Muddy flooding the car with its earthy scent.

The sign welcoming him to the town where Mose Belker had lived after leaving Weston announced *Cornell on the Mississippi* in a flowery script that would have been hard to read if he hadn't stopped to take pictures. Eddie used photos to help evoke the mood he wanted for each part of the story. That's why he never let the publisher bunch the photos together in the middle of the book—Eddie got to pick where they went and he wrote all the captions. If that wasn't in the contract, he didn't sign it. Once the contract was signed it was hard enough to get the publisher to do the little it had agreed to, much less something extra.

Eddie took a couple nice pictures of the sign from different angles. One showing the looming immensity of the river behind it. Another showing the two-lane road stretching north with small homes clustered along it. That was the shot, Eddie thought. Because that's how it felt.

Like an invitation into small town middle America.

CHAPTER ELEVEN

While Jake waited for Massey to return with the murder books, he mentally spooled through the possibilities Larson's letter raised. He didn't buy the idea that a Weston cop was dirty. Sure, some of the guys cared more about their careers than actually doing their jobs, but it was a long way from there to being crooked. He checked his watch. Where had Massey gone? As Jake strode to the counter, Massey popped into view, hustling down a long aisle of shelving with two thick binders.

"Sorry it took so long. Back room's a mess."

Jake thanked him, signed the log, then lugged the big books back up to his desk in the detective bullpen. On the way he grabbed a cup of coffee in the break room, avoiding a Cubs versus Sox debate that had been going on for as long as he had been with the department.

Back at his desk he dove into the murder books. The cases were a clear pair. Both girls had been travelling alone—Smith by bike, Brown on foot—along dark roads in late evening, disappeared, and were found dead on empty land southwest of the city. Both had been stabbed dozens of times with a slit-shaped knife between two and three inches long. Both were sexually assaulted after death.

The lead Weston detective on the cases, Ken Reed, directed a massive effort to find the killer without ever developing a solid lead. Neither girl had known enemies. No one saw either girl after they started their journeys home: Smith from work and Brown from a friend's house.

The closest Reed came to having a witness was a ninety-three-year-old woman who lived half a mile from where Brown's body was found. The woman said she had seen a van near the area but couldn't recall the day, or the color, or the make.

Reed took a hard look at every known pervert and interviewed every man who lived near either family or where they'd been found but didn't note any of them for further investigation.

Reed had worked Mose Belker hard on the Smith case—Belker had worked with Smith—which showed that Reed's instincts were good. Because the murders were identical Reed also interviewed Belker about Brown. Belker didn't ask for a lawyer during either interview and answered every question without incriminating himself or giving Reed a lever to break open his story.

The Belker part of the books—at least back in 1982—ended without mention of a possible accomplice or anyone named Mike.

Entries thinned out after a couple months. Reed's last entry in the Brown book said he had no reason to doubt Chief Stewart's theory that the crime was perpetrated by a stranger passing through town "just like with Smith." Both cases were picked up about once a year thereafter without anything significant coming up, until 1999 when Detective Sean Tate went to Iowa to collect DNA from Mose Belker to compare with the evidentiary sample from the Smith murder. By the end of that day Belker had confessed to both murders.

Jake found copies of Belker's handwritten confessions. The originals would be in the evidence vault. They read like a pair. Belker saw the girl alone on a deserted country road and was overwhelmed with a sudden impulse to have sex with her. When she refused his advance, he killed her and copulated with her body before dumping it.

Both confessions could have been written by anyone who'd read the same newspaper articles Jake had read online.

Jake turned to the forensic evidence portion of the Smith book. He knew from the news reports that the only forensic evidence that didn't belong to Smith or Brown on the scenes was the semen found on Smith's leg.

That evidentiary sample should have generated three reports: the forensic tech's report about collecting it off Smith's body, the transmission report when the sample was sent for DNA testing, and the report from the DNA lab. There should have been a similar three reports for the DNA swab taken from Belker in 1999.

None of the reports were in the book.

Jake flipped back to the chronological narrative. He found a 1982 entry for collection of the evidence and a 1999 entry for the collection of the DNA off Belker, but found only one undated entry at the end of the Smith chronology that handled the rest: *Belker's DNA matched.*

Jake closed the book then drank his coffee, long gone cold. What was there to hide in the DNA test? Obviously, that it had *not* matched.

Jake returned both books to the records room then swung by the evidence vault and checked the old logs. He found the entry for the evidentiary sample found on Smith coming in in 1982 and going *"to the DNA lab"* in 1999. *What DNA lab?* he wondered.

Jake left the station and got back in his car. The missing DNA reports told him Larson's letter, and the Belker story it contained, could be true. If it was, and Kate Ballard was abducted by the same man who'd grabbed up Smith and Brown, then she was almost certainly dead.

Jake gritted his teeth against the wave of despair coursing through him. It was rare for an abductor to keep his victim alive, or for a serial killer to change his ritual, but Jake still held onto that possibility. He would find Mike, and find Kate Ballard. Alive.

He needed to talk to the investigating detective. Reed's memory and notes might contain the link to Mike that was missing from the murder books. Jake found Reed's house on Parkway, a short street that led into the Burlington Woods Forest Preserve. It was a tired ranch with a single-car garage, a moss-stained roof of curled shingles, and a wheelchair access ramp leading to the front door. At a mile west of downtown, the neighborhood was close enough that every house but Reed's had already been replaced by a mini-mansion. Jake parked on the cracked-asphalt driveway behind a Honda Civic with sun-faded paint and took the wheelchair ramp up to the front door.

It opened as he approached.

"I'm late for work so you gotta move your car." The man exiting the house was in his twenties with a round face and soft belly that strained against a Star Wars T-shirt as he twisted to put on a beige jacket.

"Is Ken Reed home?"

"No. And I really gotta go." The man held the storm door open as he yanked the front door shut, the bottom scraping against the floor with a screech. It was as worn out as the roof. "Can you move your car?" He tried to edge past Jake on the narrow ramp but Jake blocked his path.

"After you answer my questions."

"You're a cop."

Jake flashed his badge. "I just need to talk to your—"

"Grandfather. He's dead. He moved to Tucson to get away from winter and died within a year."

Shit! "I'm sorry for your loss."

"Thanks, but I really got to get to work. I—"

"Did your grandfather leave behind any notebooks from his time on the force?"

"I don't know, man. I really gotta go."

"I need to see his work on two of his old cases. Smith and Brown."

Reed's grandson rubbed at his patchy beard. "I remember him talking about those."

Most murders in the burbs were simple domestic disputes. No planning, lots of forensics, lots of witnesses. These two were likely the only ones Reed had worked outside those norms. "He did great work there. I think—"

"Listen, Detective. I'm not kidding here. I have to go." The young Reed pulled out his phone and checked the time. "Give me your card and I'll look for any notebooks and call you if I find any. Okay?"

"It'll—"

"Are you arresting me?" The young man's voice was rising now. "If not, get out of my way."

Jake dug out a card and handed it to the man, whose hand shook with anger as he accepted it. Jake stepped aside and the young Reed shot past, jumped in his Honda and started it. Jake got in his Mustang and backed it out of the way. Reed whipped his econobox out of the driveway and drove away, the muffler rattling.

Hopefully Reed would remember to look for the notebooks.

Jake decided to drive up to the county building and talk to the assistant state's attorney who handled the cases in 1999. Maybe he had copies of the missing DNA reports in his file.

And maybe Jake would run into Anna while he was up there.

CHAPTER TWELVE

Paget County Sheriff Warren adjusted the lumbar support on her cruiser's seat yet again. She wore her full uniform when in the field, including the bulky vest and stiff belt loaded with equipment. To lead her deputies, she needed to look like one of them. She'd been wearing it a lot since climbing out from behind her desk to be a hands-on sheriff, but it wasn't getting any more comfortable with familiarity.

She keyed her shoulder mic. "Sit rep."

"Both kids are awake now, Sheriff. They're playing with some plastic cows and a barn right in the middle of the front room."

Bev clicked her mic to acknowledge the report, then sipped her coffee, her stomach twisting around the gallon she'd already downed. She had broken the task force into two teams, one for each overdose victim. After chasing leads all night, Anderson's team had reached the dealer who supplied its victim, but that man lawyered up.

So it was up to her and what her team could do right here.

Bev peered through her binoculars at the house. After rousting every person ever connected to the dead man she'd finally learned he'd been living here. Unfortunately, the woman he was shacked up with had two kids so they couldn't move in until the Department of Children and Family Services arrived.

She could see the little towheads through the front window, lips fluttering as they apparently made animal sounds. She wondered if they could hear themselves over the R-rated rap videos blaring from the TV. Then she wondered why they didn't just turn it off. But every family had its rules.

Her cell phone shuddered with a call: Fanning. "What is it, Duke?"

"I put a feeler out with the local emergency departments and just got a call about another OD."

"Still alive?"

"Yes. Her boyfriend had Narcan and the paramedics gave her two more doses when they got there. They're taking her to the hospital up in Glenbard right now."

Narcan. The Lazarus drug. It could bring overdose victims all the way back from clinical death. "Three doses means she used from the carfentanil batch."

"I'm headed to the scene right now to confirm," Duke said. "But it's a safe bet."

A car pulled in behind Bev. She recognized the driver from a woman's leadership group. Sheena something, with Child Services. The woman levered her car door open, and climbed out.

"I'll head to the hospital to question her when I'm done here." Bev ended the call, put her phone away, and got out of the car. A cold spring wind whipped against her, carrying the scent of mown grass. She waited for the caseworker then shook the proffered hand. "I'm glad you made it, Sheena."

"What—"

Bev raised a hand to stop the question. She keyed her shoulder mic. "Child Services is here. Go in."

A stream of deputies came out from behind a tall row of hedges with weapons ready. The tight pack of men flowed up the sidewalk and across the overgrown lawn in synchronized slow motion. The locked front door forced them to bunch up for the fraction of a second it took to break it open. A few seconds later shouts of "Down! Down! Down!" told her they'd found at least one adult inside. Within a minute the tactical Sergeant came out the front door. "All clear. One in the back bedroom."

"You're up," Bev said to the caseworker, then jogged across the street, equipment belt bouncing on her hips.

The house smelled like unwashed bodies and rotting fruit. The TV was off now, and the two kids sat together on the sagging floral print couch hugging each other. Their eyes were wide with curiosity, but dry of tears. Their clothes were filthy and the girl had snot crusted on her upper lip. Bev winced internally. Children like these were the uncounted victims of drug use. She left them to Sheena.

Bev found a rail thin woman in stained underwear huddled in the corner of the back bedroom. The window shades were down and the room had a deep funk, almost earthy.

"Why you break in here with all your guns? I ain't done nothing. I'm just sleeping in here."

"Where are you children?"

"They're with their dad over in Kirwin."

"What about the two blondies in the front room?"

The woman scratched her neck; the skin there looked like she scratched it a lot. "What day is it? Maybe they are here."

Bev raised the shades and the woman ducked her head, shielding her eyes from the brightness. "Why you hassling me?"

Bev knelt in front of her. "I need to know where Donny got his junk."

"I'm not telling anything about him. And why you bothering me if you're after him?" She went on like that, a long string of woe-is-me victimhood without ever mentioning the children again.

Bev slapped her, a red handprint blooming on her papery skin.

"What the hell you do that for? I don't deserve—"

Bev slapped her again, hard enough that Bev felt the sting in her own hand.

"Sheriff?" A voice from the hallway. She ignored the implied criticism of her use of force. This woman needed to talk *now*. People were dying.

"Your Donny is in the morgue. That junk killed him."

"He scored and didn't bring me none?"

The woman had missed the point. "The junk he didn't share with you killed him."

Light dawned, and the woman wrapped her arms around her knees. "Donny's dead?" She wailed and started rocking. "No-no-no-no!"

"Her name's Susan Miller according the ID on the dresser here, Sheriff."

"Susan?" Bev grabbed the woman's shoulder and shook it. "Where did he score?" But no matter how many different ways she asked it, the woman was too broken to answer.

"Search the place. Look for anything that might identify the OD's source. And if you find any of the heroin, do not get it on your bare skin."

This was a dead end. But at least child services could now protect these children. Small victories mattered. She left her team to it and headed to the hospital to talk to the surviving overdose victim.

CHAPTER THIRTEEN

Eddie drove into Cornell, the road edging away from the water, the earthy smell fading away, small wood-framed houses and well-kept lawns lining the street. Nothing about the town revealed it had been home to a murderer for sixteen years.

Before leaving Des Moines, he had printed out a map of Cornell and marked it with the places he wanted to visit. Belker's house was nearly a mile west of town just after the steady rise away from the river valley topped off. But the house didn't have a view. It was set far back from the road surrounded by a thick stand of trees with dozens of volunteer saplings growing up through the prairie that had once been its lawn.

The house had been abandoned.

Perfect.

Eddie parked on the road beyond the house to keep his car out of the shot, then walked back and started taking pictures. The single-story house gave off a vibe he needed to capture. Ominous. *The house abandoned as the town had abandoned its adopted son when he confessed to raping and murdering two teenage girls.* Close, but not exactly the right note.

Eddie stepped onto the front porch and peered in the window. A few pieces of battered furniture and empty beer cans scattered around a pile of magazines. He couldn't identify the magazines through the flyspecked window, but they'd be whatever smut local teenagers could get their hands on.

The front door was locked but Eddie circled the house and found the kitchen door standing open. Inside, all the appliances were gone and the copper pipes had been stripped out of the walls, leaving ragged tufts of drywall and insulation.

Clang!

Eddie flinched, dropping into a crouch. When the noise repeated he realized it came from outside. He stood up and shook the tension out of his shoulders.

Clang!

Eddie followed the sound.

The backyard was crowded with more volunteer trees and the woods crept up close to the rear of the yard. Another clang. It was coming from behind the detached garage. Eddie crept down the side of the garage until his view behind it opened up. Sometime in the distant past someone had torched an old van and left its scorched remains to rust and rot away on melted tires behind the garage. A sudden peal of youthful laughter and Eddie smiled with relief. Nothing to worry about here.

The van's sliding side door stood open. Eddie stalked his way up to it, then leaned in from the side to peek at the interior. The sudden spark of a lighter momentarily blinded him, then his eyes adjusted. Two boys. Pre-teens, sitting on plastic milk crates, passing a cigarette back and forth.

"Who the fuck are you?"

One boy popped up and came at Eddie with his fists clenched. He wore mud-caked jeans and dirt streaked his face. If he was a foot taller Eddie might have been worried.

"Whoa, friend. Just taking a look at the old Belker place."

"You a rapist like that sick bastard?"

"What do you know about Belker?"

"My mom's boyfriend told me all about him." The other boy—the blond—stood up now and joined his friend with his own muddy jeans and clenched fists.

"I'd like to hear everything you've been told."

"Twenty bucks."

"Ten."

"Thirty," the dirty one said, smiling.

Eddie forked over a twenty and got their stories. It was all fifth-hand gossip but he recorded it on his phone anyway because this whole scene was gold for the book. The dirty pre-teen boys smoking cigarettes in an abandoned hulk of a van, wanting to fight him, then negotiating their price. That was the kind of gritty wrong-side-of-the-tracks details readers loved.

"My mom said this is the exact van he killed all ten of them in," Pig Pen said.

"That's right," Blondie echoed.

The vehicle definitely dated from that era, back when people customized the interiors of these windowless vans. There was little left inside this one but a few scorched tatters of paneling and the frame of a bench built down one side.

"When he burned it up it was still a good van. That's what my mom says. *He* said it was a lemon. But it only has like a hundred and thirty thousand miles on it. You can still see the number on the odometer."

Eddie took a picture of that, then got out of the van and took pictures from every angle, including a dozen around the open door with the inside in deep shadow. The door the girls were dragged through when Belker snatched them off the street. Then he took some pictures from inside looking out into the light. He adjusted the focus so the doorway was a block of brightness with the woods behind it bled out of focus. *The last thing Belker's victims saw as they were pulled inside the killing box.*

That was close to perfect.

But he might have to change the name in the caption to *Mike.*

CHAPTER FOURTEEN

Jake badged his way through courthouse security and used a public access terminal in the circuit clerk's office to look up the name of the assistant state's attorney who handled the Smith and Brown cases.

Bill Fosser had been the assigned ASA on both cases. Jake didn't know the man but the SA's office was a revolving door spinning experienced ASAs out into lucrative careers in private practice. Fosser could be long gone, dead, or retired.

As Jake rode the escalators up to the SA's floor, he wondered if he would run into Anna. If he didn't, should he ask for her?

He stepped into the reception area still undecided.

"Jake?"

"Hey, Maya." Anna had introduced them at the wedding of one of their co-workers. It had been the first time Jake and Anna appeared in public as a couple.

"I don't think—is Anna expecting you?"

"I'm actually here to see Bill Fosser."

Maya shook her head, blunt cut brown hair swinging with the motion. "He's not here anymore. But you know what? Anna can talk to you about Bill."

"I don't—"

Maya held up a finger to cut him off as she made the call, her voice a hissy whisper. After she hung up, she cracked a hesitant smile. "She'll be right out."

"Thanks."

Jake paced a tight nervous circle as he waited. This might not go over well. If Anna wanted to talk to him, she would've returned his calls.

The door opened. Anna. She met his gaze and frowned. "Come on back."

He caught the door before it swung closed and followed her through a warren of cubicles. From this angle she looked the same: well put together in her classic courtroom attire of black over black, her blond hair pulled back into a ponytail that bobbed along behind her. A great view. The *same* great view. If she was pregnant, it was too early for it to show.

As soon as she closed her office door, he took her by the elbows. "Anna—"

"I was going to tell you."

"I'm sure," Jake said. "But—"

"Sit."

They sat on the guest chairs in front of her desk. Hands clasped together. Eyes locked on each other.

"I'm not sure what I'm going to do, Jake. You and me… It's been good. Really good, actually. But… " The pain in her voice carved a furrow through Jake's heart.

"But you're not sure about us," he said. "That's my fault. I've… dragged my feet telling you how I feel, because… well, that doesn't matter. I—"

"Because of Mary," she said.

Jake swallowed and nodded. "I love you. I do. And this baby… We can raise it however you want. Living together or living apart. We could get married, even."

"If that was a proposal it sucked, Houser."

He opened his mouth to try and recover from that blunder but she put up a hand.

"Give me some time. And please keep it to yourself, okay? I know you'll tell Coogan, but that's it. I mean it."

"Okay," Jake said.

"Did you really come here to see Bill Fosser?"

"He handled a pair of murders back in '99 that might shed some light on Ballard."

"How so?"

He explained Donna Larson's letter. "It's a long shot, but I have nothing else."

"You're planning to interview Belker?"

"As soon as I know enough to spot his lies."

"Bill was my mentor when I came here. He told me he took the call as the felony-screening officer in '82 when the Weston police wanted to charge Belker with Smith's murder."

"They had enough to charge him?" The murder book didn't reflect that."

"No, so Bill turned them down. Until '99, Bill used the case as an example of the SA's role to rein cops in when they become too emotionally invested to be objective. That's why felony review exists."

"And after '99?"

"Belker's confession made Bill question what he'd done back in '82. Maybe if he *had* charged Belker on Smith—even if it was tossed out—maybe that would have scared Belker away from killing again."

"You can't beat yourself up for doing your job with the information you have," Jake said.

"That's what we all tell ourselves."

"There is something specific I'm interested in." He explained about the missing DNA reports. "Would the states attorney's file have copies of all that?"

She got up from the guest chair and sat down behind her desk. "We're going through old cases to digitize them. Whatever hasn't been digitized has at least been indexed." She worked her computer keyboard. "Here we go. Two entries on

DNA. The first document is described as a DNA lab report confirming a match to a known sample. The other document is indexed as 'Weston PD certification that known sample came from defendant Belker.'"

Jake came around the desk and read the entries over her shoulder. Her hair smelled of her citrus shampoo. "Can I see those documents?"

"I'll put in a request and you'll have them within a couple days."

"A couple days?"

"We could talk to Bill. He lives right across the street."

* * *

They walked. A chill spring wind pushed away the sun's warmth and Anna hugged her jacket closed and walked quickly. Fosser didn't live in the townhomes to the south as Jake expected, but in the county home to the west.

"What's he doing in the county home?"

"Bill spent every penny he had fighting his wife's cancer. When he got dementia, this was his only option."

Jake hustled to keep up. "Dementia? Will he be able to talk to us?"

"We won't know until we get there. Every day is different."

"You visit him?"

"He's a friend. His guidance made me the prosecutor I am."

"I look forward to meeting him," Jake said, wondering what they'd get from an old man with dementia.

They found Fosser in a quiet room with big windows looking over the back yard where the spring migration swarmed a trio of birdfeeders. His face lit up when he saw Anna, and Jake hung back for a few minutes while they talked. Finally, Anna waved him over.

"Bill, this is the Weston detective who wants to talk to you. Jake Houser. He's also my… uh, friend."

Bill held out a thin hand and Jake shook it. "Thanks for agreeing to talk with me, Mr. Fosser."

"Bill, please."

"Bill, I'm interested in what you can tell me about the Amy Smith case."

Fosser looked at Anna and back to Jake. "That was the first Belker case, right?"

"Yes."

"I should have charged Belker on that one when I had the chance. Then maybe Brown would have—"

"You did the right thing, Bill. There wasn't enough to charge him until—"

"Iowa. That Weston Detective, er… Tate was his name. Yeah, Shawn Tate. He went out to Iowa to get DNA from Belker. Belker knew what that meant so he just came right out and confessed. Wish we could have had DNA my whole career. It's a magic bullet."

"Did you see the DNA results?"

"Well… " Fosser's brow furrowed. "I'm sure I did. It confirmed the confession."

"How did you confirm the Brown confession?"

Fosser's jaw went slack. He looked to Anna for help and she put her hand on his shoulder.

"Just whatever you might remember."

Fosser smiled, hesitantly and his hands fidgeted with the fringe of the blanket on his lap. "I… just don't know. I must have had something." His eyes found Anna's again. "Right?"

Anna smiled. "That's right, Bill."

"Did Mose Belker have a friend named Mike?" Jake asked.

Fosser tilted his head and his mouth opened but then it was like a curtain fell over his consciousness and his eyes dulled.

"Thanks, Bill. I really appreciate it."

Fosser didn't respond and they left him there, lost in his own mind.

The wind was even stronger on the walk back to Anna's office, the chill cutting straight through Jake's blazer. He put his arm around Anna's shoulder to keep her warm, but she shrugged it off. Jake wasn't sure if she was avoiding a public display of affection or mad that his gesture implied she needed him to keep her warm.

"Was the DNA match from Smith enough to confirm the Brown confession too?" Jake asked.

"On the theory that because the murders were identical they were done by the same person and that person is known to be Belker?"

"Yes."

Anna shook her head. "*I* would want more. But Bill blamed himself for Brown's death over his denial of the warrant on Belker in '82."

"The judge would have had to go along with it."

"Judge Wall came out of the SA's office."

Meaning he was biased in favor of the prosecution. And with no one to complain—the defendant had confessed—there was no downside. But even without considering the second murder, the DNA bothered Jake.

"If the DNA result was above board, why aren't the reports in the murder book?"

Anna shivered and wrapped her arms around herself.

Jake again reached to put an arm around her but she took a quick step to the side. "I'm just thinking of our baby—"

"It's not a baby," she said, her voice sharp. She stopped walking and looked up at him. "I'm sorry. I'm not even sure I believe that. I had… a position on all of this." A hand fell to her abdomen. "But now that I have to make this decision. That I *get* to make this decision. It's not easy."

"Whatever I can do."

"You can give me space.

They walked the rest of the way in silence, Jake thinking about her words. *Position. Not a baby.* They were cold words.

They went their separate ways when the sidewalk veered off to the parking garage.

Jake stopped and watched Anna walk away. His heart clenched.

CHAPTER FIFTEEN

Eddie found the Cornell police station in a converted house across the street from a sign for the Cornell Beach Marina. He didn't see a marina. He saw a muddy riverbank, a concrete block building, and a trailer loaded with aluminum canoes. But he'd never been into boats or the water, so knew little about marinas or about beaches.

Inside the station a waist-high wooden banister cordoned off the entryway. The sole person among the scatter of desks and filing cabinets beyond it was a pimply young man with red hair. He looked up, smiled, and stuck a pencil in the fold of the thick book he was reading.

"How can I help you, sir?" The enthusiasm brought a smile to Eddie's face.

"I'd like to talk with Officer Robert Coffey."

"The chief's down at the Go Fish having lunch."

Chief. Eddie preferred not talking to top dogs. Chiefs and sheriffs and agents-in-charge spoke so carefully he rarely got anything good out of them.

The door opened behind Eddie.

"Here he is. Someone to see you, Chief."

"Thanks, Red." The chief looked Eddie up and down, then stuck out his hand. "I'm Chief Coffey. What can I do for you?"

"Eddie Shaw." Eddie took the hand. It was large and callused, but the chief didn't overdo the grip like many large men did. "I'm researching a book and would like to talk with you about the day Mose Belker confessed."

"I know that story," Red said. "I can tell him, Chief."

"Man the phones, Red. I'll talk to Mr. Shaw in my office."

Eddie followed Chief Coffey to a square room with a pair of windows that looked out at the side of the house next door. A rank of miss-matched filing cabinets covered one wall. They sat down and Coffey leaned forward, elbows on his desk.

"I'm going to record this with my phone. Okay, Chief?" After the chief agreed, Eddie set the phone on the desk. The chief looked like he wanted to talk. Maybe it was the one big story he had to tell that didn't involve booze, drugs, or domestic abuse. Eddie leaned forward, mirroring Coffey. "How well did you know Mose Belker?"

Chief Coffey frowned. "Why do you assume I knew him?"

"I grew up down in Keosaukua, so I know small towns. Everybody knows everybody else. What car they drive and where they work and who their kin are."

"I knew him." Coffey swiveled his chair, his eyes pulling away from Eddie and going to the window. "You planning to go on about the small-town cop too dumb to recognize a killer living in his own town?"

"*Did* you recognize him as a killer?"

"No," the chief's eyes came back on Eddie's. "Maybe because Mose Belker never killed anyone."

"He confessed."

"I can't explain that. But I can tell you he was never in any trouble here."

"No one ever called in about him?"

"Never."

"Maybe people were too scared of him to complain."

Chief Coffey scoffed. "If you know small towns like you say you do, then you know that even if a complaint isn't *filed*, I still hear about what went on."

That was certainly true back home, Eddie thought. "How about after he confessed? Did any dirt come out about him then?"

"Zip."

"Tell me about the day you arrested him."

"I didn't arrest him. I just went out to the window factory—because, yes, I knew where he worked—and asked him to come down to the station. He came right along. Not because he was guilty and knew he was caught. But because we were in bible study together and he trusted me. That's why Chief Wayne sent me to do it."

Bible study! Pure gold.

"So, Belker came with you, and… "

"The detective that came out here—his name escapes me—took over as soon as I got Mose back here. The only time I saw him again was when they walked him out to their car in handcuffs a couple hours later. Then Chief Wayne sent me to tell Martha her husband had confessed to raping and murdering two teenage girls."

"How did she take it?"

"You'll have to use your imagination."

"How did you take it?"

"That's my business."

"Witnesses say one of the girls Belker confessed to killing got into a van just like the one hidden behind his garage. Maybe the killing van had been right there—here in *your* town—all that time."

The attempt to incite the chief failed. He just shrugged. "Those boys from Weston had a forensic crew out at Mose's place for two days. I'm sure they went all through it."

Eddie peppered the chief with a few dozen more questions but got nothing solid from him.

Except one last golden quote.

"Mose Belker was one of the kindest men I've ever known."

CHAPTER SIXTEEN

Jake got in his Mustang, still thinking about the DNA reports. The simple and obvious explanation for why they were missing was they conflicted with the story that Belker was the killer. That story, and Belker's confession, closed the case and removed the threat of a killer still roaming town. But only in perception, not in reality. The real killer would have still been out there and if he killed again, the lie that Belker was the killer would have been revealed.

So the people pushing the lie had known something.

Maybe, as Belker had told Donna Larson, they knew who the real killer was.

And had reason to believe he would not kill again.

The missing DNA reports could answer who that killer was and the DNA certification in the state's attorney's file would reveal exactly who was hiding that truth. Jake's money was on Abe Stewart.

Jake called Duke Fanning, Paget County's best forensic examiner. When Fanning's cellphone kicked to voicemail, Jake called the office number and learned Fanning was at a crime scene less than two miles away off north Winfield Road. Jake was there in minutes. A crowd of emergency response vehicles—county squads, a tactical van, and Fanning's big forensic van—clustered around the mouth of a gravel driveway that lead back through trees. Jake parked on the edge of the road and tried to badge his way past the perimeter but was blocked by a deputy sheriff.

"I need to talk to FIC Fanning ASAP." Jake pulled back his blazer to reveal his gold shield. "I'm with Weston Homicide."

The deputy spoke into his shoulder mic, then listened to a response too garbled for Jake to understand. "He'll be right out."

Jake paced the shoulder as he waited, scanning the trees for a glimpse of what was going on back there.

A few minutes later FIC Fanning came down the driveway. He was a thick man with a buzz cut and the no-nonsense eyes of a serious guy doing serious work. Today he looked more grim than usual, his face etched with lines and black circles under his eyes.

"What do you need, Jake?"

"Some background on the evidence in an old case."

Fanning ran a hand over his buzz cut, then motioned with his head and they moved, putting the big van between them and the bulk of the activity. "Go."

Jake explained.

"Back then Weston handled all its own forensic work," Duke said. "Had its own scene people and stored its own evidence. The DNA sample—the semen—they would have kept for a possible blood type match."

"It *was* kept."

"Back in '99 we were all using the same place out in California for DNA tests." Fanning pulled out his phone and thumbed the screen for a minute before putting it away. "I just texted you the contact information."

"Thanks, Duke." Finally, a real lead on the DNA. "What's happening here?"

Duke looked through the trees toward the distant house. Figures in Tyvek jump suits could be seen moving about. "Bad stuff, Jake."

When he didn't say more Jake got the hint the case was a need-to-know and thanked Fanning for his help. Jake got back in the Mustang and called the California lab, DNA Essentials. He eventually found the right guy, but had to hold while the man called the Weston PD to confirm it was okay to talk to Jake.

"Your chief of Ds says you're good. What can I do for you?"

Jake explained the missing lab reports. "I'm hoping your records will help me out."

"Hang on." The clack and clatter of keyboarding. "I'll have to go back into the paper files if you need more, but the transaction record—basically the inventory without the results—shows we received one evidentiary sample from an unknown person and two samples to test it against from known people."

"Two knowns?" There should have been only one; the sample from Mose Belker. "Who did they belong to?"

"They were labeled Smith Known 1 and Smith Known 2."

"Did either match?"

"I can't see that here. I'll need to pull the paper. I can tell you that we used up the samples to do the tests. That *is* on my records here."

"Can you call me as soon as you've pulled the paper?"

"Sure, but it could take a few days to get the files from offsite."

Jake gave the man his contact information and ended the call.

The DNA reports had to have been kept out of the murder book because that second known matched the evidentiary sample. And didn't come from Mose Belker.

Who had it come from?

And who the hell would allow a murdering rapist to go free?

As he reached to start the car, his cousin, Paget County Sheriff Bev Warren came out from behind Fanning's van and waved for his attention. Their dads had a big falling out when they were in their teens but the two of them had reconnected after her dad died the year before. Jake was glad to have her back in his life. He got out and joined her in front of his car.

CHAPTER SEVENTEEN

Bev crossed her arms against the breeze while she waited for Jake to get out of his car. "I saw you talking with FIC Fanning," she said as he approached her. "You find something on that missing girl?"

Jake looked her over, frowning. "You okay? Have you been up all night?"

She had been up all night but didn't want to look like she had. She shrugged and switched topics. "We've found carfentanil laced into heroin. It's—"

"That stuff's powerful."

"Three dead already." They'd found another victim in a van parked behind the bowling alley on 38. All that death and misery. A shudder started to run through her but she tensed up and held it off. "And we have sixteen ODs who've survived."

"Any leads?"

"We're making progress," she said. "What did you need Fanning for?"

"I'm working that letter you had Rieser give me. The DNA report that confirmed Belker's confession isn't in the murder book. I was hoping Fanning could help me track down the lab that did the analysis."

"So I *was* right to funnel the case to you and away from Sam Stewart as head of Weston Professional Standards."

He looked away. She pressed him. "Abe ran the department in the eighties. He came back as acting chief in '99 and still has a lot of friends and a lot of pull in the department. Sam would not have gone after his own father."

Jake glared at her. She'd made her point.

"Was Fanning able to help?" she asked.

"He remembered the DNA lab Weston used back then."

He looked away again. She knew from growing up with him this meant he'd left something out and was done talking about it.

"Good luck," she said. And she meant that. She stepped away from his car as he got in. The Mustang flung grass as its tires dug into the ground along the roadside. It slewed sideways, then straightened and shot away when its tires found asphalt.

She turned back to the job at hand. The OD who survived had dropped a name that lead to this remote house as the home of a second-tier dealer. One step closer to whoever had brought the bad batch into Weston. Progress, but it was coming too slow. And, so far, this dealer wasn't talking.

But he would.

As she walked back down the gravel driveway, her cell phone shuddered in her hand.

"Sheriff Warren."

"It's Abe," the caller said. "Abe Stewart."

She smiled. Her plan was working. "What can I do for you?"

"Your cousin is digging into some old cases. Closed cases."

"I just heard about them."

"From Doug Rieser?"

That caught Bev off guard. Her relationship with Doug was private. Secret. Abe was letting her know that he knew her secrets, too. "Jake mentioned them."

"If you got this started then you need to get it stopped."

"What are you talking about, Abe?"

"Bull showed me the file he made on me—that's how he got me to endorse you for sheriff—so I know what's in it. He also told me he was leaving it to you."

"I don't know anything about any files." Her dad hadn't even told *her* about the files. He'd always been a devious one.

"Save it, Warren."

"I have no power to stop a Weston PD investigation."

"You can destroy the goddamn file. You can do that much."

"I don't have any fi—"

"Bullshit!" Abe said. "Destroy the file and rein Houser in. If you don't, then I might have to do it myself."

"What do—"

The line went dead. She stared at her phone for a full minute with Abe's threat ringing in her ears. He had a lot of connections and wielded a lot of behind-the-scenes power like her father always had.

And Abe had his son.

Sam Stewart was Deputy Chief of the Weston PD Patrol Division, which meant the vast majority of Weston's sworn officers reported to him. She knew from her years handling Weston's Professional Standards investigations that some of them could be bent.

Abe Stewart and his network were nothing to ignore.

But Jake could handle himself; he'd proven that many times since moving back home ten years ago. And thanks to the missing DNA report he knew something stank in his own department. He would be ready and would find his way to the ultimate truth.

CHAPTER EIGHTEEN

Eddie found the window factory where Belker had worked a hundred yards up the road, sandwiched between the railroad tracks and the river. It was a cluster of white metal-sided buildings with angled parking along the street. Inside, Eddie asked around until he found the administrative offices. It was one large room crammed with people at desks talking on phones and typing on keyboards. A woman at the desk closest to the door spotted him. In her early fifties, she wore a yellow sweater and a gold chain with a small cross.

"I gotta go, honey. You'll have to find your shoes on your own." She hung up and looked at him. "Yes?"

"I'd like to talk with someone about Mose Belker." Every other conversation in the room stopped.

The woman frowned, then stood and motioned for Eddie to follow her. She led him down a narrow hallway to a small break room that smelled of donuts.

"Sit." She went to a counter crowded with a coffee maker, toaster oven, and microwave. "Coffee?"

"Please." Eddie didn't want coffee, but accepting guaranteed at least a few minutes of polite courtesy. Unless he set her off. The lines around her eyes and across her forehead made him think she could be set off. "Black. Thank you."

When they had their coffees and were seated at a table, Eddie got out his phone and set it to record with the woman's permission.

"What paper are you with?"

"No paper. I write true crime books about—"

"True crime." She pursed her lips and shook her head.

Some people did not like Eddie's chosen genre. "I have a source who thinks Mose Belker may be innocent."

"Oh." Her face relaxed and she put her forearms on the table. "Okay."

"Were you here back then?"

"I went and got Mose when the chief—he wasn't chief back then—came to get him. But he didn't say what it was about it. I was worried that maybe it was about Martha—she'd called in sick that day and—"

"Belker's wife worked here too?"

"Payroll. Died at her desk right back there in that room."

Eddie needed to get a picture of that desk.

"Was Mose surprised when the chief came for him?"

She took a moment, gazing back through time. "Not any more than I was at the unexpected visit. They were friends, you know."

"Yes. I just talked to the chief. After Mose Belker confessed, how'd Martha take it?"

"It was… hard on her."

Eddie wanted a better quote than that. "She… "

She frowned and pushed back from the table. "This was a bad idea, Mr. Shaw. I'm not comfortable talking about Martha or her husband." She stood.

"I've still got coffee—"

"I'm sorry, Mr. Shaw. But it's time for you to go."

She escorted him out. She did it politely—this was Iowa, after all—but the effect was the same. No inside scoop from Belker's employer, and no picture of his wife's death desk. Eddie asked on the way out, but the woman grabbed his elbow and kept him moving. Maybe he should have rubbed Penny's lucky dime before going inside.

* * *

Back in his car Eddie followed the map to Belker's church. It was a large traditional structure on the uphill side of 3rd street. As Eddie pushed his car door open his phone shuddered with an incoming call. His agency in New York. He sat back down but left the car door open. "This is Shaw."

"Mr. Shaw! How nice to speak with you. I'm your new agent, Haley Jones. I think Gavin—"

"I'm in the middle of something, Ms. Jones."

"Haley, please. Can I call you Eddie?"

New Yorkers were never this polite and most talked a lot faster. She sounded more Midwestern.

"Where are you from, Haley? Wisconsin? Minnesota?"

"Illinois, actually."

"What can I do for you, Haley?"

"I'm just calling to introduce myself. I've read all your books, including the cozies."

He'd used a pen name on the cozies and had never told his agent about them. "How'd you—"

"You put the copyright in your real name so it popped up. Don't worry, we aren't asking for a percentage even though your deal with us is exclusive."

Fifteen percent of his earnings on those books wouldn't buy her a cup of coffee at New York prices.

"Well, it's nice to meet you by phone, Ms. Jones."

"Gavin told me about the deadline… issues, and I want you to know I'm here to help."

Eddie grimaced and decided to start this new relationship with the truth. "That book was going nowhere so I dropped it."

"Dropped it! We have—*you have*—a contract! You already cashed the retainer check. You can't just—"

"Haley!" He interrupted her streaming objections. "It's over."

She sighed.

"I've found something else and am already on the road working it."

"Better?"

"Guaranteed."

"How *much* better?"

"A thousand percent."

"If it truly is that much better and you can get me a proposal that shows it, including the first three chapters, by Friday I can salvage this."

"Not a problem," Eddie said.

"By Friday."

"I heard you."

She ended the call without a goodbye. The Midwestern girl already had a bit of New York in her.

Eddie got out of his car and slammed the door, the weight of his decision to chase this story thrumming against his skull. He took a deep breath and pushed that distraction away. He'd made the right choice. He snapped several photos around the church, then went in through the side door marked OFFICES.

A young woman in a black turtleneck working at a stand-up desk stopped typing and smiled at him.

"Is the pastor in?"

"He is. I'll see if he has some free time." She stepped quickly away without asking Eddie who he was or what he wanted. She disappeared through an open door in the back wall and reappeared a few seconds later, her smile wider now. "He said for you to go on back."

Eddie thanked her and stepped into the pastor's office. The room was all dark woods and sunlit windows. A man in an orange and grey horizontally striped sweater came out from behind a big desk. He was thick enough through the middle that the horizontal stripes were a bad idea. He had a gray goatee and a welcoming smile.

"I'm Pastor Yates," he said, shaking Eddie's hand. "How can I help? New to town? Looking for a church to call home?"

He ushered Eddie to a group of oak chairs with red leather upholstery held on by big brass nubs. Once they were seated Eddie explained who he was and why he was there. The pastor sighed heavily, but allowed Eddie to record the conversation.

"That was a very tough time for our entire faith community, Mr. Shaw."

"Did you know Mose Belker?"

"I knew him and prayed with him and had many meals with him and Martha out at their house. He was a good man."

"Never a hint of—"

"Never."

"Did he ever tell stories of back home?"

Yates frowned, his eyes skating away as he thought back. Finally, "None that I recall, anyway."

"Maybe about a friend named Mike?"

Yates shook his head. "Sorry."

"Did you believe his confession?"

"To the police?" Yates grimaced. "I didn't but I must. Mose Belker was not a liar."

Golden. "Did Martha Belker ever talk to you about—"

"Whether she did, or didn't, I'm not talking to you about Martha Belker."

"But she's also passed on, right?"

"That makes no difference."

Eddie got no more out of the man, but he'd gotten enough. The one quote was more than worth the visit.

CHAPTER NINETEEN

Jake drove back down to Weston, his thoughts on the conversation with Bev. Talking with an outsider about someone in his department protecting a murderer had been painful. When it all hit the fan—if he gathered enough information to make the throw—he'd have to talk to a lot of people about it. It would not be good for the department, or his career.

Screw it. His duty—his *purpose*—was to avenge victims and their survivors. He would let the rest sort itself out.

Right now, he needed to find Kate Ballard. The second known DNA sample submitted in 1999 was the first solid fact that Belker might have had an accomplice. An accomplice who was never caught and who Mose Belker said had taken Kate Ballard. A person that someone within the Weston PD protected by hiding the DNA results.

Someone named Mike.

Jake's stomach growled so he swung by Potbelly's and ate a quick sandwich on his way to Coogan's office. He parked at the curb in front of the custom drapery shop that occupied the bottom floor of Coogan's building. At the top of the creaking steps the reception desk was empty. Jennifer, Coogan's right-hand, was on her honeymoon. But Levi was there, hunched in front of his giant computer screen looking at some kind of real estate records. He must have heard Jake on the stairs because his head came up.

"Hey, Jake!"

Finally. It had taken months to get Levi to call Jake by his first name. He'd met Levi while investigating a murder and been impressed by the young man's enthusiasm and skill with internet research. Since then Levi had become Jake's unofficial, and unpaid, internet investigator while working for Coogan as a paralegal and attending Paget Community College.

"Did you know—"

"I hate to interrupt you, Levi." It had to be done. Levi started a lot of conversations with those words and what followed could go on for a long time. "But I need your help with something."

Levi's eyes lit up and his smile widened. "Bring it on. These real estate tax records are boring."

Jake showed him Donna Larson's letter and explained he wanted Levi to find the Mike described there. Levi was working on it before Jake hit the stairs.

Back in his Mustang, Jake called Erin and asked her to find the detective, chief, and forensic clerk from 1999. It was approaching five, but she said she'd stay until she tracked them down.

With time to kill until Erin got back to him, Jake headed south. The second known DNA sample nagged at him. If there had been two attackers, maybe Amy Smith had known the second one, too.

* * *

Jake braced himself for the visit he was about to make. Remington and Alicia Smith still lived in the same house where they'd raised their daughter on the south side of town. The vast swaths of empty land that had surrounded their neighborhood back then were now filled with upper-middle class housing.

He parked on the street and took a moment to look over their house. It was a modest split level in excellent condition: no peeling paint or curled shingles or torn window screens. Fresh blooms of tulips ran up both sides of the driveway and other greenery clustered here and there in planting beds.

Jake mounted the front stoop and peered through the side lite window before he rang the bell. A hardwood floor spread out to a sparsely furnished living room to the right and the kitchen directly ahead. The same layout as dozens of similar houses he'd visited, first as a child, and more recently as a cop to deliver bad news and question witnesses. A carpeted staircase to the left would lead up to the bedrooms and down to the family room and a back room full of the house's mechanicals.

He rang the bell, tension building across his shoulders. Their daughter had died more than thirty years ago but seeing him on their doorstep would refresh the pain. Jake lived it himself whenever anyone asked him about his own wife's murder.

The soft thuds of feet approaching on the hardwood. The long suck of the door opening against the vacuum caused by the storm door.

"Yes?" The woman was small, with gray hair and very erect posture. She wore dark slacks and a yellow cardigan over a white, collared shirt. Pearls at her throat. The skin there smooth and taut. She had never been a sun worshiper. She raised her chin until she was almost looking down her nose at him.

"Mrs. Smith?"

"That's right." She pulled the door partly closed, blocking his view inside.

"I'm Detective Jake Houser with the Weston PD. May I come in?"

Her brow furrowed and her shoulders dropped. Her mouth pulled into a grim line. "I suppose so." She pushed the storm door open for him.

"Thank you." As Jake slipped past her, he caught the unmistakable scent of gin on her breath.

"I'll get my husband." She leaned down the stairs. "Remmy?" Her voice shook. "It's the police."

She waited there, one hand on the newel post, her gaze shifting back and forth from Jake to the empty staircase. One pant leg jiggled from the invisible motion of a restless knee.

A door opened, the smooth sounds of contemporary jazz flowing up the stairs. "The police? What do they want?"

"Are you coming?" Her words had a bite and her husband instantly thundered up the steps.

Remington—Remmy—Smith swept past his wife, but pulled up when he saw Jake. He wore loose, faded jeans and a salmon colored golf shirt. He was a tall lean man who already had a tan, the skin on his forearms thick and scaly from too much sun. He looked Jake up and down.

"You're not Detective Reed."

"Jake Houser." Jake stepped forward with his hand outstretched. Smith glanced back at his wife, then took Jake's hand and held onto it as he guided Jake to the couch under the front window. "I've got this, honey."

Mrs. Smith stepped into the kitchen.

"I'd like to talk with both of you," Jake said as he sat down.

"And I'd like you to be quick about whatever brought you here." Remmy sat down on the edge of the armchair. His weight forward as if he thought he might need to spring up and block Jake from rushing into the kitchen to talk to his wife. "Where is Detective Reed?"

"He passed away a few years ago."

"What do you want?"

"I'm looking at your daughter's case because—"

"Amy's murder. Not her case."

"Yes. I'm exploring the possibility—"

"Exploring?" Mrs. Smith ducked her head around the corner. Now she edged into the room, one shoulder pressed to the wall. "You're bothering us to satisfy your curiosity? You're no better than a reporter."

"I apologize for intruding, Mrs. Smith. But it's possible a second man was involved with what happened to Amy, so—"

Mrs. Smith lunged forward, a finger jabbing so close to Jake's face he flinched. "What *happened* to Amy was that sick bastard raped and murdered her."

Remmy stood and held out his arms as if to herd his wife back into the kitchen. "I've got this, honey," sadness softened Remmy's voice.

"You!" Her voice dripped with venom. "I told you not to let her take that job. That nothing good would come from it. That she would meet bad people. *Restaurant* people. I told you!"

"Honey, I—"

"And making her ride her bicycle everywhere she went. Never giving her a ride! To make her independent! It made her easy pickings for any degenerate who happened along."

She stormed back into the kitchen, pots and pans clanged together, then silence. And a sob.

"You need to leave," Remmy said.

Jake leaned forward and lowered his voice. "I don't want to cause you any additional pain, Mr. Smith. But if a second man was involved—"

"Tell them we want her locket back." Mrs. Smith, from the kitchen.

"What locket?"

"Amy wore a locket with pictures of her grandparents in it," Remmy said. "It's gone."

"Was it on her b—"

"You people said it wasn't."

"Did she always wear it?"

"Not always."

If Amy Smith had been wearing it that day, and it was missing, her killer had taken it as a trophy. There was no mention of a trophy in the Smith murder book, nor in the Brown book. Killers who took trophies *always* took trophies. "But you think she might—"

"You need to leave."

Jake asked the question he'd come to ask. "Did Amy know someone named Mike?"

"Mose Belker killed Amy. She avenged herself by delivering the DNA sample that put him away until the day he dies." Remmy pointed to the door. "That's it. Now leave."

Jake got up, fishing a card from the inside pocket of his blazer. "Here's my card. Call me if you think of anything or just want to talk."

Smith put his hands behind his back and Jake left the card on a small table by the door that held a shallow bowl full of keys.

And a photo of Amy.

CHAPTER TWENTY

Eddie cruised through Weston. The downtown was all high-end shopping and fancy restaurants. The residential areas within walking distance were filled with giant new houses that spread to the edges of their lot lines. "Rich people."

He drove out to the police station, one of a group of a low stone and block municipal buildings built around a manmade lake a mile west of downtown. Going inside was a calculated risk, but he needed to know whether his FOIA requests had raised any alarms. The most recent event in Larson's letter happened in 1999—twenty years ago. Maybe the dirty cops had all retired or moved on. But he doubted it: small town cops tended to stay on the force for life.

Eddie asked the woman behind the high counter for the FOIA officer. She responded with bored efficiency that she would summon him . While Eddie waited, he tried to engage her in conversation—civilian support people were often a wealth of the little details that helped him put extra color on the people in power—but this one was a closed book.

"How can I help you, sir?" The FOIA officer was a cop. A big man who stood with his chest out and hands resting on his equipment belt. He wore sergeant stripes. Sergeants didn't fall for flattery or the other types of bullshit Eddie pedaled.

"I'm Eddie Shaw. I'd like to pick up my FOIA requests." The sergeant—his nametag said Massey—flinched slightly at Eddie's introduction. He clearly knew who Eddie was and what he'd requested. Someone here at the Weston PD was still interested in these cases; Eddie was not going to be able to fly under the radar.

"I received your requests, Mr. Shaw. They're not ready, but if you give me your number, I can call you when they are."

Eddie smiled. "No need, Sergeant. I just happened to be passing through town. I'll just look forward to getting them in the mail."

CHAPTER TWENTY-ONE

Deputy Chief of Patrol Sam Stewart was not good at computer research, but could use Google. Eddie Shaw had once been a serious freelance journalist reporting on crime issues for magazines and newspapers before switching over to writing true crime books. The first one of those was a hard-hitting investigative piece that was turned into a movie like Massey said. But since then Shaw had turned into a hack, spewing out a fast book about any slaughter that hit the news by regurgitating whatever had already been reported, even crap off social media, without offering anything new or insightful.

The Smith and Brown murders seemed too old and too routine to grab the writer's interest. Shaw hadn't seen the murder book so couldn't know about the missing DNA reports. So, what was the writer's angle?

"You got a minute, Deputy Chief?"

"Come in and close the door, Sergeant."

Massey again sat down without being invited. "That writer who filed the FOIA requests on Smith and Brown is here in Weston."

"What? How do you know?"

"He was just here asking if his copies were ready."

Shit! Sam sprang from his chair and paced the area behind his desk. "Has anyone else looked at those books?"

"Houser was the first person to look at them since '99."

Someone in the know must have leaked the DNA information to Shaw. Sam sat down. "We need eyes on him."

"Give me authority over shift assignments and I'll put my guys on watching him."

My guys. The patrol officers were Sam's guys, not Massey's. But this was not the time. "I can do that, but you're staying in records for the duration."

"Agreed." Massey got up and left.

Sam sent out a command email putting Massey in charge of shift assignments.

Then he called his dad. When he had him on the line, Sam jumped right into it. His dad always said not to pussyfoot around. "What do I need to worry about in your old Belker mess?"

"What do you know about it?"

Classic dad. Never willing to give away anything without knowing what the other guy had.

"I know the DNA test is funky. I know Golden Boy Houser pulled both murder books. I know a hot shot investigative journalist has come to town and requested both books."

"What did you do?"

"I put the FOIA request on a ten-day response and have Sergeant Massey keeping an eye on the writer."

"Massey's dad was a good second for me."

Sam knew what good meant to his dad. It did not mean the man was a good cop. It meant the man did what Abe Stewart told him to do without asking any questions.

"I hear his boy is good on the street."

"Massey isn't on the street right now," Sam said. "He's working records because—"

"I heard."

The words were loaded with a disdain that made Sam squirm. "What he did—"

"What he did was make a friend on the city council. But let's not talk about how this patrol sergeant has a better eye on the future than you do. Houser's one of those guys who keeps his reports detailed and up to date. Working in records Massey can look at Houser's files, right?"

"Yes." Sam's dad wasn't even here when Houser joined up or when they installed the online reporting system and he still knew how both worked.

"Use that. You can keep an eye on whatever the hell Houser is up to by what he puts in his reports."

"I'm already doing that," Sam said.

"Slowing down the FOIA requests and asking Massey to keep an eye on the writer were good moves, son."

Sam's dad rarely called him *son*. When he did, it was a device, but Sam fell for it anyway. "Thanks, Dad. You always said I'd have to get my hands a little dirty if I wanted the top job."

A chuckle.

"It's between me and Braff for chief, Dad. If the writer or Houser stir something up on you, I'll lose the opportunity."

"And?"

"I need to know what they could find. I need to be ready to defend you and to defend myself."

Sam's dad was silent for a long minute, that began stretching into two.

"You're doing fine, son." The line went dead.

Sam slammed his phone down. *Did anyone get along with their dad?*

CHAPTER TWENTY-TWO

Jake sat in his Mustang staring at the Smith house thinking about the pain inside it. Being a parent would open Jake up to the risk of pain like that. Pain likely even worse than what he'd experienced, and continued to experience, from his wife's murder. Could he handle it?

Of course he could. If Anna decided to have the baby. *If.* It was her decision but he felt sure she would decide to have the baby.

Right?

He shook off his lingering doubts and refocused on the case. Work never failed him.

Even though the Smiths had not identified a Mike known to their daughter, the missing DNA reports corroborated enough of Larson's letter that Jake felt he had to keep looking for the mysterious Mike. He found the DNA lab's number in his notebook and called his contact there but they still hadn't found the results.

He started the Mustang and headed back into town. Amy Smith and Mose Belker had worked together at the Madison Square Restaurant on Washington Street, just south of the center of downtown. The restaurant hosted lots of lunch meetings for community organizations so Jake had been there many times to give talks on topics like burglar-proofing houses and spotting illegal drug use in teens. He'd once read the back of the menu, which explained the restaurant's history, but all he remembered was that it was family owned. Despite the decades that had gone by, someone there might remember Amy and Mose.

And a man named Mike.

He left the Mustang in the giant parking garage behind the chain bookstore and walked around front. The restaurant smelled richly of meat and potatoes. The crowd inside the restaurant was thin and he found the current owner—Traci McClure—in her office and available to meet with him. She was a good-looking woman of about sixty, with well-coifed hair and thin lips. She wore a jumble of silver bracelets on one wrist and a crowded charm bracelet on the other.

Jake introduced himself then got right to it. "I'd like to talk to you about Amy Smith and Mose Belker."

She frowned, forearms on her paper-cluttered desk. "It's been a long time. What do you want to know?"

"Were you here back then?"

"I've been here my whole life. I hired Amy. My dad hired Mouse; that's what we called him."

"What do you remember about them?"

"Amy was a sweet girl. High energy. Always smiling. She did well with tips. Everyone liked her. She covered shifts for other people and never complained about folding napkins or consolidating ketchup."

"And Mose Belker?"

"He worked in the back of the house washing dishes. Super shy and quiet—that's why we called him Mouse—but a solid worker. I considered him a nice, harmless guy."

"No problems?"

"Nope. I never believed he had anything to do with… what happened to Amy. Until he confessed."

"But you fired him."

"Word got around that the police were talking to Mouse about Amy and our lunch events—like for the Business Alliance and other groups—dropped to zero. My dad told Mouse he was sorry, but he just couldn't afford to keep him. I was okay with it because the girls were creeped out."

"He didn't creep them out before?"

"They just rolled their eyes at his differentness, if that's a word. All the girls we hire are outgoing and Mouse was not that. He had it rough, you know. His parents—I don't know specifics, but it wasn't good. When he started working here he only owned two shirts and one pair of pants. All second hand. Can you imagine? He bought the only new clothes he'd ever owned with his first check. He told me that. From Main Street Surplus."

Jake remembered the store. It had once carried army surplus but by the 80s it sold mostly no-name jeans and t-shirts that came by the dozen. "Did Amy like Mose?"

"She was always nice to him. But she was nice to everybody."

"Was everybody nice to Mose?"

"No. Girls that age, back then, weren't tolerant." She looked away. "Maybe, to Mouse, it seemed like Amy's friendliness meant she was into him."

"Did Amy have a boyfriend?"

"No."

"You sound sure?"

"I was working tables back then and all us girls gossiped in our down time. Boys was the favorite topic."

"How about a guy who was just a friend, named Mike?"

"I don't remember her having guy friends. Things were more segregated back then. At least in my part of the world."

"Did Mose have a friend named Mike?"

"I don't remember him having any friends—No… wait. I do remember someone dropping Mouse off for work a few times. A bigger guy. Drove a van."

A bigger guy who drove a van. A description of Mike?

McClure's eyes suddenly lit up and her eyebrows arched. "Have you talked to Nadine?"

"Who's that?"

"Nadine Drilling. She worked here too and was Amy's best friend. She still lives in town. I ran into her at Anderson's Bookshop a year or two ago at a signing for that thriller author, Peter Thompson."

Drilling's name was not in the murder book. "Did the police interview Nadine?"

"I don't know. She was on vacation with her family when Amy… when it happened."

"I'll look her up."

They talked for a few more minutes, but Traci McClure had nothing else to offer him.

He left her there, playing with the charms on her bracelet, her face clouded with the memories he had forced upon her.

CHAPTER TWENTY-THREE

Eddie sat in his car in the police station parking lot, thinking. The cops had noticed his FOIA request and now knew he was in town. His impulsive claim to be 'just passing through' would likely fail as misdirection. So now what? Was he going to sneak home and go back to writing the lurid crap Penny hated, or man the fuck up and get on with it? His hands trembled, so he gripped the steering wheel to steady them. He could do this. He *would* do this. A couple suburban cops were nothing to be scared of. He started the car and went to find a hotel.

He found a very nice one downtown—the Indigo—but it was a 'boutique' hotel and way out of his price range. The front desk clerk pointed north and told him to check the hotels out by the tollway or for a *real* bargain to try the Starlite on Ogden Avenue. He drank a glass of cucumber-infused water from the giant glass urn on the counter before he left.

He typed the name of the "real bargain" into his phone's map and followed the line it drew for him to a white brick motel on a busy four-lane road that felt like Anywhere, America. Every chain store you ever heard of was scattered along its length with strip malls and local businesses—like the motel—scattered among them.

But the fancy hotel's clerk had been right about the rooms being a bargain. For one-third the price of the Indigo he got a spotless room with two big beds and a long piece of multi-level furniture bolted to the opposite wall that held a desk, TV, and a chest of drawers. Being a motel, he got to park almost directly in front of his room. Eddie chucked his suitcase on the bed by the door, splashed some cold water on his face, then sat at the desk.

He re-read Larson's letter, then looked at a photo from her social media profile. She was a good-looking woman of about thirty with full lips and kinky blond hair. He called the number under her name on her letter and she answered on the second ring. Her voice matched her picture with a smoky depth that spoke of time spent in bars. He told her that her letter convinced him to take a look at her father's case and he was in town. How about a drink? She suggested they meet at the Grey Tavern at eight.

Eddie had time to kill so drove down Ogden until he found some edible fast food, fueled up, and came back to the room and got to work. He listened to the recordings he'd made of each interview that day then typed them up in narrative form, describing each scene—the people and the places—loading in as much emotional mood setting as came to him. If a book didn't connect with a reader's emotions, it failed.

CHAPTER TWENTY-FOUR

Jake called Nadine Drilling from his car. He pressed her to meet immediately, but she was tied up. He considered playing the Kate Ballard card, but didn't want the possible Belker connection leaking to the press. They set up a meeting for the next morning at the downtown Starbucks.

With nothing to work on, Jake drove home. He slowed as he cruised through the gate onto his property. The sun had dropped behind a thick bank of clouds to the west, throwing the property into an early twilight. The large concrete block commercial building he called home sat in the middle of five-acres of weed-choked gravel dotted with concrete slabs where different varieties of mulch had once been piled. Random heaps of landscaping materials—bricks and gravel and timbers—still lined the perimeter. There wasn't a stretch of grass big enough to call a yard anywhere on the property. That was great for a man living alone who didn't enjoy yard work, but would not do if a child was going to spend any time here.

His child.

He and Mary had wanted children, but they'd kept putting it off. That wasn't right—*he* had kept putting it off because he was still working the night shift. He had denied Mary her shot at motherhood. Hell, if they had been parents, they would have been at home that night with their child and Mary would still be alive.

He shook his head and pushed the past away. That had nothing to do with this. If—*when*—Anna had the baby, he needed to be ready for whatever role she allowed him.

He thumbed the garage-door button, then pulled in under the rising door and parked the Mustang. He turned on the floodlights mounted on each corner of the building, then walked the property. The land between the building and the forest preserve would make the best yard. It had the fewest concrete pads and the forest backdrop would make it shady on hot summer afternoons. He climbed over a mound of landscaping timbers and into the darkness beyond it where the forest canopy arched above him. The air was thicker here, and filled with the drone and *tick-tick* of bugs. The fence leaned and gaped open in several places so would have to be replaced. He turned back to face the building, shielding his eyes from the bright lights. Yeah. This could be a great yard.

He walked over to the building, thinking about using the timbers and bricks and gravel to put in a patio. He kicked through the weed cover along the building to see what he'd be dealing with. Gravel, packed down from decades of vehicles traffic, and a pair of parallel concrete footings jutting out from the wall. They would make a good base for a built-in brick fire pit, or—his cell buzzed with a string of texts from Erin. Excellent! She'd found both the detective and the chief from 1999.

He went inside and sat down at his kitchen island, notebook open.

He started with the detective who'd handled Belker's confessions in 1999. Shawn Tate had left Weston in 2000 and was now on the force in Denver. He answered Jake's call but wouldn't talk until he confirmed Jake's identity. Jake waited. Half of detective work was waiting. It took less than five minutes for Tate to call him back.

"What do you need?"

"I'm looking at Smith and Brown for a possible link to a missing person's case and—"

"How old is your case?"

"She's been missing for eleven days."

"Belker has been in prison for twenty years," Tate said. "How can there be a connection?"

"I can't get into that, Detective."

Tate was silent for nearly a minute, likely pissed that Jake was treating him like an outsider. But he *was* an outsider.

"I write a good book so you should start there."

"I've read both books. Reed's parts and yours."

"Then ask your questions."

Jake took Tate back through it, focusing on how he became involved in the trip out to Iowa and what had happened out there. Tate's chief had assigned him the case when the original detective, Reed, pointed out there was evidence available for DNA analysis.

"He'd mulled it over since retiring. You should talk to him, Reed. He was sure Belker had killed her. I tracked Belker down and went to get a sample from him and he ended up confessing."

"But you still got his DNA and submitted it."

"Of course. It was why I went out there, and we needed it to corroborate the confession."

"Who else did you get a sample from?"

"Who else? No one else. Just Belker."

"The DNA lab told me the department sent two known samples to compare to the evidentiary sample."

"That's not right. There was only one known sample. Belker's."

"Was the DNA a match?"

"Well, I assume so. I was gone before the result came back."

"Did you ever come across a *Mike* while working the case?"

"Mike?" A long silence. "Not that I recall. Look at the book."

"Why *weren't* you here when the DNA results came back?"

"They fired my chief, Vaughn, so I got out."

"Why was he fired?"

"Trumped-up bullshit. But I'll leave it to him to tell you."

After the call Jake wrote down what he'd learned, then stood at the windows looking across the yard to the forest. Tate had answered Jake's questions squarely, without deception or evasion. Except on the topic of why his chief had been fired.

Movement in the trees at the edge of the woods caught his eye. A deer, then another, creeping along the fence, the shine from the floodlights making them blink and falter.

He went to the panel and turned off the floodlights, then sat back down at the island to call Alan Vaughn, Tate's chief back in 1999. Jake caught his slumping reflection in the now dark window and sat up straighter. When he had Vaughn on the phone he introduced himself and Vaughn cut him off.

"I know who you are, Houser. Your family, anyway."

"Are you from Weston?" Old townies knew that Jake's mom had been a Warren—a Weston founding family that had been big and political at one time. Since her dad's death the year before, Jake's cousin Bev, the Paget County Sheriff, was the only Warren with any real power.

"I grew up there. And after what they did to me I'm done with the place. And I remember your dad, too—all tight with Stewart and his crew. In fact, fuck you, Houser."

The line went dead, Jake staring at the phone. Frank Houser had always hung out with the tradesmen in town, not the businessmen in Abe Stewart's crew.

Jake's phone buzzed. *Caller unknown.*

CHAPTER TWENTY-FIVE

Bev straddled the kitchen chair backwards and rested her forearms on its back. Sitting in a wood chair with an equipment belt any other way was impossible.

They'd opened the sliding glass door behind the kitchen table and the evening breeze wafted through, carrying the scent of wet dirt and the moldy rot of last autumn's fallen leaves. Something about the smell reminded her that she'd missed lunch and now it was dinnertime. She needed to refuel or she'd fade out on her men.

Later.

Her gaze locked on the handcuffed man sitting on the chair in front of her. Alonzo Gierhart. He was a bulky man with tribal tats, acne scars, and a topknot hairdo that didn't suit his thick features. His gaze darted around the room, eyeballing the evidence technicians who bustled about searching the three-bedroom ranch. They'd already found a pharmacy scale in the bathroom, small wax paper stamp bags in a drawer, and a box of nitrile gloves. But the panicked sweat soaking through Gierhart's tank top told her they would find more.

"Sheriff?" Duke Fanning had come in from the garage. "We found this in the trash."

An empty printer cartridge with Chinese markings. Gierhart's eyes bugged further out.

"It field-tested positive for heroin and check this out." Fanning held up a cardboard box with identical markings. "Looks like it came through the mail in this box which would hold two more just like it."

A printer cartridge through the mail from China was exactly how the disaster in Ohio started.

"Are the other two cartridges here?"

"We haven't found them, but we're still searching."

She estimated each printer cartridge held a pound of heroin, 453 grams. At one tenth of a gram per dose, that was over forty-five hundred doses per pound. Over thirteen thousand in total.

She had to find this crap before more people died.

"The heroin that came to you in this printer cartridge is killing people. You're killing people," Bev said. "It's cut with carfentanil. Your users can't handle it."

"That's not mine."

His breath stank like his insides were rotting. But he wasn't a user as far as she could tell. For one thing, he was still alive.

"When I match the chemistry of the residue in this container to the stuff that killed my ODs, I'll have you for multiple murders."

His head jerked up, eyes locked on hers. She held his gaze so he would see the truth in her eyes but it was lost on him.

"You're playing me. That's not murder. Cops are a bunch of damn liars"

"Sheriff!" The tech working under the kitchen sink. "I got something."

Bev joined him, squatting to peer into the dark recess.

"I saw this notch there." He pointed at a gap on the inside floor of the cabinet. "I stuck my screwdriver in there and pried it, like this." He demonstrated and the entire bottom panel came up. Underneath was a space about three inches deep stuffed with cash, three guns, and a notebook. The tech pulled out the notebook and flipped it open. "It's a ledger."

"Well, well." Bev stood up, kicked her chair aside, and faced Gierhart. He was blinking fast and licking his lips. "Looks like we found your business records."

Gierhart's gaze went to the patio door and then he leaned forward. Bev anticipated his move and stepped into his path as he launched himself toward freedom. She took his driving shoulder in the middle of her chest and flew backwards. She gasped when she hit the floor. She tried to rise but his boot stomped on her chest as he tried to get past her. She grabbed his foot with both hands and held on. He broke through the screen door and carried both of them over the threshold and onto the deck before she hooked his other foot and brought him down.

A fast tussle, then Bev was hauled to her feet. "You okay, Sheriff?"

She wasn't, but stood tall, pain throbbing in shoulder and down her side where it had scraped over the threshold. "I'm fine."

They got Gierhart back in his chair and a deputy stood behind him, a hand clamped on each shoulder.

"This is your one chance to help yourself, Alonzo. Hundreds of people could die from that shit you're peddling. If you help me I can—"

"Fuck you."

Bev swung from the hip, her hand flat, slapping Gierhart so hard a glob of spit flew from his mouth and hit the wall. The room went silent, then Gierhart lunged for her but the Deputy slipped his arm around the man's neck and rode him to the floor.

"Put him in a squad," Bev said. As the deputy led Gierhart away the room was silent, the forensic team frozen in place. Staring at her. She understood the stares—hitting a handcuffed man was inexcusable—but the buck didn't stop with them. Finally, Duke Fanning stepped forward.

"Let's get to back to it everyone."

Bev paced as Duke's team worked, documenting everything by dictation, photographs, and video. When they had everything out of the hidden compartment and on the table it was an impressive hall.

"Sixteen thousand in cash, Bev." Duke gestured toward the table. "But the gold is the notebook." He opened it flat on the table and stepped back.

A ledger going back three years. Street names, dates, quantities, and dollars paid. The quantities were too high to be users. This was a list of street level dealers.

Duke ran his gloved finger down the most recent page. "He gets a new batch every month or so. Here's his sale of this batch."

Bev sent out an email for every detective on the task force to assemble in the war room. They would hit their databases and snitches and identify every one of these dealers and start getting Alonzo's pound off the streets. With luck one of these street dealers would buy his freedom with other dealer's names and she could chase her way to the other two printer cartridges full of killer heroin before anyone else died.

On the way to her car her she ordered a dozen pizzas for immediate delivery to the war room.

CHAPTER TWENTY-SIX

Jake answered the unknown caller. "Detective Jake Houser."

"This is Steve Ballard. Kate's dad. You left me a bunch of messages. Has she turned up?"

The man spoke so fast it took Jake a second to take it in. Then he popped up from his stool. "Thanks for calling me back, Mr. Ballard. I—"

"I just tried Kate's phone but it's off and I texted her and sent her messages through Facebook. But she hasn't posted anything in nearly two weeks."

"She's been missing since—"

"Her mom doesn't know where she is?"

Her mom was sure she'd been abducted and was already dead. "We all hoped she'd run off to join you on that wilderness—"

"We talked about it, but she's coming out in August instead."

"She might have decided to surprise you."

Ballard was silent for a minute. "Is her stuff missing? Her backpacking stuff?"

"Her boots were still—"

"Those were too small. I was going to buy her new boots on her next trip out here. What about the rest of it?"

"Kate's mom wasn't sure. She—"

"No need to sugarcoat things. I imagine she had no idea. Listen. I can send you pictures from our hike last year and you'll see her pack and other equipment. If the stuff's missing it means she set out to come here."

"Send them and I'll check against what's at their apartment."

"There's a thousand miles between us. That's a lot of room to get… lost."

Lost. She wasn't lost—she'd been taken. Jake wasn't going to voice that thought so kept his mouth shut.

"I—here we go. A nice shot of Kate on top of Hallet Peak. You can see her pack, hiking pole, and her windbreaker. I'll send it as soon as we hang up."

"Thank you, Mr. Ballard."

"I'm home now so call me when you—or should I come there?"

Jake didn't see how that would help. "No need. I'll call you when I have anything."

"Good or bad."

"Yes."

As soon as he hung up Jake shot a text to Erin and DC Braff that he'd spoken with Kate Ballard's dad and she was not with him in Colorado.

His phone buzzed: the photo Ballard had promised. Jake zoomed in to examine Kate's equipment. A gray and orange backpack, a purple hiking pole, and a dark green windbreaker. He'd been through Kate Ballard's room and didn't remember seeing any of this stuff. Maybe she *had* left Weston for Colorado.

He needed to look through her room again.

Another call. Coogan.

"Jake, sorry I missed you this morning. How are you doing?"

Jake knew his friend was talking about Anna's pregnancy, but didn't want to talk about it. He needed to stay focused. "You okay with the work I gave Levi?"

"Not as happy as he is," Coogan said. "He does a great job finding the interesting in the mundane, but only the first time he does it. Your task should keep him happy and soften the blow when I plop another big real estate deal on him tomorrow."

"Did you read the letter?" Coogan had been studying Weston history his entire life and might see something Jake hadn't. "Do you remember the Belker murders?"

"We were kids when those murders happened, but I do remember his confessions in '99—you were in Chicago then. They freaked people out."

"What do you think?"

"If someone in the Weston PD knew that this mysterious Mike killed Beth Lachey, why let James Larson go to jail for it?"

"Because protecting Mike was more important than Larson's life," Jake said. "He must be someone important."

"Or protecting him served a greater goal," Coogan said. "Back in the eighties, this town was growing like crazy. Residential development spreading south and west, retail development along all the major roads, and corporate development along the Tollway. The bad press generated by a killer operating in Weston could have slowed that way down."

"A killer *was* operating in Weston. He killed Smith and Brown."

"Then disappeared and those crimes blew over. If the Lachey murder had been linked to the first two, it all would have been dredged back up and amplified. A lot of other towns along the transportation corridors into Chicago were competing for those corporate HQs and executive housing."

"So someone in the Weston PD knew who the real killer was but protected him to protect the city," Jake said. He had a likely candidate. "Abe Stewart."

"He *was* chief back in the eighties and acting chief in '99. I remember an interview he gave when Belker was sentenced."

Jake told Coogan about the unexplained second known DNA sample and the missing DNA reports.

"As chief, could Abe have manipulated the DNA report results?"

"Probably," Jake replied.

A long silence, but the old friends were never in a hurry to fill them. On Jake's end his silence was filled with angry heat as he thought about the corruption that allowed a killer to go free, and maybe, kill again.

Coogan broke the silence. "Have you talked to Anna?"

Jake grimaced. "Yes. She *is* pregnant."

"Wow! Okay, then. What do you think?"

"She, uh… she hasn't decided what she's going to do. I told her I'd support… whatever she decided."

"Is she considering not having the baby?"

Jake's stomach lurched and he had to swallow back a mouthful of bile. "I—" He couldn't get it out. He'd convinced himself she would decide to have their baby, but now he wasn't sure.

"I'm sorry, Jake."

"I can't do anything to stop that, right?" He knew the answer but couldn't help asking.

"No," Coogan said.

Jake wasn't even sure he would stop it if he could. The whole situation seemed beyond his ability to think his way through it. They sat in silence for a few moments before Jake ended the call. He had his work to do.

Jake again looked at the photo Kate's dad had sent him. She stood on a pile of rocks which Jake knew from experience was as good as some trails got in the Rockies. She was climbing, leaned forward, eyes on the rocks beneath her. A big smile. He needed to get over to Ballard's apartment and look for this equipment. But he would have to leave it to the morning when Kate's mom would be coherent enough to answer the door.

His phone shuddered with a text. Braff: *Acknowledged. Let's ramp this back up. I'll goose media relations, put out an Amber alert, and get the hotline running. What else do you need?*

Jake had no leads to run other than the equipment angle. But the public plea could change that. Luckily, the sergeant who supervised the hotline was great at sifting the wheat from the chaff. Jake texted back: *That's good for now.*

He turned on the TV news, but it was full of problems so far removed from him that he just couldn't engage with it and his mind wandered back to Kate Ballard, and from there to Anna.

Another phone call. Jake answered with a smile when he saw the caller ID.

"Dad!" Frank Houser had fled the cold after working outside his entire life and now lived in Scottsdale, Arizona. Jake had just been down to see him in March and had taken Anna along. Frank was a big fan.

"My boy," Frank said, in the slow wistful voice he always used when he said that. "I'm coming up for a visit."

"How come?"

"Can't a dad want to see his son?"

"Of course. You'll be amazed at what I've done with this place."

"I look forward to seeing that."

"What time's your flight? I'll pick you up."

"No, no. I'm taking the red-eye. I'll catch a rideshare out to Weston."

"You sure, Dad? It's no trouble."

"I'm sure. What's new up there in my old stomping grounds?"

"Well..." Jake hesitated because Anna had asked him to keep the news secret, but it was Jake's news too. "Remember Anna?"

"Of course! I'll never forget her catching that foul ball barehanded like that. And when she—"

"She's pregnant."

"Oh," Frank said. "I didn't know you two were headed… I mean. Congratulations, son."

"Thanks, Dad. I… "

"I'm going to be a grandfather!"

"Well… " Jake trailed off, because he now sensed his mistake. Telling his dad about the pregnancy invited him into the pain Jake was experiencing. His dad might not, in fact, end up being a grandfather.

"Talk to me, son."

And Jake spilled. About having the baby being Anna's choice and that he accepted that. About his own doubts. About needing to be ready if she did have the baby for whatever parenting scenario happened. "So, I'd need a second bedroom up here with me and maybe an apartment for a nanny downstairs."

"Won't you want a regular house?"

Somehow that hadn't occurred to Jake. But that would also work. "If she's willing to live with me we could get a house."

"You have a lot of great names in your ancestry, you know."

The conversation continued, bouncing from one parenthood topic to the next. Jake never questioned his dad's reason for coming to town.

CHAPTER TWENTY-SEVEN

Eddie left his motel room at quarter to eight to walk to the bar for his meeting with Donna Larson.

"Hey, man."

A tall skinny guy with glassy eyes stopped Eddie before he even cleared the end of the covered walkway. The guy reeked of marijuana.

Eddie looked up into the man's bloodshot eyes. "Excuse me."

"You're new." The doper didn't move.

"Are you the welcoming committee?"

"I'm Benny. I'm livin' here while I wait for my aunt's estate to get settled then I'll move to an island. Or Denver." He pointed across the parking lot to the motel's other building, a shorter twin of the one Eddie was in. "My room's right over there. That's my chair." Benny had pulled his room's desk chair out onto the covered walkway.

"I see," Eddie said.

"Stop by any time." Benny leaned in and whispered. "I've got weed."

"Thanks for the offer, Benny. But I'm meeting someone right now."

"Sure thing, man." Benny stepped aside and Eddie continued on.

* * *

The Grey was a blue-collar place with domestic beer on tap and two worn out pool tables under Budweiser lights. It smelled of spilled beer and Eddie's shoes stuck to the floor. Heavy metal cranked from hidden speakers. He sat at the bar and the bartender came right over, raising an eyebrow. He wore a Marine Corps T-shirt and sported an eagle, globe, and anchor tattoo on his left arm.

"Welcome to the Grey."

"I'll have an Old Style."

While Eddie waited for the beer, he scanned the long shelf behind the bar. It held liquor bottles and at least a dozen trophies for different sports teams the bar apparently sponsored.

"Sixteen-inch softball still a big thing here in Chicago?" Eddie asked when the bartender returned with Eddie's beer in a pint glass.

"You bet," the bartender said, eyes narrowing. "Not where you come from?"

"No, we—"

"Excuse me." The bartender stepped away to draw beers for a noisy crowd of men who'd just come inside wearing bowling shirts. Eddie sipped his beer and watched the action. Solo drinkers along the bar. Tables with two or three people huddled close around them to hear each other over the music. The rowdy bowlers around the dartboard, reliving some big bowling moment. Their shirts had the bar's name on them.

Eddie had spent time in plenty of townie bars like this one while waiting for a source or getting one drunk enough to talk. He was comfortable and settled in, enjoying the beer and the music pulsing through him.

The door opened, admitting the zip of tires on pavement from the cars going by on Ogden. Donna Larson came in. Eddie watched her in the mirror. She was taller than he'd imagined. And slimmer. The bartender called out a loud 'Hey' and she leaned over the bar to talk to him. His response included a nod toward Eddie and she came straight over.

"Mr. Shaw."

"Call me Eddie."

"Here you go, Donna." The bartender set a draft beer in front of Donna. She thanked him then picked it up and motioned for Eddie to follow her to a high table in the corner by the front window. It was quieter here, and darker. They sat with their backs to the window. She looked better than her picture, probably because of the energy in her eyes.

"First, thank you for believing I can help you and sending me your letter. Can I record our conversation?" When she agreed, he pulled out his phone and started the app.

"I can't tell you how much it means to me that you believed my letter," she said.

He smiled. "It's an interesting part of the larger story, Donna."

"What do you… " Her voice trailed off. "What's the larger story?"

"This town. The idea that the leaders of this so-called Shangri-La knew your dad didn't kill Beth Lachey but let him take the rap to protect someone named Mike." He watched her closely as he explained. She could be a great addition to his book if she was tragic enough, desperate enough. "How old are you?"

"What does that—"

"Please."

She grimaced and he knew he was right.

"Thirty-two."

"Born in '87 but conceived in '86."

"Yes." She looked down.

"The year your dad was banging this high school girl and—"

"That was just her fantasy."

This could be gold if she would say it. "But the idea of it is part of what—"

"When I was younger and believed what that girl said. Back then the idea that my dad could have made love to my mother to create me at the same time he was…. with that girl, was horrifying."

She stopped, hands in her lap.

Excellent, but he pressed her for more. "But then… "

"I lived through high school. High school girls, especially dreamers like Lachey was, have rich fantasy lives."

"They certainly do."

Larson smiled meekly before taking a long swallow that nearly drained the pint glass.

"You've been visiting Belker for a long time?"

"Since I turned eighteen."

"Tell me about him."

Larson shrugged. "I always do most of the talking. Him staring at me the whole time."

"Is he scary?"

"No, but that place sure is. The first time I went down there I almost didn't make it inside. But I'd been thinking about it so long I forced myself to go in."

"Thinking about what?"

"About getting him to admit that *he* killed Beth Lachey. He was never getting out so I was sure I could convince him to tell the truth."

"But now you think he told the truth all along."

"Because now I know Mike killed Beth Lachey."

Pure speculation, but proving it was his job. And if it *could* be proven, he *would* prove it. "Have you remembered anything else Belker said about Mike over the years?"

"No. Just the one thing about laying concrete."

Eddie needed to visit Belker but would wait until he'd locked down as much of the story as he could. Convicts were not reliable. And Eddie hated going inside prisons.

"I saw you sent a letter to the sheriff, but have you approached the Weston police?"

"I sent them at least a dozen letters asking if Mr. Belker had ever said anything about Beth Lachey when he confessed."

"Recently?" Eddie asked.

"No, this was years ago and they ignored me. Now with what Mr. Belker said, I don't trust them." She drained her glass.

Years ago. But someone there was still on alert.

"I haven't heard back from the sheriff, by the way."

"I doubt a county sheriff would want to step on the Weston PD's toes."

She shrugged. They talked some more and he kept ordering drinks, hoping for a juicy quote but she held her liquor too well for that. When her voice slowed down and her tongue got thick, she started running a finger down the inside of his forearm.

He leaned in closer and she smiled up at him.

He smiled back. *Am I about to get lucky?*

She reached under the table and squeezed his thigh just above his knee. His whole body clenched up against the sudden tickle.

He snapped out of it.

"I need to go. Thanks for meeting with me."

"I—"

"I'll pay the bartender on my way out." He paid and left, proud of himself for staying true to whatever he and Penny might have together.

But it had been a close call.

CHAPTER TWENTY-EIGHT

When the clock hit six, Jake gave up on sleep and put on his running clothes. He'd had a long night, repeatedly woken by his longest running nightmare. He never remembered his dreams for more than a few minutes after waking, but his nightmares always stuck with him. Probably because they weren't really dreams: each was the playback of a real event in his life—a dark memory of something he'd seen, done, or failed to do. His past pulled into his present by his sleeping mind.

This nightmare was about his wife's murder. They'd gone out for dinner at a restaurant down the street from the art gallery where Mary worked in Chicago. Soon after their drinks arrived, she jumped up from the table to run back to the gallery for something she'd forgotten. Mary insisted he stay put so his beer didn't go flat. Ten minutes later sirens screamed and emergency vehicles shot past the restaurant window and stopped a block away. He got there in time to see the last beat of her heart pump blood into the pool spreading across the floor from the slash across her neck.

He rarely got back to sleep after this nightmare and last night had been no different.

It was still dark out when he stepped outside, the air calm and sweet with the green scents of spring. The first half-mile was tough going, his body leaden and stiff. His belly heavy with the lasagna he'd eaten after the call with his dad. As he loosened up, he lengthened his stride and his mind cleared and his thoughts turned to Anna's pregnancy. Then back to Mary. He'd denied Mary a desired pregnancy through his own selfishness and caused Anna an unwanted pregnancy through his own desires. Maybe he didn't deserve to be a dad.

He went south on Mill, taking it through town and across the river, then cut over to the cemetery where his mom was buried. She had told him more than once that you can't wait for the perfect time to have a child, but he hadn't listened. He stopped in front of her gravestone, breathing hard. The sun was about to break the eastern horizon and had filled the sky with false dawn. "I've got news, Mom. I've told you about Anna. Well, we—it looks like I'm going to be a dad after all." Saying it out loud felt good. "I'm going to be a dad."

Jake was home, showered and dressed, before seven. He sat down with a bowl of oatmeal at the island and opened his laptop. He now had two files to update: his official Ballard case file and his off-the-books Mike file.

The only progress he'd made on Ballard that didn't include Mike was the phone call from Kate's dad, Steve. Kate was not with her dad, which meant she had disappeared here in Weston, or, if her backpacking equipment was missing from her apartment, on her way to Colorado. Jake checked his watch, but it was still too early to go visit Mrs. Ballard.

On Mike, he'd made more progress. The missing DNA reports and the second known DNA sample meant two things: Someone else had been involved in murdering Smith—alone or with Belker—and someone in the Weston PD was hiding that fact.

Jake typed all that into his Mike file, then considered whether to move this information into the Ballard case file.

Jake realized he wasn't sure who all had access to his files. He knew the ability to make entries in the file was limited to one detective and one member each from the coroner and forensic teams. But he also knew that many more people had read-only access to the file, including the other detectives in the squad, DC Braff, and Chief Arvind. But that access might go even further—to Deputy Chief of Patrol Sam Stewart, for example. Jake just didn't know. He couldn't risk the dirty cop seeing his report and interfering with his search for Kate Ballard.

He left the Mike file where it was for now.

He equipped himself and headed out. As he descended the stairs his doorbell went off, an urgent *buzz-buzzing* that chased him all the way down the stairs to answer it. Jake opened the steel service door.

"Hey, Levi." He had a green canvas messenger bag over his knobby shoulder and was still astride his bike.

"If I leave my bike out here will it be okay?"

"Probably, but bring it on inside."

Jake hit the button and waited while the big garage door rattled upward in its tracks. Levi got off the bike then ducked under the door while it was still rising. Once inside, he paused and looked around the big space for a moment before leaning his bike against the back bumper of Jake's pickup truck. Levi rubbed his hands together, his eyes dancing with light.

"You've got something," Jake said.

"I do. And you're going to find it very interesting."

"Come on up."

Levi followed Jake up the stairs and accepted a cup of coffee. They sat together at the island.

"What do you have?"

"I found a Mike, I think *the* Mike, and he worked right here." Levi patted the countertop. "In this building."

"What?"

"For Trinity Landscaping. Your dad's company, right?"

"Explain," Jake said. Cases had come close to him since moving home to Weston, but not right to the building he lived in.

"The letter mentions how Mose Belker's friend Mike got him the job laying concrete. But, that isn't the word they use for putting down concrete. It's not laid, it's—"

"Poured," Jake said. He should have caught that.

"Right. But concrete *brick*s are laid. They're used for paving; patios and roads and here in Weston, the Riverwalk."

"The Riverwalk," Jake repeated. His dad was proud of the work his company had done on the linear park that ran along the Paget River through downtown Weston.

"I looked at the old city council minutes where they discussed hiring the companies that did the brickwork. When they voted on hiring your dad's company one of the councilmen pointed out that Mr. Football would be managing the crew for your dad."

The nickname struck a chord of memory, but Jake couldn't quite place it. "And who was Mr. Football?"

"Mike Nelson. A real hotshot high school athlete back in the late seventies. One of those guys all the adult men get excited about. Potential, and all that." Levi shrugged; he wasn't into sports.

Now Jake remembered. "Nice work, Levi. Were you able to find him?"

"Not yet. He joined the army in '83, came home in '85, and disappeared soon after."

"Keep looking." The doorbell buzzed again, the sound breaking into a familiar tune: *Shave and haircut, two bits.*

Frank Houser had arrived.

CHAPTER TWENTY-NINE

Deputy Chief of Patrol Sam Stewart fumed the entire way back to his office from the chief's weekly command staff meeting. But he kept his rage off his face. When he wanted to communicate what he thought about something he did it one-on-one or through the chain of command. Facial expressions generated rumors and rumors tore through the building in minutes.

But this morning it was not easy. Deputy Chief of Detectives Braff spent the entire meeting kissing Chief Arvind's ass and the chief ate it up. The chief even asked Braff if he wanted another donut. Sam couldn't remember the chief ever doing that before. The man hoarded leftover meeting food as if he was living paycheck to paycheck instead of knocking down two-hundred thousand dollars a year and sitting on a six-figure annual pension payment.

Christ!

Maybe it wasn't just Braff who was stirring up the old Belker cases. Maybe Arvind was in on it too. Maybe he knew Sam deserved the top job—had *earned* the job—but was looking for an excuse to stiff him and give it to Braff. Those two had always been buddy-buddy. Golfing and Bears games and all that macho nonsense. Stirring up this mess until the stench slopped over from Sam's dad onto Sam would give

Arvind the cover to jump over Sam and hand the job to his buddy.

Sam would *not* let that happen.

He would work the problem and make sure his dad's misdeeds didn't screw him out of becoming chief.

Back in his office he used Massey's password to access the records database.

"Come on, Houser." Sam searched the victim's name and found the case number and clicked through to the Ballard file.

Houser had just made a new entry. "Here we go." The girl's dad had returned from his backwoods camping trip and said his daughter was not with him. The dad then suggested Houser check the girl's belongings for her backpacking equipment; if it was still there, it meant she had never left for Colorado and had disappeared in Weston. If it was gone, she had left Weston for Colorado and disappeared somewhere in between. Sam smirked; Houser should have figured that out on his own. Sam hit refresh but that was Houser's entire entry. He had written nothing about requesting the Smith and Brown files. Which meant either the files were unrelated to Ballard or Houser was keeping that part of his investigation to himself. And Braff, no doubt.

CHAPTER THIRTY

Eddie woke groggy from the booze he'd downed the night before while trying to lubricate Donna Larson's tongue. Then he remembered turning down her obvious advance and grimaced. Maybe he should have gone for it. "You're not getting any younger, Shaw."

He went to the bathroom and splashed some cold water on his face. When he saw himself in the mirror, he shook his head. Turning down Donna Larson wasn't a missed opportunity; it was an opportunity seized to do the right thing twice over. To not take advantage of a vulnerable woman and to stay true to Penny. He had a shot at something real with Penny and could not risk that on a one-night stand.

He found his phone in the pocket of his jeans draped over the desk chair and started to text Penny but had trouble finding the right words. He deleted several false starts before finding the right tone: *I'm sorry about yesterday. You were right and I knew you were right but couldn't admit it to myself. So I got angry and lashed out. Not very mature, but I'll do better. Will you give me the chance? FYI - I am in Weston, Illinois helping a woman whose father died in prison for a crime he might not have committed. If I solve it and clear his name and bring closure to the victim's family it will be because of you.*

He waited for a few minutes but there was no response. She must be working her tables. She'd get back to him when her shift ended.

He hoped.

He showered and dressed and walked down to the motel's office. He filled his travel mug with coffee and scored a couple of donuts. They were stale, but free.

He left the door open when he came back to the room. It was a cool spring day and the freshness of blooming greenery and wet dirt rode on the breeze. He sat at the little desk and opened his laptop. He had a lot of ground to cover if he was going to get this done right, and on time. He ate the donuts as he worked, washing them down with the coffee. A writer's breakfast.

His internet research said the detective who originally handled the Smith and Brown cases was dead, so he started with the detective who'd gone to Iowa to question Mose Belker in 1999. Shawn Tate was now deputy chief of the Property Crimes Division of the Denver PD. Eddie eventually got through to him, but the man did not like the press.

"You people are bloodsuckers who prey on victims and survivors to sell papers."

"I'm not with a newspaper. I'm writing a book."

"The more words you write the more pain you'll inflict," Tate said. "Forget it."

Eddie then called Tate's chief from that time. Alan Vaughn had moved away and eventually retired to a small town in Idaho.

"Mr. Vaughn, my name is Eddie Shaw. I'm researching a book about Mose Belker and how the Weston—"

"Those assholes fired me." Vaughn spoke with the breathless energy of a man with a bone to pick. Eddie smiled.

"Because of the Mose Belker case?"

"What? No. They fired me over a sexual assault allegation by some woman I barely knew who worked in the IT group.

A civilian. It was bullshit—he said, she said—but I couldn't risk the taint that would put on my record. So when Stewart offered me the deal I took it and got the hell out of there."

"Are you talking about Abe Stewart? The chief back in '82?"

"Of course I'm talking about—you really don't know shit about that town, do you?"

"Fill me in."

"Abe Stewart ran that whole damn place. As chief and over at city hall as assistant city manager. Between him and his two cronies—Lowe and Forsyth—they had a say in damn near everything. Maybe still do, I don't know. Getting pretty damn old."

Eddie scribbled notes as fast as he could, wishing he had turned on his recorder.

A long silence, then a bark of laughter. "As a cop I never talked to the press."

Another long silence. Eddie was tempted to jump in with his spiel that he wasn't the press, that his book would tell the whole story, but he kept his mouth shut and was rewarded for his patience.

"But I'm not a cop anymore so fuck 'em. What's your angle on Belker?"

Vaughn was so eager to talk that Eddie decided to push him a bit. "I'm looking at whether Belker was the right guy."

"Who says he isn't?"

"Belker says a guy named Mike was involved with him, that the Weston police knew this and protected the guy, and that Mike has started up again."

"There's been another murder?"

"A missing girl."

"That must have been why the detective called me."

"A detective called you?" Eddie knew the cops had to be working the Ballard case but not this link into the past. The sheriff must have passed on the letter Donna Larson sent her.

Getting between cops and a case, even just by interviewing people tied to the crime, could result in a charge of obstruction of justice. And that's where cops were *not* corrupt. Eddie needed to steer clear of this detective. "What's his name?"

"I'm not giving you his name. If what Belker says is true, there are dirty cops there. Probably that fucker Stewart. And I don't want any more legal trouble with them, okay? And I don't *know* the detective's dirty. He's just—he's got a conflict, is all. His mom's people were super tight with Stewart and all them old guys. And so was his dad."

Vaughn's voice had dropped. He was shutting down. Eddie was sure if he kept the man talking more golden nuggets would drop. He tried some questions that should have simple answers.

"Back in 1999 why did you decide to look at the two cold cases and why did you look at Belker for them?"

"The detective who handled them originally—Reed— came to see me. He'd retired and those two cases were eating at him. I get that now; I've got several eating at me. Anyway, he read about DNA evidence solving all kinds of old cases and thought he could finally know for sure if it had been Belker."

"And there was a DNA sample… "

"The forensic guys had taken semen off Smith's body and it was still in the evidence fridge. They'd kept it to compare against a blood type if they ever got a solid suspect. No one had imagined DNA analysis back then. Not in Weston, anyway. So I decided what the hell. Let's get a sample from Belker now and see what's what. DNA test results are determinative so warrants are easier to get. And if Belker was innocent being cleared would be good for him, too. Maybe he could move back home. All the talk of him being a suspect had forced him out of town."

"Was Abe Stewart okay with you re-opening the case and leaving the state to pursue a suspect?"

"I didn't ask him. I was chief. A chief has a lot of discretion as long as he stays within his budget."

"How about afterwards?"

"I went to Iowa with Detective Tate and when we came back home with the confessions Stewart seemed pleased. Shook my hand and thanked me for getting the parents the peace of mind that came from knowing justice had been served."

"But then you got fired."

"That was a few weeks later."

"Because of—"

"The sexual harassment claim by that civilian employee."

"But that wasn't true?"

"I barely even knew her. I don't think I was ever alone with her."

"Did Stewart believe the charge against you or did he just grab it to use as a pretext?"

"Pretext for what? I had the confessions and they stuck. Two gruesome murders closed."

"The timing is curious."

"It *was* less than a month later." Vaughn's voice had trailed off into a more pensive, tone.

"Are you sure of those confessions?"

"Didn't matter what I thought because we had the DNA."

"And it matched?"

"Right."

"You saw the test results?"

"I was gone by the time they came back, but they must have matched. Belker went down for it and his confessions were all we had other than the DNA."

"So the DNA had to match to corroborate the confessions?"

"Obviously."

"Did you ever suspect Belker had an accomplice? Or that he was covering for someone named Mike."

Pause. "People don't confess to murders they didn't commit."

"It happens all the time," Eddie said.

"In Chicago and LA, maybe. Their… demographics force them to use different tactics. But I got Belker's confessions. Me and Tate. We did everything by the book and I stand by those confessions."

"What's the woman's name who filed the complaint against you?"

"No way. I'm not re-opening that mess. Not in this me-too era. No way!"

CHAPTER THIRTY-ONE

Jake introduced Levi to his dad. When Levi left, they stood in the open garage door and watched him pedal away.

"Nice kid," Frank said. His neck and face were deeply lined from his decades working in the sun. He wore jeans and a flannel shirt and clutched a brown leather duffle bag in his left hand. Frank Houser did not go in for suitcases with wheels.

"He's a research whiz. He's helped me on a couple cases and now works for Coog."

"How *is* Bill?"

"Good. You should stop by his office while you're here."

"I will."

"Let me give you a tour of what I've done so far with this place."

"Great. But first, any news with Anna?"

"Not yet."

"Hang in there." Frank clasped a hand on Jake's shoulder. "Now show me what 's new."

Two steps into the garage Frank stopped. "Henry did a great job taking care of that truck. It looks better now than when I found it."

"You were in on this one?" Jake's friend, Henry, had never driven anything but old Chevy C10 pickups. He'd gone through a few of them because his handyman business had been hard on trucks. This one, a 1970 model in dusky red, had been his last, and Jake bought it from Henry's estate after his death. Jake had left Fox Handyman Services painted on the door.

"I spotted it in a guy's driveway while out on a run and called Henry as soon as I got home. He flew down with cash the next day."

"You can drive it while you're here."

Frank smiled. "I'd love that." He rubbed a hand down the long side of the bed as they walked into the shop area. "It smells different in here."

"I had the floor steam cleaned to remove the old motor oil and grease, then sealed it and put down a rubberized floor in the back."

"Very nice."

Jake talked Frank through the rest of his changes, his dad admiring the bar area and the remodeled bathroom more than the exercise equipment.

"If you don't mind, son. I'll stay down here while I'm in town." Frank tossed his duffle on one of the couches. "Give you your space."

Jake smiled. "I think you're more worried about *your* space." His dad always said a man needed a place to himself to do his thinking because a man had to understand his past to make sense of his present and plan his future. The older Jake got, the better he understood that.

"You got me, son. But with this nice couch and the fancy new bath this is perfect for a cantankerous old out-of-town guest."

"It's all yours for the duration." Jake led his dad upstairs and showed him through the apartment he'd built there.

"Wow," Frank said. "I never could have imagined this building as a home after how I used it for decades. All that happened in this building." He shook his head, his voice trailing off.

Jake poured them each a cup of coffee, then they sat at the kitchen island looking out the big windows to the forest beyond.

"Those windows are really something, son."

"I need to buy this building from you, Dad. I've already invested a lot in it and with the changes I might need to make for the baby—"

"I'm fine with all that you want to do with it, but I don't need the money right now so don't want to sell."

"We could trade. I've got a few other downtown properties that would—"

"Those are Warren properties," Frank reminded him. His dad had never touched a penny of his wife's old family money.

"Not all of them. Coog has bought and sold for me over the years so I have some properties a Warren has never owned. I can have Coog show you."

A long pause, and finally a nod. "I'll talk to him."

"Good," Jake smiled. "By the way, Levi—who was just here? He's been looking at a pair of old cases for me. The Belker murders back in '82."

"He confessed, right?"

"You remember that?"

Frank stood and walked to the window. "Of course."

"There's been an allegation that maybe Belker was innocent or had an accomplice." Jake walked over and stood next to his dad, watching him. "A guy named Mike who appears to be the Mike Nelson who ran one of your crews on the Riverwalk project."

"Mike Nelson?" Frank's gaze focused beyond the windows, into the past. "He did run a crew. But he was more than a crew chief."

"How so?"

"The business was failing. I'd expanded too fast and couldn't get enough business to make it work. As a last shot to save the business I put in a bid to handle the grounds of Edgar

Hospital. They rejected my proposal. As I sat in my truck digesting that, Mike Nelson showed up looking for work. Even though I wasn't from Weston, I knew who he was. I hired him and brought him along when I submitted my revised proposal. They hired me on the spot."

"Mose Belker says he laid concrete bricks for Mike. If that's true, Belker also worked for Trinity."

"Belker laid bricks?" Frank rubbed his chin. "I signed the checks and can assure you he wasn't on the payroll."

"Could he have worked for cash?"

"There *was* a budget for day laborers. We used them mostly to run bricks when we were laying them across a big expanse."

"So Belker could have been a runner."

Frank shrugged. "At most."

"What happened to Mike?"

Frank rubbed his face as he searched his memory. "He quit to join the army in, maybe '83? When he came back I didn't need anyone and he got a job at... well, I'm not sure. Maybe delivering for the lumberyard."

"He's not around now."

"I ran into him at the gas station way back then and he told me he had finally saved up enough to move west. Arizona, I think he said."

"When did he leave?"

"When?" Frank licked his lips. "It's been so long ago I can't remember, to tell you the truth. Late eighties, maybe... '88?"

"Do you think he could have been involved with Belker?"

"In killing those girls?" Frank looked at Jake. "What do you think?"

"I haven't learned enough to say."

"I mean thinking back to the guy you knew."

"What?"

"You don't remember *Big Mike*?"

Jake's face flushed as dread swept through him, making his forehead sweat and his legs tremble. "Mike Nelson is Big Mike?"

"Yep."

Jake had worked for Trinity cleaning equipment after school—in seventh and eighth grade—and had seen the big man many times. He had a quick smile and told a lot of one-line jokes. Dirty ones that Jake repeated to his buddies when he understood them. But there'd been something else between them—him and Big Mike—something had happened. Jake couldn't pull it up. He'd been somewhere he wasn't supposed to be, and—

"I'm going to catch a shower and a nap," Frank said. "Then I'm headed over to your old high school. They want my thoughts on their plan to redo the courtyard."

"I thought you liked retirement."

"They just want my thoughts, not my sweat."

Jake laughed, then got his dad the spare set of keys for the truck. Jake equipped himself before getting in the Mustang. The surprise visits from Levi and Frank had delayed him long enough that he wouldn't be able to go to see Mrs. Ballard until after he met with Amy Smith's friend, Nadine Drilling.

As he drove, the specter of Big Mike haunted him. What had happened between them?

CHAPTER THIRTY-TWO

Eddie finished typing up his notes on the Vaughn interview. His attempt to connect Vaughn's termination to the Belker case had clearly surprised the former chief. Maybe the sexual harassment claim against him had been legitimate. He *did* quit as soon as Stewart hit him with it. But Vaughn was right that even a false claim he defeated could have ruined his reputation and his career.

Eddie needed to talk to the claimant to know for sure.

Listen to yourself, Shaw. For sure? Finding enough facts to support a web of entertaining theories had been enough for a long time. But those days were over. He was going to do this book right.

He called Weston PD's IT department and introduced himself as a writer doing an article on the growth of female employment in police department technology departments. The IT manager—a man—was polite but insisted no historic employment data in his department existed.

But Eddie wasn't done. He packed his messenger bag and headed for the library.

* * *

The library was just west of downtown in a long, low building with a parking lot in front of it. Once inside Eddie paused to look over the space. It was different from most libraries he'd spent time in. Light and bright, with smooth finishes and contemporary furniture in bright colors. He stopped at the reception desk and was redirected to the far end of the building for the local history section. It was extensive, with at least thirty linear feet of six-row shelving. One hundred and eighty shelf-feet of history. He almost rubbed his hands together.

But his efforts to identify the woman who'd filed a complaint against Chief Vaughn came up empty. A bubbly young research librarian took the question as a personal challenge. She found a long run of binders with the minutes of the Board of Police Commissioners. The board handled hiring, firing, and disciplinary matters for the police department, but there was no record of the complaint against Vaughn, probably because he resigned without pushing for a hearing.

Eddie thanked the woman for her help. He hooked his bag over his shoulder and took a slow walk around the library. He stopped in front of the long wall of window on the building's south side. The ground dropped away and street level was now a story below him. Across the street a park ran along the river. The brilliant green of the budding foliage of its trees and the bright flowers under them must have been the inspiration for the colors in the library. Brick paths meandered to a covered pedestrian bridge that led across the river to a building with tall vertical windows and a giant American flag draped on one wall. City hall, maybe.

As he turned away, something in the scene caught his attention. He turned back. It took a minute before he realized what it was.

The brick paths.

Bricks used on the ground are made of concrete and are laid. Mike had gotten Mose Belker a job laying concrete. Could it have been these bricks?

Eddie found the woman who'd helped him earlier and asked her if she knew anything about that park area.

"The Riverwalk! *That* I can help you with!"

She led him back to the Local History area. "This top row is everything from the original construction which began in 1981."

That fits with Belker's murders in 1982.

He thanked her and got to work.

It had been an ambitious project. The beginning of it stretched all the way back to 1931 when the city acquired the land along the river and designated it as Centennial Park. Most of that land was left undeveloped until the late seventies when a new commission decided to commemorate Weston's 150th anniversary with the Riverwalk, a linear park to run along the Paget River and include gathering spaces, brick pathways, fountains, and public art.

The city hired professionals to pour concrete, lay the brick paths, and build the decorative covered bridge. But volunteers did all the grunt work and local businesses donated food and drink for the people doing the work.

Eddie focused on the brickwork. He found a photo album with candid and staged shots taken during construction. There were a lot of pictures of people carrying the concrete bricks, but only the staged photos had captions. He found two guys named Mike, but one was a park commissioner and the other was on the board of some foundation.

Then he saw an equipment trailer in the background of a staged shot of the landscape architect. The architect's shoulder covered part of the trailer but enough was visible for Eddie to see the company's logo was a clover.

The Irish symbol for luck.

He pulled out the dime Penny had given him. He was on this story because of her. If writing it resurrected his career it would be because of her. If Penny believed in this coin, then so would he. He rubbed it while starring at the photo. "This is where Mike had worked." He felt silly saying it out loud and stuffed the coin back in his pocket.

He dove into the records and found three companies had laid bricks for the Riverwalk, but none of them had a clover in their name and the logos were not mentioned. He flipped open his laptop and hooked into the library's Wi-Fi and googled the three companies but none of them existed anymore.

As he went to look for the librarian, he spotted a shelf of old phonebooks reaching all the way back to the mid-seventies. He pulled down the book from 1980 and found what he was looking for in less than a minute. The yellow pages ad for Trinity Landscaping included a three-leaf clover as a logo. That made sense. A three-leaf clover was an Irish Catholic symbol for the Holy Trinity of God, Jesus, and the Holy Spirit.

He went back into the Riverwalk Commission records and flipped through to where it accepted bids for the brick-laying work. With Trinity's bid, one commissioner noted that "Mr. Football would run the crew for Frank Houser's Trinity Landscaping." A Google search linking Mr. Football and Weston revealed the man's real name in less than a second.

Mike Nelson.

Superstar athlete.

Eddie found dozens of articles about Mike Nelson and his football heroics. He led his high school team to two state championships and was named Mr. Football of Illinois. He got a full ride to the University of Illinois but blew his knee out during his freshman year and came home. His parents died the next year in a car accident and he'd had no siblings.

Searching the news archives Eddie found an article when Nelson joined the army in 1983, but nothing when he came home. But he was quoted on the sports page in the fall of 1985 about the high school's dazzling new quarterback.

All subsequent articles focused on football—anniversaries of Nelson's biggest games, threats to his records posed by the latest high school talent, etc. But there were no more quotes from Nelson.

This town had loved Mike Nelson. Which gave Eddie an idea for a title if he could build a plausible story around Mike Nelson as the real killer. A killer whom city leaders shielded to protect the town from the consequences of having the town hero be a murderer: The Favored Son.

Eddie found Mike Nelson's senior year high school yearbook and flipped to the index, then looked at every page where Nelson appeared. Like every high school quarterback in America, he'd been a popular guy and had been featured in photos at nearly every school dance held that year. Always with the same girl. Grace Patino.

A high school power couple.

Eddie wondered what had become of her. He got back on his computer and googled her. She wasn't hiding. She still lived right here in town and had never married.

And she had an adult, middle-aged son: Anthony Patino.

Eddie did some math and figured out Anthony was born the year after Grace Patino and Mike Nelson graduated from high school.

Could he be Mike Nelson's illegitimate son? That had potential for some extra drama, especially if Eddie proved Nelson was the killer and confronted the son with his father's crimes. Eddie saved copies of all the articles and used the library's equipment to make high-definition scans of the relevant yearbook photos, including the covers. This stuff was gold!

Now he needed to get a better handle on Abe Stewart and the buddies Vaughn had mentioned: Lowe and Forsyth. Put a face to them. Tell their stories.

Three men.

A trinity.

A second trinity.

Eddie like that symmetry. He could wind that up into something poetic. He got on the internet to flesh out his understanding of all three men. As he worked, he had a fascinating idea: Maybe he could find a third trinity to further strengthen the imagery.

Shit! He might already have it. Three women had been murdered: Smith, Brown, and Lachey, whether by Belker or Nelson or some combination of the two.

A third trinity.

Maybe that lucky coin really did work.

CHAPTER THIRTY-THREE

Jake lucked into a parking spot directly in front of Starbucks. The trendy coffee shop had recently moved into a larger space with a new format that included higher ceilings, dimmer lighting, and darker wood finishes.

As soon as he walked in, a woman waved at him from a table for two along the window. As a contemporary of Amy Smith, she had to be at least a decade older than Jake but she didn't look it. She must have stayed out of the sun and never smoked.

"Miss Drilling?"

"Nadine, please." She gestured to the chair across the table from her. "You want to talk about Amy." She moved forward on her chair and propped her elbows on the table. "I was visiting my grandmother in Michigan when she—when it happened."

"I still want to—"

"I was her best friend. I don't know why the police never came to see me. I wanted to call them but my parents didn't want me getting involved."

"You worked at the restaurant with Amy and Mouse—Mose Belker."

"I got her the job there. Imagine how I felt knowing that's why she died. If she hadn't worked there maybe she'd still—"

"What was Amy like?"

Nadine described Amy much the same as her parents had. Which was a red flag. A high school girlfriend should know Amy a lot better than her parents did. Jake interrupted her mid-sentence.

"I need the truth, Nadine. Not just what Amy's parents want people to remember about her."

"I—" Nadine picked up her clear plastic cup. It was jammed with ice and a dark liquid threaded with streams of something milky. "Okay." She sucked in a drink with the fat straw, swallowed, and took a big breath. "Amy was all those things I said about her. But not all the time."

"What was she like the rest of the time?"

"She was a normal teenager. She liked to drink a little and smoke a little and she liked boys and... you know."

"Sex?"

Nadine nodded.

"With Mose Belker?"

"God no." Nadine grimaced and shook her head, thick blond hair bouncing. "Absolutely not."

"But she and Belker were friends."

Nadine waved that away. "Just work friends. She never saw him away from the restaurant."

"How were they together at work?"

"They weren't *together* at work. He washed dishes—the back of the house. She worked in the dining room—the front of the house. They saw each other when he helped bus tables."

"But she was nice to him?"

"She just said hello and smiled at him. She was a truly nice person."

"Were other employees as nice to him?"

A pause. "No."

"What did *you* think of him?"

"Back then I thought he was a harmless little guy scared of his own shadow."

"But now?"

"I had trouble believing he did it. But he confessed, so… "

"Did you ever meet any of Belker's friends?"

"I don't know that he had any."

"What about Mike Nelson?"

"The football player?"

"Yes. Was he a friend of Belker's?"

Drilling scoffed and shook her head. "Not hardly."

"Sounds like you know that as a fact."

"I don't *know* it. But *come on*, those two were nothing alike."

"Did Amy ever date Mike Nelson?"

Nadine pulled her head back and shifted in her seat. "Why are you asking me about him?" She wiped her mouth with a napkin.

Three deception indicators—body shifting, question as a response, and touching her face—meant she was lying, or at least holding something back.

"Where did she meet him?"

Nadine fiddled with her straw, puling it in and out through the hole in the lid of her cup. The plastic squeaked so loud a shiver shot up Jake's spine, but he said nothing. Nadine would tell him the whole story. He just needed to wait. He was good at waiting. He kept his eyes on her but let his peripheral vision roam, taking in the other coffee drinkers: four girls in Catholic school uniforms, an executive interviewing a young woman about her leadership experience, a trio of women talking with their heads almost touching.

Finally. "At the bridge. People don't hang out there anymore, but back then it's where we went."

Jake knew exactly what she was talking about. But the people who had hung out on the Washington Street bridge over the Paget River had not been high school kids. They'd been dropouts and veterans with mental issues.

Druggies, basically.

The drug subculture in Weston had begun and for many years had been concentrated on that bridge. Simpler times.

"Amy was too young to hang out there," Jake said.

Nadine shrugged. "I know that now, looking back. But at the time we thought it was cool."

"And Mike Nelson was there?"

"If we were lucky, because he would always share his pot."

"Amy—you and Amy—smoked marijuana with him? Right there on the bridge?"

"In his van."

Jake absorbed that information, thinking. Amy had known Mike Nelson and had known him well enough to get in his van. Had actually *been* in his van.

"Driving around?"

"No. Just parked in that lot behind the Cock Robin."

The mention of the old hamburger place that had stood next to the bridge brought back memories of its square ice cream scoops. "Was it ever just the two of them?"

"Never."

"But you were out of town that day."

"We had a pact to never to go there alone. We weren't idiots."

They talked for a couple more minutes but Nadine had nothing else to tell him. There had been no other boys or young men in Amy's life.

Jake thanked her and stood to leave.

"Do you think Mike Nelson was involved in… what happened to Amy?" Drilling asked.

Jake didn't want that leaking out. "His name came up so I have to check it out."

"What did Mike say?"

"I haven't spoken to him yet. Have you talked to him lately?"

She shook her head. "I haven't even thought of him in years."

Jake left her his card then headed back to his car. Nadine Drilling had put Amy Smith with Mike Nelson smoking pot in his van. Donna Larson's theory about Mike Nelson was getting legs. It was time to talk to the one man who could cut those legs off at the knee.

Mose Belker.

CHAPTER THIRTY-FOUR

Deputy Chief of Patrol Sam Stewart paced his office, ignoring his phone and three people who knocked on his door. He needed to know what the hell had happened with the DNA. That's all there was to it. He called his dad. His old man kept his phone in a holster on his belt and always answered on the first ring.

"What is it?"

"Houser's Ballard case update said nothing about requesting the Smith and Brown murder books. So either it's unrelated to Ballard, or it is related and he's keeping it secret."

"What about his other cases? Did you look at those?"

"I didn't know… hang on." Sam sat back down at his desk and got back into the system. Houser had seven open cases but the only new entry was the Ballard notes Sam had already read. "No. Nothing."

"So why did you call?"

"I'm no detective, but I know there should be DNA reports in the Smith murder book. Especially the report establishing the DNA match to Belker. Houser's interest has to be about the missing reports."

"You only know reports are missing because you've seen the book. Why did Houser request the book? And why did the writer? What sent them both to see those books at the same time?"

Sam had no answer for his dad's question so asked his own. "What did the DNA reports say?"

A long silence, which meant his dad needed to examine his own truths and lies and find the safest course forward.

"Only you and Arvind can trip me up on the DNA."

"Me?" Sam asked, alarmed.

"Remember when you took a DNA sample to Arvind for me?"

A fire erupted in Sam's belly as he remembered taking the evidence envelope to Arvind. "You told me that was to help an officer who was in a paternity dispute."

"Correct."

"That's what it was?"

"No. Your memory is correct."

"So… the sample belonged to someone… what, involved with Belker?"

"This is your moment, son. You have it in you to be a great chief. The best Chief Stewart in the history of the Weston PD. But to get there, you can't sit back and wait. A chief *acts*."

"Whose DNA was in that sealed envelope, Dad?"

His dad hung up.

Sam stewed. His father had made him do one of those little favors he asked of people to ease them down the path of being a cog in Abe Stewart's machine. His father had treated him just like any other asset.

And his father hadn't needed Sam to be involved at all. He'd been tight enough with Arvind that he could have taken the envelope straight to him. His dad had involved him because he'd known what he was doing could blow up and he wanted other people—future leaders of the department like his own son—to be invested in keeping whatever it was under wraps.

Abe Stewart always played the long game.

CHAPTER THIRTY-FIVE

Eddie spent an hour fleshing out the trinity Chief Vaughn identified as the eighties power structure: Police Chief Abe Stewart, Weston Business Alliance President Brian Lowe, and Weston Home Builders Association President Jeffrey Forsyth.

All three men were Weston natives, an identity Eddie learned was increasingly rare as the population exploded in the sixties and seventies with the super mobile executives who took up residence in the suburban Shangri-La.

Abe Stewart followed his father into the job as police chief and held the position from the late seventies through the eighties. When Stewart retired as chief, he became assistant city manager, which pissed off a bunch of fiscal conservatives in his own Republican party because it meant he started accumulating a second pension. When Chief Vaughn resigned, Abe Stewart went back to the PD as acting chief until a replacement was found.

The Stewart part of this was getting juicy: Abe Stewart hired Vaughn as chief, pushed him out soon after Belker confessed, then took over the job himself. But if Stewart's goal had been to protect the city from having its favored son fingered as a killer, why would Stewart care about Vaughn getting Belker's confession? Belker hadn't fingered Nelson.

Maybe it wasn't about that. Maybe Abe Stewart dumped Vaughn to stop him from doing something else. Or, maybe Stewart had wanted to do something that only the chief could do.

Yes. It had been one of those two things. Eddie got back to his research, a big smile across his face. These three men—who they were, what they did, and why they did it—were the key to his story.

Brian Lowe had started a flooring company, was a founding member of the Weston Business Alliance, and still sat on its board as chairman emeritus. He had worked relentlessly to bring big business to Weston, and was often cited for creating Weston's nickname of Illinois's Silicon Prairie. Lowe and his wife had three children, all of whom had moved away.

Jeffrey Forsyth's family had owned the biggest lumberyard in town and founded the Weston Home Builders Association. He'd started a construction company with Lowe and Stewart that built out many of the upscale subdivisions along the south end of town. Forsyth had married young, but he and his wife never had children and he had put most of thier assets into a trust devoted to helping maintain the Riverwalk.

In a newspaper article, Eddie found a picture of the three men on the bleachers at a football stadium watching the homecoming game. They had gone to Weston High School together and played on the Redskins football team.

Weston had a small town feel for a place with a population of one hundred and fifty thousand people.

He could use that.

* * *

Next, Eddie pulled down the Haines Criss+Cross directory from 1980. The directories listed people by street. He found Mose Belker's old address of 531 West Jackson Avenue. The listing identified the resident as Gladys Belker. She was the only woman on her block. He pulled down more directories and over time saw more women's names, presumably as their husbands passed away. Belker's address was listed as vacant in 1997, and the address itself disappeared in 2000. Two other West Jackson addresses dropped off in 2003, suggesting the mansions replacing the old housing stock sometimes spanned multiple lots.

He opened his laptop and found an obituary for Gladys Belker in 1998. She had died a year before her son had confessed. Eddie wondered if Belker would have confessed if his mother had still been alive. Had they been close? He needed to understand that relationship and learn what kind of man his mother thought he was. Old neighbors could help him do just that.

Eddie pulled up a satellite map and found Jackson. It was the street behind the library that separated it from the Riverwalk. The Riverwalk stretched along the river, spreading out to encompass a huge pool labeled as Centennial Beach. Belker's house had been directly across the street from the pool.

He dropped to a street level view and clicked his way along Jackson, passing two blocks of businesses until the houses began in the five hundreds. Where Belker's house had been now stood a giant grey house with white trim and a deep porch spanning its entire width. But three other original homes still stood along the block.

Eddie took a photo of the relevant page from the directory, then got moving.

* * *

He exited the library through the lower level, crossed Jackson, and stepped onto the Riverwalk. He took photos of the brickwork, the covered bridge, and the Dandelion Fountain. He then walked west along the curved brick walkways, taking more photos. The spring day was gorgeous, the sun warm, but the air cool and almost nippy when it puffed into occasional gusts. There were a surprising number of people on the paths for a weekday. He crossed the next street then veered off the brick and onto the sidewalk along Jackson.

He passed the Riverwalk Community Center and a couple small office buildings before the residential area began. The new houses were massive and reached nearly to their lot lines. Before crossing the street and knocking on doors, Eddie took a closer look at the immense pool he'd seen on the satellite image.

It looked even bigger up close. It had a giant concrete shallow end with a big sand beach peppered with things for kids to climb on. The massive deep end was at least a hundred yards across and looked like it had been quarried out of the limestone. Giant oak trees shaded the park-like grounds and a stone building served as the bathhouse and concession area.

Eddie took a few photos to capture the essence of the place if he decided to use it in the book, then turned and faced the houses. The three remaining original homes were dwarfed by the newer construction. One of them was empty, a big sign out front contained an artist's rendering of the new mansion that was 'Coming Soon.'

Eddie ignored that house and approached the first of the other two. According to the directory, Hazel Burke lived in the small blue clapboard house. He mounted the front stoop and rang the bell. The woman who answered met him with a pleasant smile and invited him in before he could even introduce himself.

She was short, slight, and walked with a cane. She waved him to a floral print couch under her front window and lowered herself onto a wood chair across from him. She sat with her knees spread wide and both hands on her cane planted on the floor between her feet.

Flowers appeared to be the room's theme, from the furniture to the paintings and the carpet runner that crossed the worn hardwood to the back of the house. But the place didn't smell like flowers; it smelled like cat piss and a litter box overflowing with turds. A *meow* and a longhair trotted in from the kitchen and started weaving itself back and forth through Eddie's legs.

Burke wore a pair of glasses on a chain around her neck and pulled them up now and put them on. She blinked a few times and smiled. "Daisy likes you!"

"Looks that way." Eddie reached down and gave the cat a quick scratch between its ears. The cat purred.

"How can I help you, young man?"

Eddie explained who he was and that he was there to ask her about Mose Belker. Before he was done she was shaking her head, lips pursed so tight her face looked like a raisin.

"Belker," she said with a harrumph in her voice. She launched into a tirade about Belker's parents; they were both drunks and had beaten their son. "When he was young, I'd hear him wailing. When he was older, I'd only hear his mom screaming and the smack of the paddle on Mose's bare tuckus."

It was interesting that she had started with Belker's parents instead of with the confessed killer. "What did Mose do to get the beatings?"

She shrugged as if that was unknowable, then said something under her breath that sounded like. "Typical voogas."

"What's that?"

She shook her head, lips drawn tightly together.

"Was he a bad kid?"

"Not at first." She looked away.

"But later?"

She finally looked back. "He started killing my cats in junior high school. I let them roam the neighborhood—always had—and they started disappearing."

"And you thought Mose did it."

"Of course he did it! His parents turned him into a monster. Don't make any mistake about it, Mr. Shaw; Mose Belker's parents should have been locked away for what they did to that boy."

"What about Mike Nelson?"

Her head went back. "What about him?"

"I'm working on a claim that he killed those girls with Mose."

"That's outrageous!" She pounded the end of her cane against the hardwood. "You can leave right now."

"But Mike and Mose knew each other, right?"

"Get out!"

"Weston was a much smaller town back then and they're about the same age. Did you see Mike over at the Belker house?"

"Out!' The old lady had a big voice for such a little body.

"Where did Mike Nelson live?" Eddie had searched, but found too many Nelsons to lock it down.

The cane thumped again.

Eddie left. He paused on the sidewalk and took a picture of the Burke place, and of the big house that stood where Belker's house had been. On the way back to his car in the library parking lot, he stopped off at the other remaining original house. He was glad he did.

CHAPTER THIRTY-SIX

Before driving down to the prison, Jake swung by the Ballard apartment to look for Kate's backpacking equipment. Because alcoholics have trouble moving things from short-term into long-term memory, Jake had visited Joan Ballard many times to hammer down her story.

But Jake didn't need her memory today. He just needed to see Kate's room. Again. He'd searched it twice and spent at least a few minutes in it every time he visited Mrs. Ballard, hoping to pick up something to help him understand the girl. Her room was a study of a girl maturing into a woman. Still painted pink, but all other girlish touches long gone—no flouncy bedspread or stuffed animals. Just the pink walls and a boy band poster to remember a concert Kate had gone to with her dad. Nothing Jake learned made him think she left town on her own without telling her mother.

The apartment was the top unit in a three-story brick apartment building on Spring Street two blocks east of Jake's own place. The area was nearing the tail end of the teardown craze and most of the new houses in the neighborhood dwarfed the apartment building, including a six thousand square foot "Luxury European Retreat" directly across the street that had been on the market for six years. The price had dropped from three point two million to one point eight, but still it sat.

Jake parked next to Joan Ballard's Nissan on the crumbling asphalt off the alley behind the building. On a concrete pad by the back stairs, a circle of white plastic chairs sat around a fire pit, the smell of damp ash riding on the cool breeze.

Jake climbed the wooden staircase on the back of the building and knocked on Ballard's kitchen door. Joan Ballard was slow to wake and spent a couple hours sitting in the kitchen drinking coffee and convincing herself to give it all another go.

One day at a time.

He knocked again.

"A minute!"

Jake waited, the minute stretching to two before the door opened slowly to reveal Joan Ballard in a brown terrycloth robe, one hand clenching it together at her throat, the other on the doorknob. Her hair was flat on one side and there was a pillow mark on her cheek. Jake hoped she had enough coffee in her to talk to him.

She blinked several times and sighed. "You."

"Good morning Mrs. Ballard. I need to—"

"Come in." She shuffled away, her slippers scratching against the linoleum. He followed her in and they sat at the small table in the corner of the kitchen. The room smelled of coffee and old wood. "The coffeemaker's on a timer so it's ready even though I'm not. How about you pour us both a mug? I won't be moving well for another hour or so."

Ballard was a fully functional alcoholic. She held down a full-time job and kept her apartment neat. But when she came home from work, she climbed into a bottle. Jake hadn't known her before her daughter disappeared, but sensed her despair had settled in long before that.

Jake found two mugs and filled them from the drip machine, then sat with her at the table. They sat in silence for a few minutes, Ballard hunched over and sipping from her mug.

Jake watched, waiting for the caffeine to kick in and wake the woman up. She looked wrung out.

A few sips later she released her grip on her robe and leaned back. "So, you need… what?"

"First, I heard from Kate's dad. She is not out in Colorado."

"Like I told you. Are you going to take this seriously now?"

Heat bloomed on Jake's ears. "I have taken it seriously."

She blinked. "You're right. That wasn't fair."

"But we need to figure out if Kate was headed that way."

"Hitchhiking like her little friend Angela suggested?" Ballard shook her head. "Even if Kate had decided to do that, she would have told me."

"Maybe she told you at night."

Ballard frowned. "We had a deal that nothing she told me and nothing I said after dinner counted. We talked in the morning and had no secrets."

Jake let the lie—or self-delusion—go. She didn't know about her daughter's junkyard boyfriend until Jake told her about him. "Kate's dad suggested we look for her backpacking equipment."

"What, like the big pack and her walking stick and all that?"

"Yes. If she had set out to hitchhike to Colorado it should be gone. I've seen nothing like that in her—"

"You should have thought of that in the beginning."

Jake said nothing because she was right. If her backpacking stuff was gone, he had wasted time looking in the wrong place. He didn't try to defend himself by mentioning the boots.

Ballard stood up, wobbled, and shuffled over to a set of hooks on the wall. She pulled off a key ring with the name of the local Chevy dealer and handed it to him. "You never saw that stuff in her room because she kept it in our basement storage locker. Behind the laundry room."

Jake took the key and used the building's internal stairs to descend to the bottom level. It held a small garden apartment in the front with a laundry room behind it. Three storage areas built of chain link fence ranged along the back wall. Ballard's key opened the one on the right. Jake pawed through its contents and found what he was looking for within five minutes: a cardboard box stuffed with Kate Ballard's backpack and a slew of related materials. The collapsed walking stick. Two stainless steel water bottles, a sleeping bag and pad, and on and on.

Kate Ballard had not set out to hitchhike to Colorado.

Which meant Jake's failure to look for her backpacking equipment was immaterial. She had disappeared in Weston—somewhere along the three-block stretch between her house and the library that didn't have any video cameras.

Jake took a picture of the backpack and texted it to Kate's dad with a message: *The backpack is still here.*

He returned the key to Mrs. Ballard and told her the news. She just nodded. Out in the car, Jake updated Erin and asked her to brief Braff, then headed south.

Time to talk to Mose Belker.

CHAPTER THIRTY-SEVEN

As Eddie stepped up on the front porch, a police car cruised slowly by. He watched it, his heart hammering, but the driver didn't even glance his way. When it rounded the next corner, Eddie turned back to the door and knocked. According to his research, Shirley Booth lived here alone. He heard the soft creak of footsteps on the floor inside. When the door finally opened, his heart rate was nearly back to normal and he had on his warmest smile.

"Good afternoon, Mrs. Booth. I'm a writer doing a story on Mose Belker and hoped for a few minutes of your time. Hazel up the block thought you'd want to get your two cents in."

"Oh, did she?" Booth smiled and pulled the door wide and gestured for Eddie to come in. He closed the door behind them and followed her into the small kitchen at the back of the house. It had metal cabinets and a linoleum floor and a Formica-topped table with a chrome edge running around it. It smelled like the hearty beef stew his grandmother used to make. A giant pot with a ladle sticking out of it on the stove was the likely source of that smell. His stomach grumbled. He hadn't eaten anything but stale donuts all day.

"How about a bowl of stew?"

"I couldn't—"

"Nonsense." She motioned him into one of the sun-yellow padded chrome chairs. He sat and waited as she ladled him up a hefty portion. A small TV on the counter was tuned to the old black-and-white sitcom with the maid who was always running amok. The volume was low, barely a murmur, just keeping Booth company. She must not like news radio.

She set the bowl in front of him, then ran him a glass of water from the tap. She grunted when she sat down in the chair across the table.

"Thank you." Eddie spooned up a bite; it was fantastic.

"Eat up! Then I'll be happy to talk with you."

Eddie gobbled down half the bowl before pausing to drink some water and look at the room. "This is a nice space."

"I have trouble getting out of the upholstered chairs in the living room and the dining room chairs are too hard."

"Have you been in this house long?"

"Since the day after our wedding. My Harold took us up here chasing a job. Seventy-one years it's been."

"Where from."

"New Orleans."

She pronounced it *Naw-lens*, like a native, but she'd lost her southern drawl. "Great town. Okay if I record this?" She nodded and he set up the phone app, then took another bite.

"Did Hazel really tell you I'd want to talk about Mose?" Booth's eyes pierced Eddie's. "I think that might be a tall tale, young man."

He swallowed. "She wouldn't have done that?"

"Not for a minute. We never saw eye to eye on the Belkers. She never gave none of them a chance. Especially not the boy."

"Why's that?"

"The old biddy's prejudiced—a racist."

Eddie was confused. "What, uh…?"

"Hazel always thought Mr. Belker—Mose's father—was black. He *was* dark-skinned but he wasn't a Negro. He was

Sicilian or Greek or something. Got real dark in the summer from working outside. He was a roofer. Even if he was, so what? The way she carried on!"

Eddie couldn't help thinking how Mose Belker being black would have added another layer to his story.

"Mrs. Burke called them *voogas*," Eddie said, remembering the word Burke had muttered.

"*Shvoogs*," Booth corrected. "Yiddish version of the N-word."

"I heard it was an unhappy home."

Booth frowned. "They were drinkers and maybe something else. Whatever it was they kept it inside. Doors closed and blinds drawn."

"How did they treat Mose?"

She fidgeted. "Not good."

"Would you happen to have any old neighborhood photos with the Belkers in them?"

"The Belkers never socialized in the neighborhood. Like I said, they did their drinking at home."

"How about Mike Nelson?"

"How about him what?"

"I hear he hung around with Mose."

"Did you ask Hazel about Mike Nelson?"

"I did and she didn't like it."

"I bet! She and Nelson are cousins."

This story had a lot of layers. "Do you know Grace Patino?"

Booth glared. "I do."

"Does she still live on Laird?"

"Yes. And she still runs her hair salon in that alley off Washington, too."

"How about her son, Anthony?"

Booth's mouth pulled into a hard grim line. "What about him?"

"I've been told Mike Nelson is his father."

A deep frown. "If he is you couldn't tell it by how he treated him."

"How *did he* treat him?"

"He was never a father to that boy. Never lived with him. Never spent time with him. Ignored him as far as I can tell." Her eyes were dark with anger.

"Does Mike Nelson visit Hazel?"

"Well, not in so long as I can remember. I'm not one to spy on my neighbors—can't really see anything from here in the back of the house, anyway—but seems like I would have noticed if'n he'd come by. Or she would have bragged on it."

"Were Mike and Mose friends?" The conversation was going too fast for Eddie to take another bite of his stew.

"I saw him over there in his van a few times; dropping Mose off or picking him up for work. That little fella was a damn hard worker. Reminded me of my Harold."

"You liked Mose?"

"I did. And you can write that in your book. Don't care who knows it."

"Could he have killed—"

"Mose Belker was a meek soul. Never hurt nobody and never would."

"He killed Burke's cats."

"I killed those damn cats. Poisoned them. Got tired of them crapping in my flowerbeds. Took the hardheaded old biddy about a dozen cats to get the hint and keep them inside. You can put that in your book too. See what she does about it. Though I'm not sure she knows how to read."

CHAPTER THIRTY-EIGHT

Jake took a minute to gather himself before stepping inside the prison. Stateville Correctional Center was a Level 1 Maximum Security Facility. Inside, the visitor-fronting spaces were built of concrete blocks painted in dull earthy colors and smelled of industrial-strength cleaner. The tile floors gleamed with polish. The air felt heavy, so dense that sounds seemed muted.

Jake badged his way through the first level of security, then locked up his gun and knife in a one of a small bank of lockers provided for that purpose. He got hung up with the other cops and lawyers requesting their visits and signing into the warren of rooms where private meetings were held. As he waited, he wondered what he might get from Belker. Larson's letter implied the man had descended into some kind of bible spouting incoherence. Jake hoped that was just an act.

He would soon see. What he'd learned about Belker so far seemed inconsistent with a twice-confessed rapist and murderer.

Eventually a guard ushered Jake to a small interview room and left him there. The air was even thicker here, too warm, and sour with the smells of stale sweat and dried vomit. Jake waited in the open doorway, where the air was cooler and moved down the hallway. A few minutes later the guard returned with

Mose Belker. He was short, wiry, and completely bald, walking with shoulders back and chin up. His dark eyes gave off an almost tangible energy. He clasped a thick book bound in black leather with gilt-edged pages.

Jake stepped into the room and the guard followed with Belker, who sat down without looking at Jake. The guard chained Belker's hands to an eyebolt in the middle of the stainless-steel table. When the guard left, the door clanged shut behind him with a thunderous echo that made Jake flinch.

Belker looked up at Jake. "You're the cop?"

"I am." Jake put his business card on the table and slid it over until it was directly in front of Belker. Belker ignored it and squared his bible to the corner of the table.

Jake sat down in the steel chair across the table from Belker. The man's eyes locked on Jake's. The Illinois Offender Database said Belker's eyes were blue, but Jake saw only black. Flat and bottomless.

"Your friend Donna Larson got people all riled up." Jake's words echoed slightly against the cinder block walls.

Belker leaned back, his chains dragging across the metal table. "For children are innocent and love justice. Donna is a nice girl. Thinks her daddy was innocent. Wouldn't you want your kid to think that?"

"You told Miss Larson—"

"Wouldn't you?"

"Wouldn't I what?"

"Wouldn't you want your child to think you're innocent?"

Jake didn't want to talk about hypothetical children or how a child's love for him would affect her judgment. Not today when he'd been trying not to think about his own possible fatherhood; trying to focus on his work which had saved him from many similar introspections over the years since Mary's murder. "I don't have any children."

Belker's chains rattle as he held up his hands in apology. "Sorry. Weston's a family town, so I just assumed."

"You told Miss Larson her dad was innocent."

"I don't remember saying that." Belker's right hand slid across the steel table, dragging the chain with it. He put his hand on the bible, one finger rubbing the embossed title.

"You told her Mike killed the Lachey girl." Belker hadn't said that exactly, but had sure implied it.

"For all have sinned and fall short of the glory of God."

"You told her someone in my police department knew her dad was innocent and let him take the rap."

Belker's gaze dropped to the table. He picked up Jake's business card and read from it. "Detective Jake *Houser*. Weston Police Department. Major Crimes." A smile pulled his mouth into an awkward line like he didn't know how to do it. Or had forgotten how. "Are you Frank's boy?"

The casual, knowing way Belker said his dad's name made Jake's hands shake. He pressed them to his thighs.

Belker tapped the edge of the card on the table, chain clanking. "I worked for Trinity, you know. I cut in the bricks around the Dandelion Fountain."

Jake read no deception. Frank Houser would not have allowed a day laborer to do that important detail work. His dad had lied to him. Jake fought off that distraction. "Mike Nelson got you that job, right?"

Belker froze, then his bottomless gaze bored into Jake.

"Mike Nelson killed Beth Lachey," Jake said.

Belker's eyes narrowed, but he said nothing.

"And you think he's now responsible for Kate Ballard's disappearance."

A rattle of chains as Belker pulled the bible across the table and held it in both hands, the muscles along his forearm popping into relief. "I never said that."

"You told Miss Larson that 'Mike is at it again.' What does your bible say about lying?"

Belker said nothing.

Jake leaned forward. "Do yourself some good, here. Help me catch this guy and I can get you a better cell. More yard time."

Belker shook his head.

"You made such an impression on Miss Larson that she now thinks you're innocent and Mike Nelson killed Amy Smith and Linda Brown. Thinks you're too meek to hurt a fly."

Belker's eyes flashed like lightning sparking across the dark sky of his irises. "What comes out of a person is what defiles him. All evil comes from within and defiles a man."

"I think you did kill those girls, but Mike was right there with you."

Belker didn't answer and seemed to retreat inside himself; his breathing slowed down and the veins in his neck and forearms lost definition as his pulse slowed. Jake considered hitting him with the DNA evidence, but to use it effectively he first had to lock down where it led.

Jake could come back any time; Belker wasn't going anywhere.

CHAPTER THIRTY-NINE

Bev worked the luncheon crowd: shaking hands, making small talk, and accepting congratulations for her nomination. She wore the uniform she'd been in since before dawn, so felt a little ripe. Polyester did not breathe.

After she'd covered enough ground that people would remember her being there, she parked herself against the wall, eyeing the table in front of her. She needed to sit down. Her back was killing her from all the time in the squad car and the heavy equipment belt and her run-in with the drug dealer the evening before.

She checked her phone and read through the updates that had built up during her mingling. Teams were executing search warrants all across the county. So far, they'd found eleven more overdoses and four dead bodies. Area hospitals reported twenty-six overdoses during the last twenty-four hours but no deaths thanks to the quick use of Narcan by emergency responders and ER staff. That stuff saved lives.

She looked at the table again, then straightened up, pressing a fist into a hard knot of pain at the top of her butt cheek. She scanned the room but not a single person had sat down; the many departments of county law enforcement didn't get together that often and liked to swap stories.

The subject of one of those stories would have to take the stage and accept this stupid award and make a humble brag of a speech. She sure as hell hoped she didn't get it. She had no interest in amassing a slew of meaningless awards like her dad had. He'd belonged to so many clubs it seemed like their main purpose was for members to take turns giving each other man-of-the-year awards.

"I don't like your odds."

Assistant State's Attorney Anna McKay was suddenly at Bev's side.

"My nomination is just a bone Borgeson threw my way," Bev said. "Did you read it?" It was full of flowery praise for things like achieving cross-department synergies. Even Bev couldn't explain what he was talking about.

"Tried to," Anna said. "Maybe there's a gender discrimination claim percolating out there and he's trying to change his image."

"I think he's a few years too late."

"I heard about what you did yesterday," Anna said.

"What did I supposedly do?"

"Tackled some drug-maddened dealer. Maybe next year *that* will win you this award."

"I grabbed his foot as he ran me down."

Anna laughed. "Well, *the boys* say you tackled him."

Bev shook her head, but what *the boys* thought mattered more than it should.

"Shall we sit?" Anna pointed to the table.

"Let's."

They sat. Bev turned and twisted, realigning her spine. Better. She reached for the white wine, poured herself a healthy slug, and reached to fill Anna's glass. Anna covered it with her hand.

"Not today."

"Oh?" Bev set the bottle down. "Are you in trial this afternoon?"

"Just talking a break."

Anna shifted in her seat, eyes darting to look at Bev, then away. Bev reached down the table and grabbed the basket of bread and crackers and set them both in front of Anna, who immediately dove in.

Hmm…

An announcement from the podium and the rest of the crowd found seats. A flush of waiters descended on them in courses—soup, salad, entrée and a chocolate tart for desert so amazing it almost made wasting two hours here while her men were busting heads, worth it.

The conversation around the table centered on law enforcement issues, but often spiked off into taxes, retirement plans, the union, and, as always, sports. There was no talk about the pending award. Everyone except the person who won it was just there for lunch and conversation.

Anna cleaned her plate on every course. Bev had watched enough friends and co-workers get pregnant to recognize the symptoms. Well, good for her. Not all—Bev suddenly remembered that Anna was dating Jake. Which meant Anna's baby was a Warren. Bev's own relative. An intense wash of emotion flowed through her and her eyes suddenly welled with tears.

"Are you okay?" Anna asked, leaning in to keep her question confidential.

"I… just realized… " Bev's voice broke and she waved at Anna's plate and her wine glass.

Anna's face flushed red.

"Jake's?"

Anna nodded.

"Jake's my cousin."

"Oh," Anna sat up straighter. "I knew that. I guess I forgot."

"That's my second cousin once removed in there." Bev poked Anna lightly in the stomach under the table. Then pulled her hand back. "Sorry. Just caught me by surprise."

"It's okay."

"Jake's got to be out of his mind," Bev said. *Lucky bastard.*

"What do you mean?"

"He thought he'd missed his chance. His wife died, you know. And since then he's been single and he's a bit old for—"

"He's not that old."

Bev smiled. "I am *so happy* for you. Both of you."

"Well, it's not a done deal."

Before Bev could ask Anna what that meant, County Board Chairman Borgeson took the podium and started his lame speech about the award.

Before he announced the winner—a male commander in the Glenbard department—Anna had snuck off. When the recipient finished his acceptance speech, Bev headed for the door, slowed by another round of greetings.

Halfway to the exit she spotted Abe Stewart's son. Sam had volunteered to take on Professional Standards when she'd returned it to the city. No real cop wanted to investigate other cops. But that was Sam… a by-the-book kind of cop. His father had been the opposite as the file documented: the ends justified the means. And then some. She stopped and watched Sam. He was alone, scanning the crowd, frowning. He looked like his father and wanted to be chief like his father *and* grandfather had been. The family business. Did Abe tell him everything? Did Sam tell his father everything?

Maybe she could stir them up. Action could be very revealing.

CHAPTER FORTY

Deputy Chief of Patrol Sam Stewart was not surprised when the award went to an officer from Glenbard. Someone from Glenbard always won it. Sam—and every other Westonite from a founding family—hated Glenbard as their ancestors had hated it since 1868 when Glenbard literally stole the county seat from Weston in a midnight raid.

"What's got you so deep in thought?"

Sam startled, then turned toward the voice. Paget County Sheriff Bev Warren. She was from Weston and had moved back into her family home when her father died a few years before. Her father had been a real bastard, maybe even worse than Sam's.

"Weston keeps getting stiffed in these awards," Sam said.

"They're meaningless."

"They're recognition. When we never win, it looks like we aren't as good."

"Nobody pays any attention to these things, Sam. They're just an excuse to get together and eat a big meal and tell tall tales."

If she didn't get it, he couldn't explain it to her. Maybe growing up with the Warren silver spoon in her mouth and then working in the county her entire career meant she couldn't see how the county treated her hometown. Always taking, never giving. But Bev herself was a solid cop. "How's the task force doing? Are you closing in on the source?"

"We're making progress."

"We stand ready when you need us."

"I know you do, Sam. And I appreciate hearing it." She turned to go, but stopped.

"I ran into Jake yesterday. He told me about the case he's working."

"Kate Ballard." He'd forgotten Warren was some kind of cousin to Houser. Her gaze scanned the crowd, her face calm and relaxed. She had that professional something that made him want to be better around her. *Leadership*. How did she do that? he wondered. "How's he doing on that? Any leads?"

"Jake's working a nonsense tip from some crackpot that the man who was really responsible for those old Belker murders is still out there and took Ballard."

Sam froze, tendons in his neck flexing. He shot a look her way, but she wasn't even looking at him.

"Do you remember those cases? Back in the eighties?"

"Vaguely." Sam felt sweat beading on his upper lip and his forehead. He wanted to wipe it away but now felt her eyes on him. "How about you?"

"Not really."

She waved at someone across the room. Even in her patrol uniform she looked good. Her posture so straight she could be in the military.

She continued. "I was young when they happened and working for the county when Belker confessed. I bet your dad remembers."

"Wh-why… er—" Sam's voice broke. He cleared his throat. "Why would he?" Sam had never been good at deception. That's why he'd been a poor detective. Interrogation relied on lies and manipulation and he could never pull it off.

"He was chief when the murders happened, right?"

"He was." Sam crossed his arms, then dropped them to his sides. "But he hasn't said anything to me about those old cases."

Bev patted him on the shoulder. "Good to see you, Sam. Say hello to your father for me."

When she was gone Sam realized he hadn't acknowledged her goodbye. He'd been caught up in wondering if Houser had sent her to probe him about his dad and those cases. Was there a real connection between Kate Ballard's disappearance and the closed Belker murders? And if Houser was investigating a connection, why hadn't he included that in his Ballard case file? What was he hiding? And who was he hiding it from?

CHAPTER FORTY-ONE

Jake drove slowly on the way back to Weston from the prison visit, unsettled by Belker's claim to have been an actual employee of Trinity Landscaping. Had Frank lied? He needed to talk to his dad.

Halfway back to town, Jake's phone buzzed with a text from a number he didn't recognize: *I found gramps' cop box. I'm home if you want to come look through it.* Reed's grandson. Jake replied that he'd be there within a half hour and sped up. The entries in Reed's notebook could be a more unvarnished look at what the man had been thinking than what was in the murder books. Detectives often left speculation and uncomfortable truths out of the book.

Jake made it to Reed's house in twenty minutes, parked behind the Honda, and walked up the driveway. The sun had dropped below the tall trees to the west and the deep afternoon shadows chilled the air.

The garage door was open, revealing dozens of slumping cardboard boxes and a jumble of furniture that didn't look worth saving. A voice from the dim depths said, "Come on through here, Detective." An overhead bulb popped on, illuminating a slim path that wound through the packed space.

Reed's grandson stood at the open door into the house. "I brought the box inside."

Jake sneezed away the dust Reed's search had stirred up, and followed the young man into the house. They snaked through a tiny laundry room and into the kitchen where a grimy box sat on the worn oak table.

"You want something to drink?" The young Reed opened the refrigerator and bent into it. "I've got Bud Light and—"

"I'll just take the box and bring it back when I'm done."

The fridge closed with a *whump*. "No way. That's the only thing I have of his time as a cop. Look at it here, or forget it."

"Okay." If he found anything important, he could get a subpoena. "A glass of water would be great. What's your name by the way?"

"David."

"I appreciate this, David." It was too warm in the house and Jake took off his blazer and draped it over a chair.

"Sure." David set down a glass of water. Today he wore cargo shorts and a Star Trek T-shirt. "Gramps would have wanted me to help."

"You wore a Star Wars t-shirt the other day," Jake said. "I thought you super fans picked Star Trek or Star Wars."

David shrugged. "I love them both."

Jake smiled, then pulled the box over and took off the lid, careful not to dislodge the dust onto the table. The box was packed tight with forty years of calendars and detective notebooks. He got started.

Reed had clear handwriting, but he didn't write much. The calendars had simple notations to remind him when he was due in court. The months covering his Smith investigation were blank, except for a blocked-out vacation that had "cancelled" written across it in red ink.

Jake set the calendar aside and pulled out the notebooks. Reed had dated them and Jake quickly found the book covering the Smith and Brown murders. He pushed the box away and sat down with it.

"You find something?" Reed was leaning against the counter, watching Jake.

"This is the notebook from when he investigated the cases I'm interested in."

"What does it say?"

"I don't know, yet."

Dave Reed frowned, then busied himself in the kitchen.

Jake's phone buzzed with an incoming call. He didn't recognize the number, but that wasn't unusual. He gave his number to a lot of people during an investigation. He considered answering, but decided to stay focused and let the call go to voicemail.

Jake opened the old notebook and flipped through it until he found the first mention of Amy Smith. From there he read every word. The vast majority of it had been in the murder book, but he found two things that weren't.

After interviewing the two old women who were neighbors of Belker's parents Reed had written *?Belker is Black?* then scribbled it out. Maybe he had disproved it. Or maybe he was reminding himself to keep it out of the murder book. No one else Jake had talked to mentioned Belker's race and the man certainly didn't look black. He was nearly as light-skinned as Jake.

At the end of interviews with over a dozen of Smith's friends and fellow restaurant employees Reed had written: *"?Was Belker friends with Mike Nelson?"* The very next page contained notes of Reeds interview with Nelson who had confirmed the friendship then apparently convinced the detective that Belker was not the killer: *"Mike says I'm barking up the wrong tree."*

Jake leaned over the table, held the notebook directly under the light, and took photos of the relevant pages.

Why wasn't the Nelson interview in the murder book?

CHAPTER FORTY-TWO

Eddie headed for Grace Patino's hair salon, alert for cop cars, but he saw none. It was a short walk east on Jackson and north on Washington. He'd finished the stew before leaving Boothe's and his belly felt heavy. Totally worth it. Making stew like that was a lost art.

The alley was barely three feet wide and he might have missed it if he hadn't been looking for it. A sign screwed to the interior wall read GRACE'S HAIR CHAIR with an arrow pointing into the alley.

Eddie took a photo of the sign, trying several different angles to get the lighting just right. When he was done, he scrolled through the photos using the screen on the back of the camera, thinking about a caption. *Grace Patino, hidden in a dark alley off the town's main street.* Or maybe, *The unwed mother's shame still ran so deep she hid in the dark alley.*

The chill in the shadowed alley raised goose pimples on his arms. He made a mental note to get that feeling into the book. Foreboding, he'd call it—of what awaited him at the hair salon. With luck he'd learn something that made that work.

The salon was small with three chairs and one shampoo sink. It had that heavy chemical smell of a just completed perm. A window looked out over the wasteland of dumpsters and pot-holed gravel where several alleys converged behind the commercial buildings that encircled the entire block.

He opened the door to the high-energy chatter of women enjoying each other's company but it disappeared as he crossed the threshold. Two hairdressers worked clients while a third sat in the idle chair. An older woman sat on a high stool behind a cash register. All eyes were on Eddie.

"Grace Patino?" he asked as he approached the woman behind the register.

Her eyes narrowed. "Yes?"

Behind him, the talking resumed, the volume lower.

"I'm a writer doing a story on Mose Belker and I understand you knew his friend, Mike Nelson. I'd like—"

"Get out." She spoke in a low voice through clenched teeth.

"I would just like to—"

"Now!"

The voices behind him went silent. Eddie glanced that way and five sets of eyes stared back.

He left. But on the way to the door the idle stylist gestured with her head. He took it to mean she had something to tell him so he waited for her in the alley. A few minutes later she came outside, hugging herself against the chill. She lit a cigarette as she approached and blew out the first lungful with a sigh.

"Why are you asking about him?"

The woman hadn't come out here for the cigarette, she wanted to talk. So, he answered with his own question. "What do you want to tell me?"

She took a drag, elbow propped on the other forearm. She tapped off the ash. "If you write about it, you can't say it came from me. Grace is a good person and a good boss. It's her story to tell, but she's never told it and it needs to be told. Me too, and all that."

"Nelson abused her?"

"They went to the turnabout dance and he talked her into leaving early. Then he raped her. Said he was tired of waiting for her to give it up. Anthony come from that."

Eddie's pulse ramped up. The favored son is a rapist. The yearbook photo of Grace Patino hanging on Mike Nelson's arm at the Sadie Hawkins dance was taken the exact night it happened. Pure gold.

"Did Grace tell you this?"

"My mom told me. They were best friends. They were on a double date that night. Nelson left Ma and her date stranded at the high school. The next day Grace told Ma what happened. But only that once. She never talked about it again."

"Why did your mom break that confidence to tell you?"

Another long drag on her cigarette as she thought through her answer. "My son was getting to be a hotshot football player and it was going to his head. She told me the story as a warning to make sure I kept his feet on the ground. Didn't want him to turn out like Mr. Football."

"How did your son turn out?"

She took another hit off her cigarette, the tip glowing hot red. She dropped it to the pavement and twisted it under her shoe. "So far, so good."

"Can I talk to your mom?"

"She's passed on."

"Does Anthony know about… that night?"

"I sure as hell never told him."

"Do you know Anthony?"

"He works here sometimes when he gets fired from whatever shit job he manages to scrounge up."

"Where's he working now?"

"He's not. If you walk back around the corner, you'll likely see him holding down the bar at the Jackson Avenue Pub."

CHAPTER FORTY-THREE

Jake checked his phone when he got back to the Mustang and found a voicemail from Bentley at the California DNA Lab asking for a return call. Finally. Jake jumped right to it when Bentley answered. "What did you find?"

"We received three samples for testing. A semen sample from an unknown person that was swabbed off a victim's body in 1982, a cheek swab taken from a known individual in 1999, and dried blood off a white handkerchief from a known individual dated 1988."

"And?"

"The second known sample—the one from '88—matched the evidentiary sample taken off the victim's body."

Jake's heart sped up. "Did you send these results to us?"

"Yes. With an invoice that was paid."

"What email address did you send them to?"

"Forensics at Weston PD dot I-L dot gov."

"Can you resend the report?'

"Just give me your email address."

Jake did so, and they hung up.

Belker's DNA had *not* matched the DNA found on Amy Smith. And at least one person in the Weston PD had known that since 1999. That person also must have known who the blood on the handkerchief belonged to. That dirty cop knew who killed Amy Smith.

And let him walk.

And let Mose Belker take the rap.

The dirty cop had to be whoever got the email with the DNA results. Erin was working on chasing that down. He called her. "Did you figure out who was handling forensics in '99?"

"I have a name but haven't confirmed it."

"What's the trouble?"

"The duty rosters are gone, so I went to the annual report sent to the city council, but that didn't have enough detail. So, then I started talking to people and got a name. I think it's the right name, but… "

"Just give it to me."

"It was the chief."

"Arvind?" Jake asked, but it was entirely possible the chief had once worked forensics. Weston prided itself on cross-training its officers.

"Yep."

"How sure are you?"

"I never found it in writing, but my sources are sure."

"Thanks, Erin."

Jake started the Mustang and headed for the station.

Chief Arvind was either the dirty cop or knew who was.

CHAPTER FORTY-FOUR

Eddie walked back around the corner. The Jackson Avenue Pub occupied the ground floor of a brick building sandwiched between an Argentine steakhouse and a high-end kitchenware store. The pub's wide multi-paneled front window had been opened accordion style to take advantage of the fine spring day. Before he went inside, Eddie set up his phone to record and stuck it in his shirt pocket, not willing to take the chance Patino would turn down his request to tape the interview. He hadn't needed its luck at the hair salon, but gave Penny's dime a quick rub.

Just inside the front door was a sun-splashed and breezy space that held four empty round high-top tables. The bar narrowed as he walked past the walk-in beer cooler, then opened to the main room, a deep space with the bar running down the left-hand wall and square high-tops butted up to the brick wall on the right. All the tables were empty, but three men held down the bar, each alone, huddled over a tall draft. No odors of stale beer or vomit like the place where he'd met Donna Larson.

A young woman came out of a back room hauling a case of Molson in bottles. She took it behind the counter and set it on the floor in front of a trio of counter-height, glass-doored refrigerators on the wall behind the bar. She slid a menu in front of him. "Sit wherever you want. Kitchen's open if you want a burger. Shout when you're ready to order."

"Thank you." Two of the three men watched this exchange, but then went back to watching the sports news on the TV above the bartender's head. The third man had kept his focus on his beer, and now lifted it and drained the last swallow. Dirty jeans, unkempt beard, thick hair that hadn't seen a comb, or even a smoothing hand, since the spring wind had stood it up. He was the right age and had wide shoulders like Mike Nelson. Eddie took the stool next to him and signaled the bartender, "I'll have a glass of whatever Anthony's drinking and please refill his, on me."

"Nothing to eat?"

Eddie shook his head and she scooped up the menu and went to pull their beers.

"I don't know you so you must want something," Patino had a worn, raspy, voice, but his eyes were on the beer the bartender was pulling. Or maybe he was watching her. She was worth watching.

"I want to ask you about your father."

Patino squinted at Eddie. "I don't have a father." He accepted the beer from the bartender with a nod and took a long drink.

"Mike Nelson," Eddie said.

Patino swiveled his stool to face Eddie. He licked beer foam off his mustache, his eyes narrowing. "Who told you he's my father?"

"Several people."

"Not much of a secret, I guess," Patino said, his voice slow and sorrowful.

"He was an amazing athlete."

"In high school."

"How far might he have gone if—"

"That was his favorite topic, too."

"You talked to him about it?"

"*He* talked to *me* about it."

"Can you tell me how to get ahold of him?"

Patino swiveled back to face the bar. "I have no idea."

"When's the last time you saw him?"

"Why do you care?"

"I'm writing a book about Mose Belker and I've heard from several people that your dad knew him pretty well."

Patino shook his head, but said nothing.

"Did *you* know Belker, Anthony?"

"A bit. He worked the Riverwalk project for Big Mike—that's what he told me to call him." Patino's gaze lifted from his beer then seemed to cloud over. "He took me with him to watch some of that. I got to carry some bricks." Patino blinked rapidly and looked back down at his beer.

"Did Mose Belker carry bricks, too?"

"He was the detail guy. Cut in the curves and like that."

"What did you think of him?"

"He was a weird little dude. Fidgety. Too much energy."

"What did your dad think of him?"

"I've already given you a beer's worth." Patino held up his empty glass. Eddie ordered him another one. After the first long drink from his fresh beer, Patino said: "Big Mike wasn't a dad to me. Not like the dads my friends had."

"What do you mean?"

"My mom and me were a *family*. Big Mike was just the guy who came around once in a while with a six-pack he'd drink while he told me stories about his glory days. He'd throw some cash on the table when he left like he was a big shot."

"Did you like him?"

"I thought he was a god. He was so big and those stories… "

"But?"

Patino stared at his beer. "He didn't treat my mom right."

"How so?"

Patino shrugged. Eddie wondered if Patino's mom had told her son what happened after the dance.

"Do you think your mom might know where he is?"

Patino spun to face Eddie. "Leave her alone."

"I—"

"I mean it," Patino said, his voice dropping so low it vibrated. "You stay away from her."

Patino locked eyes on Eddie and didn't release his stare until Eddie nodded. Then Patino went back to looking at his beer.

"Did it surprise you when Belker confessed to killing two women?"

Patino drained his beer and got up from his stool. He stepped away, then turned back. "Stay away from my mom."

Eddie watched him go, mentally working on a description of Patino and his drinking hole for the book. But he had trouble nailing it down because Patino didn't fit the place. The pub was… too nice. Maybe he could find a way to work with that. Something about—

"Another beer?" the bartender asked.

Killing an hour or two drinking beer in this nice bar was appealing, but Eddie didn't snap back from day drinking like he used to, so it would shoot his day and he had a lot to do.

"Just the tab."

CHAPTER FORTY-FIVE

Jake drove to the station. If Chief Arvind hid the DNA results back in 1999, he was involved in protecting a murderer. Jake hoped the chief had an explanation, but whether he did or not, just asking Arvind about it could be a career killer.

As he walked through the detective squad room, someone caught him by the arm and yanked him to a stop. Callie Diggs. He'd been so focused he hadn't seen her coming.

"Who do you have in your sights?"

"What do you mean?"

"Come on, Jake." She released his arm, then shot a look around the room. He did too. No one was looking at them. "I know that look. You're in your zone. Ready to attack."

She was right. And going into Arvind's office so obviously primed would make the man defensive. Jake took a deep breath and realized his arms and shoulders were tight. He rolled his shoulders and shook his hands out. "Thanks."

"Is this that juju you warned me about?"

"It looks bad."

"Do you want me to—"

"I've got this, Callie. I'll let you know if I need help."

She smiled grimly and left him there. He took another moment to decompress before he continued on. As he passed Braff's office, Erin looked up from her work. "Good luck."

He nodded and kept moving.

These questions had to be asked.

And they had to be answered.

Arvind's assistant was not at her desk. Jake knocked on the chief's door and when Arvind shouted "Yes?" walked in and closed the door behind him.

* * *

Chief Arvind sat at his desk, suit jacket off, his blue button-down shirt crisp.

He looked up from reading a bound report. When he registered Jake's identity his gaze went to the door. "What can I do for you that Deputy Chief Braff can't handle, Detective Houser?"

"I have a few questions on the Amy Smith case."

Arvind stuck a pencil in the bound report and closed it. "Why are you digging around in a closed case when you have Kate Ballard to find?"

"They're connected." Jake said with absolute conviction as he sat down across from Arvind.

The chief leaned back, the setting sun catching him square in the face. He didn't even squint. The man loved the sun and was always the first person with a tan every spring. His office reflected that love. Where Braff's nearly identical office was all dark woods and deep brown leathers, Arvind's was lighter, with a blond carpet, light wood furniture, and the blinds all pulled high and out of the way. "How so?"

Jake ignored the question. "You were the forensic tech in '99 who sent Belker's cheek swab to the lab to be tested against the DNA found on Amy Smith in '82."

The chief's Adam's apple ran up and down his throat as he swallowed. Worried, now. He knew what was coming. He crossed his arms.

"You also sent a bloody handkerchief to test."

Arvind's chair squeaked, and he licked his lips. "I honestly don't remember a second known DNA sample." Arvind cleared his throat. Pebbles of sweat had beaded on his forehead and one ran down along his nose. He wiped it away and then tried to smile.

Three deception indicators after Jake's question: anchor point movement, lip licking, and the claim of honesty. The chief was lying. "I didn't say the bloody handkerchief was submitted as a known."

Arvind said nothing, his gaze darting to the door. But no one was there for him.

"The lab matched *that* sample to the killer's DNA," Jake said.

Arvind's lower jaw dropped and his mouth hung open. The man had not known about the match. "I uh… became a school safety officer—we had just started that program—right after I sent the samples out."

"Whoever *did* get the lab results hid them. They're not in the murder book." Jake let that sink in. "*That* action protected Amy Smith's *real* killer. That killer may now have Kate Ballard. That's the connection."

Arvind balked, his head cocking back. He swallowed, and wiped the sweat from his forehead.

"Who gave you the handkerchief for testing, Chief?"

More sweat ran down Arvind's face and stained his collar a darker hue where it met his neck. The chief stuck a finger behind his tie and pulled at his collar. But he said nothing.

"Protecting whoever gave you—"

"I know the department means nothing to you, Detective. But to the rest of us, it stands for something. And being part of it is the most important identity we have."

"Think long and hard about this, Chief. Do you really choose to protect the department over saving Kate Ballard? The department exists for the people, Chief. Not for us. When it fails to protect and serve Weston's citizens it needs to be called to account."

"The people we protect need to believe in us."

The chief was not going to talk. "I will get to the bottom of this." Jake left Arvind there, his collar soaked and his armpits stained.

Jake headed home. Time to force Frank Houser to cough up the truth about Mose Belker working for Trinity.

CHAPTER FORTY-SIX

Eddie went back to his car and scrolled through the photos he'd taken so far. He had some good stuff to sprinkle throughout the book but he was missing a key photo. Donna Larson's letter had helped him find Mike through her reference to laying concrete. Eddie now knew Nelson and Belker had worked together for Trinity Landscaping laying concrete bricks on the Riverwalk project. Trinity appeared to be long gone but he needed a photo representing Trinity. Something more than a shot of its yellow pages ad or the partially obscured image of the equipment trailer he'd found in the library's files.

Maybe the company had left something behind. He pulled out his smartphone and entered Trinity's old address into the satellite map. It was less than a mile away at the end of a dead-end street along the railroad tracks.

As he turned north on Ewing, a police siren screeched behind him and his rearview mirror filled with flashing red and blue lights.

"Shit!" He pulled to the curb, his heart hammering wildly. That cop he'd seen from Booth's porch *had* been following him. But why would they pull him over? He took a quick inventory of his interior. "Get a hold of yourself, Shaw!" It had been at least a decade since there had been the stub end of a joint in his ashtray, but an adrenaline dump still made his pulse soar. He wiped away the sweat beading on his forehead and forced himself to settle into his seat. "Fucking cops!"

The cop got out of his cruiser and lumbered forward. Eddie watched him in the side view mirror and lowered the window as the man approached. He stopped a few feet back from Eddie's window. He was a stout man with a belly that pushed his equipment belt down at an angle that made Eddie wonder how his pants stayed up.

"License and registration."

Eddie thumbed his license out of his wallet and handed it over. "Registration is in the glove box."

The cop leaned down, his right hand on the butt of his gun. His nametag read Welch. "Go ahead."

Eddie retrieved it and handed it over. "Why'd you pull me over?"

"Sit tight."

The cop took the documents back to his cruiser. Eddie watched him in the rearview mirror as he talked on his cell phone. Cops used radios, not cell phones. The cop met Eddie's gaze through the mirror. The cop continued talking on the phone, eyes locked on Eddie's until his call ended. The cop got out of the cruiser. He had a clipboard with Eddie's license and registration clipped to the top of it.

"I pulled you over for failing to come to a complete stop before turning the corner off Jackson," the cop said. "But now I smell beer on your breath. Have you been drinking?"

Bullshit. Half a beer didn't give him beer breath. "I was just at the—"

"Get out."

He made Eddie walk a straight line and lean back and touch his nose. Eddie had no problem with either field sobriety test.

"Get back in your car and pull the trunk release."

"Why would—"

The cop put his hand on his gun and unsnapped the leather strap that held it in its holster. "What are you hiding in your trunk, Mr. Shaw?"

"I just don't see why I have to open it. You've got no right to—"

"That's an argument you can make in court if I present something I find in your trunk as evidence. What am I going to find?"

"I can make a civil rights claim."

"Another argument for court. Right *now*, you need to open the trunk."

Eddie got back in the car and pulled the trunk release lever. *This cop was going to plant something!*

Welch pulled a small flashlight off his belt and shone it into the trunk, then disappeared from the image in the side mirror. Thuds and scrapes as Welch searched through the trunk.

The lid slammed and Welch came back around to the window.

"I want to check the operation of all your lights on this old car."

Eddie released a breath he'd been holding. The cop hadn't planted anything. "Okay, officer."

The cop walked around the front of the car and started shouting out directions for the various lights. Eddie complied. Someone inside the Weston police department—or with enough power and connections to make the Weston PD do his bidding—didn't like Eddie digging into Mose Belker and Mike Nelson. Most likely Abe Stewart. This meant Eddie was on to something. And it had to be pretty damn juicy for Stewart to risk a civil rights lawsuit. Eddie smiled. He was right about this story. Now he needed to keep from getting killed so he could write the book. He pulled out his phone and shot a quick text to Penny: *I am going to crack this case!*

Finally, the cop came back to Eddie's window. He finished writing the ticket then tore it off and handed it over with Eddie's license and registration.

"Have a nice day, Mr. Shaw. And watch that day drinking. The buzz can sneak up on you."

"Thank you, Officer." Eddie waited for the cop to drive away, wondering why he was pulled over. Was this minor inconvenience the suburban equivalent of harassment? Eddie shrugged. Maybe these cops weren't worth worrying about.

He continued to the old address for Trinity Landscaping. Ewing ended at Spring, a giant concrete plant looming up on the other side of the street. Beyond it, a commuter train roared past. Eddie turned west.

The road angled toward the tracks where a tow truck yard was pinched in the narrowing slice of land, penned in by giant blocks of concrete. The back of some fancy townhomes rose up to the left, veiled by a thin row of trees. Where the asphalt ended, he found the address he was looking for on a sign attached to one of the posts that held a pole gate.

The gate was open so Eddie crept forward, the car bumping as it dropped off the asphalt onto gravel. Twenty feet in, the tall stands of weeds around the gate thinned out to reveal a concrete block building centered in a large piece of land scattered with concrete pads. Eddie frowned. He had hoped to find a sign still on the building or some old equipment with the clover logo painted on the side. But the absence of weeds near the building meant someone was keeping the place up. Maybe he'd get lucky.

Eddie parked, slung his messenger bag over his shoulder, and got out of the car. Even without the logo he could use pictures of this place. He pulled out his camera and started circling the building at a distance, camera clicking away. He veered toward the railroad tracks, getting the front of the building squarely in view: Two tall garage doors and a service door. The right-hand side of the building had windows on two levels.

The window on the second floor was a box window like people put over a kitchen sink. Was there a residence up there?

"What are you doing?"

Eddie lowered the camera. A man near the building. Coming fast.

"Hello," Eddie called out and started walking forward, holding his camera chest height. Clicking away. "I'm looking for Trinity Landscaping."

"Stop right there."

The man wore gray pants and a black blazer over a shirt with narrow blue and white stripes. He was about Eddie's height, five-ten, and fit. Good posture and no belly.

"Who are you?"

"I'm a freelance writer doing a piece on the men who built the Riverwalk. One of them owned Trinity Landscaping." He pulled out his notebook and searched for the owner's name. "Sorry, bad memory. Frank Houser."

"Trinity closed down years ago."

"I know. I hoped for some history, background, maybe an interview."

"Frank isn't here right now."

"But he lives here?" An interview might be even better than pictures. Eddie pointed at the second-floor windows. "Upstairs?"

"Who hired you to write the article?"

"It's a spec piece. I'd like to talk with the other men on his crew, too. Where they are now, how they feel about what they helped create, that kind of a thing."

The man nodded, but not in agreement. More like he knew Eddie was full of crap.

The wind gusted. The man's blazer flapped, revealing the gleam of a badge on his belt. Another cop! Abe Stewart did not want Eddie looking at Trinity.

"Give me your card. He'll call you if he's interested in talking." The cop held out his hand.

Eddie hesitated, but the cops already knew who he was. He found a card in his wallet and handed it over.

The man held it up. "Eddie Shaw," he said it as if he was entering Eddie's name on a list of suspects.

"Please do have him call me. I'd love to talk with him." Eddie walked back to his car, turned the Mercedes around and left.

As he passed through the gate and bumped up onto the pavement, he checked his mirror. The cop was still watching him.

CHAPTER FORTY-SEVEN

Deputy Chief of Patrol Sam Stewart spent the day thinking about what Bev Warren had told him: Houser was looking for a link between the missing Kate Ballard and the Belker murders.

Sam could not see any way for them to be connected.

He signed back into the system with Massey's credentials to look at Houser's Ballard file. The man apparently only updated the book in the morning. Sam had checked the Weston Police Manual and it said the file should be updated as new material became available so all stakeholders had the information they needed to do their jobs. Sam read that to mean Houser should update the book every time he learned something new. And why not? The man carried a smart phone that could access the system. Houser's morning-only entries kept Sam a day behind what Houser was doing. Sam needed to edit the manual to make this requirement clearer.

The intercom buzzed. Chief Arvind wanted to see him immediately.

* * *

Sam found Chief Arvind pacing along his windows. When he saw Sam, the chief pointed to his desk and Sam sat in a guest chair, watching the chief trek back and forth. Sam only paced when alone, afraid it made him look emotional. But he now realized it could be an effective device. Arvind's pacing captured Sam's full attention and sent a low scale dread creeping through him about what was coming.

Finally, Arvind stopped pacing and clasped his hands behind his back, his chest thrust out. "Detective Houser was just in here asking me questions about the Amy Smith case and the DNA I sent to that lab in California when I was the department's forensic tech."

"I, uh, remember the Smith case." Sam hoped the chief didn't register the pause while he worked out what to say. His dad was so much better at this.

"Then you will also remember the bloody handkerchief you asked me to send to the lab for DNA profiling."

"I remember delivering a sealed envelope to you for my dad," Sam said, reminding Arvind that the favor he had done was for Abe Stewart, not for Sam.

"Whose blood was on that handkerchief?"

"I didn't even know it *was* a handkerchief," Sam said.

Arvind frowned. "Houser says *that* DNA—not Belker's—matched the semen found on Smith's body."

That was the issue with the DNA reports, Sam thought.

"You didn't know about the results either?"

Sam shook his head.

Arvind sat down behind his desk.

"Abe assigned me a new job before the results came back and he didn't fill my old job for three or four months. I think he intercepted the results when the lab sent them back and that's why they aren't in the murder book."

Sam's father knew who killed Amy Smith. Maybe he hadn't known back in the eighties, but when those results came back in '99 he knew for sure. But he still let Belker take the rap; the man must have been involved. "But Belker confessed, right?" Sam asked.

"That's right."

"Then he was in on it and just didn't leave any DNA behind."

Arvind frowned and dialed a number on his phone, putting it in speakerphone mode.

Sam knew Arvind well enough to know exactly who the chief had called. He hoped it would go to voice mail.

Abe Stewart answered so fast it seemed like he'd been waiting for their call. Voices rumbled in the background, the clatter of tiles. Sam knew those sounds; his father was at the senior center playing dominos with his friends. Chief Arvind jumped right in without preamble.

"Tell us whose blood was on that handkerchief and where you got it."

"Who's us?"

"I'm here with Sam."

Abe Stewart chuckled, the background sounds fading as he moved away from the din. "How perfect is this? I involved the very two men who ended up running the show."

"Involved?" Arvind's voice rose. "In what?"

"You'll just have to trust me that leaving things as they are is best for everyone."

"Houser won't agree," Arvind said.

"You need to handle that problem."

CHAPTER FORTY-EIGHT

Jake watched the Mercedes's taillights disappear. He didn't buy the writer's story and he didn't believe in coincidence. Larson must have sent a letter to this guy, which explained why he'd played coy with Jake. He'd clearly made Jake as a cop and with Larson's dirty cop allegations the writer wasn't about to talk to some random cop he ran into while researching his story.

Back inside Jake sat down at the kitchen island, staring west out the big picture window, the sun dropping behind the woods. The writer wasn't the only one lying. Frank Houser had lied about Belker's connection to Trinity Landscaping. Thinking about why his own father had lied turned Jake's thoughts to fatherhood.

The smear of orange above the forest canopy shrank to a sliver, then faded away, his reflection in the darkened glass sharpening into focus. He looked away.

Anna was pro-choice. He knew that. And so was he. Now she had to make that choice. The only thing he could do was make sure she knew he would be there for her in any way she would have him.

He pulled out his phone and called her. She answered on the first ring.

"I'm surprised you waited so long to call."

"I wanted to give you time to think. I—"

"A whole day." The lilt in her voice sounded like the playful teasing he was used to. Her mind was now freed from the turmoil of indecision.

"You've made your decision?"

"I'm going to have the baby."

The weight of his earlier thoughts fell away. He stood up. "I know that decision wasn't easy. I want you to know I'll be there for you and our baby however you want me to be."

"I… haven't made any decision beyond that, Jake." She was silent for a beat. "I think given time for our relationship to advance naturally we might have ended up together. But now, I don't know if what I feel, or what you feel, is about us. Or about the baby."

Her confusion was his fault. If he had told her he loved her when he first felt it, things would be different. He was about to say so when he heard the soft click of the call terminating. He'd been too slow to speak up, yet again.

* * *

As Jake was finishing up a plate of reheated lasagna, the garage door screeched up in its tracks.

Frank was back.

Jake pulled two beers from the fridge and went down to meet him. The garage door had just finished its loud downward descent when Jake reached the garage. Frank popped out of the truck.

"Hey, bub."

"Heard you pull in." Jake held up the beers and his dad took one. They walked over to the couches and sat down. Jake opened his bottle and took a drink; the sharp coldness washed away the lasagna's tomato acidity and felt good on his tongue. "I need to talk to you about Mose Belker and Mike Nelson."

"We already talked about them."

"This time I need the truth, Dad."

Frank grimaced. His chin dropped and his eyes pulled away from his son's. Jake was glad to see it; A man *should* have an emotional reaction to being caught lying to his son. When his dad started talking, his voice was low and he kept his eyes on the blank TV screen.

"Mose Belker did work for me as a part-timer. He had some other job… I don't remember what it was. He was small, but a good worker. After those girls died, I was told—your Uncle Bull told me—that Mose was a suspect. I cut him loose."

Frank took a long drink, then looked down at the bottle in his hands.

"Why lie to me?"

"I just… I got used to lying about Belker. In '99 a reporter learned Belker had been on my payroll in '82 and I had to buy a ton of advertising to keep my name out of the paper."

"Were Nelson and Belker buddies?"

Frank shrugged. "Mike brought Belker in, so I guess so."

"Were they tight enough for Belker to bring Nelson in with him on killing those girls?"

"I can't see that," Frank said, his voice suddenly soft. "And Belker confessed."

"He did. And over the twenty years since then he's never claimed his confessions were coerced."

"Then it was him," Frank said. "End of story."

Jake detected no deception from his dad. He held out Shaw's business card. Frank took it. "What's this?"

"This guy came by looking for you today. He claimed he was writing an article about the men who built the Riverwalk."

"You think he was really here about Belker and Nelson?"

"Too much of a coincidence otherwise." Jake drained his beer and set it on the table. "I'm going up. I have some work to do."

"Okay, Jake." Frank reached for the TV remote. "Wait. What's happening about Anna?"

"No change," Jake said, his face warm from his deception. But he suddenly felt like his dad didn't deserve the news.

On his way up the stairs he got a text from Detective Fallon with the Glenbard police department: *I've caught the case of a young woman's body found dumped on an abandoned railroad siding off 64. Could be Kate Ballard.* The attached image was of a map.

Jake texted back: *On my way.* He dashed up the stairs, equipped himself, and headed north.

CHAPTER FORTY-NINE

Eddie sped back to the hotel, anxious to start pulling together his thoughts about the cops harassing him. He was working the key into his hotel room door when a shadow appeared over his shoulder. He jumped, still wound up from his encounters with Weston cops.

"Whoa, man." It was Benny, the hippie who introduced himself the night before. He backed off a step, hands up. "Didn't mean to scare you."

"What do you want?" Eddie pulled the key out of the door. He wasn't going to let this doper bum-rush him into the room. Whatever this was, he'd keep it out here.

"I wanted to tell you about what happened here today, man."

"I don't need to know what everyone's up to in this place."

"Not the place, man." He pointed at Eddie's door. "Your room."

That grabbed Eddie's attention. "What happened?"

"The cops, man. They—"

"Hold it." Eddie keyed the door and ushered Benny and his reefer stench inside. The room looked the same as when Eddie'd left it.

He sat on the bed, pointed at the desk chair, and Benny sat down. Mike Nelson was real and the Weston cops had protected him. The thought shot through Eddie's mind and made his hands shake.

"So, like an hour ago I was sitting in my chair out front of my room and a cop car pulled in. I'm good at noticing cops because, you know."

"You're usually carrying some weed."

"Bingo. It'll be legal next year but right now I gotta watch it. I met a guy who's got a doctor who will get me a prescription but—"

"The cops?"

"Right. So the cop car pulled in and parked. The cop—there was just one of 'em—went into the office then walked straight to your room. He must have had a key because he went right in. I clocked him on my phone and he was in here for eleven minutes."

This was why he'd been pulled over. To make sure he wouldn't walk in on the cop searching his room. Let them search; all his notes had been with him in his messenger bag. "Then what?"

"He came out and left. But I thought you should know." Benny looked around. "Looks like he tossed the place."

"This is how I left it." Eddie never let maids into his motel rooms and didn't pick up after himself until he was packing to leave.

"I follow that organization lady on YouTube. You might want to check that out."

"Did the cop have anything with him when he came out?"

"Not that I could see, but he could have had something in his pocket."

"Thanks, Benny."

"Sure, Eddie. We got to stick together."

"Against the man," Eddie said.

"That's right." Benny stuck out his fist and Eddie bumped it. "Let me know if you want the pictures."

"What pictures?"

"Of the cop and his car."

Eddie smiled, a spike of energy shooting through him and making his fingers and toes tingle. He had them. These photos confirmed the Weston cops were corrupt. Now, just about anything he said about them would ring with truth. But he would still play it straight. This story had enough on its own without help from him. "I do want them, Benny. Right now."

They exchanged cell numbers and as soon as Eddie had the photos, he ushered Benny out of the room. Then Eddie zoomed in on the cop's face and marched to the motel's office. Before he went inside he started the recording app on the phone. The man behind the counter had not been there when Eddie checked in. This guy was short and skinny with a rash of pimples across his cheeks.

"Can I help you?"

Eddie held his phone with the photo displayed close to the man's face. "Why did you let this cop into my room?"

"Where'd you get that picture?"

"That's not an answer."

"I… I just gave him a key."

"Why?"

"He said you were suspected of being an opioid dealer and he wanted to see if that was true before ruining your reputation by arresting you."

"So you let him in to protect my reputation?"

"Exactly. If you were innocent, which he said you are when he came back with the key, then no problem."

"You didn't do it for the fifty bucks?"

The man's mouth opened and closed, his eyes skating away. He scratched his face. His fingernail raked open a pimple, leaving a red trail down his cheek.

"How much *did* he pay you?"

"Twenty."

"What was the cop's name?"

The little man shrugged. "He was just a cop."

"I'm leaving my surveillance camera up and if this happens again, I'll call in the FBI."

Eddie took a picture of the clerk with his phone. The idiot smiled for it. Eddie wondered if the clerk would tell the cop about being busted but doubted he'd want to make that call.

Back in his room Eddie locked the door and sat at the desk. He was onto something here that reached deep enough into the police department for them to commit crimes to protect themselves. He got back up and latched the security chain. As he was walking back to the desk, his cell phone vibrated in his pocket and nearly gave him a heart attack.

A message from his agent. She was much more direct by text: *Clock's ticking. How does the new story look?*

He replied: *Dirty Cops!*, then explained what had happened.

She sent him back a string of ridiculous emojis. He hated emojis.

He sat down and started writing. Fuck these cops.

CHAPTER FIFTY

Deputy Chief of Patrol Sam Stewart snorted in disgust. Houser still hadn't added anything new to his Ballard file. What the hell was he working on? Sam called Massey into his office to see what he had on the writer.

"What's he up to?"

"I've had someone on him all day. He got a late start, then spent hours at the library looking through the local history stuff. I went in and talked to the librarian after he left and she said he was interested in the Riverwalk.

"From there he went to visit a couple old ladies who were Belker's neighbors on Jackson back in the eighties. Then he spent about a minute in a hair salon in the alley off Washington, talked to one of the stylists out in the alley for a minute—might have been hoping for a hook-up—then had a beer at the Jackson Avenue Pub where he talked to some loser at the bar."

"Who was Shaw looking for in the salon and the bar?"

"The bar was just on his way back from the salon. Maybe he's a drunk. A lot of writers are drunks."

"*Maybe* he's a drunk? You need to do better than that."

"I—"

"Who was he looking for at the hair salon?"

"He talked to the woman behind the cash register for about a minute, then left."

"And she is?"

Massey looked at his notes. "Grace Patino. A nobody."

The name rang no bells with Sam. "Find out who she is. And I don't buy that Shaw was just getting a drink. Find out who he talked to in the bar."

"Will do. When Shaw left the bar, I had one of my guys pull him over to keep him busy while another guy searched his motel room."

"You what?"

"Don't worry. I timed it so there was no way Shaw could surprise my guy there and we were in and out in a couple minutes. Plus, we had the desk manager's consent so we're covered if it hits the fan."

Sam squeezed the arms of his chair. Massey must have missed their training on what constituted a legal search of a motel room. All getting the desk manager's consent had done was create a witness. "What did you find in the room?"

"Nothing. Shaw must keep whatever he has on this in that bag he carries everywhere."

Sam swiveled his chair to look out the window, the long view across Lake Osborne normally brought him some calm, but it was dark out and he only saw his own reflection. He popped up from his chair and paced along the window.

"There's something else boss. And you're not going to like it."

"You think I like what I've heard so far?"

"No, I—"

"Spit it out."

"Shaw went to see Houser."

Sam froze in his tracks. "What?"

"Straight from the traffic stop he drove to Houser's place on west Spring Street. He converted a commercial building—a warehouse or something—into a bachelor pad. I think it—"

"How long did they talk?"

"Not long. They didn't even go inside. Shaw took a couple pictures of the building then Houser came out and they talked for maybe three minutes. Then Shaw gave Houser a business card and left."

Shaw taking pictures of the building might mean he was there because he was interested in what had been in the building: Trinity Landscaping. Running into Houser had to be an accident.

"How did they leave it?"

"Houser went back inside and Shaw picked up a sandwich on the way back to his room and that's it."

"No visitors?"

"My guy had to leave him at that point. Family thing."

"Get someone else."

"You wanted to keep this small. I already got two other guys working it. Any more, and I'm spreading it beyond guys I'm sure about."

"Use overtime."

"I have, boss."

Sam sat down. He did not know enough, that was clear. Who was Grace Patino? Who was the guy at the bar? *Were* Shaw and Houser working together? He hoped not.

Massey was still there, slapping a manila folder against his thigh.

"What is it?"

Massey handed the file over without comment. Inside was a brutality complaint against Houser and a stack of photos showing a nasty gash above a man's eye and wrists torn up by struggling against zip cuffs.

"Where did this come from?"

"The complaint was filed against Houser last year, but was never resolved."

"Last year? When the sheriff' was still handling these matters?"

"Exactly. Houser's own cousin was in charge of investigating him."

"How'd you find out about it?"

Massey's eyes skittered away and came back. "I talked to the investigating deputy. Hogan."

Sam checked the form and found the name, Warren Hogan.

"Look at the bottom of the form, boss. Bev Warren killed it before the injured guy even signed it."

Massey was right. Sam rubbed his thumb over the empty signature line.

Sam reached to hand it back to Massey. "Take it out there and get this Woodling guy to sign it now."

"Can't. The dirt bag was a serial domestic abuser and his girlfriend killed him on Christmas Eve. She got off. Self-defense."

Shit!

"Hogan will say he went out and got it signed back then," Massey said.

Will say. Sam thumbed the blank signature line again. "Can you count on Hogan?"

"Absolutely one-hundred percent. He hates Houser."

A personal vendetta was a powerful thing. "Maybe Woodling *did* sign it. Which would imply the sheriff substituted this unsigned version to preserve the record but make it impossible to adjudicate," Sam said.

Massey smiled. "I like it boss. He pulled a pen out of his pocket and held it out to Sam. "But we found the signed one and now we can push it."

Sam did not reach for the pen. Forging this document was one thing. Doing it in front of Sergeant Massey was another. He was already in deep with Massey. Too damn deep.

"You're dismissed."

After Massey left, Sam stared at the complaint form for a long time. If he forged Woodling's signature he could talk

Arvind into suspending Houser and the Ballard case would be re-assigned to Detective Diggs. Diggs had ambition. People with ambition were sensitive to upsetting the organization within which that ambition resided. Which meant Diggs would be willing to listen to reason when Sam finally figured out exactly what his dad had done, and for who, and what had to be done to keep it all in the past.

He hoped.

But that slim hope was better than dealing with Houser.

He picked up his pen, but set it back down.

Massey knew this document wasn't signed and presumably so did Bev Warren. Which meant he would keep this copy as it was and create a signed version and a plausible story about how he found it.

Sam made a copy of the unsigned form, then pulled up Woodling's driver's license on the state system. He practiced the signature on a blank legal pad until his forgery looked passable and signed the form. It looked pretty damn close to Woodling's actual signature. Sam stuffed the signed form into one of his crowded file drawers and pulled it out again, over and over, until it was wrinkled and its corners bent. Then he put it in the file with the original.

And sat staring at it.

He couldn't do it.

Could he?

Is this what it took to be chief?

CHAPTER FIFTY-ONE

Bev took off her equipment belt and draped it over a hook on the coatrack, then went to the kitchen for a glass of wine. She'd earned one. The dealer's ledger had been a goldmine. They'd translated the street names into real identities and obtained search warrants—forty-three so far—and taken fourteen ounces of the bad batch off the streets. The rate of overdoses was dropping and they were still talking to nine of the street dealers. One of them would crack and know enough to help the task force chase the two pounds of heroin in the missing printer cartridges.

She poured herself a large glass of the dark, oaky cabernet. The first sip was so heady she had to sit down.

Her phone vibrated with a text from Doug. He wanted to come over. She smiled at the little thrill it sent up the back of her neck. Maybe she and Doug had a shot, and maybe they didn't. But for now, it was good.

She called him.

"You got my text."

"I did."

"So… ?"

"I *would* like to see you but I'm beat," she said. "Been wearing my browns all day with the equipment belt. I need a bath and an early night."

"Sure," he said. "Tomorrow night?"

"Yes, subject to—"

"Duty calling."

She smiled. She'd dated plenty of men who didn't accept that her job came first. "That's right."

"I'll let you—oh, I have news."

"What's that?"

"Your uncle is in town. Jake's dad. My dad saw him at the diner over lunch."

Had Abe Stewart called in help? Maybe that's all Abe had meant by taking action to rein in Jake if she didn't.

"I'll have to stop by Jake's place for a visit."

"I don't know if that's where he's staying."

"He always stays there."

"Oh, okay. Well, enjoy the bath and good luck tracking down that tainted smack."

After the call, Bev retreated to her dad's old office. She had kept all his furniture so it still felt like his room. She sat in his old chair, sipping her wine, thinking about Jake and Frank together in that old landscaping building. They were very close. But it didn't matter; nothing Frank Houser could do would stop Jake.

Her cell phone rang. Her department's liaison to the task force.

"We got a lead," he said. "Two of these fu—dealers, cracked and have bought stuff from the same guy. We have his street name—Peddler—and his address. We're headed there now."

"Give me the address."

Bev buckled her equipment belt back on and grabbed her keys.

* * *

The address led to a tight pack of three-story apartment buildings near Paget Community College. A smart spot for a drug dealer. Lots of turnover. Lots of young people. People in-and-out all day. Hell, Peddler probably didn't even have to give his real name when he rented the place.

She did a slow roll past the building, then met her team in the parking lot behind the CVS on Roosevelt Road. She listened to the tactical sergeants plan their entry, then rode along in their big black van and followed them inside after they called *All Clear*.

They found the empty printer cartridges on a card table dusted with white powder. The table also held a pharmacist's scale and a box half full of the small wax paper stamp bags that would each hold a tenth of a gram. It looked like the two pounds had been broken down. They would stretch to more than nine thousand deadly doses.

"Get Fanning in here." While she waited for Fanning to confirm the powder was the bad smack, she searched the place. In the bedroom the dresser drawers were all pulled out and most of the clothing was gone. Peddler had run and taken the bad doses with him. It wasn't on the street or the ODs would have kept climbing. But basic economics said the dwindling supply would create a desperate demand that would spike prices. When the price rose high enough, Peddler would come out of hiding and start selling. Bev clenched her fists. She needed to find this stuff right now!

On the way outside, Fanning stopped her. "It's the same stuff. And there's no evidence he's cut it with anything so we're still talking lethal doses."

She accepted the bad news and continued outside. Three of her squads were now holding the scene while the tactical team got back in its van. A scatter of twenty-somethings had come out of adjacent buildings. As she watched, they edged closer, the pack getting denser. A scatter of shouted insults. "Jack-Booted Nazi Motherfuckers!" But her tactical men were seasoned pros and ignored the abuse.

She looked over the crowd. At least one of these assholes would know something about the man who'd lived here. One of them may even have a hot dose in his pocket right now, itching to go home and use it.

She stepped over to the crowd. "We would like your help here. We—"

"Cops suck!"

An empty beer can hit her in the shin. She scanned the crowd and found the likely offender staring at her from a group of unwashed men in heavy metal T-shirts. She locked eyes with Beer Can and held his stare until he broke it off. Wimp.

She turned back to the crowd, now bunching in front of her. "The smack being sold out of this apartment—"

"Allegedly!" A shout from Beer Can.

"—is killing people. Eight dead so far and dozens in the hospital." Bev scanned the crown as she talked, trying to catch the eye of as many people she could. They were all young. Some scared. A few angry. "We need to stop him. Who can—"

Beer Can stepped forward and threw another can. She swatted it down before it reached her but this can hadn't been empty and fluid splashed against her neck and chin. It wasn't beer. It was chewing tobacco. A warm stream of tobacco spit ran down between her breasts.

She waded through the crowd, grabbed Beer Can by the throat, swept his legs out from under him, and slammed him into the ground.

"That's assault on a police officer, dickwad." She squeezed. He grabbed her arm with both hands, his face turning red. His mouth gaped open and his eyes bugged out. "Sheriff." A tug on her shoulder. "Sheriff!"

Bev released Beer Can and stood back. He took a long sucking breath. A deputy edged past her and flipped Beer Can over and cuffed him. Another grabbed her by the elbow and walked her toward the van. Her head buzzed with adrenaline and her hearing felt fuzzy. The people were shouting again. *Brutality! Cops Suck! Nazi!* Cell phones were out and filming.

"You better go, boss. We'll hold the scene until forensics clears it."

CHAPTER FIFTY-TWO

Jake drove north, the lasagna roiling in his stomach with the certainty the dead girl was Kate Ballard. He wiped sweat from his face and rolled down the windows, the crisp evening air filled the car.

Because her body was found in Glenbard, Jake would be sidelined unless he could talk Fallon into letting him stay on the investigation. But he didn't see that happening; Weston and Glenbard had never worked well together on anything.

But damn it, Kate Ballard was from Weston and Jake wanted to deliver her justice.

As he drove, the night sky filled with a low sweep of clouds and the humidity climbed. A storm was coming in. He hoped it would hold off until forensics finished up and Kate's body was moved.

He would have to tell Kate's mother—the Glenbard cops would no doubt be happy to let him handle that unpleasant task. He'd do it in the morning, when she sobered up.

As he crossed over North Avenue, he spotted the emergency lights reflecting off the low cloud cover. A squad blocked the intersection with Randy Rd. When Jake flashed his badge, the uniform shouted for him to come in from the north. "Left on Kehoe, then south on Gresevske."

Jake waved his thanks and followed the instructions, badging his way past another squad to enter an industrial park of long low buildings with large parking lots spread around them. Ahead, the road was clogged with emergency vehicles, their combined lights a blinding display. Jake pulled into the last parking lot before the scrum and parked.

As he walked toward the scene, the emergency lights blinked off one-by-one, leaving behind the white glare of headlights and the soft yellow glow of a street light that hung over the gathered vehicles. A generator on a trailer chugged away, a snake of electrical cables running east from it along the abandoned train siding. Jake scanned the vehicles. Four squads, three unmarked, two civilian rides, the forensic van and the coroner's wagon.

The gang was all here.

A uniformed officer stood between the rails with his hands on his belt.

"Are you Detective Houser?"

"Yes."

"Detective Fallon told me to escort you to the crime scene."

"Let's go."

The officer trudged off down the tracks, following the trail of flattened weeds that showed where those ahead of them had trod. As they exited the spill of light around the responding vehicles the shine of floodlights rose ahead of them. Overhead the flat slapping of helicopter rotors *thwupmed-thwumped*. Jake gazed upward but saw only low clouds reflecting back the floodlights. The news choppers would fly back to Chicago with nothing to show for the effort.

Jake's phone buzzed with a text. Erin: *Is it Kate?*

Erin had first-class resources so it didn't surprise him that she knew about the body. But her question meant either Detective Fallon ran a tight crime scene or there was still doubt about the victim's identity.

"What can you tell me, officer?"

"I've been working the perimeter so haven't seen the, er… body. But I heard that a guy searching for glass insulators—you know, like on old telephone poles?—found it. I mean, her."

"Anything else?"

"That's all I know."

They pushed through a stand of sumac and into the harsh glare of the tripod-mounted floodlights. The humidity had risen further and Jake sweated despite the cool temperature.

The forensic team had erected a canopy over the body to protect it in case it rained and a trio of Tyvek clad specialists worked under it, cameras flashing.

The dead girl lay on her side facing away from Jake. Her knees were drawn up as if curled to sleep. She wore low-cut jeans and a light blue T-shirt. The same clothing Kate Ballard had worn in the video footage of her at the library. The shirt had ridden up, and the skin was mottled with the blue stains of lividity. When she died, she had lain on her back long enough for blood to pool there before being dumped here.

"Over here, Houser."

Detective Fallon was a gaunt man in his early sixties with a bushy mustache that he worked ferociously with thumb and forefinger when he was thinking. He gave it a scrub as Jake approached. "If she's your girl I'd appreciate you sending me what you've pulled together on it."

"The clothes match. No ID on the body?"

Fallon shook his head and waved toward the body. "Take a look and see if you can give me a preliminary."

Jake had spent enough time staring at Kate's photo that he was sure he could. He approached the body, circling to see her face. One arm was trapped under her and the other was up near her head. As the dead girl's face came into view he braced himself for animal predation. But he saw no damage, just the blotchy and bloated pallor of a dead Kate Ballard. Acid bubbled up from his stomach, burning his throat and fouling his mouth. He swallowed it and squatted in front of her. She was in an advanced stage of decomp and her clothes were stained with the fluids leached from her body and maggots writhed in the puddles. The smell was god-awful.

These were definitely the clothes she'd been wearing. But her jean jacket was missing, and her necklace. A plain gold cross on a gold chain. Her mom had said she always wore it. Which meant the killer had taken it. A trophy.

He returned to stand next to Fallon.

"You're almost as pale as the—"

"It's her," Jake said. He told Fallon his observations about Ballard's clothing and the missing jacket and cross. "I want in."

"It's my case, Jake."

"You can see from the lividity in her back that she wasn't killed here," Jake said. "I've narrowed her abduction to a three-block stretch—"

"This is a murder, not an abduction."

"I can help with—"

"I called out the task force so have plenty of manpower."

The Paget County Major Crimes Task Force was an inter-agency group that worked together on serious crimes across the county. Weston was not a member of the task force.

"If you have a relationship with the family, they would likely appreciate you handling notification," Fallon said.

"I do, and I will."

"I appreciate that, Jake." Fallon looked at Jake as he scrubbed his moustache. "And you'll send me what you've got?"

"Of course," Jake said.

"Did you have anything solid?"

Belker's comment about "Mike" having Kate Ballard wasn't solid. Not yet. "I've been working an old boyfriend, but only because she kept him secret. He came forward on his own."

"Maybe he wasn't a real boyfriend."

"It was real. He had plenty of photos and text messages to back it up. It'll all be in the file." The men fell silent, watching the forensic team. The humid air thick and cold. Fallon worked his mustache, then stepped away to take a call.

The tech squatting next to Ballard's body turned around, her gaze searching for someone. Probably Fallon.

Jake stepped forward. "What did you find?"

"Clear evidence of sexual assault. We can get DNA off semen for seven days, and sometimes longer. How long has she been missing?"

"Thirteen days."

The tech shrugged. "Maybe we'll get lucky. It's been a cool spring, especially at night and she's in the shade of these tall weeds we knocked down."

Jake suddenly remembered Glenbard was part of a pilot program for an ultra-fast DNA analysis machine. "If you find viable DNA you'll put it through that new technology?"

"Yes. If the guy's in the system, we'll have his name in a day or two. It's supposed to take ninety minutes, but there's a backlog."

Weston either needed to get one of these machines or join this task force to get access to it. "Will you text me?"

She pointed to Fallon. "I'll text him."

Jake thanked her. He asked Fallon to keep him in the loop, then reluctantly left. It didn't feel right to leave Kate, but standing there did nothing for her.

CHAPTER FIFTY-THREE

Jake drove home, windows open, hoping the fresh air would drive the decomp smell from his clothes and clear it from his nostrils. On the way he detoured to Ballard's apartment and parked at the curb. He shut the Mustang down, and looked up at her windows. A low wattage bulb glowed in a back bedroom and the vibrant wash of a big television lit the living room drapes. But by this hour Kate's mom would be deep into her bottle and Jake didn't want to talk to her while smelling like this. His bad news would keep.

He pulled out his phone and called Kate Ballard's dad. When the man answered, Jake didn't waste time with preliminaries. "I'm sorry to tell you Kate's body was found today."

Ballard sighed, then choked back a sob. Jake waited for the questions. When they came, he answered what he could, then referred him to Detective Fallon.

"I guess I need to talk to Kate's mother to make arrangements for the... body."

"I haven't told her yet. I planned to tell her in the morning."

"When she's sober."

"Yes," Jake said.

"I know it's weak of me, Detective Houser. But I'm going to let you do that. I'll call her tomorrow afternoon."

"You're just letting me do my job."

Ballard hung up.

When he got home, Jake sent emails to Erin and Deputy Chief Braff explaining that Katy Ballard's body had been found in Glenbard and he was forwarding his Ballard case file to, and cooperating with, Detective Fallon of the Glenbard PD. Braff would no doubt shoot this news up the chain of command where it would be received, at least in part, with relief because it was no longer a Weston case and would not register on Weston's crime statistics.

Jake put his clothes in a plastic bag to take to the dry cleaners then took a long hot shower and put on sweat pants and a T-shirt. He sat down at the island with a beer and updated his Ballard file with the discovery of her body in a neighboring jurisdiction and the identity of the detective now handling her murder case. Next, he reviewed everything. Had he missed something? If he had, he still couldn't see it. He was sure of her route home from the library and the three-block stretch where she had to have disappeared. No one except the boyfriend had popped, and as hard as Jake tried to squeeze blood from that stone, there was nothing there.

He leaned back and considered also sending his Mike file to Fallon.

Though Jake had identified Belker's mysterious Mike, he couldn't prove Nelson had been involved back in the eighties, or now. Hell, he couldn't even prove the man was still alive. And though Jake knew Kate Ballard was most likely dead before her disappearance was even reported, he still felt like he'd failed her. And her parents. Finding Mike would in some small way atone for that.

And he couldn't forget that Larson's letter alleged Weston PD corruption; The manipulation of the DNA reports confirmed that claim. Dropping it on Fallon without briefing Braff would be a mistake.

He'd hold the Mike stuff. For now.

He converted the Ballard case file into a pdf and sent it to Fallon. He then grabbed another beer, turned off all the lights, and sat looking across the yard to the forest preserve. The low cloud cover had begun to break up and shafts of moonlight illuminated the scene. He hoped to see a deer or fox or coyote but saw nothing. No, that wasn't true. He saw a weak reflection of himself in the glass. A man sitting alone in the dark. Drinking.

This was his life—his present—but it would not be his future. The baby was his future. And maybe Anna. He pulled out his phone, but then put it away without calling her and went back to drinking beer and staring out the window. Three beers later he gave up and went to bed.

He jerked awake at 3:16 a.m., drenched in the familiar sweat of his nightmares. He'd been young in this one. He remembered the metallic taste of his braces when fear sent an electric spike through his body. And he'd been somewhere damp and dark, the floor gritty under his tennis shoes. Somewhere he wasn't supposed to be. Alone.

Then he wasn't.

Someone very big. Coming closer… looming over him… then he woke up.

He lay back down until the windows lightened with the coming dawn. He checked his phone and email for any word on the DNA on Ballard's body, but found only an acknowledgement from Fallon that he received Jake's investigative file.

Sitting at the kitchen island sipping coffee, the nightmare came back to him in vivid detail.

Which meant it was a memory, not a dream. Of what, and when, he didn't know. It would come to him. Eventually. But not until he experienced it several more times.

He fixed a bowl of oatmeal and ate it while he turned things over. He needed to get to Kate Ballard's mom before some reporter stopped by for a quote on how she *felt* about her daughter turning up dead.

But first he had to tell Braff about his Mike file.

He opened his laptop and updated the file with what he'd learned the day before then went through all of it, starting with Donna Larson's letter introducing Mose Belker into his Ballard investigation. Jake had identified the mysterious Mike as Mike Nelson. Nadine Drilling had put Amy Smith in Nelson's van having sex and smoking dope with him. Detective Reed had documented in his notebook that Nelson was a friend of Belker's. Jake's own interview with Mose Belker had confirmed Belker knew Mike Nelson.

And someone in the Weston PD—maybe current Chief Arvind—had hidden the 1999 DNA results, which said the DNA found on Amy Smith did not belong to Mose Belker but to an unidentified man. Someone in the Weston PD had also lied to the state's attorney and certified the DNA did match Belker.

Had Anna been able to get those documents?

He called her and got her breathless on-my-way-to-court voice.

"Hey, Jake."

"Good morning. I'm wondering—"

"I only have a few seconds."

"That certification from the Weston PD on the—"

"Oh, that. I got it this morning by email but haven't even opened it. I'll forward it to you right now."

"Perfect. Thanks—"

But the line was dead. He looked at his phone and briefly wondered whether she actually was on the way to court or just avoiding him. He *had* promised to give her time. As he stared at his phone it buzzed. The email.

He opened it and then clicked open the pdf attachment.

Abe Stewart, Acting Chief of Police had signed the certification. A flat out lie.

Jake attached the DNA lab's results and Abe's false certification to his Mike file then summarized them in his narrative report.

There was one thing missing from what he'd written. Belker and Nelson both had worked for Trinity Landscaping at the time of the murders. Jake couldn't leave that out—it was a key fact in identifying Mike Nelson as the "Mike" in Larson's letter. Jake had to play this straight. His dad answering some tough questions was a small price to pay for getting the dead girls the justice they deserved. Jake typed in the connection to Trinity and Frank Houser and loaded his Mike file into the Ballard case file as a supplemental report.

He then typed an email to Braff: *I just updated my Ballard file with a supplemental report tying her abduction to Belker's murders and a Weston PD cover-up.* Before he hit send, Jake read back through it and considered amending the message to alert Braff that the cover-up was in the past. But Arvind's refusal to tell the truth about what happened in 1999 had extended the cover-up to today.

As Jake hit send, he wondered what Braff would do.

Take it slow, was the answer. He would wait to see what happened when Arvind read this report and give the chief an opportunity to act on what it said: come clean, or cover it up.

Rope to hang himself, in other words.

As Jake showered and dressed, he thought about who else would see that supplemental report. If Sam Stewart saw it, things would get interesting.

He equipped himself and headed out to notify Mrs. Ballard that her daughter's body had been found. He remembered his own devastation when his wife was murdered. How much worse it must be to learn that your child was killed.

Now, Jake was going to be a dad and open himself up to the risk of that kind of pain. He had given up on being a dad when Mary died and had accepted—or at least grown used to—being alone. Then he met Anna and his thinking started to change. Maybe he wouldn't be alone. Maybe she could be a part of his life. But this pregnancy changed everything. For him, for Anna, and for the two of them as a couple.

Maybe it would have been better if Coogan had never called him and Anna had made her choice alone. Would she have gone the other way?

Jake grimaced and shook away the dark thoughts bubbling in his mind.

He could do this. He wasn't too old. And he wasn't too set in his ways. If she didn't put the baby up for adoption, he could handle it. Would handle it.

He laughed quietly to himself. "Have you convinced yourself, Houser?"

CHAPTER FIFTY-FOUR

Deputy Chief of Patrol Sam Stewart read Houser's update to the Ballard file. Her body had been found partially decomposed in Glenbard. She hadn't run away. She had been abducted and killed and unless they could prove she was abducted somewhere else, the people of Weston would be scared.

Until the killer was caught.

Another update popped up. A supplemental report. Sam's heart started to hammer as soon as he began reading it. Houser had linked Ballard's disappearance to the Belker murders based on a tip letter that alleged a man named Mike had been involved with Belker back then and had taken the Ballard girl. Houser identified this accomplice as high school football legend Mike Nelson. Houser tied Nelson to Belker and put Amy Smith in Nelson's van smoking dope and maybe having sex with him.

On the DNA, Houser had the original lab report that showed the semen found on Smith did not match Belker's cheek swab, but did match the second known sample, the one Sam himself had delivered to Arvind. Houser also had a document Sam's father filed *in court* certifying that the evidentiary DNA matched Belker. Houser even had documentation to show that Sam's father had controlled the forensic department when the lab result came in before it disappeared.

The second known sample must belong to Mike Nelson.

Houser also learned that Nelson had fathered a son—Anthony Patino—with a high school girlfriend named Grace Patino. That was the woman Shaw had talked to at the hair salon!

"Shit!" Sam got up and closed the door. Both Houser and Shaw knew more about what the hell was going on than he did.

He needed to *do* something. He pulled the Woodling complaint file out of his briefcase and looked at the signature he'd forged, shame flashing across his face. He didn't want to do this… to be this guy. But it was all he had. He headed for Arvind's office. If Arvind had read Houser's update, he would see this complaint as the tactic it was. But the chief was not that hands-on, so chances were good he had not read it.

* * *

When Sam explained that he needed to discuss an Internal Affairs matter, Chief Arvind agreed to see him immediately.

"What do you have, Sam?"

"Take a look, Chief." The Woodling complaint and the photos were more powerful than anything Sam could say. He dealt the photos out, first the gash above the eye, then the wrists.

"I can't believe one of our officers did this."

"Not an officer," Sam said. "A detective."

"Who?"

Sam handed over the complaint.

Arvind took his time reading it, shaking his head by the time he got to the end. It was an ugly claim. Houser had mus-cled his way into the guy's house by kicking in the door, resulting in a serious eye injury. Arvind tapped an entry.

"This all happened in Kirwin?"

"Yes, Chief. But in Paget County. South of the mall."

"This happened last year. While the county was handling our internal affairs complaints?"

"Right."

"How was it resolved? I never heard about it."

"Well, that's the issue, Chief. It appears to have been dropped."

"We don't *drop* complaints, Sam."

"I agree, Chief."

"Where did you find it?"

"The file had an unsigned copy of the complaint. It's there at the back. But I found this *signed* copy on the bottom of the drawer under the hanging files holding the other complaints Sheriff Warren's department had handled."

Chief Arvind leaned back. "Jake's cousin."

"That's right," Sam said. He was sure Arvind was thinking exactly what Sam wanted him to think: Sheriff Warren killed the complaint to protect her cousin. "Sergeant Massey talked to the former deputy who investigated the complaint."

Arvind looked at the complaint, then glanced up. "Former?"

"He moved back east, but he says the complaint was credible. He convinced Woodling not to sign it while he tried to get Houser to resign quietly to avoid it becoming public."

"But?"

"Houser called in his union rep and fought it, so Hogan went back out there and got the complaint signed."

Arvind picked up the phone and dialed a number from memory. He leaned back and looked at Sam while waiting for whoever he called to answer.

"Sheriff Warren? I'm putting you on speaker phone. Deputy Chief Stewart has brought me the Woodling complaint filed with your IAD department against Detective Houser last year. Apparently, it was never adjudicated. What can you tell us about it?"

"As I recall, the complainant wasn't credible. In fact, when Hogan, the deputy assigned to it, pushed the man to sign it, he refused. Which meant, technically there was no complaint."

Sam spoke up. "Deputy Hogan says just the opposite. He said *he* believed Woodling's story so went back out and got it signed."

"That's news to me, gentlemen. Deputy Hogan himself recommended the complaint be dropped as No Cause. Our records will show that."

"I'm sure *your* records do—" Sam stopped talking when Chief Arvind held up his hand. Arvind held the complaint up, eying Sam over the top of the document.

"The document I'm holding in my hand *is* signed, Sheriff."

"That's not right."

Arvind gave Sam the hairy eyeball again. "What did you think of the complaint, Sheriff?" Arvind asked.

"I was surprised. It was the only complaint we ever had against Jake."

"Did you ask Jake about it?"

"That would not have been appropriate."

"No. That's right, Sheriff." Arvind looked at Sam. "Any other questions for the Sheriff, Sam?"

"No, sir."

They ended the call and sat quietly. Chief Arvind thumbed the edge of the complaint, eyes boring into Sam's.

"I understand your concern here, Sam. And I share it. There was an apparent conflict that I think meant Bev should have recused herself from handling the complaint at all. To have it die, without being adjudicated or formally withdrawn, just makes it look worse. And now that it's landed with us, we need to make sure that impropriety doesn't stain us."

"Agreed, Chief."

"Adjudicate it. By the book."

Sam left before the chief could change his mind.

CHAPTER FIFTY-FIVE

Eddie woke to find a text message from Penny: *Apology accepted. I believe in you! Can't wait to read your book and know the truth!*

He looked at the text for a long time. She was the one. When he got back to Des Moines, they would be together.

He went out to the motel's front office, which was empty. Maybe the clerk was avoiding him. Eddie filled his travel mug with coffee and took the last three donuts. Writing took energy.

Back in the room he flipped open his laptop. He had two days to deliver a proposal that would convince the publisher he could write a book that would sell. That meant a beginning that sucked the reader in with the promise of a big payoff, and a narrative outline that revealed that payoff.

Eddie's problem was he didn't yet know the complete story. He was especially thin on what was happening now, with Kate Ballard. But he could write around that by focusing on the solid handle he had on what had happened in the past. He had the boogeyman, Mike Nelson, and he had the men in the shadows protecting him—Stewart, Lowe, and Forsyth. And now he had the Weston PD harassing him and violating his civil rights because he was asking questions about Mike Nelson. All good juicy stuff, though none of it *proved* Mike Nelson was the killer or *proved* the three men covered up Nelson's participation to protect their beloved city from the stench of his crimes.

But he had enough to get started. He began by describing the two murders in Weston and the common perception that the same man—Mose Belker—committed them. Then Eddie laid out the young Mose Belker—his parents, his home life, and the claims he was a cat killer. From there he jumped forward, to the Mose Belker who had lived in Iowa, the church-going man, with a wife who loved him. A man beloved by his pastor and the police chief who was in bible study with him. A nice guy, but a nobody.

Eddie pulled his hands off the laptop and flexed them, then leaned back and stretched. That was a solid start. Now he needed to prove Mike Nelson was the killer and that Abe Stewart and friends railroaded the nobody to protect Weston's favored son.

He finished the last donut, showered, dressed, and got moving.

* * *

Eddie left the Mercedes in the parking garage next to city hall, then crossed the street to the Weston Settlement Living History Museum. It was on a large parcel of land that contained dozens of original homes and businesses moved there from across the city, all connected by brick paths that wound through beautifully landscaped grounds. The place crawled with visiting school groups screaming their way between buildings. But the main building, a re-creation of the original Preemption House where Abraham Lincoln once gave a speech, contained a second-floor archive that was blissfully quiet.

Eddie introduced himself to the curator of research who was as eager to help as the librarian Eddie met the day before.

"I'd like to see anything you have on Police Chief Abe Stewart, Weston Business Alliance President Brian Lowe, and Weston Home Builders Association President Jeff Forsyth." Eddie knew something about each of these men but he needed more to make the reader understand *why* they would protect a killer.

The curator's face lit up. "You must be writing about Weston's building boom!"

"That's exactly what I'm interested in." Eddie smiled; every building boom involved money and influence.

And corruption.

The curator showed Eddie to a large table in the corner, then started delivering a stream of magazines, newspapers, city records, and marketing materials.

Eddie started with newspaper profiles of the three men. They had known each other their whole lives, growing up on the same block where this library currently stood. Brian Lowe started his own flooring company, which still existed. Jeff Forsyth had built his father's small lumberyard into the biggest supplier of residential building products in town. Abe Stewart had followed his own father into the police department, rising up to chief, then retired and worked as assistant city manager. Together the three men had also owned a development company that bought up farms and turned them into some of the dozens of subdivisions that spread south and west from downtown.

Eddie whistled. When the girls were being murdered, the three men were heavily invested in Weston and its continued success. Having the town's favored son labeled a rapist and serial killer might have ended the building boom and destroyed them financially.

The marketing materials played up Weston's low crime rate, touting it in every brochure the city put out during the boom years, along with blurbs about the schools, parks, commuting distance to Chicago, and Centennial Beach.

"Here's another brochure," the curator laid down a larger publication, thick and glossy like a magazine. "This went to developers we hoped to lure to town."

This brochure was a lot more detailed. The school section laid out every school's headcount and capacity, the land already designated for new school buildings in the expanding southern and western areas of the city, and the money set aside for their construction.

The crime statistics were equally detailed, broken down by types and neighborhood. It also touted the Weston Police Department's clearance rates and the innovative techniques and equipment it used. Chief Abe Stewart had even started a countywide task force for pooling resources on serious crimes.

Eddie scrolled his focus forward from the time of the murders to when Mose Belker was arrested in 1999. The building boom was over and the focus had turned to redeveloping the downtown. None of the three appeared to have direct stakes in that redevelopment, but they had standing. Reputations. There were pictures of them at every type of social event the town had: Business Alliance luncheons, Fourth of July parades and festivals, Labor Day parades, and a carnival called Last Fling. They'd even judged the annual barbecued ribs contest on multiple occasions.

Eddie pulled out his laptop and opened the document he'd started that morning. With what he'd just learned his narrative outline would slay.

Eddie laid out Weston: its multiple "Best of" awards, the great library, the excellent schools, low crime rate and the phenomenal growth this generated. From there he described the police department: its size, its training excellence, the awards it had won, and its low crime rates.

Then Eddie dove into the police department's behavior since he arrived in town: the runaround with the FOIA requests, pulling him over, posting a plain clothes cop to protect Frank Houser, and, finally, searching Eddie's hotel room.

This direct intimidation was the nail in the Weston PD's coffin. The publisher would undoubtedly use that in its marketing materials—how suburban Shangri-La would go to any lengths to keep its sordid criminal history and corrupt police department buried. Pure gold.

Then he asked the next logical questions: Who in Weston was scared of Eddie getting to the truth and could control the police like this?

Stewart, Lowe, and Forsyth. The local power structure that controlled the town at the time of the murders and still controlled it today.

That should leave the reader burning to know *why* these men would protect a rapist and murderer.

Once that question landed, Eddie asked the reader to wonder *who* the men *would* be willing to protect. Certainly not Belker, a nobody who didn't even live in town anymore. Then he used Donna Larson's letter to introduce his investigation identifying Mike Nelson. Mr. Football. Local hero.

Excellent. Now all he needed was proof that Mike Nelson was the killer. Eddie made copies of the best of the archived materials using the curator's color copier. It was well worth the thirty cents per page. He thanked the curator for his time and walked back to his car.

* * *

On the way, a phrase Eddie just read popped into his head. *Task force.* He'd come across another mention of a police task force sometime in the last few days. Maybe when he was back in Iowa first digging into the case.

He left his car in the parking garage and walked across the covered bridge to the library. He found the same reference librarian who helped him before and she found what he was looking for. According to minutes of a meeting of the Board of Police Commissioners, in 1988 Chief Abe Stewart pulled Weston out of the county-wide task force he had started because "Weston no longer needed the help of neighboring departments and couldn't afford to work on other city's cases."

It sounded like bullshit to Eddie; Abe Stewart just didn't want outsiders in the task force looking at Weston cases anymore. Because he was protecting Mike Nelson.

But what triggered Stewart in 1988?

Eddie flipped through the entire book of meeting minutes and a binder full of police department reporting charts and manpower statistics. He didn't find an answer but he did learn that the current Deputy Chief of the Weston PD patrol unit was named Sam Stewart and there was a Weston detective named Jake Houser.

A few minutes on Google confirmed that Jake Houser was Frank Houser's son and that Sam Stewart was Abe Stewart's son. He found a picture of Jake Houser; he was the cop who'd braced Sam at the old Trinity Landscaping building. The sons, Sam Stewart and Jake Houser, were protecting their fathers. Former Chief Vaughn's suspicion that the detective who called him was dirty looked true.

Diving into the newspaper archives, Eddie learned something even more interesting. The Lachey murder in 1986 was not an isolated case. Four other murders followed it in Paget County within a two-year span.

All unsolved.

CHAPTER FIFTY-SIX

Bev kept checking her watch as she paced. This was taking too long. "When will Judge Mather be back?" she asked the judge's assistant. "I've got a lot going on today."

"As soon as she gets through her court call, Sheriff."

The judge had demanded a face-to-face before she would sign any more search warrants. Bev didn't blame her. Some of their warrant applications had been thin. A bad warrant application meant anything found could not be used at trial. Bev could live with that if it helped get the deadly smack off the street. But a bad warrant also made the judge who approved it look bad and Mather had signed a lot of warrants.

Bev sat down to wait.

The call from Weston's Chief Arvind about the Woodling complaint against Jake had surprised her, especially Sam's implication that she shut down the complaint to protect her cousin. She *had* manipulated the complaint, but not to protect Jake. She'd used the complaint to try to control Jake when he'd come after *her* father. When that failed, she'd buried it because it was generated in circumstances that would not survive close scrutiny and that made her absolutely positive the complaint had never been signed. Which meant the signature Arvind had been looking at was a forgery. That tactic smacked of Abe

Stewart. Was by-the-book Sam getting bent by his father? She knew from her own experience how hard it was to stay on the straight and narrow when it came to what a father had done. Or asked his child to do for him.

"Sheriff? The judge is ready to see you now."

CHAPTER FIFTY-SEVEN

Jake leaned back in his Mustang's seat and rubbed his face with both hands. Every notification was different. Kate Ballard's mom had been sure from the first day Kate was missing that she was dead so had been ready, and stoic, to start. But when she asked Jake where her daughter had been found and he was honest with her—in the forgotten wastelands behind an industrial park—the tears had come. Then the rage.

His phone buzzed with a message. Levi: *I've found something. Call me!*

Jake decided to stop by instead. Coogan's office was only a few minutes away. After he talked to Levi maybe Coog would have time to talk about the baby and help Jake get a handle on his own feelings.

As he parked on the curb down from Coogan's office his phone buzzed with another text. Erin: *DC Braff had me look into access to your supplemental report. He wanted you to know that it was accessed by Sam Stewart's computer using Sergeant Massey's credentials ten minutes after your update this morning. Sam then ran straight to Arvind's office. But it must not have been about the report because Arvind <u>still</u> hasn't read it.*

Jake smiled. His report about Mike Nelson, the DNA tests, and Abe Stewart's lies had stoked the fires. But either

Arvind was too smart to pull up the report on his own computer and create that trail, or Sam had talked to him about something else. Time would tell.

Coogan wasn't in the office but Levi's news was worth the visit.

"That murder Larson's dad went up for? Out in the county? The one she wanted to pin on Mike Nelson or Belker?"

"Yes."

"That wasn't the only murder up there. Over a two-year span five young women were abducted, raped, murdered, and dumped through the north half of Paget County. Only that one was ever solved."

"Where are you getting this?"

"Newspaper archives."

"Were the murders ever linked up?"

Levi shook his head. "But I heard a radio report on a new body found off North Avenue last night and that sounds like the exact same dump site as the murder Larson's dad went to prison for."

"That was Kate Ballard," Jake said.

Levi went pale. "Okay."

"Send me what you put together on those five."

Levi worked at his keyboard, finishing with a flourish. "There you go. Note that all five happened after Mike Nelson came back from the army."

"He came home in what, '85?"

"That's right."

"What about while Nelson was gone?"

"No unsolved murders of young women in the county."

Circumstantial, but informative. "Belker was living in Iowa during that time, right? Less than two hours away."

"He was," Levi said. His color was returning and he sat up straighter. "I checked and there were no unsolved murders of young women out around the river."

Serial killers didn't take time off unless they were interrupted. By going to prison or going into the military.

Jake went into the conference room and stood at the wide window looking out over the Riverwalk as he called an old friend.

"This is Major Kotzan." Mark Kotzan was a lawyer with the Judge Advocate General's office at Fort Bragg. They'd been friends since middle school.

"Marcus, I need your help."

"Again? I'm starting to think the Weston PD should put me on the payroll."

"I'm working a case tied into a pair of murders back in the eighties and—"

"Belker?"

"Right, but—"

"Isn't he still in prison?"

"Yes, but there might have been another man involved back then. And he might be responsible for a victim found last night."

"Who?"

"Mike Nelson."

A long silence. "Mr. Football?"

"Exactly."

"And you're calling me because he joined the army?"

"While he was gone, there were no murders. There were five murders over a couple years after he came home."

"Then what?" Kotzan asked. "He just quit? Like that BTK killer in Kansas?"

"It's possible."

"You want to know if he controlled himself while he was with us?"

"Yes." Jake waited. Kotzan was not susceptible to argument or begging. If he decided to compromise his ethics and give Jake information on Nelson's service, he'd do it on his own.

A long silence, followed by a sigh. "Linda Brown was a friend of my oldest sister."

"Emily?"

"She barely left the house for a year."

"I didn't know that. I'm sorry."

"This will have to be off the record. Not documented *anywhere*. Until you send me a warrant."

"Agreed."

The soft clacking of computer keys came over the phone. Within a minute the clacking stopped. "Nelson was picked up while overseas on suspicion of sexual assault. We negotiated his freedom and rushed him out of the service. We even gave him an honorable discharge to keep it quiet."

Silence as they both absorbed this news. Mike Nelson, Mr. Football, was not the golden boy of memory. Mike Nelson was a sexual predator.

"Thanks, Mark."

"Let me know how this shakes out."

"I will."

Jake jogged back to his car and hustled south to see Belker.

CHAPTER FIFTY-EIGHT

Eddie was juiced. Five murders in two years. The only one solved was the Lachey case against James Larson, Donna Larson's father. Eddie pulled out his phone and shot off a text to his agent: *Found a second string of unsolved murders that were never connected to these.*

Within ten seconds the little dots popped up and then her response: *This book is going to change everything for you!*

Eddie smiled. He liked his new agent.

He pulled out his laptop, clicked into the library's Wi-Fi, and started googling each of the unsolved cases. But a flood of after school groups suddenly poured into the library and their noise was overwhelming. He went to the reference desk and was able to reserve a quiet study room. There he read dozens of stories spanning the years of the murders and the long string of follow-up articles each murder generated. The same reporter wrote the best of them: Marlene Max of the Chicago Tribune. He knew that name. He'd read her articles while researching earlier books and had even met her at a journalism conference years ago. Hopefully, she'd remember him *and* not hold anything against him. As a young journalist he'd often gotten carried away with free booze.

Eddie called the Tribune. Max had retired nearly five years before, but she wasn't hiding; Eddie found her within minutes and she answered her listed number when he called it.

"Hey… Maxine." A sudden memory that he'd called her Maxine all one evening and she hadn't corrected him until he was so drunk he refused to stop doing it.

"My name's not… Is this Eddie Shaw?"

He laughed. They caught up for a few minutes before he got to it. "I'm calling about the articles you wrote on the five women murdered in Paget County in the mid-eighties."

"I remember them," she said, her voice suddenly wary. Journalists didn't like to share information on stories. "What's your angle?"

Eddie didn't like sharing information, either. But if he didn't, this conversation would end before it really started. "I'm looking at a link to a pair of murders in Weston earlier—"

"You can't pin these five on Mose Belker."

Her certainty gave Eddie pause. "Why not?"

She was silent for so long Eddie started to worry that her journalist instincts were kicking in and she would refuse to tell him more. After a sigh she said, "I have no interest in polluting my life with that kind of depravity anymore, Eddie. I'm a grandmother now, and that's all I want to be."

Eddie waited. It was coming.

"Mose Belker had alibis for those murders."

"And the alibi was… ?"

"What the hell," she laughed. "His time cards at the window factory. I have copies if you want them."

"I do." Eddie gave her his email address. "What else can you tell me?"

"You're an investigator. At least ask me some questions."

So he did. She had worked all five of the murders hard, in the eighties and again in '99 when Belker confessed, hounding the assigned detectives and begging her editors for more column inches and front-page photos to keep the murders in the public eye.

"The articles generated lots of phone calls to the hotline the task force had put together, but nothing came from any of them."

"Is this the same task force the Weston police chief started in the seventies then pulled his town out of back in '88?"

"That's right," she said. "You have a theory about that?"

That, he wouldn't share. "Did the task force consider whether the killings were the work of a serial killer?"

"Of course. But these five weren't like Belker's two. Only one was a stabbing. The others were strangulation and blunt force trauma."

"But all the murdered women were nabbed while walking or bicycling along empty roads after dark."

"Which could have meant they were random crimes of opportunity."

Eddie saw her point. "None of the five women were from Weston or found in Weston."

"That's right."

"Weston is the largest town in Paget County by both population and land area—back then and now. So that seems more than a coincidence. And those areas to the west and south of downtown were rural back then. Plenty of room for dropping bodies."

"Like where the two Belker victims ended up?"

"That's right."

"So, your conclusion is that one man killed all seven girls and after the first two he stayed away from Weston."

"Exactly," Eddie said. The killer—Nelson—had been protected by Stewart and his pals in Weston, but didn't want to test that protection so when he came back from the army he moved his 'operation' outside the city limits. Yeah, that worked. Or better yet, maybe Stewart had made a deal with the killer to stay out of Weston. That implied Stewart knew the man would keep killing. Was that pushing it too far? Maybe.

"That one man can't be Mose Belker."

"Right."

"But you have a theory," she said.

"More than a theory."

A long silence while she worked it out. "You think someone in Weston knew the real killer and protected him."

Eddie said nothing, wanting to see where she would go.

"Someone who had something to lose if it came out who the killer was."

Another silence that Eddie broke with a prompt. "And?"

"And that someone had the power to protect him. Who and why, Eddie?"

"Those are the big questions, Maxine."

"Abe Stewart," she said. "He's the one who pulled Weston out of the task force. You think that was about protecting this guy, don't you?"

Eddie said nothing.

"You'll have another best seller if you play this right."

"Connect me with the cops handling the open cases and I'll put you in the book."

"I'll give you the names but only if you promise *not* to put me in your book."

Eddie spent the next hour calling the detectives handling the cold cases without learning anything new. Two refused to talk and the detective handling the county cases was tied up on a different task force.

CHAPTER FIFTY-NINE

Eddie's conversation with retired Tribune reporter Marlene "Maxine" Max energized him. Her quick mind had latched on to the same thread he was pulling: someone in the Weston power structure had protected the killer. Eddie was sure, as Maxine had been, the protector was Abe Stewart with the help and support of his cronies.

Eddie parked outside the restaurant and waited. A simple Google search had revealed that Abe Stewart was inside lunching with his lead team, which the Business Alliance website said was a cross-marketing group for area businessmen. This town loved doing business.

Eddie had plenty of practice, so waited patiently.

A thin stream of men in business suits started trickling out. A break, a trio of women, then Abe Stewart in khakis and a brown leather jacket cut like a sport coat. Small and intense, he walked quickly, head up, wearing a confident smile.

If Abe Stewart was behind the cover-up and the Weston PD's harassment, talking to him would be like kicking a hornet's nest. Eddie rubbed damp palms on his thighs, started his phone's recording app and put it in his shirt pocket. He got out of his car and cut across the parking lot to intercept Stewart. The retired chief spotted him and stopped; cops are always aware of their surroundings. Eddie had seen the same thing many times before.

"You must be the writer," Stewart said.

"I'd like to ask you a few questions about Mose Belker."

"Let's sit in my car. This wind has a bite to it." Stewart led the way without waiting for an answer and Eddie followed. He had little choice if he wanted to talk, and was impressed with how smoothly Stewart moved the conversation to his own territory. Stewart drove a Cadillac coupe. Shiny and new.

Eddie paused with a hand on the door. He cast a look around and saw several other small groups walking through the parking lot. A man yelled a greeting to Stewart and Eddie relaxed. He'd been seen; Stewart would do nothing to him now. Not here, anyway. He got in. The car smelling richly of its fine leather seats.

"Go ahead," Stewart said, once the doors were closed.

Eddie started with a hand grenade. "You fired Chief Vaughn on the pretext of a sexual harassment complaint."

"Not a pretext." Stewart started the car, the radio blaring into a loud report on a Cubs game. Stewart turned it down.

"I talked to the complainant. She—"

"This will go faster if you don't lie to me."

"How many people did Mose Belker kill?"

"He confessed to two," Stewart said.

"But may have killed more?"

"There were four other murders out in the county after Lachey."

"Mose Belker had alibis for those four murders, and for Lachey."

Stewart's face froze, then his eyes narrowed as he searched Eddie's face to see if he was telling the truth. When he found it, his expression registered panic. Belker's alibis hadn't come out until after his arrest in 1999—eleven years after Stewart had pulled Weston out of the task force. So Stewart had not known about this vulnerability in the story he had planned to push on Eddie.

"Did Mike Nelson have alibis?" Eddie asked

Stewart licked his lips. He opened his mouth, but closed it again without saying anything.

"Yes, I know about Mr. Football and that you and your buddies protected him when he raped Grace Patino. That's where it all started, didn't it? You protected Mike Nelson again when he killed Smith and Brown so when he came back from the army he moved his raping and murdering outside Weston."

"You've got nothing."

Attacking Eddie's evidence instead of denying the accusation was a guilty man's move.

"I know the DNA results prove Mose Belker didn't kill Amy Smith."

Stewart grimaced and didn't answer. He tried to hold Eddie's gaze, but shook his head and looked away. "You're bluffing, Mr. Shaw."

Eddie held his breath. He could spin that evasive lack of a denial in any direction he wanted to. Time to end this before Stewart said something that closed off the opportunity. Eddie opened his door and got out, but couldn't help leaning back in for a parting shot. "I will get to the bottom of this, Mr. Stewart. Call me if you want to get on the right side of it."

He slammed the door before Stewart could say anything else and quickstepped back to his car. He pulled out his phone and checked the recording app. It had all come in loud and clear. He owned that old bastard.

CHAPTER SIXTY

Jake spent the drive to the prison thinking about the Weston Police Department cover-up to protect Mike Nelson from a murder charge. A cover-up that may have cost the lives of five more women in the eighties, and, if Mose Belker could be believed, Kate Ballard.

Abe Stewart was clearly the leader of it all. Chief Arvind, only a patrolman and evidence tech back then, had definitely been surprised to hear about the DNA match. Realizing now that he'd been a dupe back in '99 is what had made him respond so defensively. Jake had hoped Arvind would think it over and come clean. But Sam running to him this morning after reading Jake's report might mean Arvind was Sam's ally. Or at least that Sam thought their interests were aligned.

Against Jake.

The Chief of Police and Deputy Chief of Patrol were a formidable pair. Jake's boss, Braff, would be on Jake's side. But not until things came to a head and Sam and Arvind committed themselves to a course of action that left them no wiggle room.

Entering the prison for this second visit to see Belker was easier. Maybe a person could get used to this place. Guards must, or they couldn't show up day after day.

When Jake finally made it through security, they put him in the same interview room, which now smelled of bleach.

But it still felt the same. As if the air had weight.

He sat down to wait, but it didn't take long.

The guard chained Belker's hands to the table again and left, never even looking at Jake. Jake braced himself for the thunderous echo when the door slammed shut but this guard eased it closed without a sound.

Belker spoke first. "He isn't going to last long," Today his eyes were clear of whatever demons had darkened them last time Jake visited and looked blue like they were supposed to. "Heard his uncle's the warden. I don't think getting the kid this job is doing him any good. Too timid." Belker squared the bible up to the edge of the table. "Why are you back, Detective?"

"You raped and murdered five more young women in the late eighties."

"I moved to Iowa in '82."

Jake shrugged. "It's only a two-hour drive."

Belker grimaced and his hands swept over to the bible, the chain dragging across the metal table top. He rubbed the embossed cover. "It wasn't me."

"All five were identical to your two in every way that matters."

"I'm telling you—"

"If you didn't kill those five, then you didn't kill Smith and Brown. The same man killed all seven women. And it wasn't you. Your DNA did not match the DNA found on Smith's body."

Belker stopped rubbing the bible.

But he didn't quote from it. Jake realized Belker hadn't offered up any bible quotes. So, it wasn't just his eyes that were different today. Maybe he was on medication and hadn't taken it before Jake's prior visit. Maybe Jake could get through to this Mose Belker. It was worth a try.

"Amy Smith was your friend," Jake said. "For twenty years people have believed you raped her. I talked to the woman who runs the restaurant where you two worked together and she blames herself for Amy's murder because she gave you that job and you met Amy there. Nadine Drilling blames herself for Amy's murder because she was Amy's best friend and was out of town the weekend Amy died. Amy's mother blames Amy's dad because he let her take that restaurant job where she met you and because he forced her to ride her bike to work. Don't they deserve the real truth? That Amy was murdered by Mike Nelson and it was not connected to her job at the restaurant? That whatever your role in Amy's death, you yourself didn't rape her?"

Belker shifted in his chair and Jake knew that last point had hit home. Belker did care what people thought about him. Or at least what they thought about how he had treated his friend. Belker looked up at Jake and bit his lip, but said nothing.

"Help me find Mike Nelson and I'll make sure they learn the truth."

Belker was still. His gaze dropped to the table. He pulled the bible in front of him and placed both hands on it, one over the other.

"The truth will alleviate their guilt and change how they think of you."

"You'll tell them the truth no matter what I do."

"Only if you tell me about Nelson."

Belker shook his head. "We have access to the internet in here, you know. I looked you up and learned enough to know you'll tell the truth without me making any deal with you. Justice, and all that."

"You've read me wrong, Belker. Justice doesn't drive me; vengeance does. I want to punish the man who killed Amy Smith. I don't care about you."

Belker said nothing.

"We found Kate Ballard's body last night. Exactly where Lachey's body was found. And her killer left behind DNA."

"I don't know anything—"

"You told Donna Larson that Mike Nelson abducted Kate Ballard."

"I thought… I thought he'd told me. But I… " Belker grabbed the bible and hugged it to his chest. "I've done bad things and I deserve being here. This book helps me deal with that, but it doesn't… " Belker stabbed the side of his head with a finger. "It doesn't quiet what's up here. And what's up here isn't always the same as what's in front of me."

Belker was describing hallucinations. "You thought Mike Nelson told you he took Kate Ballard."

Belker nodded.

"In a dream?"

"I thought he came here to visit me."

Jake's pulse accelerated so fast he had to take a deep breath to stay oxygenated. "But someone did come visit you. Your hallucination, your mistake, was thinking it was Mike Nelson."

"Looked just like him. That's what I thought, anyway."

Jake needed to see the prison's visitor log.

CHAPTER SIXTY-ONE

Deputy Chief of Patrol Sam Stewart dove straight into researching the fastest way to use the Woodling complaint to get Houser off the streets. Procedure was cumbersome—state law, department rules, prior hearing decisions, and the detective union's contract—all applied. It was the kind of intellectual puzzle he normally loved, but not today. After two hours of careful analysis Sam found the fastest path to be a summary procedure that allowed him to suspend Houser immediately and hold his due process hearing within the next seven days.

With Woodling dead there would be no hearing, but that wasn't his goal. Delay was the goal. Seven days should be long enough that Braff would reassign Diggs to Houser's cases. Sam at least had a shot at working with her. Smearing Houser might even taint Braff enough for him to lose his job, opening his slot up for Diggs and assuring Sam of Arvind's job when the chief retired.

If Sam could survive this mess himself.

Unfortunately, the suspension could not begin until Sam notified both Houser and his superior officer in person.

Sam ignored Braff's secretary and walked right thorough the open door and closed it behind him.

"Sam." Braff stood and came around his desk. "What's up?"

"I need a few minutes. A Professional Standards issue."

Braff pointed to his guest chairs. "Please have a seat." Braff sat down behind his desk and closed a binder he'd been reading.

Sam sat, then leaned forward and laid the photos out one by one on the desk, letting them tell the story. The tactic had worked on Arvind, but Braff appeared completely unfazed. When the last photo was in front of him—the ugliest one, showing Woodling's fractured eye socket and the gaping wound—Braff looked up.

"This again?"

Sam balked. Warren had not mentioned that Braff knew about the complaint. Sam pulled the complaint out and put it on top of the photos. "I know you believe in your detectives, but we need to take this seriously. It shows—"

"The sheriff took it very seriously when the complaint was made and assigned it to a special investigator. I took it very seriously when that investigator brought it here to my office. Detective Houser took it very seriously and turned it over to his union rep. Then the complainant—" Braff glanced down at the form. "Woodling. Dropped it. Never even signed it."

"I don't want to speculate on what happened back then, but when Deputy Hogan re-interviewed him, Woodling signed it." Sam reached across the desk and tapped the form. "The disciplinary investigation should not have been dropped. It makes the result look tainted."

Braff snatched up the form and looked at it. He frowned. "Did you talk to—"

"Chief Arvind and I both talked to Sheriff Warren."

Braff frowned. He had doubts, clearly, but would he get in the way?

"We need to be above board about this," Sam said. "We need to start over and do it right to protect the integrity of our department and of the process."

"I'll advise Detective Houser you've reopened the investigation and—"

"I will contact him myself, Deputy Chief. I'm following the summary suspension procedure so we can do this quickly. Dragging it out would only attract attention we want to avoid for the sake of both the department and Detective Houser's reputation."

Now Braff smiled. "No."

Sam didn't like the smile. "What do you mean, no?"

Braff slid the complaint across the desk. "I won't hide something this serious. We'll do it publicly."

"Chief Arvind and I already spoke and he agreed to my approach."

"I'm sure Detective Houser will request a public hearing as is his right."

* * *

Sam closed his office door and sat down heavily behind his desk, his legs wobbly. Step one was completed, but Braff had surprised him with wanting the proceeding to be public. The signature he'd forged would not survive public scrutiny. Did Braff somehow know that?

The answer dawned on Sam—Braff had read Houser's report and knew Sam's father was dirty and now assumed that Sam was too.

Damn it! But Sam still had Arvind on his side. Thank god his father had corrupted him with that DNA test back in '99.

Sam forged ahead. He typed up a message for Houser on the intra-office system: *Please report to Deputy Chief Stewart's office immediately.* His hand trembled as he hit send. Houser would not take this lightly. Sam was good at confrontations when he was in the right. Holier than thou, his dad used to say. But Sam wasn't sure he could pull up that same stridency for this.

His door flew open, but it wasn't Houser. It was Detective Callie Diggs, Houser's union rep.

CHAPTER SIXTY-TWO

Eddie found the other two members of the Weston power trinity in less than twenty minutes. Forsyth thought himself fascinating and kept up a near constant stream of social media posts about where he was, what he was doing, and who he was doing it with. Right now, he was at the Riverwalk Community Center playing dominoes with Lowe.

Eddie had walked past the center when he visited Belker's old neighborhood so knew exactly where it was. He parallel parked along Jackson. Before going inside, he set his phone to record and stuck it in his shirt pocket. Old white men who had lived long lives of privilege were liable to say just about anything. But they would deny it just as quickly when someone pointed out how crazy they sounded. A recording killed such claims quickly.

The center was in what to Eddie looked like a Frank Lloyd Wright style stucco building with long lines, multi-paned windows, and a run of stacked grey flagstone along its base.

The interior was all tile and hard surfaces. Eddie followed the signs upstairs and the click of domino tiles to the game room. It was a bright, open space with groups of senior citizens sitting around tables playing cards and dominos. Someone shouted "Uno" from the corner. Thanks to Forsyth's social media posts Eddie knew both men were wearing red cardigans and found them quickly.

He pulled out an empty chair at their table and sat down uninvited. Lowe to the left, bald and thin with a flapping waddle and big teeth. Forsyth to the right—a full head of silver hair and big glasses, his belly pushing against the front of his sweater.

"Who are you?" Lowe asked.

"Eddie Shaw. I'd like to ask you some questions about Mose Belker and Mike Nelson."

Lowe looked across the table at his friend. "This is the guy Abe told us about."

"Warned us about is more like it," Forsyth said, shaking his head.

Clearly, he had not liked getting the warning. It implied he couldn't handle himself and he was a man who was sure he could handle himself. And now, maybe, he'd want to prove that. This was his town and his turf and he was playing a relaxing game in the company of his lifelong friend. Eddie could not have imagined a time or place that would make the men more likely to talk.

"Tell me about Mike Nelson."

"Mike Nelson is a legend in this town. You wouldn't believe the crowds at his football games. Tickets were resold for a hundred dollars."

"That's a fact," said Forsyth. "I sold some myself."

Lowe laughed. "My niece worked in the athletic office and got us a big block for every game. We did very well."

"Back-to-back state championships," Eddie said. "That must have been something."

"It certainly was."

"So, when he raped Grace Patino you swept it under the rug."

Lowe slapped a tile down loudly. "That old rumor slurs Grace and Anthony as much as it does Mike."

"That's exactly right," Forsyth said.

These old men talked like they were living in *The Scarlet Letter*. "How do you figure that?"

Lowe leaned back in his chair and looked at Eddie like he was an idiot. "Can't you see that rumor calls her a damaged woman and her son a bastard?"

"It calls Mike Nelson a rapist."

"If that was true, why didn't he go to jail?"

"Because you and Abe Stewart made sure he didn't. You three ran the town back then."

"Not just then," Lowe said under his breath.

Eddie hoped his phone caught that. It had a good microphone, so maybe.

"Mike Nelson killed Amy Smith," Eddie said.

"Mose Belker was the bad apple, Mr. Shaw."

"Did you know the detective who got Belker's confession took a DNA sample off him to compare to the DNA found on Amy Smith?"

"Of course we know that."

"That DNA test proved Mose Belker did *not* kill Amy Smith." Abe Stewart's reaction when Eddie made this allegation convinced him this was true.

Lowe looked across the table at Forsyth, but neither said a word. Another soft confirmation the DNA did not match Belker. How much further could Eddie take them?

"Did Abe tell you who the DNA *did* match?"

"Mike Nelson did not kill anyone," Lowe said.

Eddie almost smiled at where Lowe's mind had immediately gone. Did he *know* the DNA matched Nelson, or just suspect it?

"Listen, Mr. Shaw." Forsyth leaned toward Eddie, his voice dropping into a low rasp. "That Mose Belker was a goddamn bad influence."

"Because he was black?" Eddie threw the possibility out to see if anyone else in town believed what Belker's racist old neighbor did.

"Is that old witch that lived next to them still alive?" Lowe jumped in, stabbing a finger at Eddie. "Belker wasn't any blacker than you so you can't blame his race for what he did. He was just plain bad. We never did figure out why an outstanding young man like Mike even talked to the little fucker, but we fixed it way back in '82."

"By driving Belker out of town."

"Damn right. And we sent Mike off to join the army. Came back a new man."

"And started killing women outside Weston city limits," Eddie said. "Mose Belker had alibis for those county killings. Mike Nelson did not."

"That's not—" Lowe caught himself and leaned back.

Forsyth took up the denial. "Mike Nelson never killed anyone."

"Maybe you want to double check that story with Abe Stewart."

"It's not a goddamn story."

Eddie left them there, staring after him. As soon as he got outside Eddie listened to the recording on his phone. He'd captured everything, Even Forsyth's admission that the three still ran the town.

He was going to bury these geezers.

CHAPTER SIXTY-THREE

Jake texted both Erin and Levi from the prison parking lot: *Who is Anthony Patino and how is he linked to Mose Belker and Mike Nelson?* Patino was the only visitor Mose Belker had received other than Donna Larson, so had to be the man Belker had confused with being Mike Nelson. Hell, maybe it was Mike Nelson. The man had disappeared for thirty years so could easily have changed his name.

While driving back from the prison, Jake received a text message from Deputy Chief of Patrol Sam Stewart: *Please report to Deputy Chief Stewart's office immediately*. Coming straight at Jake instead of going through Braff meant Sam was using his role as head of Professional Standards to protect his dad. Maybe he'd talked Arvind into filing an insubordination complaint against Jake. Which would confirm that Sam and Arvind were working together.

He pulled into the station's parking lot and was opening his door when he got a text that confirmed his suspicion. It was from Callie, who also happened to be his union rep: *CALL ME RIGHT NOW! Don't come to the station!*

He closed the car door and called Erin to see what was happening at the station. Her desk was in the thick of things on the command staff corridor and she had the best network in the building.

Erin answered. "Have you talked to Callie?"

"I got a text—"

"Call her right now."

"First, tell me what happened after Sam Stewart went in to see Chief Arvind this morning."

"A couple hours later Stewart walked in on Deputy Chief Braff."

"Which means Arvind is supporting what Sam is doing," Jake said, thinking out loud. Braff's play was working. Arvind was going to hang himself with Sam.

"I think so. As soon as Sam left his office, DC Braff had me call Callie as your union rep. It's about the Woodling complaint."

Woodling! A year ago, back when the Sheriff's Office handled complaints against Weston cops, Woodling had claimed Jake had beaten him. It was bullshit and Callie killed the complaint. She could probably kill it again. Jake doubted the union's contract with the city allowed a second bite at the apple. But it did mean Sam was taking the gloves off.

"I'll call Callie," Jake said. "What have you found on Anthony Patino?"

"He's a lifelong Weston resident. Lives with his mom in a little house on Laird. Works at his mom's hair salon on Washington. No criminal record. No apparent connection to Mike Nelson or Mose Belker. He's too young to have known either of them."

"Stay on it."

Jake then immediately called Callie, wondering if Braff had let her in on the whole story with the Stewarts.

Callie said, "Don't come to the station."

"Erin told me."

"Stewart dredged up that Woodling complaint but suddenly it's signed. When I met with Deputy Hogan on it last year it was not signed and I took a photo at the time just to prove it. I threw that in Stewart's face and he told me to call Hogan if I had any questions. So Hogan is in on it."

"Didn't Hogan move back east last year?"

"He did."

"What about talking to Woodling?"

"I'll go there if I have to, but a guy like that could say anything."

"Agreed."

"Anyway, I had a preliminary meeting with Stewart. Can you believe he went straight to Braff and tried to cut me out? I'm still working it, but for now even his interpretation of the summary suspension rules require him to give you face-to-face notice. So avoid him."

"I just got a departmental system message to go see him."

"Ignore it," she said. "Can you believe this?"

He could. They were scared; Arvind, Sam, and Abe. A formidable trio. But they would not win. "Stick to the complaint, Callie. Don't go off looking at why it's coming up now or who's pushing it."

"Braff said almost exactly the same thing."

Which meant Braff didn't tell her the whole story.

"If you guys would tell me the why and who I wouldn't have to go off looking for them," Callie said.

"You need to play this straight and knowing the why and who would make that impossible."

Callie paused. "I'd make you promise to tell me the whole truth when this is over, but the last time you made me that promise you didn't keep it."

She was right. "Thanks, Callie."

Jake started the Mustang and sat with the engine running. He needed to talk to Anthony Patino. Belker had fingered his visitor, the one he'd thought was Mike Nelson, as confessing to Kate Ballard's abduction. That visitor was Anthony Patino, a man too young to be Mike Nelson with a new name. But with Sam Stewart out to suspend Jake, he had to stay out of the man's grasp until Callie had that threatened suspension handled. Talking to Anthony Patino would have to wait.

* * *

While Callie worked on quashing the suspension threat and Levi and Erin worked to develop background on Anthony Patino, Jake got out of town. He drove north to talk to the detectives handling the four cold cases Levi had discovered. Two of the cases were with the county, one was in Poplar Grove, and the fourth was in Lynn Stream. He started there because it was the farthest away.

He lucked out and hooked up with the cold case detective immediately. But calling that murder a cold case was being generous. The assigned detective hadn't looked at it in three years. But he didn't hide that fact and let Jake read the murder book.

When Mose Belker confessed to the Smith and Brown murders in 1999, the detective took a look, but Belker had an alibi—a time card from his factory job was in the book with the detective's notes on interviewing the factory's personnel director.

Mike Nelson's name was not in the file and there was no mention of the killer taking a trophy.

Jake also had luck when he got to Poplar Grove, but the detective handling that cold case insisted on sitting with Jake as he went through the book. He was an old-timer and a talker. This was distracting, but his back-in-my-day monologue pulled Jake's attention away from reading the book.

"Say that again?"

"I said your chief started the task force so it's weird you guys aren't in it anymore."

"Weston used to be in the Major Crimes Task Force?"

"That's what I'm saying. Your guy started it. Stewart."

"Abe Stewart?"

"Yeah. Same guy who pulled you out of it in the late eighties."

Jake mulled that over. The late eighties. The second known DNA sample was dated 1988. Maybe Stewart pulled Weston out of the task force to limit the number of eyes on what he was doing.

Jake kept working through the book and stopped when he found Belker's name.

"What caught your eye?" The detective leaned over the table to see what Jake was looking at.

"When Mose Belker confessed to the Lachey murder you took a look at him."

"For this and every sex crime we had open. But he lived two hours away and worked a lot of well-documented overtime. He was clean of them all."

"It looks like he's as close as you've ever come to a solid suspect."

"Random crimes are like that. If we don't get lucky with a witness or forensics—that's getting more likely every day—then you're about done. You know how that works."

Jake knew *exactly* how that worked. "I don't see anything in here about the killer take a trophy."

"He might have. The parents said no, but her boyfriend said she'd been wearing his class ring, which wasn't on her body. He had a rock-solid alibi, by the way."

Jake frowned. These visits were not getting him closer to the truth. But they had to be done. He made a note of the class ring.

"What brought you here?"

"Nothing concrete," Jake said.

The detective leaned forward, his coffee breath spilling over Jake. "Listen. I'd love to be able to tell her parents that we got the guy who did this to their daughter. They come in here twice a year to go over our progress. You know how hard it is to make a case this cold sound active? I mean I look at it and put the case details through the databases, but I can't just keep re-interviewing everyone."

The pain in his voice was palpable and familiar.

"I *do* know," Jake said. "But I have nothing for you." He left the man there with the murder book in his hands, his gaze locked on the victim's name on the cover. Jake knew the haunted look in the detective's eyes because he often saw it in his own mirror.

The last two cold cases were with the sheriff's department because the bodies were found on county land. The sheriff's office was in the county complex on County Farm Road. Jake parked and badged his way inside and walked up to the detective squad room without needing an escort. He'd attended enough cross-department meetings here to know where to go.

Detective Anderson was assigned both cases. Jake had only met the man a few times but knew he was competent and diligent.

Jake stopped at Anderson's desk. "On your way to see your cousin?" Anderson asked.

"I'm here to learn about two of your cold cases." Jake gave him the names.

"I can tell you, or let you look at the books."

"How about both?"

Anderson walked them to a small glass-walled conference room that smelled of coffee and donuts. They sat down at the small round table and Anderson laid out both cases very succinctly.

"Did you look at Mose Belker for these two?"

"Of course, but Belker had solid alibis."

"And you got his time cards and that was that."

"We also went out there—I was the junior man on that team back then. We talked to Belker's boss and co-workers and the personnel officer. We also examined the time card system and another set of documentation that tracks each worker's production. Belker was definitely there when the time card said he was."

"Any other suspects?"

Anderson frowned. "No. We put all our local known perverts in the box but got nothing."

"Can I see the murder books now?"

"Jake?" Sheriff Bev Warren stood in the doorway wearing her tactical browns complete with a heavily laden equipment belt.

Anderson and Jake both stood. "Hey, Bev."

Bev smiled, then looked at her detective, who explained: "Detective Houser wanted to talk about our two cold cases from the eighties."

Bev's eyebrows went up "Were you able to help him?"

"I'm just heading over to get the murder books now." Anderson left the room.

Bev stepped inside and sat down. She rested her forearms on the table, hands flat, fingers interlaced. Her 'tell-me-everything' pose.

CHAPTER SIXTY-FOUR

Deputy Chief of Patrol Sam Stewart paced in front of his office window. He had not anticipated that Houser would get his union rep involved so quickly. But Diggs couldn't really do anything until the hearing and she'd left his office when he convinced her of that.

A knock on his door. "Come in."

"You wanted me, Deputy Chief?," Massey stood in the doorway.

"Come in and close the door."

Massey entered and closed the door behind him. "I called Houser in on a summary suspension but he's ignoring it. I want you to go out and bring him in."

"Absolutely, boss." Massey shifted on his feet. "What's my authority?"

That was the problem. There was no rule that authorized arresting Houser, but he might not know that.

"How about I put out the word and when my guys find Houser, I take you to him?"

Sam frowned. Again with *my guys*. But Massey's idea had a lot less potential for blowback if—

The door burst open. Callie Diggs. Again!

Massey turned to face her, widening his stance to block her from approaching Sam's desk.

Sam stood. "I'm in a meeting, Detective Diggs."

"Out of my way, Massey." Diggs lunged and when Massey moved to block her, she spun the other way and stepped easily around him.

Damn it! "You're dismissed, Sergeant."

Sam waited until the door closed, then: "Barging in here—"

"You screwed up, Sam." Diggs held up a thick softbound book.

"It's Deputy Chief." Sam recognized the book: the disciplinary hearing manual. He checked his credenza, but his copy was still there. Diggs came around his desk and stepped so close to him that he backed away, the back of his knees hitting his chair. He fell into it. "We already discussed this, Detective. Until the hearing you have no—"

"There won't be a hearing." She slapped the book on the desk, open to a page with a single sentence highlighted.

CHAPTER SIXTY-FIVE

"The cold cases from the eighties?" Bev had been briefed on her department's cold cases when she took the job, but had never read the files or spent much time looking at the detective division. *If it ain't broke, don't fix it.* "Do you think they're connected to what was in Donna Larson's letter?"

"I made it clear to Doug Rieser when he gave me that letter that I would not report to him, or you, about my investigation."

"But now you're looking at two of my cases. That changes things."

He frowned as he examined her logic. A small nod. "We've identified Larson's mysterious *Mike* as Mike Nelson. He—"

"Mr. Football? *That* Mike Nelson?" Her dad had been a football junkie and compared every quarterback at the high school to him. "You're sure?"

"Yes. Nelson was a crew boss for Trinity and he hired Belker to help lay the brick walkways on the Riverwalk project."

"Ah… the concrete work the letter mentioned."

"Exactly," he said.

She had not seen that coming. "Could Mike Nelson actually be the real killer?"

"I believe so. Maybe alone, maybe with Belker."

"And he's good for our cold cases, too?"

"They fit his timeline and loosely fit the MO of the Belker murders—young women snatched off the roadside, raped, murdered, and dumped."

Solving two cold cases was a result she had not anticipated. Closure, and justice, for two more families.

"By the way," Jake said. "There's a writer named Shaw sniffing around. He came out to my place, the old Trinity building, pretending to be writing an article about the Riverwalk."

"That's the first I've heard of it," Bev said. But she didn't think a writer would get in the way.

They went silent with their own thoughts. Then she saw Jake's lips tighten and his brow furrow. He had something else on his mind. "Is there something else?"

"I might need your help with—"

"Here they are!" Anderson came in and set two heavy binders on the table with a thud.

"Give us the room for another minute, Detective."

Anderson looked back and forth between them, then left and closed the door behind him.

"What's going on, Jake?"

"You know Deputy Chief Stewart took over our Professional Standards function when you dropped it, right? He's resurrected the Woodling complaint."

"Chief Arvind called me about that earlier today—with Sam on the line. I told them we dropped it because Woodling wasn't credible and never signed the complaint."

"Did they dispute the lack of signature?"

"Yes. They said it *was* signed.

"Maybe they tracked Woodling down and talked him into signing it now," Jake said.

"Impossible. The woman you were protecting him from, Sheila something, killed him in self-defense a few months ago." She left the implication unsaid because Jake didn't need it spelled out—the signature was a forgery. Sam wanted to sideline Jake to protect his dad and to protect his own shot at becoming chief. Ambition over service. A Stewart move if ever there was one.

"Sam is pushing to have me suspended immediately pending a hearing."

"A summary suspension is bullshit. And how is he going to have a hearing without Woodling?"

"Callie's on it for me as my union rep."

Bev smiled. "She really busted Hogan's balls when she repped you the first time."

Jake returned the smile, his more rueful than amused.

"I'll let you and Detective Anderson get back to it. With a little luck, maybe you'll solve our cases, too." Bev stood. "By the way. I ran into Anna at a luncheon yesterday. She ended up telling me her, uh, secret."

Jake's eyebrows rose and he straightened in the chair. "So, what did she say about it? Did she—"

"I'm not going to betray any confidences. Women in law enforcement have to stick together."

"Of course." He looked down, embarrassed. "We… she and I, we're working through… things."

Bev smiled. "I'm happy for you. And a bit jealous to be honest." More than a bit. Her own biological clock had run out and the window to adopt was beginning to close. She still didn't feel ready. Her life was far from settled enough to bring a baby into it.

"Thanks, Bev." Jake's smile was real this time. And wide.

She left him there and went back to her own office and the opioid chaos awaiting her.

* * *

Judge Mather had given Bev an earful on the warrants but continued to sign them. Some wouldn't stand up if challenged in court, but saving lives was the goal and the warrants were already doing that. The rate of ODs and associated deaths was way down since they'd started serving the search warrants on the dealers named in the ledger. But if Peddler had kept a ledger for his network, he had taken it with him when he disappeared.

A text: *One of the dealers says he overheard that Peddler's source was a man known on the street as Kingpin.*

She entered the name into the system but found no one using it.

A knock. Her assistant. "I have Chairman Borgeson on the phone for you. A video broke on what you did—what happened—yesterday."

Bev winced. "Have you seen it?"

"I emailed you a link."

Bev opened the link and watched the video before taking her boss's call. The video started after the cans hit her so it looked like she'd acted without provocation. But the worst of it was the look on her face. Eyes wide, teeth bared. Beer Can's arms raised to ward her off but she swarmed past them, grabbed his neck, and slammed him to the ground. She could see her knuckles turning white as she squeezed his throat, his pipe-stem arms scrabbling at her hands. Then a deputy stepped in and touched her shoulder and it looked like her switch had been flipped. She released Beer Can and her face calmed and she stepped away.

Bev looked at her assistant. "Put the chairman through."

He jumped right at her. "Why would you let someone take a video of you like that?"

"I can't control how members of the public use their phones."

"You look crazy, Bev. Do I need to pull—"

"I'm fine. The guy threw a can of tobacco spit on me and that was the second can he hit me with."

"That's not on the video."

"It never is. But I saved my uniform shirt to prove it, just in case."

"I'm getting a lot of calls. I can't just say the guy deserved—"

"Refer the calls to our public information officer."

"Give me the number."

She did and he let her go with a final warning to keep her cool.

* * *

Jake took his time going through the murder books. Like the other two cold cases he'd reviewed that day, the similarities to the Belker murders were superficial. And like the other two, Belker had an alibi and Mike Nelson was not mentioned by name or implicated by any piece of evidence or witness testimony.

But he did find another possible trophy. The mother of one girl was "almost sure" her daughter had been wearing a silver ring etched with human footprints around the circumference. Jake remembered that design as a barefoot, free love hippie thing back in those days. It was painted on vans and printed on T-shirts.

He left the sheriff's office feeling the weight of the crime scene and autopsy photos he'd examined. The four failures to avenge the dead twisted his stomach in a knot that would likely be there for a while. How would taking stuff like that home with him impact Anna and their baby if they all lived together? Other cops managed to keep their work and home lives separate.

When he was back in the Mustang his phone vibrated with an incoming message. Callie Diggs: *You are in the clear! I found a disciplinary board decision that says a complaint must be both signed and dated to be valid. This complaint was not dated. If Sam had done his homework before forging that signature he would have forged the date, too! Complaint is VOID! He's PISSED.*

Saved by a technicality. He'd take it. He responded: *Thank you. I just learned that Woodling died months ago. He could not have signed the complaint for Stewart.*

Callie: *Bastard!*

He smiled and headed back to Weston. With Sam Stewart off his tail, Jake could now find the man who had visited Belker in prison. Anthony Patino—the man Mose Belker said had taken Kate Ballard.

CHAPTER SIXTY-SIX

Eddie's hand was on the door of his Mercedes when someone grabbed his shoulder and spun him around.

Anthony Patino: eyes wide, spittle crusted in the corners of his mouth. "I told you to stay away from my mom."

"I talked to her before you said that." Eddie yanked free of Anthony's grasp. "But listen, I was just in the senior center talking to a couple old-timers who had a lot of good things to say about your father."

"Don't call him that!" Patino swung a punch at Eddie, missed, and staggered, grabbing the car's side view mirror for support. A car sped by and Patino flinched away from it, thumping up against the Mercedes. His face was pale and sweaty despite the cool temperature. He looked to be on the verge of puking.

"Let's get you home, Anthony." Eddie took Patino's arm and walked him around the car and up onto the sidewalk. Eddie opened the passenger door.

Patino said nothing, but got inside. Eddie darted back around the car, eager to get Patino home before he puked in the car. Eddie had puked in it himself, years ago, and the acidic sharpness still leached from the carpet from time-to-time.

Eddie started the car. "Which way?"

Patino pointed forward. Eddie pulled away from the curb and followed Patino's directions. It was short trip.

"Here." Patino pointed at a big house surrounded by a chain link fence. A large sign behind the fence showed an artist's rendering of the mega-mansion planned to be built there.

"You can't live there, Anthony. It's set to be demolished. It doesn't have any doors or windows."

"*He* lived there."

"Your father?"

Eddie couldn't evade Patino's punch in the tight confines of the car and took it on the meat of his shoulder. "Mike Nelson? Is this where he lived before he moved away?"

"In the basement." Patino shrugged. "Maybe he took it with him, I don't know."

It? Eddie kept his voice calm and even. "Took what with him?"

"I saw him do it once." Patino licked his lips. "To a woman."

Eddie's pulse ticked up. This was it. He reached for his phone to turn on the recording app but stopped for fear of disrupting the moment if Patino caught him doing it.

"Did you see that here?"

Patino nodded. "I used to come over here and watch him through his little window. He was supposed to my *dad*."

"I understand, Anthony."

"I just wanted to know about him."

"Then, one time, you saw him do… something, to a woman."

"Right there in his apartment. He stuffed a sock in her mouth and held her down and… did it."

Silent tears welled in Patino's eyes. He fought off a sob and wiped his eyes. "I was young but old enough to know what he was doing and I… got a boner. From watching that. I… " He shook his head, gulping back another sob, his shoulders shaking.

Eddie waited and when Patino quieted, said: "That doesn't make you like him, Anthony. You were young and your reaction was natural."

"I had to throw away my underwear so my mom wouldn't see."

Eddie said nothing.

"He kept her panties and put them in a box with a bunch of other panties and little things."

Trophies. Eddies breath caught. That was the proof he needed that Mike Nelson was a serial killer. *The* serial killer.

"I've looked for it a bunch of times."

"Didn't he take it with him when he moved?"

"He didn't take anything with him," Anthony said. "The landlord stored his stuff for a while then threw it in the garbage cans in the alley. I got all his football plaques and stuff, but the box wasn't there."

Eddie looked at the hulking mess of a house behind the chain link fence. The box could still be in there.

"Let's go look for it."

Patino burped, the sourness of half-digested beer wafting through the car. Then he nodded.

* * *

Eddie took a few photos from the street, then slung the camera over his shoulder and approached the fence, a temporary construction of long sections inserted into heavy metal stands. Eddie wedged himself between two sections and slipped inside. Patino followed, but got snagged and fell down, cursing. Eddie helped him up and hustled him into the deep shadows of the pine trees hunkering over the back of the house. More pictures. Eddie stepped up onto the back porch. He paused at the doorway into the house. "Your… uh, Nelson lived in the basement?"

Patino nodded from where he stood on the edge of the porch.

"Are you coming?"

Patino shuffled forward, following at a distance as Eddie walked through the stripped-out kitchen and into the living room. The worn hardwood floor remained, but the windows, baseboards, and crown molding had been removed. A large fireplace was the central focus, but the opening had been bricked over in the distant past, yellow paint now flaking off.

"Down there," Patino said. He pointed to a stairway that dropped into gloom from a doorway near the fireplace. Eddie pulled out his phone and started the flashlight app. The stairs were bare wood, darkened by age, the treads worn in the middle from long decades of use. Eddie eased his way down, sweeping the light ahead of him, stopping every couple steps to shine it behind him for Patino. When they stood together at the bottom of the stairs, Eddie scanned the basement. Light entered through several small windows high on the walls. He turned off the flashlight app. The basement smelled damp and musty and was unfinished, except for one room boxed in against the far wall. The rest of the space was cluttered with decrepit furniture, cardboard boxes, and bundles of newspapers with hulking laundry machines standing along the rear wall.

"Was it… nicer when he lived down here?"

Patino shrugged, then stepped into the walled-in space and nodded at the window in the opposite wall. "That's where I was when I… saw him. There." He pointed to the corner, where a stained mattress slumped on a metal and wire bed frame.

Eddie pulled his camera off his shoulder and was stepping forward to take a picture when Patino bolted, a sob escaping him as he pounded up the stairs. Eddie let him go and got to work, snapping pictures of the room and the window. Then he re-slung the camera and searched every nook and cranny of that large basement. It took hours, and Eddie was about to give up when he noticed the small metal door in the cinder block wall. Ashes from the fireplace above could be shoveled down a hole and collected down here. But the upstairs fireplace had long been out of commission.

He opened the metal door.

A wooden box.

CHAPTER SIXTY-SEVEN

Jake's phone buzzed with a text. Erin: *Call me on Anthony Patino!* Jake pulled into the parking lot of an office building on Diehl Road and called her.

"What have you got?"

"Anthony Patino is Mike Nelson's secret, illegitimate son. The mother, Grace Patino, was Nelson's high school girlfriend. Anthony lives with her on West Laird. I'll text you the address."

His son; that explained why Belker mistook Patino for Nelson. "If he's secret, how'd you find this out?"

"One of my oldest sources," Erin said. "My Aunt Edith was two years behind Mike Nelson and Grace Patino in high school. Mike and Grace were *the* pinnacle of cool at that time."

Jake thanked her and hung up. Now that he had confirmed Mike existed and that Belker had a visitor who could have told him about Kate Ballard, Jake needed to call Fallon and tell him about Larson's letter.

He scrolled through his contacts for Fallon's number and called him.

Fallon answered on the first ring. "You a mind reader, Houser? I was about to call you."

But Fallon's voice held anger, not wonder at the coincidence.

"What about?"

"The DNA we found on Kate Ballard was viable and is a familial match to both an evidentiary and comparison DNA sample your department put into CODIS in '99 for the Amy Smith case. You never put names on them but they must have belonged to Belker since he went to prison for it. Who is Belker's son?"

Fallon's news confirmed Erin's rumor; Patino was Nelson's son.

"Houser?"

"Back in 1985 a man named Larson was convicted of killing Beth Lachey. Larson died in prison but his daughter has maintained his innocence and had been visiting Mose Belker in prison. She was convinced Belker actually killed Lachey and was trying to get him to admit it. Belker apparently brought up the Kate Ballard case with her on her last visit and said *Mike* was at it again. She wrote the sheriff about it who sent it to me outside the chain of command."

"Why outside the chain of command?"

"Belker claimed that someone in the Weston PD had known this *Mike* was Lachey's killer but let her dad take the rap."

"Your PD covered for a murderer? Who *is* Mike?"

"I worked it and identified him as a Mike Nelson. He was—"

"Mr. Football?"

"Yes. He was a friend of Belker's and Belker's DNA did not match the DNA the killer left on Amy Smith."

"Was it Nelson's DNA?"

"I can't prove it yet, but it seems likely."

"Belker said *Mike* was at it again, but the DNA says it's his son."

"Belker isn't all there."

"Who is Nelson's son?"

"I just learned Nelson might have had a son through a high school girlfr—"

"Name?"

"Anthony Patino. And I checked the prison visitor log and Anthony Patino visited Belker, not Mike Nelson."

Silence on the other end. Finally, "You should have told me all of this in the very beginning. It—"

"First, I had to—"

"Don't try to justify it by saying you had to confirm it because Larson and Belker weren't credible. Doing that was my job."

Fallon was right.

"Send me all of this. Right fucking now. I'll put an APB out on Patino. You need to stay the hell away from all of this."

"I'll send it as soon as I get to my laptop," Jake said. "I'm heading there now."

"My chief isn't going to like this, Houser. And he's a noisy bastard. You'll be hearing about this through your chain of command."

Fallon hung up and Jake headed home. It was Fallon's case now.

* * *

Back on Spring Street, Jake pulled into the giant garage and parked next to the pickup truck. His dad stood near the front of the truck, looking over the big space. Jake joined him. Frank clapped a hand on Jake's shoulder and squeezed. Forty years of landscaping work had given him a vicelike grip. "I was lost in memories. Worked with some very good men out of this building. This," he waved toward the basketball court, "looks so different, but it works."

"It *did* work," Jake said. He wasn't sure how well it would work going forward. Anna might refuse to live in such an untraditional space, or—if she didn't move in—might think it wasn't a good place for a child. But every house had a garage and this was just a giant garage. And the residential part of the building was perfectly normal and could easily be remodeled to add rooms.

"Anna's coming over for dinner," Frank said. He'd always been good at knowing what Jake was thinking about.

"You called her?"

"She called me, but dinner was my idea. Can you give me a hand pulling something together?"

"Absolutely," Jake said. He needed this diversion from the manhunt going on without him. "I just need to spend a few minutes on the laptop first."

As they ascended the stairs a smell coming from the kitchen interrupted Jake's thoughts.

"Have you already been at it?"

"I filled up your pantry and fridge today, Mr. Cereal and Sandwiches. So we have lots to work with."

"What did you cook?"

"I roasted some diced carrots."

"Ahh," Jake said, now recognizing the smell. It was an ingredient in his dad's Houser Special salad. The rest of the ingredients were heaped in a colander in the sink, draining from having been washed.

"You can handle the salad when you're finished with your work," Frank said. "I'll put some potatoes in to bake and build my famous meatloaf."

Jake opened his laptop on the tall table under the big window. The sun had set and the last glow of twilight backlit the forest canopy. A deer and fawn walked along the fence, and bedded down in the flattened weeds where he'd seen them before.

He pulled his eyes off the scene and sent his complete supplemental report that contained the Mike Nelson information to Fallon, not filtering out a single word of what he'd found.

Not even about his dad. Next he shot Braff an email about Fallon's DNA results and what they meant, and about sending Fallon the supplemental report.

Jake washed his hands and joined his dad at the kitchen island. He wasn't great with a knife so it was slow going but it gave him time to think as he worked his way through the kale, cucumbers, onion, grapes, celery, and three varieties of peppers. He cast long glances at his dad, still unsure of why he'd lied to him. "Did you really come home to consult on the courtyard project at the high school?"

Frank stopped kneading the meatloaf. "You know I like springtime in Illinois."

The evasion caused Jake to jump right to his big question. "Who called you about me looking at the Belker murders?"

Frank looked away, lips pressed together. The truth seemed to weigh on him, but would he tell it, or serve up another lie? A small nod as his eyes locked on Jake's. "Abe Stewart."

"What did Abe want you to do?"

Frank stared out the big window. But the sun had dropped so there was nothing to see but his own reflection. He shook his head, but said nothing.

"He wanted you to handle me, didn't he?"

"No one *handles* you, Jake."

"He wanted you to convince me to leave the past alone?"

Frank was silent, then nodded.

"Why?"

"He thinks it's best to let things lie as they are, that's all." Frank bent back over the bowl, kneading his loaf mixture.

"Don't Amy Smith's parents deserve to know who killed their—"

"They *know* Mose Belker did it. And they *know* he's being punished for it."

Jake understood his dad's point. The survivors thought they had their justice. Revealing it to be a lie or a partial truth would only hurt them. But Jake believed in more than justice.

He believed every victim deserved her vengeance. Amy's was still due.

"Abe Stewart had the DNA evidence to prove someone else was involved in killing Amy Smith. Mike Nelson."

Frank froze, but said nothing. After a long pause, he resumed kneading the meat.

Jake wondered just how much his dad knew. "It's all going to come out, Dad. I can't protect—"

"Don't!" Frank punched the meatloaf. "Just… let the chips fall."

"Okay, Dad." They worked silently after that. Jake finished chopping the vegetables, built a big salad in his largest bowl, zip-locked the extras and put them in the fridge.

Frank patted the meat into a loaf pan, spread his special tomato mixture on top, and slipped the pan into the oven.

The doorbell rang. "Anna's here," the Houser men said in unison.

"Let's stay away from Belker and Nelson tonight," Jake said. "And she doesn't want to talk about the, uh… pregnancy."

Frank agreed, and they both kept that promise.

It was a nice evening spent with Jake's two favorite people who also liked each other very much. But Jake had trouble enjoying it. While they talked—about basketball, healthcare reform, Machu Picchu, Gobekli Tepe, and the Bears—he was mostly quiet, looking at one or the other of them and asking himself two questions over and over. What was his dad hiding? Was Anna going to keep the baby or give it up?

At the end of the evening he walked her out to her car.

Anna put a hand on his chest. Her hands were always warm and he could feel her heat through his shirt. His heart rate sped up. "I was afraid you and your dad were going to gang up against me tonight. Thank you for not doing that. But the two of you weren't in sync like you normally are. You want to talk about it?"

He'd rather talk about the baby, but he did need to talk. "Dad's mixed up in this Belker thing."

"What? How so?"

"Both Belker and Mike Nelson worked for Trinity Landscaping. My dad lied to me about that the first time I brought it up."

"That's not like him." She rubbed her hand on his chest on small circles. "What's he hiding?"

"I don't know," Jake said. They were both quiet for a minute, then his mind shifted to his second question. "Have you decided—"

She patted his chest and he stopped talking. He looked down into her eyes.

"I'm having the baby. Your baby. Our baby. That decision is made and I will not change it. After that I just… I'm having trouble wrapping my head around the idea of being a single mom. I—"

"You don't have to be a single mom. We can—"

"You've said." She stepped back. "A little more time."

"We can live together right here. I—"

"Here?" Her voice had an amused lilt. "In your bachelor pad?"

"Just throwing it out as one possibility," he said.

"A little more time, Jake."

He smiled and she opened her car door, leaving him there, staring after her, suddenly wishing he'd asked to touch her belly.

CHAPTER SIXTY-EIGHT

Eddie snapped a picture of the box, then slung his camera over his shoulder and eased the box out of its hiding place. He dusted it off, then started up the stairs.

At the top of the stairs Eddie remembered Patino and paused to listen for him. The house was quiet; the only sound the whisper of tires on Jefferson and a car door slamming in the distance. A dog barked. A breeze wafted through the gaping window frames, carrying the scent of the pine trees out back. A dry leaf scuttled across the floor.

He exited the house, scurried across the yard, and slipped through the same narrow gap in the fence he'd forced open to get in, the chain links clanking. He crossed the street to his car and got in, locked the doors, and headed back to the motel.

He had writing to do.

* * *

Eddie filled his travel mug in the motel's front office. The same pimply faced kid who sold the cop a key to Eddie's room was behind the counter.

"Have the cops been back?"

A headshake.

"If my camera caught them, or you, in my room I'll—"

"I swear, man." The kid raised his right hand and put his left over his heart.

Eddie kept his eyes locked on the little man. Sweat beaded on his forehead and he lifted his right hand higher. Eddie bought his sincerity, and went back to his room.

Benny sat in his chair across the parking lot. He held out a thumbs-up Eddie took to mean all was clear. Eddie returned the gesture. Once inside his room he locked the deadbolt.

Eddie set the box on the bed. Penny had been absolutely right. He still had it. He could still find his way to the heart of a story and peel back the layers to the ultimate truth. This box proved that.

And proved Mike Nelson was the killer.

He took photos of the box from every angle. He then eased the top open: a jumble of panties and jewelry and a small Timex watch.

Classic serial killer trophies. Almost a cliché.

He used a pen to slide each trophy out onto a clean sheet of paper. He took photos of each item and put them back in the box.

He laid out his notes and typed up a long narrative stream, the words flowing like water from a fire hose. When Eddie stopped typing an hour later there were dozens of typos to correct. He went back through the whole thing, making sure his narrative hung together. Then he sent it off to his new agent by email along with the photos of the box and its contents. It was way past five, but New York book people worked all the time. And his email subject line—*I solved the murders!*—should grab her attention.

He wondered if she'd call her boss. If Haley insisted on bringing Gavin in, Eddie would drop her. This book would land him any agent he wanted.

He waited for Jones to get back to him and thought about the missing girl. He had avoided getting into that too deeply because… because he'd been afraid. But if he was going to be what he had once been, if he was going to write the whole story, he needed to nail that down. But what he had was more than enough to sell the book. Once his proposal was accepted, he'd break that part of the story wide open, too.

His cell phone rang. His agent, Haley Jones.

"You solved it!"

"Yep."

"Mike is the killer just like the daughter said in her letter?"

"Yes, but her father is only off the hook if one of the trophies ties into Beth Lachey. It'll be up to the State's Attorney whether to clear his name. And nothing proves Belker was innocent."

"You can take the box on the road with—"

"I have to turn the box over to the cops."

"Of course, of course." Haley was thinking so hard Eddie could hear gears grinding. "Your publisher is going to be—"

"Let's buy out my existing contract and put this book up for auction." This story was worth way more than what they'd paid him for the book he'd abandoned. And it deserved a lot more marketing than that contract required. Getting a publisher to spend on marketing was writing's biggest challenge.

A pause as she absorbed that. "I'll talk to Gavin and—"

"Screw Gavin. You're my agent."

"But—"

"If you can't go it alone let me know now and I'll sell this book myself, Haley. He stays out of it."

"Okay," she said, her voice subdued. Then the energy came back. "How does the dead girl work into this?"

"Which dead girl?"

"The one they found last night. The guy in prison—Belker—told the daughter that Mike had her."

"They found Ballard last night?"

"You writers!" Haley laughed through the phone. "You get in the zone!"

Eddie grabbed the TV remote and flipped it on and found an all-news channel, but saw nothing about Ballard. He needed to see what he'd missed. "I have to go."

"How fast can you get me the first three chapters?"

Eddie had already written them, but with his ending locked down he could now add in more texture and foreshadowing. And to generate big auction bids, his writing had to sing. "Tomorrow."

"Perfect."

Eddie got on the internet and found the Ballard news in seconds. The spot her body had been dumped sounded familiar. He checked his notes; the Lachey girl had been dumped on that same railroad siding. Either Mike was still here in Weston or someone was copying his moves.

He kept searching and found a discussion on the local "Patch" website that the Glenbard police had put an APB out for Anthony Patino.

Eddie leaned back. *Patino?* Eddie had just been alone with the man in an abandoned house. Anything could have happened.

But nothing did happen. *Man up, Shaw! You got this!*

Maybe he could get to Patino before the cops did. He had the man's cell number. And he had bait Patino would not be able to resist.

He sent Patino a text: *I found the box. If you want to see what's inside meet me at the Grey Tavern on Ogden at 10pm.* He attached a photo of the box. There was no way Patino could resist that invitation. And the bar's seedy vibe would lend great atmosphere to the meeting. Words to describe the place began scrolling across his mind, but he didn't write them down. He would get a fresh impression when he met Patino at the bar.

* * *

Eddie got his portable printer out of his trunk and printed out the best photos of the box and its contents. He played with various effects until the colors popped. Then he hustled over to the bar, notebook in hand, photos in his pocket.

He was twenty minutes early.

The same bartender stood behind the bar; today's Marine Corps T-shirt even tighter than the one he'd worn the previous night. "Old Style draft, right?" The bartender pointed at Eddie, head cocked.

"Please." Eddie waited for the beer then took it to the same tall table in the front corner where he'd sat with Larson. He pulled out his notebook and sipped the beer while he wrote down every sensory detail he was experiencing; the dim lighting, the scarred pool tables, the yeasty odor of old beer, the hard-driving heavy metal piped through giant black speakers. He wrote out quick descriptions of the two regulars at the bar, and of a trio of woman laughing in a booth by the bathrooms.

Donna Larson came in and took a seat at the bar. He should have anticipated that. This was her regular spot.

The bartender brought her a short glass half filled with dark liquid, a whiskey or bourbon, and pointed toward Eddie. She rose from her stool and came over to his table. Eddie stuffed the notebook in his pocket.

"They found Kate Ballard's body last night," she said.

"I heard."

"Did you find Mike?"

"I've confirmed Mike was real," Eddie said. *Finding* Mike was the cop's job. "His name is Mike Nelson. He was a local sports hero who—hang on."

Anthony Patino had stepped into the bar. He stood by the door, sweeping his gaze around the room. He looked like he'd recovered from his day drinking with a nap, his hair pressed flat on one side of his head. Had he been drinking to forget what he'd done to Kate Ballard? Or to remember it? Eddie held up a hand and Anthony caught the motion and headed their way.

When he spotted Donna, his step faltered. His left hand swept over his hair in a lame attempt to flatten it down. His right hand was clenched around something that he worked with his thumb.

"Who's that?" Donna asked.

"I'll introduce you," Eddie said. Conflict drove drama, so adding Larson to this meeting just might work out. The bartender—Donna called him Rick—brought her a fresh drink and took Anthony's order for a draft beer. Eddie drank in the moment. Anthony moved his stool a couple inches farther away from Donna. Donna ran her eyes up and down Patino's rough form, then shot Eddie a questioning glance.

"Donna, this is Anthony Patino. Mike Nelson is his birth father. Anthony, Donna's father was convicted of the 1986 murder of Beth Lachey. A murder your fa—Mike Nelson most likely committed."

Donna wrapped her hands around her glass and leaned into the table. "I knew it!"

Eddie waited for Anthony to say something, but the man's expression never changed and he kept his mouth closed. His thumb worked whatever he held.

"Where is he?" Donna asked. "Did you find him?" Her gaze shot to Anthony, who still hadn't moved. "Can you *prove* he was the real killer?"

"I *can* prove Mike Nelson was a killer," Eddie said. "I found his box."

"What box?" Donna asked.

"Mike Nelson kept trophies. Small personal items that belonged to the women he—"

"Where?" Anthony licked his lips, then cleared his throat.

"In the ash trap at the base of the chimney."

Anthony's gaze pulled away into a memory, maybe, of where he'd searched, and where he hadn't. The bartender walked up with Anthony's drink and they were all silent until he was back behind the bar. Anthony reached for the beer, a thin gold chain dangling from his clenched right fist. When Anthony realized the hand was occupied, he switched hands and grabbed the beer with his left.

Was the chain a trophy he'd taken from Kate Ballard? Eddie locked in the image.

"How many?" Anthony's voice croaked as if he wasn't used to talking. He put the beer down. "How many *things* are in the box?"

"Fourteen."

"You mean Mike Nelson killed fourteen women?" Larson's voice was thick with sadness.

"That's for the police to say," Eddie said. "Some might be for memories of something… less." Like the rape Anthony had witnessed as a young boy.

"You're giving them the box?"

"I have to."

"I want to see it," Anthony said.

Eddie pulled out the stack of photos. Anthony stuffed whatever he'd been holding into the pocket of his jacket and snatched the photos from Eddie's hand. Donna leaned to look over Anthony's shoulder, but he turned his back to her and lowered the photos under the table. His breathing became husky.

"This *is* the box I saw my dad put them in." His voice dropped and got hoarse. "This is them… the pink ones."

"What's he talking about?" Donna asked.

Eddie didn't answer. He was memorizing the scene. The tone, the words: "my dad," "the pink ones." And especially *this is them* and the weight the words carried of a long-treasured memory. Donna still trying to look over Anthony's shoulder. Anthony's breathing, raspy and uneven. The shuffle of the photos under the table.

"What does seeing them mean to you, Anthony?"

Anthony ignored the question, his breathing becoming faster. He leaped off his stool and fled with the photos. He bumped into two men near the door, spun off the impact and was gone.

Donna turned back to Eddie. "That box proves my dad was innocent and your book will explain that, right?"

"The box proves Mike Nelson was *a* killer. If there's a trophy in there from Beth Lachey that will prove Nelson killed her, it doesn't prove—I can't prove—that your father wasn't involved. It will be up to the State's Attorney to—"

Whiskey splashed against Eddie's face. Larson's lips pressed together and her eyes darkened. She ran from the bar. Eddie sat still, the heady sharpness of the scotch filling his nose, and stinging his lips. He licked it off. Maybe it was better that she hadn't let him finish.

"You're smiling like you wanted Donna to do that." The bartender appeared with a towel. "Here."

"Thanks." Eddie patted himself dry, but not too dry. The scotch added a texture he wanted to keep with him as he wrote this up. "What kind of whiskey was that?" Details mattered.

"Wild Turkey."

Perfect. Eddie dropped two twenties on the table and headed back to his motel room.

He had writing to do.

While he walked, he googled the Weston Crime Stopper's number and called in an anonymous tip that he had just spotted Anthony Patino in the Grey Tavern.

CHAPTER SIXTY-NINE

Jake tried talking to his dad after Anna left, but Frank begged off. "Let's talk in the morning. Okay, buddy? I'm beat."

After Frank went downstairs to the garage, Jake cleaned up the kitchen and handled the leftovers. When he was done, he sat at the island sipping a beer and looking at his reflection in the big window. He didn't like what he saw. A man whose dad was lying to him. A man who got his girlfriend pregnant and wasn't sure he could handle the responsibility of having a child. A man who had failed to find Kate Ballard while she was still alive.

"What's wrong with you, Houser?"

He drank another beer but had never found an answer in a bottle and tonight was no different. He turned out the lights and went to bed. Thankfully the alcohol dulled his brain enough to put him under.

But it didn't last.

He woke gasping, disoriented, body shot through with adrenaline, heart pounding.

He was in bed, sitting up, the ceiling fan spinning, the downdraft cold on his sweaty skin.

He lay back down on the damp sheets.

It felt like when he woke from one of his nightmares, but he remembered nothing. He closed his eyes and took long slow breaths, flexing and releasing each muscle, searching for peace.

He drifted off…

He was cold. A thick penetrating wetness in the air. But sweat ran down his forehead, a salty sting in his eyes. He shivered, from the cold and from the fear rising up through him. A big shadow blocked light and a sharp roar and—

He woke again.

Drenched.

But he remembered this time—the same nightmare he'd had the night before. But he still didn't recognize the place.

He took a short cool shower, changed the sheets, and lay back down.

That was not a dream.

It was a memory of a time in his childhood. He'd been alone—somewhere he wasn't supposed to be—and been caught.

But by whom? Where? And what happened next?

CHAPTER SEVENTY

Eddie refilled his travel mug, the coffee in the motel office's pot now thick and bitter.

He asked the new kid behind the counter to make some more, then went back to his room.

The writing was going well. He'd finished revising the first three chapters and the narrative outline was coming together exactly liked he'd hoped. It would lay out a puzzle with an answer only he had ever provided. An answer that exposed the corruption at the heart of this suburban Shangri-La.

He thought about calling Penny. She had inspired him to research this story and be the writer he had once been. He would dedicate this book to her. He smiled. She would love that. He pulled out his phone but when he saw the time decided not to call her. She got up early to handle the breakfast rush at the diner.

Tomorrow.

The phone on the nightstand rang. It was the kid at the front desk. "The fresh coffee's ready and I just told a woman which room was yours. She's not a cop—I heard about that. She had a bottle of whiskey with her."

The kid hung up before Eddie could respond.

A soft knock. "Eddie? It's Donna."

He opened the door. Donna smiled shyly then held up a bottle of Johnnie Walker Green Label. The good stuff.

"What's going—"

She pushed past him and put the bottle on the desk. She bent down and looked at his laptop screen. "Lot of typos. That's what the red mean, right?"

"Donna?"

She straightened, looked around the room, her gaze darting into every corner, then focusing on the dresser. Probably looking for the trophy box.

She sat down on the bed, leaned back on her hands, and crossed her legs. She'd changed into a short skirt and a tank top and the look worked. She had the taut legs of a runner. He licked his lips. But this was wrong. He had something with Penny. Something real. This was nothing

"Why are you here?"

She uncrossed her legs, giving him a view into the shadow between them. His pulse accelerated as his resolve crumbled. *Pull yourself together, Shaw!*

"I wanted to apologize for throwing my drink on you."

"You didn't let me finish what I was saying. If there is a trophy from Beth Lachey in that box then chances are good your dad will be exonerated."

She sat up straight, then leaned forward. "Eddie! That's great."

He tried to keep his eyes off her breasts, but they were eye magnets. His face got hot. Too much writing adrenaline. Too much caffeine.

Eddie cleared his throat and refocused on Donna's face. "The news reports back then don't mention a trophy taken from Lachey, so if there was one taken the cops kept that to themselves. I'll work on Lachey's parents with the photos. See if anything belonged to her."

"Thank you, Eddie." She licked her lips and held out a hand, palm up, inviting him to take it. Her arms were slender, tanned, firm.

Eddie hesitated. He and Penny had a shot, but that was separate from this, wasn't it? He'd earned this… like… he deserved it. He took her hand and they didn't talk about anymore. They just drank and screwed. She was as athletic as she looked. Surprising, really, for a woman who drank like she did.

After their second round he fell back, his body loose and tingly. He closed his eyes and a boozy fog drifted in and he was out.

* * *

Eddie woke suddenly.

A sharp, pain on his neck, a burning line of fire.

He tried to breathe but choked on… something. He gasped and a torrent of fluid poured into his lungs. He coughed, bucking in the bed, and a spray came from his mouth.

He tried to scream but only coughed more fluid. He reached out and slapped the bed next to him.

Donna wasn't there.

But he wasn't alone. Someone was in the dark room with him. A shadow hanging back, but watching.

Eddie tried to breathe again, but only sucked in more fluid. He touched his throat, it was slick with hot wetness that welled rhythmically against his fingers. Blood. He probed the flow and found the pain. His throat was cut.

His vision dimmed; the room grew darker.

The shadow watching him moved away. Eddie raised a hand but the light faded and he saw only black.

Penny would have loved the dedication he was going to write to her.

If only his luck had held.

CHAPTER SEVENTY-ONE

Jake pulled on a set of running clothes when he woke then hustled downstairs to talk to his dad, but Frank was already gone. Jake had *never* beat his dad to the new day. Frank Houser loved the dawn.

On the way back upstairs Jake noticed the truck was still in the garage. Either Frank was on foot or someone had picked him up.

Jake checked his messages and found nothing on the search for Anthony Patino. But maybe Fallon just wasn't sharing.

He drank a glass of water, stretched, then went for his run, hoping for the clarity that often came as his feet pounded pavement. He slipped through a gap in the back fence and ran down the path into the woods. The air was heavy with moisture. He passed the swamp, red-winged blackbirds trilling as they darted from one tall clump of reeds to the next. Just before he got to the gravel entrance road, he spotted a flannel shirt off to the left. His dad, seated on a log, staring at the ground. Jake didn't stop. His dad liked his quiet time and they could talk when Jake got back from his run.

Jake took the gravel road out of the forest preserve, swung around the curve on Douglas, and got on the Paget River Trail heading north along the bank. As the sun rose higher the humidity thinned and the sky cleared. Birds sang and chirped and squirrels darted from tree to tree. The river ran high, thick and brown with spring run-off.

Clarity came.

Anna was going to have the baby; she had said so and wouldn't change her mind. Which meant he was going to be a dad.

The thought bounced around his head, catching on images of Jake and his own dad playing catch, wrestling on the floor. Then his mom was there, too. On road trips, and playing Yahtzee, and baking apple pies. Good memories.

He wanted that. All of that. A family with Anna. And wanting that was not being disloyal to Mary. It was being loyal to the future he had planned with her. She would want him to have that. Mary had not had a selfish bone in her body.

If he *had* told Anna he loved her before… this, maybe they'd be in a different place now. But thinking about could-have-beens did him no good. He needed to plan for what was in front of him. And although the baby put stress on their relationship, it didn't have to kill it. The baby might even bring them together, eventually.

Whether he and Anna ended up together or not, Jake would be a dad.

Finally.

Emotion surged through him so hard and fast that his stride faltered. He came to a stop, hands on his knees, tears welling.

"You okay?"

Jake nodded, but didn't look up.

"Okay, man."

The runner continued on and Jake stepped off the path onto the grass. When he had himself under control, he wiped his eyes and straightened up. His senses reopening to the gurgle of the river.

He needed to make some changes at the Spring Street property or find them a real house to live in. Whatever Anna wanted.

*　*　*

Deputy Chief of Patrol Sam Stewart got to work even earlier than normal and sat at his desk, laptop open in front of him, waiting for Houser to update his Ballard file. Detective Diggs had destroyed his plan to suspend Houser so the man was still out there, finding truths that would only hurt Sam. He needed to—

Bam!

Sam flinched away from the noise, his hand launching the computer mouse against the wall. He needed to start locking the damn door.

"What is it, Sergeant?"

Massey scooped up the mouse and put it on the desk. "Dead body out at the Starlite. It's Shaw. The writer."

A wave of nausea flowed through Sam. Massey stood still, unaffected. Stoic. "What did your guys do?"

"Nothing, boss. We—"

"Who caught the case?" Sam asked, holding his breath.

"Diggs. She's on the way over there now."

Sam exhaled. At least it wasn't Houser. "Your guy who searched the room. Get him on scene and in the room without gloves on ASAP. Just in case."

"I need to take over the scene to get that done."

Sam opened the deployment program on his computer. "Go. By the time you get there the scene will be yours."

CHAPTER SEVENTY-TWO

Jake turned around and ran home. He showered, ate, dressed, and equipped himself. He had a message on his phone from Braff summoning him for an eight o'clock meeting. No doubt to talk about his Mike file and Abe Stewart. He had thirty-two minutes to get there.

Jake sat down at the counter and flipped open the laptop to update his Kate Ballard file. He started with the supplemental report, summarizing what he learned about Mike Nelson's army service, the reason for his discharge, and the second string of murders that occurred after he got home from his Army service.

Then he walked through his analysis of the DNA evidence. Belker had a visitor who claimed to have abducted Kate Ballard. That visitor was Anthony Patino. Anthony Patino was rumored to be Mike Nelson's son. The DNA found on Kate Ballard's body was a father-son familial match to the second known sample submitted for DNA analysis in the Smith murder. Conclusion: the second known DNA sample from 1999 belonged to Mike Nelson, Mike Nelson killed Amy Smith, and Anthony Patino killed Kate Ballard.

He hit *publish* and got moving.

As he descended the stairs his cell phone rang. Erin. She jumped to it as soon as he answered.

"Callie just caught a murder out at the Starlite Motel."

"Did she ask for my help?"

"No, but the victim is a writer who I just learned has been poking into the Mose Belker murders that—"

"I met him. Shaw. He came out to Spring Street to talk to Frank. Tell Braff I'm going out there so won't be in this morning as he requested."

"Will do."

Jake jumped in the Mustang and headed for the motel. Shaw was murdered because of what he'd learned. Or because of what someone was afraid he would learn. That someone was either Abe Stewart, or Mike Nelson.

* * *

Deputy Chief of Patrol Sam Stewart refreshed the page he had open, waiting for Houser to update the Ballard file.

He picked up his coffee mug, but it was empty, again. He stood to go fill it, but hit refresh one more time. "Finally!"

He pushed the mug aside and hunched over the screen. There was a lot there.

Houser had confirmed that Mike Nelson was a rapist and murderer and that his son, Anthony Patino, had killed Kate Ballard.

Sam reread the entries, but found no holes. Houser's analysis was irrefutable.

And damning for Sam's father.

Abe Stewart protected Mike Nelson from being charged for the Smith and Brown murders and sent him off to the army where he abused women in South Korea. Houser speculated that when Nelson came home, he continued with his disgusting crimes with five more murders through the rest of Paget

County. A reasonable conclusion based on what he had been able to confirm.

Those murders—if Nelson had committed them—were on Sam's father.

Why the hell had he protected Mike Nelson? To protect Weston from being labeled as the home of a sexual predator and serial killer? Or much more likely, out of his own self-interest.

But his father could not have known Nelson would commit more crimes. The fact that his father ran Nelson's DNA in 1999, meant he had only suspected Nelson before that. But by 1988, the date the DNA report said the blood on the handkerchief was collected, his dad's suspicions became strong enough that he saved that sample.

Where did his father get that handkerchief?

CHAPTER SEVENTY-THREE

Jake found the Starlite awash with emergency response lights. It was an old motel on Ogden Avenue that consisted of two narrow white brick buildings facing each other across a parking lot.

He pulled in and parked near the entrance so he wouldn't get blocked in when the coroner and forensic teams arrived. The parking lot was less than a third full, but at least a dozen guests were outside their rooms watching the show from the covered walkways that ran the length of both buildings. Patrolmen stood clustered halfway down the right-hand building.

As he approached, Callie Diggs's angry voice broke through the general din.

"Where did you learn to handle a scene?"

The throng dispersed, leaving behind Callie and a young patrol officer Jake didn't know. The officer was trying to take a clipboard away from Callie. She pulled it away and held it behind her. She spotted Jake and held it up. "Look at this!"

"What?" Beyond her shoulder Jake spotted a tall man with long, unruly hair and a braided beard step off the walkway of the other building as if to come their way. The man stopped, then went back and sat in a chair he'd pulled out of his motel room. A witness, maybe.

"Seven of these bozos stepped all over this crime scene already. At least seven." She jammed the clipboard into the cop's chest, but yanked it back when he reached for it. "How many people went in who didn't make the list?"

"Everybody who went in is on it."

"Did *any* of these people—seven of them for Christ's sake—wear gloves and booties?"

The answer was obvious because no boxes of gloves and booties were set up for use.

"No, ma'am."

"It's Detective." Callie turned to Jake. "Can you believe this?"

He couldn't. Patrol officers received excellent training on crime scene preservation. He checked the officer's badge. Holcum. He was no more than twenty-five with a square jaw and big eyes. His face glistened with sweat despite the cool morning air. His gaze darted after the group of officers now retreating to their squad cars. "Which of them ordered you to let those men into the room, Holcum?"

"It was—" Holcum's Adams apple bobbed as he swallowed what he'd been about to say.

"Are you shitting me, Holcum?" Callie asked. "One of them *told* you to contaminate my crime scene?"

"Not contaminate it, but—"

"What's your question, Detective Diggs?" The sergeant from the records room approached. Massey. "I'm managing this scene."

"Well it's a fuster cluck, Massey." Callie stepped in and rose on her toes, eyeballing the much bigger cop. "Straighten this out. Right now."

"I'm on it, Detective." Massey stepped between her and Holcum. "Get your gloves and booties, Holcum. I'll hold the door."

"Too little, too late, Massey." Callie turned toward Jake. "What are you doing here, Houser?"

Jake pulled her a couple doors down and explained about Donna Larson and her letter. About Belker, Mike Nelson, the DNA, and Anthony Patino. Then he told her about Chief Arvind's involvement and about Abe Stewart.

"This is the bad juju you warned me about in the beginning." She shook her head, hands on hips. "If—"

"Here you go." Holcum held out boxes of booties and gloves. Jake and Callie pulled on a pair of each and went inside. Jake paused just inside the door; he liked to see the whole scene before shifting his focus to the body.

The room was bigger than Jake had expected, deep enough to hold two queen-sized beds with narrow spaces to move around them. A half-empty whiskey bottle stood on the night table between the beds with two empty glasses. The rim of one held a light smudge of lipstick. The air was rich with the sweaty tang of sex and the metallic taste of spilled blood.

The bed closest to the door was still made and held an open suitcase with a jumble of clothing spilling out of it. The other bed had been slept in. The nearest pillow held a head print and a makeup smudge.

The body was on the other side of the bed.

Along the right-hand wall of the room ran a long piece of built-in furniture that served as a combination dresser, TV stand, and desk. The desk held a laptop, a small portable printer, and neat stacks of notebook paper.

"Is this Shaw?"

Jake looked at the dead man. "Yes."

"He had a guest. A woman," Callie said. "But I don't think a woman did this."

Jake had to agree.

"You know this guy, so why don't you take the room and I'll start in on the clerk and the other motel guests?"

"Start with the tall bearded man across the parking lot."

"You know him?"

"I saw him as you were dealing with Holcum. He wants to talk."

Callie smiled. "Maybe we'll get a fast start."

After Callie left, Jake went through the room, taking his time. He started with Shaw's personal effects—his suitcase and clothes and toiletries—but found nothing interesting. Then he turned to Shaw's writing materials. The laptop and the stacks of notes look undisturbed. But the messenger bag Shaw had with him when he'd come out to Spring Street was missing.

What did it contain that his laptop didn't?

Jake found Shaw's phone in the pocket of a pair of pants puddled on the chair by the window. Jake hit the home button and the screen lit up but it wanted the passcode or a "Touch ID."

He looked at Shaw's body. The touch ID security protocol "read" a fingerprint by detecting the variations in electrical current between the ridge and trough of a fingerprint. Dead bodies sometimes retained enough electrical charge to trigger the system.

He tried it, and got in with the right thumb. A text message from "haley-agent" appeared on the screen: *Update?!?!?!?* Jake went into the phone's setting and removed both the passcode and touch ID requirements before reading the text message. It was from earlier that morning. Jake scrolled back through the message string and found a message from Shaw: *DIRTY COPS! A cop named Welch pulled me over for no reason and illegally searched my car to keep me busy while another cop SEARCHED my motel room. A guy staying here got pictures!! This is pure gold!*

Christ! Proof of dirty cops in the patrol unit. Sam Stewart's division.

Shaw had attached two pictures to the text message. One, of a squad car parked by the motel's front office, and one of a uniformed patrolman coming through a door clearly identified as belonging to this room by the number on the door. Jake did not recognize the cop in the picture but the name of the cop who'd pulled Shaw over—Welch—rang a bell. An older guy with a barrel shaped beer belly.

Jake forwarded the text string to his own phone and then sent it on to Callie with a message: *READ ASAP!*

She called him within a minute.

"This burn-out told me his whole story without ever mentioning these photos, can you believe it? That cop in the photo is Graham," Callie's voice rumbled with anger. "He's on Holcum's list. I'm looking at him right now standing next to his squad talking to Massey."

"That explains the contaminated crime scene," Jake said. "The dirty cop—apparently Massey or whoever he works for—"

"Sam Stewart," Callie said.

"—wanted to get his man on scene. Now any forensic evidence Graham left behind when he searched the room can be explained by sloppy crime scene management."

"Fuckers," Callie said.

"We need to clear this place out," Jake said. "Graham and Massey are dirty, at a minimum."

Callie was silent for a minute. "You've been here longer than me. Who can we trust?"

"For sure? No doubts? Braff. Grady. Erin."

"That club's too small."

"I'll put Grady on the door here and ask the sheriff to send some units to guard the scene."

"You trust her?"

"A hundred percent," Jake said. "Have you called for forensics and the coroner?"

"Deputy Corner Chen and FIC Fanning are both en route."

"Excellent," Jake said. Chen and Fanning were the best.

"I'll call Braff," Callie said.

CHAPTER SEVENTY-FOUR

Bev stepped into the shade cast by the tactical van to read the screen on her phone. The murder victim at the Weston motel was Eddie Shaw, the writer Jake said was digging into Larson's letter.

Her hand shook and a sudden chill shot through her. Was Shaw's death her fault? She hadn't brought the writer into it, but she did stir things up by getting Jake involved.

She stepped back into the sun, letting her polyester uniform absorb the heat and erase the chill. She set things in motion and had to let them play out. When it was done, she'd examine her responsibility. For now, she had a job to do and got back to it.

Her long string of search warrants had brought her here. Two different dealers had identified this end unit in an empty strip mall on Roosevelt Road as Peddler's hideout. With any luck the dealer and the rest of the tainted batch would be inside and this raid would be the last. As the tactical squad leader briefed his men, her thoughts turned back to the dead writer. Had she underestimated Abe Stewart's threat because of his age? Her own father had been a force all the way to his deathbed. And it had to have been Abe. She couldn't see Sam Stewart taking it that far.

Her cell phone vibrated with an incoming call. Jake.

"Did you catch the Shaw case, Jake?"

"Callie's primary, but I'm helping out and we've run into a snag."

"What do you need?"

"Help securing the scene. Can you send three units down—guys you know are solid?"

"Why? What's going on?"

"Those issues we talked about with the department. We need to keep this scene clean. Keep Sam's people away from it."

"Sam Stewart is the dirty cop?"

"Sam and at least a few of his patrolmen."

"I'll send help now, Jake. What else I can do?"

"That'll do it."

"The men will be on their way within five minutes."

Bev climbed into the cruiser and used the dash-mounted laptop to pull up her deployment chart. She went through her on-duty patrol officers and diverted the best three to secure the scene at the Starlite, telling them to answer only to Houser or Diggs. Then she called in three off-duty officers to cover those beats.

She thought about Sam Stewart falling into Jake Houser's sights and almost pitied him.

Almost.

"Sheriff?" The tactical sergeant stood at her open car door. "We're all here and ready."

"Let's roll."

CHAPTER SEVENTY-FIVE

Jake called Grady and told him to suit up and get to the Starlite immediately. Grady heeded Jake's urgency and asked no questions. After the call, Jake took a closer look at Shaw's laptop. He opened the lid and the screen came on to display a background photo of Shaw holding a trophy in one hand and a hardback book in the other. *Trackside Hunter.* Jake remembered the movie, but hadn't known it was based on a book by Shaw. In the center of the screen a box awaited a password. Maybe Fanning could crack it.

He turned to the stacks of notes. Shaw's handwriting was clear but the notes were too brief to be helpful—nothing more than what Shaw needed to jog his memory when typing the notes into his computer.

Memory.

When they'd met, Shaw pulled out his notebook to look something up, explaining he had a bad memory. Jake found Shaw's wallet in his discarded pants. Stuffed in a pocket inside it were eleven pieces of paper with little reminders: grocery lists, prescriptions, paint colors. He also found three passwords, obvious by their combinations of letters, numbers, and symbols. He hit the right one on the second try: prOWriter!#.

Remembering his luck with Shaw's text message, Jake started with the email program and hit pay dirt. Shaw sent an email to Haley Jones at 8:04 the previous evening with the subject line "I solved the murders!" Jake opened it and found the email blank but there were attachments: a document titled "Narrative Outline" and sixteen photos. The photos were of a wooden box and the fourteen items found inside it. The sixth photo was of Amy Smith's missing locket, the eighth depicted the silver ring circled by footprints worn by one of the two county victims, and the last photo was of the class ring taken from the girl from Poplar Grove.

Trophies.

Jake opened the Narrative Outline and skimmed it for the word "box." Shaw had learned about the box from Mike Nelson's son, Anthony Patino. Patino had witnessed his dad raping a woman and putting the woman's panties in a wooden box with other similar souvenirs. Shaw found the box hidden in the ash trap of the boarding house where Mike Nelson had lived immediately before moving west in 1988.

That box—proof that Mike Nelson was a serial rapist and killer—was not here in Shaw's room. Which meant the killer had it.

Jake went back to examining the laptop. He noticed the icons of three open documents along the bottom margin of the screen. They were labeled as Character Profiles, Narrative Outline, and First Three Chapters.

He opened the Narrative Outline and found an expanded version of the one attached to the email. The narrative was in roughly chronological order, so Jake scrolled to the end to see if Shaw added anything after he sent it off to Haley Jones. He had. Shaw heard about Ballard's body being found and the APB on Patino and arranged to meet the man at a bar. While waiting for Patino, Donna Larson showed up. Apparently the bar Shaw had selected was her regular spot. The narrative ended mid-sentence.

Shaw had been interrupted.

Jake went back to the email program and selected Shaw's last email to his agent then attached the three newer documents to it and sent it to himself. Then he deleted the copy of that sent email. He trusted Fanning and his forensic team, but with dirty cops in the mix, it was smart to play it safe and preserve this evidence.

He opened his phone, forwarded the email to Callie, and sent her a text: *Shaw found Mike Nelson's trophies. They are not here so Shaw's killer has them. See photos attached to email I just sent you.*

A minute later she sent back a thumbs-up emoji and a string of exclamation marks. The news did deserve exclamation. The contents of that box solved many cold cases. And when they found who had it now, would also solve Shaw's murder.

A horn sounded from the parking lot.

Jake stepped outside. Fanning's forensic van and the Coroner's wagon had both arrived, lights flashing. The scrum of Weston officers hopped into their squads and backed them out of the way, allowing the vehicles to pull right up to the door. Beyond them Jake saw Grady roll by in his Jetta. He skirted the far side of the parking lot, parked, and jogged over.

"You're dismissed, Holcum." Jake snatched the clipboard from him. "Stand up against the wall."

"What do you—"

"Shut up." Jake handed the clipboard to Grady. "No one inside but me, Diggs, and the pros."

"Got it," Grady said. He eyed Holcum, who then looked away and leaned against the wall.

Forensic Investigator in Charge Duke Fanning stepped up with a team of three Tyvek jumpsuit-clad scene technicians. Jake briefed them and they went in. Deputy Coroner Chen waited by her wagon and Jake walked over and explained the scene to her.

Then the three county squads Bev had promised arrived.

The Weston patrolmen shouted questions at Callie, who waded into their midst. Jake resisted going over to help her. It would make her look weak and she wasn't. He stayed where he was, but ready, just in case.

"What's going on, Jake?" Deputy Coroner Chen looked from Jake to the phalanx of Weston officers surrounding Callie. She had one man by the arm: Massey. She stepped close and rose on her toes, face inches from his chin, her mouth moving, but Jake couldn't hear what she said. Callie stopped talking and the two stood still.

"We have some dirty cops, Chen."

Ten seconds passed, twenty more. Then Massey shook his head and left the parking lot to stand next to Holcum. Massey said something to Holcum, who shook his head and stepped away from his sergeant.

The other Weston officers clustered around Callie, who now held another man by the arm. The officer from the photo: Graham. She levered his arm up high behind his back and reached for her cuffs. Voices raised. *Bullshit!* and *You can't do that!*

Jake stepped down onto the parking lot, but the group suddenly dispersed, tossing more profane shouts at Callie as they got in their squads. She cuffed Graham, then grabbed the link between the handcuffs, put her other hand on the middle of his back, and walked him over to Grady's car. Graham balked when she opened the back door, but she forced his head down and shoved him inside.

Jake stepped back up onto the covered walkway and faced the cops against the wall. Massey stood over Holcum, whispering into the man's ear. Holcum's eyes were wide and he was shaking his head.

"Massey!" Jake yanked the Sergeant away from Holcum. "What the hell are you doing here? Did Deputy Chief Stewart pull you out of records to handle the scene of this homicide?"

"Yes, Detective."

"Did he order you to have Shaw pulled over and harassed by Officer Welch while Graham searched Shaw's room?"

"What?" Holcum stepped farther away from Massey. "I had nothing to—"

"Shut up, Holcum!" Massey said.

Jake smiled. Holcum was the weak link. He would talk. Jake doubted he would know enough to deliver anyone beyond Massey, but that's how conspiracies were unraveled. You pick on the low man and work your way up. It just took time, and making deals with the lower level offenders.

Callie joined them. "When Graham talks, you're going down, Massey."

"I don't think so."

"You think Deputy Chief Stewart is going to protect you?" Callie shook her head. "Don't be an idiot. Shit flows downhill, Massey."

"I'm not taking anyone else's hit."

"That's the first smart thing you've said. Take yourself to the station and report to Deputy Chief Braff. He knows you're on your way in. If you aren't there in ten minutes, I'll have a deputy sheriff haul you there in cuffs."

Massey clamped his mouth shut. His face was a deep red, sweat popping on his forehead and running down both temples. He shook his head, then slunk off.

"What about me?" Holcum asked.

"You heard what I said about getting in front of this?"

"Yeah," Holcum said, wary.

"You are now my confidential informant," Callie said. "I'm going to put you in the car with Graham and you're going to get him to talk. Every last thing he knows."

Holcum nodded. Jake cuffed him and put him in the back of Grady's car with Graham.

When he got back to the hotel room door, Grady asked him: "You gonna tell me what's going on?"

"Eventually."

"I'm going to talk to the motel clerk," Callie said.

"I'll stay here in case we get some fast news from the pros." Jake motioned toward the open door, where a camera flash pulsed. While he waited, Jake pulled out his phone and scrolled through Shaw's photos. Nelson's trophy box held four panties, two watches, and eight items of jewelry. Fourteen victims deserving vengeance. They would need to link the trophies to specific victims through DNA, trace evidence, and family testimony. That evidence would be good enough to identify the victims, but to use the information against Mike Nelson, Jake had to establish that it was his box. The man hid it where he could easily get to it so probably handled it a lot. And Jake doubted he wore gloves when doing so. Hopefully it would be plastered with his filthy prints.

Jake needed the box.

CHAPTER SEVENTY-SIX

Deputy Chief of Patrol Sam Stewart paced his office. His stomach burned and he'd already finished a roll of antacids. His efforts to protect his father had failed. Instead, he'd ensnared himself and put his career at risk.

That damn Massey. Sam should have taken the scene himself. Staying here gave him a small level of deniability, but that was planning to fail. He should have planned to succeed and gone out there himself.

Finally, his cell phone rang with a call from Massey.

"What the hell, Sergeant. You've left me flying blind."

"We're screwed, boss. Someone took photos of Graham when he went into Shaw's room. Shaw had the pictures and wrote up the whole thing. The traffic stop to keep him busy, the room search, the twenty Graham gave the clerk."

Sam's stomach clenched and his bowels burned. "How do you know?"

"Diggs told me right before she called in sheriff deputies to take over the scene. She told Braff the whole thing and ordered me to go see him. She says if I don't go straight there she'll have a deputy sheriff arrest me. Can she even do that?"

A bubble of bile rose into Sam's mouth. He managed to force it back down.

"Boss?"

"Don't say a damn thing to Braff. Ask for your union rep and keep your mouth shut."

"I will. And Graham and Welch will both hold fast."

Three people. One of them would flip. Who was the weak link? Not Massey.

"I'm not sure about Holcum," Massey said.

"How is he involved?"

"He was first on the scene and held the clipboard so I had to leverage him to get Graham in the room."

"What does he know?"

"Nothing more than that. If we don't talk, we'll be all right."

Sam was not so sure. In fact, he very much doubted it.

"I'm pulling in now, boss. I'm going into Braff's office, but don't worry. Me and my guys will say nothing."

The line went dead. That was it. He was done. Suspension and disgrace. The best he could hope for was to avoid prison. That's how his career would end.

His cell again. His father. "Dad?"

"The shit's hit the fan, son."

"Was it worth it?"

"Was what worth what?"

"I protected you from what you did to protect Nelson and it's now cost me my career. Was it worth it?"

"You made your own choices."

That was true.

"And you're not done yet. Houser is sniffing my way. You need to—"

Sam hung up. He grabbed his keys and left the station, feeling the eyes following him. His secretary didn't even look at him. Word had obviously already gotten out that the sheriff had taken over the crime scene and the detective division had sequestered Sam's men.

His career was over.

CHAPTER SEVENTY-SEVEN

Jake read through the documents on Shaw's phone while the forensic team worked. Shaw developed a theory that Abe Stewart and his two cronies, Bryan Lowe and Jeff Forsyth, knew Nelson was the killer from the beginning and protected him to protect their own financial interests. Shaw confronted all three men with different levels of this accusation. Their responses convinced Shaw he was right; good enough for Shaw's book, but far short of courtroom admissible admissions. The threat of seeing the accusations in print could have triggered this murderous reaction from any of them, but Abe Stewart was their leader and the falsified DNA evidence used to convict Belker was hanging over his head.

So they had three suspects in Shaw's murder: Mike Nelson, Anthony Patino, and Abe Stewart.

"Jake!" Callie jogged toward him from the motel office. "Guy working the desk says Shaw had a female visitor around midnight. Blond curly hair. Slender. A looker."

"That's how Shaw described Donna Larson in his character profiles."

"That's the woman who wrote the letter? Her father went up for the Lachey murder?"

"Yes," Jake said. "She's staying at a boarding house on north Main." Her return address had been on her letter and Jake was familiar with the place because a recent case had taken him there several times.

"Let's go."

They drove separately to preserve mobility and Jake beat her there. He parked and waited, leaning against his front fender, scanning the boarding house and the neighborhood.

The big old house looked as it had the year before. Worn out. The bare dirt yard fringed by the bright green of new spring grass. The house held six people and as many as four more could live in the converted garage. Jake didn't know whether Larson was staying in the house or the garage apartment, but Carl, the guy who ran the place, would tell them.

Jake's phone shuddered with a text. Erin: *Sam Stewart ran out of here right after Massey showed up.*

If Sam was headed out to do damage control, he was too late.

Callie parked in front of Jake's Mustang. She hopped out, adjusted her jacket. "Let's go." She took off, quick strides propelling her toward the house.

Jake bounced off the fender and jogged to catch up. "I know the guy who runs the place. Carl."

"Then you take the lead with him. I'll lead with Larson." Callie's voice held the edge it got when she was heading for the home stretch in a case. Donna Larson was in Shaw's room the night he died so had the opportunity to kill the man. And she had the means; it didn't take much strength to slit a man's throat when he was asleep or passed out. But it did take nerve. And guts. Did she have motive? Shaw had done what she asked by finding Mike and proving he was the killer or at least *a* killer.

Jake stepped onto the back stoop and heard the loud drone of a TV coming from inside. Carl loved daytime TV. They knocked.

"Come in," the words came to them faintly through the closed door.

Jake led the way through the kitchen and the wide arch into the living room. Carl sat in a battered recliner, feet kicked up, head back, watching a woman's talk show on a giant TV.

"Ha!" he laughed. Then he saw Jake. "You're that cop from when those boys were staying here."

"Good to see you, Carl."

Callie walked into the room. Carl sat up straight, then slammed the recliner's footrest down and came out of his chair faster than looked possible.

"Hello!" Carl's smile was so wide you could almost see teeth through his wiry gray beard and droopy, food-stained mustache. He smoothed the front of his fleece jacket and ran a hand down his face, pulling his beard into a point. "I'm Carl."

"Callie Diggs." She read Carl's obvious interest in her and took over. "We hope you can help us, Carl."

"I'm sure I can."

"We'd like to speak with Donna Larson."

"Sure." Carl went to the bottom of the front stairs and shouted, his eyes never leaving Callie. "Donna! You have a visitor!"

A visitor. Carl had forgotten Jake was even there.

Carl turned back to them. "She's usually at work but she must have called in sick today. She was out late last night. This morning, really."

A door closed above them. Feet padding down the stairs. "Who is it, Carl?"

"Police." Carl stepped back into the living room and waved toward Callie as Donna entered the room. She looked as Shaw had described her—tall and slender, attractive in a barfly kind of way, with frizzy hair and skin scaly from too many hours in smoke-filled bars. She had circles under her eyes and the hair around her face was stuck to her skin by dried sweat. She wore a Cubs T-shirt and a pair of faded jeans ripped across both thighs and was barefoot, her long toes gripping the hardwood floor.

"I'm Donna." She crossed her arms and her gaze shot back and forth between Jake and Callie.

Callie asked, "Carl, is there a quiet place where we can talk to Ms. Larson alone?"

"All my other tenants are out, so the kitchen will be quiet. I'll turn off the TV for ya." He did so then went through a door at the base of the stairs. "I'll wait in here until you're done."

Jake and Callie introduced themselves to Larson and they all took seats around the scarred Formica table in the kitchen. The room was clean and smelled of hot water and dish soap. A stack of clean pans and dishes mounded out of the left-hand sink. With the TV off the house was so quiet Jake could hear the *pap pap pap* of water dripping off the dishes.

"Are you here about clearing my father?" Her voice was high and hopeful and the question felt honest to Jake. She had thought of her dad first, not Eddie Shaw.

Larson was looking at Jake, but Callie answered before he could.

"We're here about Eddie Shaw," Callie said.

Larson's gaze shifted to Callie. "I know Eddie. I asked him to write about my father's case."

"When's the last time you saw him?"

"I met him at the Grey last night." Larson crossed her arms. "Out on Ogden."

"Was he alone?"

"Eddie found out who Mike was and—"

"Was he alone?" Callie interrupted.

"Mike Nelson's son showed up. That's the Mike Mr. Belker meant. Mike Nelson actually killed Beth Lachey. Not my dad."

"The son; You're talking about Anthony Patino?"

"That's right." Larson re-crossed her arms, and shot a glance at Jake. "If you know, why are you asking?"

"Did Mr. Shaw invite you both there? You and Patino?"

Larson shook her head, then hugged herself. "I just happened to be there. Mr. Shaw probably went there because it's the only bar he knew in town. We had met there a couple nights ago."

"Did it bother Shaw to see you there?"

"He seemed fine with it. I sat down with him and then the other man showed up. Mike Nelson's son."

"Why did Shaw want to meet with Patino?"

"Eddie had found a box full of things Mike Nelson kept from his victims. He'd brought pictures of the box and what was in it. He showed them to this guy—Patino—and the guy got excited."

"And?"

Larson shifted in her chair, eyes bouncing back and forth between them. "He snatched them out of Eddie's hands and ran out of there."

"What did you do?"

"I stayed. We had a drink, but Eddie said he needed to get writing and that was that." Larson shrugged, brushed at her hair, and licked her lips. Thanks to the motel clerk putting her at the scene, Jake didn't even need those indicators to spot her lies.

Callie said nothing. Waiting.

Larson looked back and forth between them; her lips compressed and turned white.

"Donna, we know you went to his motel room."

Larson blinked and swallowed. "I did go to his room. I had thrown a drink in his face and I wanted to apologize."

"Why'd you throw—"

"I thought he said the box didn't clear my dad."

Callie caught Jake's eye and nodded. Larson had just provided a motive for killing Shaw. But Jake didn't buy it.

Jake spoke up. "What happened in his room, Ms. Larson?"

"He explained that the box *will* clear my dad when the police match something in it to Beth Lachey. So we...

celebrated. Drinking and … stuff. But when he fell asleep, I left."

"But you had the bottle with you even when you thought Shaw wouldn't clear your dad."

Larson grimaced. "I was going to try and bribe him, I guess."

Jake detected no deception. This was the truth. And it explained how the killer got past the security lock on the hotel room door. Larson had disengaged it as she left. Anyone with a key or lock picking skills could walk right in.

"What time did you leave the room?"

"It was almost three."

"Did you see anyone outside the room as you left?"

"What? No?" Larson's gaze snapped back and forth between Jake and Callie. "What happened?"

"Eddie Shaw was murdered last night."

Larson covered her face with her hands and started to cry, sobs shaking her shoulders.

Jake got up and tore a square off a roll of paper towels on the counter and handed it to Larson. When her sobbing quieted and her hands came down from her face, Callie started in again.

"Did you see the box when you were in Shaw's motel room?"

Larson nodded, wiping her cheeks with the paper towel, now a crushed soggy mess. Jake got her another sheet and put the wet one in the trash.

"Where?"

She swallowed, then spoke so softly Jake had to lean forward to catch it. "Under the bed."

"The box isn't there now," Callie said.

"I…"

"Where is it?"

"In my room upstairs," Larson said. "I trusted Eddie. I did. But I thought if I took the box I could make sure, you know?"

"Show me." Larson got up and led the way, her shoulders hunched and head down. Bare feet slapping the hardwood and leaving behind damp footprints. Her room was at the top of the stairs. It was large, with a worn oak floor, a four-poster bed, and a private bathroom. The box was on a small table between two upholstered chairs. Donna pointed to it, then crossed her arms.

"Did you touch anything inside it?"

"No. I opened it when I got back here. I thought maybe I could tell if something in there meant my dad didn't... do anything. But seeing those... things. I just couldn't..." Her eyes teared again and she pressed the paper towel to them, her shoulders shaking with another string of sobs.

Callie reached into the inside pocket of her blazer and brought out a pair of zip cuffs. "Hands behind you, Miss Larson."

Larson's eyes went to the cuffs and her eyes grew larger. Her mouth fell open as she backed away, a hand reaching for the doorjamb. "No, no, no. I didn't kill Eddie. I—"

Jake grabbed Larson and spun her around so Callie was behind her. "We'll straighten this out at the station, Ms. Larson. Please cooperate and this will be faster and easier."

"Okay, I just... " Larson put her hands behind her and winced when Callie tightened the cuffs.

Callie led her to one of the chairs and settled her into it. She pulled her phone out and called for a forensic team.

"Can I see you in the hall, Detective Diggs?"

Out in the hall, Callie stood facing the room, an eye on Larson through the open door. "Jake, I can see you did your truth-detecting thing and believe her story."

"More than that. I—"

"She lied about going to the hotel room, she had motive, she had opportunity, and she has the missing box in her possession. Which she admitted to stealing. I have to take her in."

"I agree," Jake said. "But she readily admitted to taking the box and killing Shaw destroys the opportunity to clear her dad—the one thing most important to her."

"She was the last one to see him alive."

"When she left the motel room, she couldn't re-engage the internal security lock so anyone with a key or lock picking skills could get inside. We already know at least one of the clerks sells access to the occupied rooms."

"Who then? Mike Nelson?"

"Or Patino. He was the only other person who knew about the box and he's a killer. His DNA was found on Kate Ballard." This was about the box and Abe couldn't have know about the box—or he would have found it—so wasn't a viable suspect anymore.

"Okay, Jake. I like it. Want to put out an APB?"

"Fallon, up in Glenbard, issued one on Patino for killing Ballard. He hasn't picked him up yet, so Patino must not be where Fallon expects him to be. But I have an idea. Let me work it."

Diggs considered, then nodded. "I'll take Larson in and talk Braff through all of this."

"He's going to want to talk about Massey and the rest of it."

Callie grimaced. "Wish me luck."

Jake went back out to his car, thinking through his theory. Patino had been so aroused by his dad's crimes he stole the photos of the trophies and fled the bar, likely to go somewhere to enjoy them in private. But their power waned as he thought about the real trophies. So, he broke into Shaw's room to steal the box and when it wasn't there freaked out and killed Shaw.

Frustrated at not finding the box, Jake could think of one place Patino might go to amplify the power of the pictures.

CHAPTER SEVENTY-EIGHT

Jake started the Mustang and pulled away from the curb, tires squealing.

The large white house where Shaw said he found the trophy box was only a block off the route Kate Ballard walked on her way home from the library. It once belonged to a Weston founding family but had long since been carved into tiny rooms rented out to single men who had nowhere else to live. The place had generated so many police calls the city council finally outlawed boarding houses. That law was still on the books but moot. As soon as real estate prices recovered from the 2008 downturn, investors started tearing down the boarding houses and replacing them with mansions. Carl's place was now the only one left.

Jake parked across the street. The sun was bright, but the big house was in deep shadow under the huge pine trees that hung over its backyard. A six-foot tall chain-link fence circled the property. Behind it, a large plywood sign on a pair of posts held an artist's rendering of the mansion that would replace the old house. It was a monster with more gables and dormers than one house should have.

Jake's hand fell to his waist as he approached the fence, pushing back his blazer to rest on his gun. He didn't like carrying the gun and had not for nearly a decade. But recent events had convinced him it was necessary. His suburban uto-pia had warts and some of them were dangerous.

The fence was temporary, built in sections, the vertical posts sleeved over pipes welded to wide, flat bases. The sections were not connected to one another so when Jake levered two apart the top of the gap was wide enough to squeeze through.

Thud!

Jake dropped to a crouch and waited, but the sound didn't come again.

He moved forward, stepping lightly, the ground a spongy combination of rain-softened dirt and fallen pine needles. Nothing moved, even the air was still. The only sounds the flitting of bugs and chirps of birds and tires on nearby Jefferson Avenue. He put a foot up on the porch and paused as his eyes adjusted to the shadowed darkness. The doors and windows had been removed, the openings gaping darkly open.

Thud!

The sound came from inside. He stepped onto the porch. *Squeak.* He paused, fearing detection from inside, but heard nothing. Maybe—hopefully—the noise he'd made didn't carry into the house. He pulled his Glock from its holster and held it along his leg, trigger finger extended along the barrel, ready, but hoping he wouldn't need the gun. He continued on, step-ping as softly as he could.

He went through the empty doorframe and into the foyer. A sudden breeze sent a piece of paper skittering across the floor and he flinched.

Calm down, Houser.

Thud!

The sound was closer, now. And beneath him.

Two more steps.

Thud!

The floor shuddered beneath his feet.

Then the impacts fell into a slow, floor-quaking rhythm. Jake sped to the basement stairs, sure the thunderous blows would mask his footsteps. He flattened himself against the wall, then stuck his head around the jamb. A long stretch of wooden stairs descended to a red-painted concrete floor. Paths were worn into it leading away in several directions.

The blows continued, now followed by smaller sounds of something hitting the floor and scattering.

Jake sped down to the bottom stair and leaned around the corner. Light spilled in through a couple small windows high on the walls.

A man stood in the center of a large room. Tall, wide shoulders, and a thick beard. He wore jeans, a flannel shirt, and thick lugged-sole work boots. Patino.

Patino held a long metal bar, the end resting on the floor. A brick pillar rose in front of him, supporting the ends of two massive timbers stretching across the ceiling. Chunks of brick lay scattered across the floor.

Patino was breathing hard, shoulders rising and his chest expanding. He lifted the bar and swung it against the pillar. More bricks flew, the bar emitting a low *wo-ong* as it vibrated from the blow. The idiot was going to bring the whole damn house down.

Jake raised his gun and edged along the wall, opening up his view of Patino. Blood, dried and flaky, streaked his hands and forehead.

Another blow.

Crack.

The pillar compressed an inch, bricks shooting out, one hitting Jake in the knee and knocking the leg out from under him.

He must have shouted with the impact because Patino looked at him, then grinned and gave the pillar another mighty *whack.* It buckled, bricks flying, one knocking Patino across the head. Blood welled and the light faded from his eyes and he dropped to the floor, the metal bar rolling away.

The giant timbers dropped a couple inches, long groans across the ceiling as the house drooped downward. Jake scrambled to his feet, weight on his uninjured leg. He holstered the Glock, took a look at the sagging beams, and hobbled over to Patino.

A *screech* and the front timber sagged, a *crack* as it dropped again.

Jake rolled Patino onto his back, hooked his hands under Patino's armpits, and dragged him to the stairs. Then he hauled Patino's body higher, grasped his hands together around the man's chest, and started up the stairs.

Stair by stair he climbed, his knee aching, the house shuddering and creaking, the massive beams continuing to droop. A *crack* so loud that Jake felt it in his chest and a tumble of wood and plaster spilled into the basement. A dust cloud swelled up and engulfed them. Jake kept moving, one stair at a time, his knee throbbing, his lungs burning, eyes gritty with dust.

At the top of the stairs he set Patino down and straightened up, flexing his injured leg. The front of the house came down with a mighty *crash*, a large section of shingled roof spilling into the dining room.

Cra-ck.

The floor dropped under his feet, but caught on something and stopped with a jolt. Jake fell, landing on Patino. The man groaned, but didn't open his eyes. Jake got back up, panic flushing through him, the open door at the back of the house a few steps away.

Patino groaned again.

Jake grabbed Patino's wrists and hauled, jerking him across the floor in stages. As he crossed the kitchen, the floor shifted under him again, angling down toward the center of the house.

Creeeak! A long, protracted *screech*.

The back doorway suddenly leaned toward him. Jake lunged for it, a mighty heave on Patino's wrists and they shot through the door. Patino landed on top of him as he fell backwards onto the porch, Patino's weight driving the air from his lungs.

Shouts. Then hands grabbed and pulled them off the porch and dragged them across the lawn, pine needles spearing through his pants and into his legs.

The ground shook and a cloud of dust billowed out and engulfed them. Jake closed his eyes and held his breath.

Quiet.

Jake opened his eyes and blinked away the grit. He breathed deeply and when his head cleared, stood up. The house was now a mound of rubble topped by the point of one roof gable.

"Are you okay?"

Three teenage boys clustered around him, faces covered in dust. One coughed and wiped his mouth.

"Thanks to you three," Jake said.

"I think this guy's coming to." One of the boys knelt next to Patino who rolled over onto his stomach and started to push himself up. Jake dove onto Patino, knocked him to the ground, and cuffed him with the zip cuffs from his blazer pocket.

The three teens just stared. "He's a murder suspect," Jake explained.

One of the boys smiled through his dirt-caked face. "We helped catch him!"

Sirens approaching, followed by flashing emergency lights coming down the street. A fire truck and a paramedic van. Patino coughed a few times then started cussing. Jake hauled him to his feet and moved him toward the Mustang. A crowd had assembled and pulled the fence aside and all their eyes were on Jake. Then a massive honk from the fire truck. When the crowd looked that way, Jake edged around it.

"Injured men over here," someone yelled, pointing at Jake.

Jake kept moving but glanced down. His clothes were ruined. Blazer torn, white shirt filthy, blood soaked through from various scratches and cuts. Gray pants bloodstained and ripped where the brick had hit him.

Patino struggled against Jake's grip, eyes darting, looking for space to run. Jake tugged on the cuffs, wrenching Patino's shoulders behind him.

Jake stopped next to the Mustang and read Patino his rights. As he finished, firemen swarmed them. "He's a cop." One shouted. "Are you okay, Detective? Can you hear me?"

"I'm fine, but check this guy over before I take him in."

The paramedics walked them both over to their unit, sitting Patino on the back bumper. Someone pressed a water bottle into his Jake's hand. He used the first mouthful to rinse the dust out of his mouth, then drank it down while two paramedics started in on him.

"I'm fine," he said.

"Then it will only take a minute."

Jake succumbed, keeping his eyes on Patino who was getting similar treatment: Concussion check. Body examined for wounds.

Jake winced, flinching away from whatever the paramedic was doing to his side.

"Hold still, Detective. You've got a lot of superficial cuts but nothing serious. Keep them clean and they'll heal up fine."

"How about my knee?" Jake lifted the offending leg then set it back down as the paramedic examined it.

"You don't need emergency treatment, but you should see your doctor tomorrow in case you tore something in there."

"Your prisoner is going to be okay," said the other paramedic. "Head wounds bleed a lot but it's superficial. He has some other blood on him that's already dry but I don't see a wound."

"Leave that alone. That's not his blood and it's evidence," Jake said.

The paramedic grimaced and stepped away from Patino.

A squad car pulled up, lights flashing. Jake didn't recognize the two patrolmen who got out of it, but they ignored him, jumping into the crowds and moving them away from the house.

Jake thanked the paramedics, then hauled Patino to his Mustang and stuffed him in the back seat. It was a tight fit. Then he called Callie.

"I got Patino and he's covered in Shaw's blood."

"Stealing my glory, Houser?"

"Just got lucky."

"Bring him in and I'll take over."

"You'll need to call Fallon."

"I'll handle it."

CHAPTER SEVENTY-NINE

Jake handed Patino off at the station and drove home. As the garage door rose in its tracks, he found himself hoping to see the truck parked inside. It wasn't

"Where are you, Frank?"

Jake parked, then lowered the door behind him. He levered himself out of the Mustang and limped across the garage. His knee had stiffened during the short ride, which made climbing the stairs painful. He emptied his equipment onto the kitchen counter then eased his way to the bathroom, stripped down, piled his clothes in a dirty mound, and got in the shower. He examined the knee. A dry crust of abrasion surrounded by a dark bruise marked the spot where the brick had struck him. He raised and lowered his leg, his range of movement improving quickly. It was just a bruise. He would be fine.

He washed thoroughly, remembering the paramedics' caution to clean his cuts and there were a lot of them. The only injury he remembered was the brick hitting his knee. He finished with the water set to cold and when he stepped in front of the mirror none of his wounds bled.

He patted himself dry then wrapped the towel around his waist and walked into the kitchen. His limp was already getting better. He took two Aleve, then went back to his bedroom and dressed in jeans and a quarter-zip over a Bears T-shirt.

Callie could handle—and wanted to handle—Patino on her own. But Deputy Chief Braff would need Jake's help with Abe Stewart, Sam Stewart, and the corruption in the patrol unit. Jake called in, but got Braff's voicemail. He left a message that he was available whenever the DC wanted him.

Jake stretched out in his recliner, legs shuddering with exhaustion. He closed his eyes. Hauling Patino up those stairs had taken a lot out of him. His cellphone skittered across the kitchen counter, went still, then skittered again. A phone call, not a text. He lurched up and answered it, his knee protesting the sudden movement. "Houser."

"This guy—Mike Nelson—he's our killer?"

Jake recognized the voice—the detective from Poplar Grove. The old timer who talked too much. "I think so."

"Not a hundred percent?"

"Not until a jury says so."

"Is there really a box of trophies?"

"Who told you that?" That should not have gotten out.

"Ten different people. This is huge news, Houser. People are talking. The killer took a ring from our victim. If it's in that box—"

"For your ears only. No leakage."

"Absolutely."

"There is a ring in the box like the one you described."

Silence. "I need a picture of it."

"Callie Diggs took the box into evidence for her case against Patino for killing the writer. She controls it. You'll have to go through her for access to the box."

"A picture, Houser. Her parents have been waiting for thirty years."

"We need to go by the book."

Another silence, but Jake didn't hang up. The detective said: "I'm going to put out an APB on this Mike Nelson."

"You should." The box nailed Nelson and they could now demonstrate that it was his. Patino could put the trophy box in Mike Nelson's possession in his basement room. Shaw's email to his agent established that he found the box in that same basement. Donna Larson took the box from Shaw. Callie took it from her. With luck, forensics would also find Nelson's prints and DNA on the box and its contents.

"Later, Houser."

After the call, Jake scrolled through the trophy pictures until he got to Amy Smith's locket. With this trophy and Abe Stewart's false certification of the DNA results, they would have to re-open Smith's murder. Maybe Jake could coax more from Frank's memory about where Nelson had gone. But Abe Stewart might also know something. According to Shaw, the man spent a lot of time at the senior center on Jackson. On the way out, Jake left a note for his dad on the couch he was using as a bed. *We need to talk!*

* * *

Jake was familiar with the senior center but had never been inside. It was on the block west of the library and like the library, the back entrance was one level lower than the front. Jake walked up the hill and entered through the center's front door.

The building was a bright clean space of shiny tile and freshly painted walls. A woman sat behind a reception desk but the clack of dominoes to his left told him where to go.

Jake paused at the door to the card room and scanned the space; ten or more tables about half-filled with seniors playing cards and dominoes. Most drinking from Styrofoam cups, the smell of overheated coffee riding on the air.

Abe Stewart sat with his back to the windows. He laughed, then slapped down a string of dominoes. Jake wasn't familiar with the game, but whatever Stewart had done ended things. The other two men groaned and one of them started flipping the tiles facedown.

Stewart leaned back in his chair, and watched Jake cross the room. Jake lowered himself into the empty chair, favoring the knee, and put his forearms on the table.

"Whoa, youngster." The man working the tiles pushed at Jake's forearm. It was Bryan Lowe. He was thin and bald. "We aren't looking for a fourth."

"I'm not here to play. I need to ask Abe a few questions."

"This is Detective Jake Houser, boys," Abe said.

"Frank's son?" This from the third of the trio. Forsyth. He was much heavier than the other two, and looked older, his eyes red-rimmed and watery behind thick glasses, big belly pressing against the edge of the table. "Your dad stopped by to see us just the other day. He—"

"What brings you by our game, Detective?"

Jake wondered why his dad had come to see these guys and why Abe didn't want to talk about it. These guys weren't Frank's people. Frank had always hung out with the other tradesmen in town: he'd never trusted men with power like these three.

"I'm looking for Mike Nelson."

"Why would I know where he is?"

"You three protected him."

"This town owed him better than he got," Forsyth said.

"This town treated him like a hero," Jake said.

"Until he got hurt. And that was our fault." Abe leaned forward, elbows on the table. "He played hurt to win us that second championship and when he got to the next level, he had nothing left. That knee was done. When he came home from that he mowed lawns for your dad. That's a hell of a fall."

"Mike Nelson is a rapist and murderer, Abe. You knew that in 1983 when you made him join the army."

"I knew no such thing in '83."

The *'83* hung in the air as if the words echoed. Abe swallowed and scratched his temple. He'd slipped and he knew it.

"But you knew when you got the DNA results in 1999."

"I don't know what you're talking about."

"Where is Nelson?"

Abe chewed his lip.

"You've put your son and Chief Arvind in the middle of your mess. Do you think they'll continue to lie for you when it puts them at risk?"

A minute passed, Abe chewing his lip. Finally, he said, "You need to talk to your dad."

"My dad doesn't owe you, Abe. He's not going to—"

Abe sprang up, hips bumping the table, dominoes flying. "Just talk to him goddamn it."

Abe stalked off. Jake looked at the other two men. Forsyth kept his eyes on the table. Lowe said, "Son, maybe you should do like Abe suggested."

Jake stood up. "Maybe I will." His dad *had* been hiding something. Something serious enough to make him to lie to his son.

* * *

Back in the car Jake noticed he'd missed a text from Braff: *Good work on Patino! Rest up today. Tomorrow at 7AM in my office. To talk about your supplemental report, our mess here, and about Fallon.*

Tomorrow was going to be a long day.

Another text from Braff: *And stay away from the press.*

That warning wasn't needed; Jake hated the press as much as Braff did.

Jake had also missed three calls and a string of texts from Anna that all said basically the same thing: Call her immediately. Had something happened to her or the baby?

He called her, almost dropping the phone because his hands were suddenly slick with sweat. *Be okay. Be okay. Be okay.*

"It's about time!"

"What's wrong?"

"You tell me. You're the one who was almost crushed by a collapsing house while hauling a killer out of it."

"You're okay? And the baby?"

She sighed loudly. "You promised to give me time."

"I know. I just… your messages were so urgent I thought something had happened."

"Something *did* happen."

"What?"

"To you! Something happened to you!"

"I'm fine."

"You should've called me."

"I'm just a little sore."

"That's not good enough, Jake."

Jake said nothing, unsure what she was mad about.

"If we're going to do this together, you'll have to do better."

Jake smiled and his heart rushed to a faster beat. "Together," he repeated. "Yes ma'am."

"I need to know my daughter's father is okay. I can't be worrying about you all the damn time."

"Daughter?"

"That's my mom's theory based on what food I'm craving."

"You're keeping the baby—her—that's what you're saying?"

"Yep."

"And we'll raise her together?"

"Let's give it a shot. Strike that. Let's give *us* a shot."

Jake couldn't speak. His throat had closed and his eyes filled with tears that started running down his cheeks.

"You're tearing up, aren't you? You are such a softy. Kids are hard, Houser. If our girl is anything like me, we have a tough couple decades ahead of us until she grows out of it."

"I… it's going to be amazing."

"Yes, it is." Her voice lowered. "I've got to go. I've been called into your department on this thing with Stewart and Massey. But with a deputy chief—and maybe the chief himself—involved, the state will likely take over."

"It's a mess."

Her voice dropped. "I'm glad you're okay."

"I… "

The line went dead.

Jake drove home and collapsed into his recliner. He looked out the window at the woods across the yard. The sun had fallen behind them but it was far from dark. Birds flittered from branch to branch and a giant raptor floated above it all, likely watching Jake's yard for movement. Sleep overtook him.

CHAPTER EIGHTY

Bev was so tied up with seizing the rest of the bad batch that she didn't hear about Jake rescuing Anthony Patino from a collapsing house until she was home and halfway through her first glass of cabernet. The cab had been a birthday gift from Doug that she had saved and was the best she'd ever tasted.

Or maybe it was her victory that made it taste so good. She'd gotten ahead of this thing. They'd recovered all but six ounces of the bad batch with Peddler at his hidey-hole and finally convinced him to give up his dealer network or face murder charges. He claimed not to know Kingpin, so she would not be able to chase arrests farther up the food chain. But getting the deadly smack off the streets was her first priority. Teams were busy chasing Peddler's people now. And, best of all, only three new ODs had been reported today and no fatalities.

There was a lot of work left to build cases against the people she'd arrested, but that could all wait until tomorrow. Some of those cases would fail because of her weak warrant applications, but it was an acceptable trade-off for the lives saved. Borgeson wouldn't be able to see that. Lives saved was not measurable.

She refilled her wine glass. If Doug didn't hurry, she might finish the bottle before he got a sip of it. As if her thought conjured him, the front door opened.

Yeah, he might be the one. She smiled, anticipating the smile he always cracked when he saw her.

He did smile when he saw her curled up on the end of the couch, but not his normal full-face smile. This smile was small, of relief. Like she was a lifeline saving him from drowning in the despair of a long ugly day.

"That bad?"

He dropped onto the couch next to her, lifted her feet, and put them in his lap. He immediate started rubbing them, his strong thumbs carving away the ache of the days spent on her feet in tactical boots. She groaned involuntarily, which made him laugh. He called it her purr.

"Sergeant Massey, the patrol sergeant who directed his men to make that traffic stop and search Shaw's room, already flipped on Sam. I never would have pegged Sam as dirty," Doug said. "With a deputy chief in it, the Board of Police Commissioners had an emergency meeting and called in the state's attorney."

"What about Arvind?"

"He's cooperating. He knows the only way to survive this is to open the kimono and let us shine a flashlight into every dark corner."

"What's Sam saying?"

"He disappeared."

"He *ran?*"

"It looks that way. And Abe lawyered up before we even called him in."

"Did Patino confess?"

"Diggs is working him, but he was covered in Shaw's blood, so it's a slam dunk whether he confesses or not. And his DNA was on Ballard, so he'll never see the light of day again."

Bev's phone buzzed with a text message.

"You better check it," Doug said. "Lots going on."

Bev picked up her phone. The Weston PD had put out its own APB on Mike Nelson in addition to the one the Poplar Grove department put out an hour earlier. She showed it to Doug.

"Diggs said Nelson had a trophy from Amy Smith in that box." Doug shook his head. "And from more than a few other young women across the county."

"I need to talk to Jake." She pulled her feet off Doug's lap and headed for the front door.

"You deserve a night off, Bev." Doug followed her down the hall.

She stepped into the study and scooped the file off her dad's old desk. The file had Abe Stewart's name on the tab, because that's who her father had used the leverage against.

"I won't be more than an hour." Bev slipped on a pair of tennis shoes.

Doug's gaze dropped to the file in her hands, then flicked to the cabinet where the safe was hidden and back. "What's in the file?"

"A lesson."

CHAPTER EIGHTY-ONE

Jake woke with a start. He was in his recliner in the great room. The windows were dark and showed him his reflection, half his face in shadow, the other half lit from the lights over the kitchen island. His face looked puffy with exhaustion. He limped to the kitchen sink and splashed cold water on his face. Better. His cellphone lay on the kitchen island, its screen glowing with a text from Callie Diggs. *Call Me!*

He walked up and down the hall a few times, stretching the leg, getting blood pumping through it and into his brain. His thoughts were thick, foggy, like after one of his dreams that weren't dreams. He remembered nothing about having dreamt while in the recliner.

He called Callie.

"Patino confessed."

"Good work, Callie."

"It was the box. When I let him see it to confirm it was the same one he saw Nelson with, he freaked out. He *wants* to be locked up."

"Or dead," Jake said.

"What do you mean?"

"He was trying to take that building down on top of himself."

A long silence. "He got a boner when I showed him the box. Stained his pants," Callie said.

"That's… "

"Yeah," Callie said. "Fallon is in with Patino now."

"What about Massey?"

"He flipped on Stewart, who is now missing."

"What about Abe?"

"He lawyered up and is holding fast."

"And Arvind? He was involved at some level when he sent those forensics to the lab in 1999."

"He says he did that as a favor to Abe, who told him he needed the DNA profile for a hush-hush paternity test for a friend. Oh, and Anna is here. One of the patrol sergeants who didn't like seeing Massey in cuffs gave her some lip and she about took his arm off bending it behind his back. Gave him a bloody nose when she slammed his face into a desk."

Jake gritted his teeth. "Is she okay?"

Callie scoffed. "Your girl can handle herself, Houser."

"How's Braff taking it? He told me to come in tomorrow morning."

"Like the pro he is except for the cussing. Mostly about the press. There's gotta be a dozen news vans in the parking lot. If you turn on your TV, you'll see it all."

"No thanks."

"Jake, you solved a bunch of cold cases and cleaned up the department in less than a week."

"The cases aren't closed until we have Mike Nelson in cuffs." And no one was going to be happy about the department's dirty laundry hitting the news. Jake sure wasn't.

"Braff put an APB out on Nelson based on the box, what Shaw wrote, and the DNA reports. You need to use this media attention while you have it. Let them see the box and they'll give you as much air time as you want." She sounded envious of the exposure Jake would get. Any cop looking for a boost up the ladder would be.

"You want to partner on cleaning this up?" Jake asked. Time in front of the cameras bringing peace and closer to victim's families would be good for Callie's ambitions. "I'll focus on Nelson and you handle Patino, the press, and talking with the other departments?"

She hesitated a moment. "I've already got three departments calling me about their cold cases."

"Good," he said. "I'll come by tomorrow after I talk to Braff."

After the call, Jake walked the long hallway until his knee was loose enough to take the stairs. He went down to the garage. His dad still wasn't back from wherever the hell he'd gone. The man was almost as much of a ghost as Mike Nelson.

Jake sat on the couch and his thoughts drifted back to Anna. Her calls worrying about him had felt nice, but it reminded him of something he'd forgotten over the long years since Mary was murdered. A family man had responsibilities beyond himself. To stay safe, to come home, to protect his family, and to not bring the uglier parts of his work home with him.

All of that would be much harder than finding a place to live if he couldn't convince her to live here. It was unconventional—he got that. But it was also big enough that they could add anything she wanted.

He opened the door into the crowded storage area under his apartment to check it out. Finishing this area off would double their livable square footage. It was musty in here, damp, and smelled like wet concrete. The smell evoked a memory and he closed his eyes to hold on to it, dread slowly filled him as it unfurled. The basement again. The big man.

It was here!

But this place didn't have a basement.

Did it?

He turned on all the lights and examined every inch of the floor looking for a staircase or a trap door. He moved boxes and old landscape company office furniture and rusty lawn care equipment and a small mountain of fertilizer bags, but found nothing.

He sat down in an old wicker garden chair. Was he wrong about the memory? Was it just a dream after all?

The garage door screeched upward in its tracks.

Frank was back.

Jake was about to yell to his dad that he was in here when he heard Frank's feet pounding up the stairs to the apartment. His eyes tracked the sound, focusing on the staircase.

Of course! The basement stairs should be directly under that staircase.

He pushed his way through the junk and looked under the stairs. Nothing but a couple boxes of old tax records on a concrete floor.

This concrete looked newer than the rest.

He got a sledgehammer from the garage, folded a couple empty burlap bags to kneel on, then swung the sledge in a tight arc to avoid the sloping ceiling and struck the concrete.

In rang hollowly. *A basement.*

CHAPTER EIGHTY-TWO

Sam Stewart stood on the balcony looking across Wrigley Drive to Geneva Lake. He'd learned that distinction on his honeymoon when he and his bride occupied this same room. The town was Lake Geneva; the lake was Geneva Lake.

He and Barbara had come back to Lake Geneva and this room at least once every year while their marriage lasted. He hadn't been back since the divorce. He knew she still came to Lake Geneva because she posted about it on social media and had never blocked him from her accounts. Did she leave their accounts connected because she wanted him to see all the fun she was having without him, or because once she was done with him, she forgot all about him? A memory easily released.

A chill breeze blew across the lake, stirred up small white caps, then came ashore and slapped against Sam on the fourth-floor balcony. He shivered, but stayed outside. To *feel* the cold. It was something.

Tears came and he wiped them away. His father would tell him to 'man the fuck up.'

When the cold penetrated to his bones, Sam went back inside and sat on the bed, eyes still on the lake. Maybe he should do it out there. Go to a hardware store and buy a hundred pounds of chain then rent a boat and take it out to the deepest part of the lake and sink himself, letting the boat drift away. Disappearing.

He liked it. It had drama. And a little mystery.

His phone rang. His dad. He decided to see what the old man had to say. Would he apologize? Could he? Abe Stewart didn't admit to mistakes so never had to apologize.

"Hey, Dad."

"Where are you, son? You need to fight back. You can't let them—"

"It's over, Dad."

"It is *not* over. You have cover. Stick it to that Massey. Say he was taking money from Shaw and something went south between them. You only ever spoke with Massey, right? You're the *goddamn* DCP. Your word trumps his! The other three—Graham, Holcum, and Welch—all did what Massey told them to do. Let Massey take the weight."

"Dad!" Sam yelled so loud he startled himself, but his father went quiet. "I'm not going to lie about what I did," Sam said, "or why."

Sam hung up, then turned off his phone. His dad would call right back, demanding to know what Sam meant by *why*. Let him worry, Sam thought. The man had protected a serial rapist and murderer which allowed the man to rape and kill more women through the eighties. His argument that he didn't know *for sure* that Nelson was the killer until 1999 would not have much weight with the press or the public.

Sam sat down at the desk and picked up his gun. He was a cop. This was the way to go.

CHAPTER EIGHTY-THREE

Jake swung the sledge again. A chunk of concrete shot off and stuck in the drywall. He kept at it, closing his eyes at each blow to keep from being blinded—he should have grabbed his safety glasses.

"Jake!"

Jake turned to find his dad watching him, his face flushed, eyes wide. "What are you doing?"

"There's a basement under here, isn't there?"

"Why does that matter?"

"There *is* a basement down there." A familiar voice from behind Frank.

Bev.

"What are you doing here?" Frank asked.

"The Weston PD put out an APB on Mike Nelson, Frank. You and I both know that's a waste of resources." She held up a manila file folder.

* * *

Bev held the file and waited.

Frank looked at the file, then at her, eyebrows furrowed and forehead creased. He apparently knew enough about her father's files to imagine what was coming.

"What's in the file?" Jake got up from the floor with a long groan, and stood, weight on one leg, the other bent. He limped over and sat on an old wicker chair.

"My dad kept files on people. He used them for leverage to get things done."

"To blackmail people into doing things he wanted done," Frank said.

Jake looked at his dad. No doubt wondering what Bull had forced Frank to do. Then he looked at Bev. "Is that file why you gave me Larson's letter?"

"Do you want to tell the story, Frank?"

Frank met her gaze then looked away. "This is your show."

Perfect. "The file contains a tape recording, five photographs, and a signed statement. I transferred the tape recording to a digital file." Bev pulled out her phone, opened the voice memo app, and hit play. Although she'd listened to it a dozen times, hearing her dad's voice—so strong and vibrant... so *alive*—still brought a lump to her throat.

"This is Bull."

"Bull, this is Abe. I need your help with Frank Houser."

"Help doing what?"

"I need to know you're in before I tell you."

"Tell me or I hang up."

"Frank has... done something. He called me to confess it. He wants to go public. But if this gets out—the whole truth of it—well, the truth has a long tail that will pull a lot of us into it and hurt the city."

"What did Frank do?"

"Maybe he'll listen to you because you guys are family, right?"

"He married in, but yeah. What did he do, Abe?"

"Remember those two girls, Smith and Brown?"

"Abe, I told Frank we thought Belker did that and to dump him."

"Belker didn't do it, not alone anyway."

"It was Houser?"

"Of course not. But Frank caught the real killer in the basement out there on Spring doing it again and—"

"You mean attacking a girl?"

"Yes. But Frank was too late. She's dead."

"Christ! What did Houser do?"

"Frank killed him."

"What? Who did Houser kill? No, don't answer that. I don't want to know.

Click.

Jake's face was ashen. He looked at his dad, who had turned away and now stood with one hand on the wall, head bowed. Jake put his hand out for the file. "Let me see the rest of it."

* * *

Jake's hands shook as he took the file from Bev and his heart hammered. His dad had killed someone and Abe Stewart had covered it up to protect himself and his buddies. That's why Abe Stewart had called Frank to come back and handle Jake. He needed help and Frank Houser had as much at stake as anyone. Yet once here, Frank had done almost nothing to stop Jake. He must still want the truth to come out.

Jake slid a box in front of himself and placed the file on top of it. Before he opened it, he looked at his dad but Frank had gone to the window where he faced out, his own reflection looking back at him. What did he see? Jake wondered.

Bev stood with her arms folded across her chest, watching Jake.

He opened the file and started with the photos.

The basement. The camera's flash had drawn out more detail, but it was the same place as in his dream. Grit on the floor. Water stain on the concrete wall. The cot.

It also showed things he hadn't seen in his dream. A pair of panties rolled down and discarded at the foot of the cot. One white tennis shoe on its side. A knife with a serrated edge lying beside a splash of blood. More splashes on the wall by the cot.

He read the statement.

> *I Bull Warren, certify that the words below are the truth, so help me God.*
>
> *On August eighth I received a phone call from Chief of Police Abe Stewart. A recording of that phone call is included with this statement. Abe wanted my help in talking with Frank Houser. Abe explained that Frank had found a man killing a young woman in the basement at Trinity Landscaping and that Frank then killed this man. Abe appeared to know the identity of this person, but I did not. Frank confessed this to Abe*

and apparently wanted to submit himself to Abe's authority as Chief of Police. Abe thought this would hurt "us" and the city. Abe did not say so, but I suspect that "us" to Abe, would include Abe, Lowe and Forsyth. Those three are together in everything they do. I refused to help Abe and hung up the phone.

I then drove over to Trinity and found Abe's car inside the building but the garage door was up. I snuck up to the opening and saw that Abe's trunk lid was open. He soon came up the basement stairs with a woman's body wrapped in a blood-soaked sheet. He put the body in his trunk and drove away. I snuck down the basement stairs and took the photos in the file. Frank Houser was not there, nor was the person Abe said he had killed. But there was a lot of blood.

I hid outside the building and ninety minutes later Frank Houser came through a gap in the fence that abuts the woods with a shovel in his hand.

I kept this information to myself because I trusted that Abe was right that going public would hurt our town's reputation. I admit that I was also sensitive to Abe's reminder that people see Frank Houser as a member of the Warren family and him being a killer could hurt my family.

I do not think Frank Houser was involved in killing these girls.

Signed this 9th day of August, 1988.

/S/ Bull Warren.

Jake read it all again, then looked at his dad. His back still turned.

A killer. Or a hero?

Bev uncrossed her arms. "I thought you should know."

"I understand," Jake said. She wanted him to see this side of his dad that he could have never imagined. Just as, the year before, a case Jake investigated forced her to see a side of her own dad she'd been reluctant to acknowledge.

A small, rueful smile. "I'll leave that file here and we will never speak of it again." She turned and left.

* * *

Bev felt lighter as she left the building. She had twenty-one more files in that safe. Would turning each over give her the same sense of relief?

Her dad had marked this file for—and apparently already used it as—leverage over Abe Stewart. But he had used it against Frank Houser, too. This file had to be why her dad had suddenly excluded the Houser family from all Warren family gatherings. He'd known Frank Houser was a killer and couldn't invite a killer into his house.

In the car, her thoughts turned forward, to what awaited her at home. To Doug, and the possibility of a future together. And, maybe, a family of her own.

CHAPTER EIGHTY-FOUR

Jake waited for his dad to speak. Frank had opened the file and read the statement. Now he was holding the photos, a tear running down one cheek, then the other.

"I never suspected Mike back in '82," Frank said. "Bull warned me about Belker, but I never believed that either. Mose was a good worker once you got him started but he didn't do things on his own. There was no way he had done what Bull suspected."

Frank flipped through the photos again. "Then one night I came in to pick up some company records the accountant needed for an IRS audit. The paperwork was down in the basement. I walked in on this." Frank gestured with the photos. "Nelson didn't come back to work here after the army, but he must have kept a key. I surprised him. Otherwise I couldn't have… he was big, you know. But I got lucky and got the knife and… I killed him."

"And buried his body in the woods," Jake said.

"I called Abe and confessed just like the tape said. But Abe immediately put it together and knew Mike must have killed those other two girls, too. And who knows how many more. Abe said telling the world that our local hero was a serial rapist and murderer would have hurt our town."

"Especially since Abe and his cronies protected Nelson when his name first came up."

"What?"

"From the beginning Abe suspected Nelson of being in on killing Smith and Brown. He and his pals forced Belker out of town and made Nelson join the army."

Frank shook his head. "I didn't know that. So, hiding what happened here protected him, too."

"It also protected you and your business."

Frank looked down. "And your mother. And you."

Jake absorbed that and was grateful for it. His mom would have been devastated.

"I sealed up the basement to forgot about what I did down there. But it's time for the whole truth to come out. About Belker, about Nelson, and about what happened in the basement." Frank turned away, arms folded. "I'm ready, but what'll happen to me, son?"

"If you killed Mike in self-defense or in defense of the girl, you'll be fine," Jake realized he was coaching his dad, but didn't stop. He just hoped his dad understood what he was telling him. "But if there was no threat, you will do time."

Frank shook his head. "I've fought against reliving those moments, against seeing those images, every day for over thirty years. I remember clearly that she was alive when I first saw her, Mike was on top of her. By the time I did… what I did… she was dead."

Jake called Coogan and asked him to come over. When Coogan asked why, Jake handed the phone to his dad and left the room.

EPILOGUE

Jake moved out of the Spring Street property that night and back into the apartment he'd first lived in when he returned to Weston. It happened to be empty and he'd always liked the location n the center of downtown Weston. But it didn't have a yard or even a balcony so it would not do once his daughter arrived.

Their daughter. Together.

He swiveled the recliner away from the bay window and looked at Anna. She lay sprawled on the leather couch, one hand holding a paperback novel, the other stroking her belly. Stretched out like that he could see it was just starting to get some roundness to it.

"Quit looking at me like that."

"Like what?"

"Like a fat cow washed up on a beach."

"That's not how I was looking—"

His phone rang. Coogan.

Jake answered the call with a question: "How did it come out?"

"The forensics in the basement didn't refute Frank's statement so the state's attorney accepted it."

"So, he's in the clear."

"Yep. The Paget County Hero was free to go and he's already left. He directed me to have the building torn down and to sell the land to that townhouse developer who's been pestering him."

"A clean break." Jake knew that had to feel good.

"Jake, they found Sam Stewart."

"Where?"

"In a hotel room in Lake Geneva. He ate his gun. He'd rented the place for a week and put a DO NOT DISTURB sign on the door, so he was pretty far gone when they finally went in."

"Abe ruined him. Can they get to Abe without going through Sam?"

"Not for harassing Shaw. But the DNA documents and the file Bev gave you contained enough to kill his pension."

"And the other three? Massey, Welch, and Graham?" Jake had written up every last sordid detail and turned it over to Braff.

"The SA rolled them all up with deals to get Sam before they found his body, so no jail time. But they'll lose their jobs and pensions."

"So that's that," Jake said.

"Yep."

Frank had led the coroner to the spot where he'd buried Mike Nelson. The remains were exhumed and reburied in Weston Cemetery.

Mose Belker was still in prison. The state's attorney was re-examining his case because the confession was only accepted on the strength of the DNA match that was now known to be a lie. But nothing Jake—or Shaw—had found established that Nelson had worked alone.

"Your department will have a state investigator on site for a while, but otherwise it's done. The TV vans are even gone."

"We'll survive it," Jake said.

"How are Anna and the baby?"

"Great!" Jake glanced toward Anna who was looking right back at him with her I-know-what-you're-talking-about smile.

"Is it going to work out between the two of you?"

"I think it might."

"Your rental house on Douglas is going to be empty at the end of June."

Jake had always liked that house. Coogan had picked it up in a swap with the city for some empty land near the south side library. "That would be perfect."

"I'll keep it empty," Coogan said. "Good luck."

After the call Jake stared out the window, then leaned over and cracked it open. As the lonely widower just moved back to town, he'd loved sitting in this spot. It had a great view of the street and with the window open he would listen to the bustle below and feel like a part of his town even while his pain kept him apart from it.

Now he had a new life, and it was just beginning.

"What are you thinking about over there?" Anna asked. She sat up.

He smiled and joined her on the couch, one hand on her belly.

He closed his eyes, lulled toward a nap by the distant sounds on the street below and the warm spring air flowing through the windows.

"I think we still have a shot at an *us*, Jake."

His eyes popped open. "Me too." He sat up straighter.

They talked for hours. About the baby. About the two of them. About the three of them. They had a future to plan.

THE END

**If you enjoyed this Jake Houser mystery,
please consider posting a review on amazon.com.**

ACKNOWLEDGMENTS AND A HISTORICAL NOTE

This book was a bear. In the middle of revisions my wife and I decided to sell our home of twenty-one years and move into a smaller house closer to downtown. The new house needed work, and the distraction of the move and renovation delayed this book by several months.

This book was inspired by an online group discussion of a string of murders of young women in DuPage County, Illinois in the 1970s. When I started googling to learn more, I fell down the rabbit hole. Many of those murders remain unsolved to this day. I brought the murders forward a decade, but used many facts from the original cases in this book.

I received help from early readers Irene Reed and Peter J. Thompson. Pete has published a string of hit thrillers. Irene is a "pre-pub" whose debut novel will knock your socks off.

I also enjoyed help from the following professionals, without whom this book would not look as good, or read as well, as it does. Thank you!

Ron Edison, Editor.
Kevin Summers, Book Formatting and Design.
Jeroen ten Berge, Cover Design.

ABOUT THE AUTHOR

Bo Thunboe is a suburbanite—born and raised—and still lives in Chicago's western suburbs. When bad eyesight killed his dream to fly helicopters for the Marines, he went to college. It didn't go well, and a few lost years later Bo was out in the world laying bricks and repossessing cars. Then he met his wife, Diane, got his head on straight, and went back to college, where he earned a BA in Economics and a JD from Northern Illinois University. (Go Huskies!) After a couple decades spent lawyering he is now a full-time writer.

Please visit www.thunboe.com to sign up for news and to learn more about Bo and the Jake Houser Mystery Series.

www.ingramcontent.com/pod-product-compliance
Lightning Source LLC
Chambersburg PA
CBHW051203190726
48288CB00006B/1792